BEWILDERNESS

BEWILDERNESS

BOOK ONE

KEVIN COX

CHAPTER 1

VEILED MONSTERS FROM the remnants of a dream gathered in the corners of her mind. Whispers that called to her, echoed through her soul. The image of a blue glow coming through a swirling vortex was burned into her brain. She sat in the orange-and-gray sand, unsure where these thoughts came from, for there was nothing in this lush oasis that resembled anything sinister. In fact, there was nothing living here except for some plants. Strange trees rose above her, their green-and-red spine fronds hanging low to the ground like weeping willows. They dangled in the gentle breeze coming off the waters of the crystal-blue spring.

Beyond this lush oasis lay miles and miles of barren desert. To her right there was a sea of windswept dunes; to her left the sand gave way to cliffs of crusted sand and rock. For what seemed like a week, she had been here, pondering who she was, unable to recall anything about herself or this deserted world of sand and dust.

Sitting in the orange-and-gray sand, the girl lifted her head from her hands as she rested her elbows on her knees. Cleaning the sediment out of her long, caramel-colored hair, there was little left to do but dwell on her predicament. She tried to remember what had happened, but her thoughts became a jumbled mess. Vague memories twisted together until they met and short-circuited inside her brain. There was an emptiness that weighed heavily on her. While there was no memory in her mind to accompany it, her heart had not forgotten. She dared not shine a light on this dark place, dreading the day she would have to turn and face it.

She feared that no one was here, which was possibly worse than any fear of unknown inhabitants. The good news was that she had water and a source of food. There were berries that were not poisonous. They didn't taste good, but that didn't matter. She was able to survive here, physically. Mentally, she was less certain.

There was little to keep her going. Loneliness was her enemy now. There had been no signs of any living creature on this planet, neither a tiny insect crawling on the ground nor a bird flying across the sky. The oasis was an anomaly on this dead planet. She figured that if there were animal life here, this place is where it would want to be.

Drawing pictures in the sand was her new pastime. She drew rough stick drawings of people, but she did not remember anyone else. Sometimes she would draw words, big words, right outside the oasis, hoping someone would find them. As she drew greetings like "hello" or "help" in big, bubble letters, after a momentary flash, a memory surfaced of doodling on notebook paper. It wasn't much to go on.

Brushing back a clump of hair that fell over her mahogany eyes, she realized how oily and tangled it had become. It had not always been like this. She wished that she could wash it. The waters of the spring helped but did not get it as clean as she thought it should be.

This place was not home. She must have a home out there somewhere but did not know where to find it. Leaving the oasis was something she would have to do eventually if she wanted to get back, but this was her sanctuary, her haven in the unknown. For now, she decided that she would stay with the water and food to survive. Perhaps after she slept, she'd have fewer reservations about taking that risk.

A gleam of yellow, orange, and red filled one side of the sky between the trees. It had been that way since she first recalled being here. She remembered a world where the light traveled across the sky until it splashed behind the horizon in streaks of glorious colors. The world would grow dark for a while as she slept, and then its sun would climb into the sky when she awoke. Not like here, where it was stuck forever between light and dark.

Moving over to a big, flat stone that had become her sitting spot, she overlooked the waters of the spring. The stone was smooth except for some cracks and scratches on the top. Another gust of wind passed through, animating the trees and disrupting the glassy surface of the water. The girl watched the ripples until they dissipated and the spring settled back into its solid form. When the dark waters were calm, they flattered the skies with their imitation. The red-outlined clouds that stretched for miles, the soft array of blazing colors, and the field of bright stars at its ceiling held a serene beauty that had only her to appreciate it.

Leaning forward, she interrupted its reflection with her shadow. The water was crystal clear. In the shallows, there were enormous stones at the bottom, while the deepest part of the spring radiated with a blue glow. It stimulated her curiosity, but not enough to swim down into the freezing water to inspect it.

The air in her mouth tasted horrid. Leaning down a little closer to the water, she stumbled off the stone. After she took a drink, something on the stone caught her eye. The scratchings from this angle were like letters. She could make out two Ls, a W, and an H. Inspecting the scratches, she tried to find more letters against the rest of the scrapes in the rock. She wondered if it was her mind attempting to find patterns in random markings, but there were more of them. Altogether, she found the letters T H E H O L L O W written on the rock.

If these truly were letters, it meant there had been someone here before her. Maybe they were still around somewhere. She could find only one way to decipher the combination of letters in the order presented. *The Hollow,* she thought, *but what does that mean?*

The longer she stared at the letters, the more they looked like random scratches. She turned back to the rock again, but the words did not appear in the way they had at first. Her excitement faded to disappointment. She was alone here. The girl remained perched on the stone, her throne in this vacant land, queen of this world by default.

She lifted a hand to the collar of her white sundress, and her fingers found the silver necklace, with its icy-blue jewel. She lifted it into view as it sparkled, even in this dim light. When she touched it, it made her feel comforted and happy most of the time, while also regretful and sad. She remembered being given the necklace as a gift but couldn't remember by who.

Her attention was drawn toward the dark horizon through the trees, but she turned away. Something out there made her uneasy. It was like she was being watched, even though there was nothing out there but dried, crusty sand and formations of rock. As silly as it may be, she knew she would never travel in that direction if she left to search for home.

She hoped for some movement in the glow of the other horizon, someone to rescue her from this lonely world. But as usual, there was no one. Only her and the trees. It made little sense for her to stay here and wait for something.

The thought of leaving her haven frightened her. What if nothing else was out there and she couldn't find her way back? But then, what if she stayed here? She imagined herself growing old and dying here, while the entire time a civilization was just over one of the dunes.

The first steps toward the unknown are always the most difficult. She had to make herself do it. There is no success without risk. She decided that she would rest once more, and then she would begin her quest. There was one advantage to this twilight; she wouldn't have the sun beating down on her as she crossed the desert. Making one last drawing in the sand, she wrote herself a reminder of her decision.

She lay down on a pile of sand that she had been using as a pillow, and the bright stars winked at her through the trees. As she counted them, the loneliness subsided a little. There could be someone else out there, far from home, gazing up at these same stars. She wished that she could talk to them and tell them they were not alone, that they should not give up and they would find what they were searching for. She wished someone would tell her that right now, as she drifted off to sleep.

⤲

After some time had passed, strands of her hair blew across her face, tickling her freckled nose. Waking from her light sleep, she saw the reminder she had written in the sand.

Start walking, the message said.

She got to her feet and stepped over to the spring, splashing the icy water on her hair, face, and body until she was wide awake.

It was time. She removed her shoes and socks, taking the socks and soaking them in the spring. She picked a handful of dark red berries and poured them into the socks. The girl stuffed her socks underneath the sash of her white floral-print sundress and put her shoes back on. A sense of dread came over her, as there was nothing left to do but start walking and begin her journey.

She set out toward the glowing light and away from the sanctuary of the oasis. The sand was softer out here and her feet sank into it. After she had walked down the first dune and up to the top of the second, she turned back once more to glimpse the oasis that had been her temporary home since she had been here. From this distance, it was out of place among the endless sand and rock.

She continued, facing whatever might lie ahead, with no sign of hope yet on the horizon. Slope after slope of dry sand awaited her. She told herself there was no turning back until she found something out here. Crossing over endless sand and dirt, she reached the top of the next dune and turned back again. There was no longer any sign of the oasis behind her.

She kept a steady pace—she wanted to get as far as she could before needing food, water, or sleep. The socks under her dress were still damp. She wasn't sure how long that would last, so she squeezed some water into her mouth, being careful not to crush the berries inside.

With the spring out of sight, she hoped the hardest part was over with. She allowed herself to imagine the interesting places that must be out here that she would discover. There was the possibility that she may need to go back at some point, and she made sure that she maintained a straight path so she could find her way if she needed to.

As she trudged down another hill, she came to a formation of gray-colored rock at its base. The rock was between two dunes. Upon examination, the pockmarked stone had a symmetrical pattern to it, almost like honeycomb. Was this a natural formation or a sign that someone else had been here? She touched it, and a piece of it broke off easily in her hand. The outside of the rock was hard and crusty, but the inside was soft, like limestone. Was she getting close to water?

As she crossed over another dune, she began finding more rock formations peeking out of the sand. She didn't want to get too excited, but she was getting closer to something. The risk of leaving the oasis needed to be worth it.

The sand turned into a rock-covered landscape ahead. She speculated that perhaps a civilization would build in this area. Aside from the uneven surfaces, this was much faster terrain than the deep, silting sand. She was enjoying the sense of wonder and exploration.

She came across some cliffs and walked around to more sloping ground. She quickened her pace whenever she had the opportunity over sections of flat surfaces. Her legs were tired after all the resistance from the thick sand, but she pressed on.

Up ahead, the stone surface was ending as sand stretched over it. A bit farther she walked, until she saw something at the horizon. As she got a little closer, she could make out what it was. There was a patch of trees ahead. She couldn't believe it! There was more life here. There could be people here too.

Excited, she picked up her pace, eager for a new discovery. The trees did not stretch out far, but they gave her a sense of hope. As she hurried toward them, an odd rustle moved toward her. It came gently on the breeze. A voice filled with intangible words that she strained to decipher.

She stopped and turned toward the sound but saw nothing there. As she began moving, the noise appeared again. It was faint, but she was sure something was there. She paused again, focusing all attention on the sound. Scanning the dunes around her, she was filled with the creeping sense of someone watching.

The breathy wind grew louder, closer. It was so near, yet invisible. The voice drew ever closer, until it slithered its way into her mind, the words echoing in her soul as it spoke.

You're going the wrong way, it whispered.

Oddly, the creeping terror inside her was numbing with the calmness of the voice. She started walking again but was facing toward her recent footprints in the sand. This wasn't the direction she had been walking. This would lead her back to the oasis she'd started in. How did she get turned around in the opposite direction? Her thoughts became fuzzy as her focus waned. The voices coiled around her in a tight but unwelcome embrace.

Let us guide you, it said.

Control over her own actions was slipping away, but she resisted. Her brain seemed to be shutting down, as if she were very drowsy. She couldn't sleep again, not now. No matter what these whispers spoke to her, she had to know what was ahead.

That's it . . . Let it all slip away . . . We are here with you. Open your eyes and see.

A chill ran down her spine as her calm turned to fear. She could not bear to face the thing that was speaking to her. Panicked, she turned and ran as fast as she could toward the group of vegetation ahead. There were familiar trees with the red, drooping fronds here, and the whispers faded. Turning her head in all directions to make sure nothing was there, she began to relax a little. The voices had completely stopped now.

Moving ahead to explore this new discovery, she realized there was a spring here as well. It was the same size as the spring in her own oasis. Weaving through the trees and berry plants toward the water, she made it to the spring and realized that it was exactly like the one in her oasis.

She walked toward the new water source and noticed a smooth stone like the one she had used as a seat before. She sat on top of the stone; it was exactly the same in every way. The shape of the spring and the configuration of the surrounding trees. Everything about this was the same.

How could this be? There was a swelling inside her throat. She had been suppressing negative emotion and thoughts for as long as she could remember being here. She tried to hold it back now, but it kept coming, slow and steady, like a freight train, and she could not outrun it forever. She had no choice but to let it rush through her. She waited for it to subside, but it did not.

Panic and desperation hit her. She was on a deserted world, lost somewhere out in the universe. She couldn't breathe. Even though they were only vague images, somewhere out there were people she once knew and loved. She had to get back to them, had to find some way to talk to them again.

She tried to steady herself, gasping for air, but couldn't get anything. Her heartbeat accelerated, and her skin became wet with sweat. She focused on the spring. The waters made her calm and at peace. On the positive side, she was back in her haven, but there was no way she had walked in a circle. She'd made sure that she maintained a straight path. Finding her necklace, she cradled it in her fingers. As she began to settle down, she took a few deep breaths.

She walked over to the spot under the trees where she slept. There was no sand pillow, no words saying, "Start Walking." This wasn't the same location but an exact duplicate of it. Did that mean there were copies of this same area all over this world? If that were true, then there really was no hope.

This must be a dream. Nothing about this place makes any sense.

She had experienced realistic dreams before, but nothing compared to this. She had been here too long to have been asleep. She remembered all the details of days of boredom, of staring at the spring. On the other hand, she couldn't remember how all this started. It didn't make any sense for her to be here and not remember how it happened. In dreams there is never an origin; they simply form into a random event. Not being able to trace events back to a reasonable beginning was a sign that it was a dream.

But there was something before this. Hazy memories, emotions that haunted her. She remembered a world where the landscape was varied. There was more than a place that kept repeating itself over and over. A world where the sun lit up the sky and . . . Earth! That was it! Her home was on a place called Earth. It wasn't a dream. Now she needed to remember how to get there.

Carved into the stone where she sat was the word HOLLOW again. The letters were unmistakable this time. As she excitedly traced over the markings, she made out even more letters than before. A R E THE HOLLOW; it wasn't making any more sense, but knowing that she wasn't the first being here gave her some comfort. It was the second sign of life here, but hopefully this had nothing to do with the Whisperers.

As she began to recognize the square style of the carved letters, they were getting easier to pick out from the random scratches. BEWARE THE HOLLOW is what she finally came up with. She wasn't sure what it could mean other than a warning.

After thinking on the words for a while, she began growing weary-eyed, and she decided to try to rest. She would come up with a new plan. She was pleased with this new mystery. She welcomed the challenge. Counting the stars at the top of the sky, she laid her head on the soft sand and drifted off to sleep.

⤶

A new sound nearby awakened her. She sat up, listening intently to it. There was someone crying. Her pulse quickened as she backed away. She calmed herself to keep from running. She needed to know who was there. Quietly, she moved toward the direction of the sound.

Creeping between the trees on the other side of the spring, she searched for the source of the noise. Curiosity and fear fought a battle inside her as she drew closer to the sobbing. To her own surprise, curiosity was winning.

When she reached the edge of the oasis, she saw a girl sitting on the stump of a tree, looking out at the desert wasteland before her. The girl did not appear completely human, as she had dark gray skin with magenta-and-red hair that pulsated and glowed like embers. Dark bruises covered her face and arms as though she had been beaten.

She stood there watching her for a moment, debating how she should approach the situation, until finally she got brave enough to speak.

"Are you okay?" she asked the girl.

The girl spun around and drew a two-pronged blade that resembled the forked tongue of a serpent. She was obviously ready to defend herself at any cost.

"Sorry, I didn't mean to intrude," she said. "I've been alone for so long and was beginning to think there was no one else here."

The girl studied her, as if trying to determine whether she should run or attack. After a few moments, she relaxed and put away her knife.

"Where do you come from?" the girl said. "I haven't seen your kind before."

"From what I remember, I come from a place called Earth," she replied.

"I have never heard of such a place. I am Sidaire. What is your name?"

"Um . . . well, I don't know. It was something like . . . Ammm . . . I can't quite remember."

Sidaire looked directly into her eyes. "Not long ago, I had lost who I was too. Only recently have I begun to recover."

"That's good. Maybe I will, too, then."

"You may wish you hadn't."

"What do you mean?"

"I lost myself . . . in The Hollow. It took everything I knew, my thoughts, feelings . . ."

"The Hollow? Were you the one who wrote that message on the rock?"

"I don't remember writing a message."

"What is The Hollow?"

Sidaire looked out in the distance. "Darkness . . . Oblivion. It consumed me . . . Left me with no control."

"How did you get out?"

"I don't even know." Sidaire turned back, eyes focusing on her again. "It was like something caught its attention, and its domination subsided for a moment. I don't yet remember anything more than that."

"Caught who's attention?"

"The monster."

"Monster? Is that what the whispers came from?"

"The whispers??" Sidaire's eyes widened as she stood up to take a few steps back. "Have you heard them?!"

"Yes, when I was walking over here . . . They seemed to be—"

"You brought them here?!" Sidaire said with a mix of anger and fear.

"No, they—they left when I got here . . ."

"Get in the water!" Sidaire commanded. "Hurry! I'm going to take a look around."

Unsure of what else to do, she went back through the trees toward the spring. Hesitantly, she pulled off her tennis shoes and dipped her feet into the ice-cold water. The sensation was a shock at first, but as she got used to the temperature, it was quite refreshing.

As she began to submerge herself in the spring, she wondered if getting in with her sundress on was a bad idea. Based on Sidaire's reaction, this was not the time to be concerned with that. Once she was out of the shallows, she quickly dunked her head under the water. Was she supposed to hide under the water of the spring? After taking another breath of air, she went under the surface again.

She was surprised at how deep the water was toward the center. If nothing else, it gave her a chance to investigate the blue glow at the bottom. It was coming from a large opening in the rock.

Bringing her head above the water again, she waited for any sign of Sidaire. Still nothing. She dove back under, swimming down a little farther to investigate the opening. There was a light coming out of the tunnel that shone momentarily and then vanished. It reminded her of the last image she could remember, the blue light coming out of a vortex.

She surfaced again. "There's something down here!" she yelled, hoping Sidaire would know something about it. There was no response.

She lunged forward and swam down toward the blue glow. Around the walls of the cavern, she noticed there was white stone with a honeycomb pattern. It was like the rock formations in between the dunes on her trek across the desert. Inside the cave, the light moved across again, illuminating the inside for a moment. She wanted to move in a little farther, but first she needed to breathe.

Taking a deep breath and holding it, she went back under, down to the cave. The mouth of the cave opened into a larger space inside the rock. There were three smaller tunnels ahead of her. The honeycomb-patterned stone covered the entire cavern. The light brightened again, coming from the tunnel on her right.

She went back out of the cave, surfacing again to get another full breath. This time when she reached the three tunnels, she swam through the one on the right. The tunnel remained tight, making it difficult to turn around. She should not have entered, but it was too late now. She went from cautiously moving through the passage to using her feet on the bottom to propel herself through faster.

She finally came to a wider opening, immediately turning around and going back through to get more oxygen. She had second thoughts about going back but decided to go a little farther, wanting to find the source of the light.

She went back through the smaller tunnel again and came to the larger opening. There were two more tunnels here, but one was too small to enter. The other was about the same size as the one she had come through.

The light was much brighter when it appeared again, and she decided to go through. This tunnel sloped upward at an angle. She used her hands and feet to propel herself as fast as she could through it. As her back began to scrape the ceiling of the tunnel, she realized that it had become smaller than it was when she first entered.

Holding her breath began to get uncomfortable now. She had to consciously resist inhaling. The tunnel kept stretching onward, and she began to panic. She tried to turn around in the small cave but could not do it. She clawed at the ceiling of the tunnel. Fear was setting in now but was a waste of energy. Trying to calm herself, she went back to propelling herself forward in the tunnel.

She was now at her limit. She couldn't hold her breath any longer. She involuntarily gasped for air, but nothing entered her lungs. It was as though her body no longer needed air. Suddenly her entire world flipped over. Her sense of equilibrium went haywire. The water disappeared, and she began to feel completely weightless. A thousand voices whispered in her mind. The girl struggled to decipher the words as they blended with each other in disarray. Her body was numb as she floated aimlessly through the void. There was a vastness to it that she had never experienced. It was as if it had no beginning or end. There was a sense of falling and hitting water again, and her body's need for oxygen returned. The girl quickly held her breath as everything started spinning.

Once she had regained her balance, she realized that she was floating in a much larger space than the tunnel was she in. Above her, rays of light danced through the liquid medium. Was this the light she'd been chasing? It must be really close now. She swam upward toward the surface, finally breaking through and getting some much-needed air.

She immediately closed her eyes. The light was intense. She squinted. It was all a white blur. Once her eyes dilated, details started coming into focus. What was there did not make any logical sense. This wasn't the spring in the oasis, or even the desert planet at all. It was an entirely different world.

CHAPTER 2

THE WARMTH OF sunlight embraced her, a sensation she had not experienced in a long time. A violet sky and large, puffy clouds welcomed her into this new environment. She found herself swimming in a lake that sparkled in the bright sunlight. A landscape of blue-green vegetation surrounded her.

To her right were grassy hills and open meadows. To her left were tall stone banks that led to thick forest. But the most obvious landmark was the monolithic black mountain ahead of her. The mountain went nearly straight up, tapering off as it reached its apex. Two waterfalls cascaded from the mountain into pools that fed into the lake.

She swam toward the banks on her left, heading for the forest side closest to her. The water was nice, but the thought of unknown creatures being under her inspired her to quickly get to land. She wanted to make it to the shore as fast as possible, but the more she hurried, the more panicked she became. It was like something was chasing her.

The banks of the lake ahead were formed into white, rocky mounds. There was a flattened, semicircular area that cut through the mounds. There were three symmetrical inlets there that the lake was flowing into. This appeared to be the closest accessible spot for her to climb out.

She reached shallow water and walked the rest of the way toward the shore. The floor of the lake was hard and slick to her bare feet, slowing her down. When she reached the shore, she noticed something different, a heaviness to her body, as though weighed down by something. Perhaps the gravity was stronger in this world, but it wasn't hurting her or impeding her movement. She found a sizable rock to sit down and rest on. Now she was wet, cold, and uncomfortable as the water began to evaporate from her skin and clothing. The sun was small in the sky here, about the size of a dime in an outstretched hand, but so much brighter than the sun on Earth.

As she sat quietly, the melodies of birds singing in the trees nearby came into focus. There were other sounds, too, the buzzing and clattering of insects. She focused on one sound at a time amid the cacophony and made out a single bird vocalizing five sharp staccato notes, closing with a trill. Another bird made the sound of a low whistle that slid into a higher note at the end. One was like the sound of breath blowing into a bottle.

There were a variety of different animals on either side of the lake gathered to drink. One that caught her attention was a tan-colored animal on four legs about the size of a cow. It had an armored head like a triceratops and a long snout like an elephant trunk. It was using the trunk to drink from the lake.

Now, this was a place worth exploring. She stood up and walked toward the forest line into the thick brush. Most of the foliage on the ground was fernlike plants that grew among the tall grass like weeds. The ferns had an unusual color similar to cyan or aquamarine.

She approached the forest and its thick underbrush. Several vocalizations rang out through the trees around her. The announcements of creatures living in the woods. The trees at the edge of the forest were tall with thick leaves, a variety including yellow, green, orange, and blue.

Towering above them all were gigantic trees with a thick, black bark that was rough and jagged like stone. They had crooked limbs that trailed outward like lightning bolts. These massive trees added an extra layer of canopy over the deeper parts of the forest.

She took a few steps through the first line of trees, grabbing some of the branches to move them away from her face as she moved farther in. Rays of sunlight beamed between the roof of branches and leaves. Leaves fluttered down like falling snow as she explored the wooded area.

The ground began sloping downward as she reached the shadows of the enormous trees overhead. The forest under them was as dark as night. She hesitated to go farther but noticed some lights ahead, glowing around some of the distant trees. Her bare feet crunched on dried leaves as she walked into the dark.

She headed toward the glowing lights until being alerted to another source of crunching leaves behind her. She turned around as a creature came toward her. It walked on six spindly legs and had a long, cylinder-shaped body. Its head had big, yellow eyes, staring right at her. This thing was nearly double her weight.

The creature came closer, stalking her. A garbled growl came from its toothy mouth. It was insect-like in shape, but its skin was scaly and reptilian. Her body felt limp, as though sparing her from the pain it was anticipating. Her breathing turned to gasps as she turned to run. The creature pounced and knocked her to the ground before she had taken more than a few steps. It pinned her down as it stood over her, baring its fangs.

She screamed and closed her eyes. There was a whooshing sound through the brush and then a loud collision. She opened her eyes again and saw the creature fighting with another animal. A few seconds later, the reptilian creature stopped moving, letting out its final breath. The animal that had killed it was a four-legged beast with a dark gray coat of fur. A spiky black mane covered the top of its head and back. Its ears were swept back and pointed, and it had a furry but long, snakelike tail with a rounded tuft of fur on its end.

Its bright blue eyes gazed at her as it sat down on the fern-covered ground. Her situation had not improved. She checked to make sure that her necklace was still there as a new rustling of leaves drew closer.

"Are you all right, dear?" said a voice from somewhere in the woods.

The girl stayed put, unsure whether she should answer or not.

"If you need help, say something," said the voice.

"Help! There's a . . . an animal over here!" the girl shouted as the beast continued staring at her.

A figure in a violet cloak appeared through the trees, walking on two legs in a peculiar, staggered fashion. It went over to the beast and stopped. The beast stood up and nuzzled against the two-legged being. The being moved its head toward her. It had light gray, wrinkled skin. Its face was oblong, with rust-colored eyes containing black slits. It had a ridged brow and flattened nose. Underneath each side of its small mouth were protrusions.

In one hand it was holding a shiny black staff with a sharp metallic point on each end. On its other shoulder, it carried a cloth satchel. Its long, slim legs bowed out behind it underneath the cloak. The thing's backward knees remained bent even as it stood, and it wore leathery sandals on its feet. It was creepy, but sounded friendly.

"Don't be frightened, my dear. This is Blaez. He's mostly friendly," said the cracking, but distinctly feminine, voice.

The being studied the girl for a moment in obvious surprise. "What kind of creature are you? I've never seen anything like you before," she said, her slit eyes blinking as they fixed on the girl. The girl was surprised that she could understand the language of such a strange being.

"Um . . . human," said the girl, her eyes moving back to the beast.

"Never heard of human before," said the being as she examined her. "Where do you come from?"

"Earth."

"Never heard of that either. How far is it?"

"I don't really know how far it is. I'm lost."

"What direction is it?"

The girl pointed up. "I think it's out there somewhere, in space."

"Now is not the time for jokes. I'm trying to help you, dear."

"It wasn't a joke, I just—"

"Let me start over. My name is Maetha," the female said as she held her hand up beside her head with her palm toward the sky. Her hand appeared to have two thumbs, with three fingers in between them and spiny ridges on its palms.

"Thank you for saving me, Maetha," said the girl as she curtseyed, holding the ends of her dress outward. She wasn't sure what made her do that. It was a natural inclination.

Maetha waited for a few moments. "What kind of a greeting is that?"

"The curtsey?" She demonstrated again.

Maetha laughed. "No, you're supposed to introduce yourself."

"Oh . . ." said the girl. "Well, I don't remember my name."

"How do you not remember your own name? Does your brain work?"

"It works just fine, thank you very much!" said the girl as her timid tone quickly changed to an irritated one. "I've been through a lot the last few days. I was stranded alone in a never-ending desert, followed by something invisible, almost drowned in a spring, and then I was attacked by a monster and this beast you call a pet."

"An expression, dear. I meant no offense."

"All I remember is that it started with Am."

"You must have a name, something that identifies you. Let me think of something . . . You're definitely not Kavekkian, so you shouldn't have a Kavekkian name. I don't really know any non-Kavekkian names, though . . . Wait, I do recall something," Maetha said.

"Do you think we should get out of the woods first? Are there any more monsters out around here?"

"Am . . ." Maetha mumbled to herself.

"Please don't call me Am . . ."

"Am . . . Amm . . . brielle. Ambrielle . . . Yes, that's perfect!"

"Hmm, that doesn't bring back any memories, but it's not bad."

"It means 'unique beauty,' or 'beautiful jewel.'"

The girl's cheeks blushed. *Is this creature saying that she thinks I'm beautiful?*

"That crystal you wear around your neck is unique. We have many crystals, but I've never seen one that sparkles in the sunlight in that manner," said Maetha.

The girl rubbed the jewel between her thumb and index finger, now blushing from a different kind of embarrassment. She was relieved that she had not thanked her for the compliment.

"Oh, the necklace," the girl said. "Yes, that's clever."

"And it even starts with Am," Maetha said.

"Yes, it does."

"Do you like it?"

"I do like it . . . It's different."

"Good, I will call you Ambrielle."

"Great . . . I'm kinda nervous being in these woods, with the monsters and stuff."

"I suppose we can leave. I've about got all the fruit I can find around here."

They began walking out of the forest into the brightly lit fields in front of the lake. Several animals remained around the lake, stopping to drink or cool off in the water.

"Let's retrace your steps, Ambrielle," Maetha said, stopping once they left the tree line. "Before you were in the forest, were you out here?"

"Yes."

"Before you were in the field?

"I was in the lake."

"And before that?"

"Underwater, in a tunnel."

"What were you doing underwater in a tunnel?"

"It's . . ." said Ambrielle, "a long story."

"What about before this tunnel?"

"I get where you are going with this, but believe me, logic doesn't apply here."

"Please, to help me get an idea of the situation."

"I was in a desert. There was a spring with a tunnel, and the tunnel led to this lake."

"I suppose you are right. That doesn't make sense, but maybe if you go back through the tunnel, you can get back to your desert and be home again."

"That lake is much deeper than the spring. I don't think I could find the cave again. Besides, that's not my home. I don't want to go back to that desert again." Ambrielle worried about Sidaire. She hadn't intended to leave her there alone.

"How did you get to the desert from your home?"

"That's the part I can't seem to remember."

"So, you're saying that Earth is not part of Anatharia?"

"Anatharia?"

"Yes, all this . . . everything . . . the whole world." Maetha's face contorted in apparent confusion.

"No, Earth is another world on its own."

"This is a wild story, indeed," Maetha said, "but then, I have never seen your kind here before. So I can't completely dismiss that yet. Where do you plan to go for now?"

"I'm not sure," said Ambrielle. "I don't really have anywhere to go."

Maetha stared off into space for a moment, deep in thought. "You may come with me if you would like."

"You don't mind?"

"It may take other Kavekkians a bit to warm up to an outsider, especially a breed we've never seen before, but it should be fine," said Maetha, "Just don't break the rules."

"What are the rules?"

"The basics," Maetha said. "Don't lie, cheat, or steal. Don't hurt anyone."

"That's easy enough."

"Oh," said Maetha, "and if you see a Darterran, don't talk to them. It's forbidden."

"What's a Darterran?"

"They live around here in the caves, but most Kavekkians do not trust them."

"All right, that shouldn't be a problem."

"Good," said Maetha as she hobbled through the fern-covered field, followed by Blaez. Ambrielle caught up to walk beside her.

"Where is this place we are going?"

"Up there, on Mekkinspire." Maetha pointed toward the mountain.

"What all is up there?"

"The Kavekkian city and my home."

"You're Kavekkian?"

"Yes," Maetha said as they walked around the banks of the lake toward the mountain. When they got closer, the sheer face of the mountain sparkled in the sunlight. It was as if the whole face of the mountain was a prism, refracting the light into an array of colors. As fascinating as it was, the reflected light hurt Ambrielle's eyes.

"So, what is your Earth like?" Maetha asked.

"Well, from what I am remembering . . . there's lakes, grass, and trees, but they look different. Most of the vegetation is green, and the sky is light blue. There's—wait! What is that??"

For a moment the blue vortex flashed in front of her as she remembered a time on Earth, crouched down, behind a tree. As she reached down to tie her shoe, she saw a giant, long-legged thing on her leg. Her skin crawled as she stood up and ran, wiggled, and danced around, trying to get it off, but it was still there. Only moving slightly in its creepy, stuttering motion. A spider . . . She hated spiders . . . Why couldn't she remember something good?

"What?" asked Maetha.

"Right there!" Ambrielle said, pointing at something on the back of Maetha's shoulder.

"Oh," said Maetha, brushing off a long-legged, yellowish insect with a curly tail. "You've never seen a flaeg before?"

"No! Thankfully." The insect flew away. "But at least it isn't a spider."

"What's a spider?" Maetha asked.

"Oh, you don't want to know," Ambrielle said.

As they walked toward the mountain, Ambrielle's mood was improving. She needed to make whatever she could out of this situation. She realized this was probably the most interesting part of her life so far. Whatever happened, she should take the time to enjoy this rare gift. She was probably the first human to set foot on another world full of life. Hopefully, she would have the chance to make it back one day and be able to tell the story to . . . whoever she knew back on Earth.

She wished she had brought her shoes for all this walking. The grass, sand, and dirt were soft, at least. There was the occasional rock, but fortunately nothing sharp yet.

"I'm not certain your Earth story will be believed in my city," Maetha said. "But your being here can't be explained either. It's best to be honest when you are asked, regardless of it being believed or not."

Ambrielle nodded, her eyes moving toward the waterfalls as they approached, but she couldn't keep her eyes open in the bright sun.

"Your sun is so bright," Ambrielle said. "Is that what you call it, a sun?"

"Its name is Versoh, but yes, we refer to it as a sun or star."

"Wow, two moons!" The moons rose above the trees behind the mountain. One was about the size of a quarter, higher in the sky in a first-quarter phase; the other was the size of a Frisbee in a waxing gibbous phase. In the sunlit day, they were like a chalk drawing on the sky.

"Oh, yes. Miraeda and Pathea. The big one is Pathea."

Earth had a moon, she recalled, but she didn't remember it having a name. The path took them onto the rocky stone at the base of the mountain, under a recess behind the waterfalls. The falls poured into two deep pools that flowed down into the lake. Once they were past the roaring water, they came to a ridge thirty feet above them.

"We go up from here," Maetha said.

"How do you get up there? Is there a secret path?" Ambrielle grew excited at the prospect of a secret path leading to a city.

"No, you have to climb up."

"What? There's no way I can climb that," Ambrielle said, a bit worried.

Maetha smiled. "There are few creatures that can. I wasn't sure whether humans could or not. It is part of our defense. We're the only ones that can get up the mountain into the city."

"But how will I get there?"

"I will take you on my back. It's only a short way up, and then there is a path that you can walk."

"Okay," Ambrielle said. "How should I get on your back?"

"Here . . ." Maetha bent forward onto her hands to lower herself and make it easier for Ambrielle to climb on. It was awkward reaching out to touch a stranger, especially an alien one with strange bony, hard, wrinkled skin.

She put her left hand on Maetha's robe, grabbing a handful of the cloth, while putting her right arm around Maetha's upper body. She then swung her leg across her waist to support herself. Maetha's upper body was ridged and uncomfortable. There was something like small ribs up close to her chest and neck. Blaez went ahead and climbed up the rocks ahead of them, using its claws to dig into the rock.

Maetha put her hands on the wall of stone, the ridges of her palms digging into the hard rock as she pulled herself up, burrowing her feet into the rock. She started climbing the straight face of the ridge. Her body was ideal for climbing; the backward bend to her legs suited it perfectly.

Her climbing movements were creepy, like a spider, making Ambrielle uneasy. She considered asking her to stop and let her back down but hated to say anything now. Fortunately for Ambrielle, it didn't take long for them to reach the top of the ridge, and Maetha lowered her body close enough to the ground for Ambrielle to climb down.

Ambrielle stood there for a moment, her arms partly out, as though she were still holding on to Maetha.

"You all right?" Maetha asked.

"Oh . . . yes, I'm fine," Ambrielle replied, trying to relax her body.

"You must be afraid of heights," Maetha said.

"Only a little," said Ambrielle, but truthfully, she was freaked out by the insect-like climb she had ridden up on.

"This is the wrong place if you don't like being high off the ground. You sure you want to continue?" Maetha asked.

"Yes, I'll be fine," Ambrielle said.

"Good, it's quite a view up there."

Maetha began walking up the steps carved out of the black stone. Her back was to Ambrielle. She was hunched over, knees bent. Her bowed-leg, hobbled walk made Ambrielle far more comfortable. Ambrielle followed behind. Although the rock was uneven and jagged, the edges were rounded off and surprisingly smooth under her bare feet, which she was grateful for.

The rock was dark in color, black and shiny. When Ambrielle knelt closer, she saw it had tiny metallic sparkles. It was almost like quartz. The flat, smooth edges flashed the same prismatic light that gleamed from the mountain at a distance.

"It's called mekkadium," Maetha said. "This mountain is the only source that we know of. It goes deep under the ground too."

"It's unusual. I bet you could make some amazing jewelry from it," Ambrielle said, thinking out loud more than anything.

"Yes, you can." Maetha smiled. "It's easy to carve and shape but doesn't break easily. We mostly use it for tools, structures, and other decoration."

They started along the dark, rocky path and then came to a doorway carved into the side of the mountain. Ambrielle was eager to get there and peer inside. When she walked through the opening, she entered a large room carved into the rock. There were several chairs, with a table surface in the front. The walls of rock had detailed, precise designs carved into them.

"This was all carved out of the mountain?" Ambrielle asked.

"Yes, this is where the Darterrans used to live," Maetha said. "This particular room is where they would gather for different discussions and events. Many Kavekkians would come as well."

"Why aren't they here anymore?"

"There was a big disagreement many cycles ago. They ended up leaving the mountain," Maetha said with a sadness in her voice.

"Where did they go?"

"They moved into the caves and have remained there for more than sixty cycles."

"What was the disagreement?"

"Some of them stole an important item from us. None of them would return it, and the vaesari had them all banished from Mekkinspire. They could not be trusted any longer."

The room was bathed in a blue light. Along the perimeter of the room's ceiling, there was a trench at a higher level than the rest of the ceiling. The floors were the opposite, with a stepped area all the way around. The corners had a half-circular inset that softened the sharp edges.

There was a ray of light coming into the room around a hole in the cave, which was causing a blue crystal that was positioned in the opening to glow. A blue beam came from the crystal and traveled toward the ceiling. Small crystals in the ceiling reflected toward each other in a zigzag of focused light.

Ambrielle went up to the opening, seeking the source of the light. Peering into the hole in the cave, she saw there was a beam coming from somewhere higher on the mountain.

She walked over to the chairs. They were carved out of this same mekkadium. Some were standing high and others were lower and wider, with cushions lying on the seats. She climbed into one of the tall chairs out of curiosity. The back of the chair was slender and slanted forward, and her feet didn't touch the floor while she sat in it. It was an uncomfortable chair for humans. The lower, wider chairs were better but would be uncomfortable for her after sitting there for a while.

There were drawings carved all over the walls that attracted her attention. There were some precise multilayered triangles that were like arrows pointing down toward the floor. Inside the triangle patterns were lines and circles that Ambrielle interpreted as the sun with rays coming down to the surface of the world. Under this was a carving of two trees intertwined together.

Some of the grooves of the carvings were encased in a light gray, sandy substance. The light gray offset the dark black stone. There was one drawing of a large, dark object with several figures that were fighting it.

"What's this about?" Ambrielle wondered.

"The Darterrans love their stories," Maetha replied. "That one, I think, is about a dark spirit that was able to turn the ancients of this world against each other."

"Oh, interesting."

Maetha was waiting at the doorway. "Ready to continue?"

Ambrielle nodded, and they continued walking up the path. "Do you make everything out of this same rock?"

"Mostly. It's so accessible on this mountain, and it's strong," she added, "but we also use palaetha wood and korkal stone."

"It's going to take me a lifetime to learn everything about this place," Ambrielle said, almost excitedly.

Maetha smiled. "I'm sure you will be fine."

The path led them behind one of the waterfalls as it lent its calming thunder to the quiet serenity of the mountain. Ahead of them were large openings in the side of the mountain. There was a plateau here between the bulk of the mountainside and a large rock face on the other side. Large openings were carved into the sides of the rock around them.

"This is the Darterrans' marketplace," Maetha offered. "Kavekkians would also come here to trade with them."

Wooden structures made with a yellowish-colored wood lined the plateau. Ambrielle imagined a busy street with creatures walking to different shops and picking up new merchandise, some exchanging money, some eating food, children playing. In reality, it was completely deserted. There were no signs anyone had been here in a long time.

Ambrielle couldn't resist peeking in some of the dens. They were simple but round on the inside. There was a larger main room, a bedroom, a small room, and then an area that must have been like a kitchen, where food was stored and prepared. The wooden structures were mostly like shelving, which she imagined were part of the market area. They walked through the street market area and passed what must have been around fifty small dens, all about the same size.

"How many of them lived here?" Ambrielle asked.

"I'm not certain. It was a whole pack," Maetha said. "There's another pack of Darterrans that have always lived underground in the caves at the base of this mountain. The Darterrans that left here moved into the caves with them. I was very young when it happened. I barely remember it."

Ambrielle's feet had become sore from all the walking, and the uneven terrain in certain places hadn't helped. They came upon a wide pool of crystalline water formed into a semicircular shape around the base and into an alcove in the rock. The pool was the source of two of the falls, and the rushing sound of water met them again.

"Oh, that is so lovely," she said.

Maetha seemed to enjoy seeing her reactions. It seemed as if she were experiencing it all again for the first time through Ambrielle. There were two other Kavekkians relaxing in the water. The Kavekkians turned and gasped at the sight of Ambrielle as she and Maetha entered the area.

"What is this . . . creature you bring up here?" one of them asked.

"Calm down, she is peaceful," Maetha said. "She has lost her way home, and I am trying to help her find it."

They continued to stare at Ambrielle as they moved through the alcove. Ambrielle raised her hand to wave at them, but they only continued staring. She understood their reaction, but it still made her uncomfortable about being there.

Another upward path led to crudely carved stairs heading toward a cavernous hallway. There were more glowing crystals along the ceiling, shining the way. As they reached a curve in the hallway, they came upon another Kavekkian sitting there. This one had more pronounced facial features and more wrinkles than Maetha.

The Kavekkian sat by a widened part of the hallway, where there was a cutout that let in light from the outside. The large field and lake stretched out from the mountain through the small window as he carved something out of a small piece of wood.

"Welcome dawn, Maetha. How did your gathering go today?" asked a rough, masculine voice.

Maetha smiled. "Welcome dawn. I got enough, but it's getting harder to fill my bag."

"Those pesky Darterrans, going out every day at sunset. One of them doesn't even seem to mind the sunlight," he said.

"Why would the Darterrans take more fruit than they need? It's going to spoil," said Maetha.

"To punish us," he said, almost apathetically.

"I don't know," Maetha said. "They've never done anything like that before."

Blaez ran up and started sniffing the older Kavekkian. "Why must you bring that thing everywhere with you?" the Kavekkian asked.

"He likes you, and he may be the only one in Lon Kavekkia that does," said Maetha, laughing.

"What is this you have with you now, a new pet?" he asked as he squinted at Ambrielle.

"Taunsin, this is Ambrielle." Maetha gestured toward her.

"How do you do?" Ambrielle said as she curtseyed. She decided that if she was going to be representing all Earthlings here, she should use her best etiquette and manners.

"Oh, this one talks," he said.

"Taunsin, she's not some animal that followed me home from the woods. She's intelligent," said Maetha.

"She doesn't look so smart," he mumbled.

"Could you be a little more welcoming?" Maetha said.

"What are you, and where did you come from?" Taunsin asked.

This was not the type of conversation she'd imagined having with alien life, but things rarely go quite the way you envision them.

"I'm human," she said. "From Earth."

"Earth? Never heard of it," Taunsin said.

"It's another world, far away from here, I think," Ambrielle replied.

"If it's so far away, how did you get here?" Taunsin asked with a demanding sort of tone.

"Well, I don't really know," said Ambrielle. "I mean, it doesn't make any sense, but I was swimming to the bottom of a spring, looking to find a shining light. I followed it into a cave, and when I came out the other side, I was out there in the lake."

"That sounds rather foolish," Taunsin said.

"Well, under the circumstances—" said Ambrielle.

"I thought you said this one was intelligent." He turned to Maetha.

Ambrielle tried to mask her annoyance; she needed a place to stay and needed them to like her. It always made her mad when someone called her stupid or treated her as if she were.

"Taunsin, you had manners once. Perhaps you could remember how to use them—at least for our visitor," Maetha said.

"Yeah, all right. We don't get many visitors up here, so we may be a little distrusting of new creatures," he said.

"So I've heard," said Ambrielle.

"Don't take it to heart. I'm not that trusting of anyone," Taunsin said.

"What's that you're making?" she asked, hoping to direct the conversation to something a little more friendly.

"Hmm? What does it look like I'm making? It's a carving, a figurine. It's going to be a likeness of Baetian's mother. It doesn't seem like much yet, but you can bet it will. Once I get the basic shape right, then I'll start on the detailing."

"Baetian is a good friend of ours," Maetha said to Ambrielle.

"Of course he's a good friend of ours. Everyone knows that," Taunsin replied.

Maetha sighed. "I was telling Ambrielle. She doesn't know Baetian yet."

"I thought you would have mentioned Baetian," said Taunsin. "He's one of our closest friends. How was I supposed to know you don't talk to anyone about Baetian?"

Maetha put a hand over her face. Some gestures are universal. Ambrielle found Taunsin amusing, when he was directing his frustrating remarks toward someone else.

"Well, I think it is beautiful," Ambrielle interjected. "The figurine. I hope I get to see it again when you have it finished," she said, smiling, and Taunsin's lips curved ever so slightly into a hint of a smile of his own.

"We're going to head on, Taunsin. Enjoy the daylight," Maetha said.

"All right, you do the same," Taunsin replied.

Ambrielle waved to him before turning around to follow Maetha as they walked past him down the hallway.

"You'll have to excuse ole Taunsin. He can be a bit difficult," Maetha said as they got out of earshot.

"He's fine. I kinda like him," Ambrielle said.

Maetha smiled. "I do too. Sometimes I'm not sure why, but we've been friends my whole life."

They walked on farther toward the end of the hallway, as sunlight appeared, into a large, open area.

"We're almost to the city now," said Maetha.

Ambrielle's eyes lit up. She was beginning to like this place. "I can't wait to see it!"

CHAPTER 3

THE SOUNDS OF talking, laughing, working, and building filled the air as Maetha and Ambrielle approached the city. Beams of white and blue light radiated in all directions above them. There were two natural formations of mekkadium on the plateau standing several feet high, each with a white crystal on top.

Shafts of white light shone down onto smaller blue crystals that were set atop tall posts crafted from the black stone. They were spread out around the perimeter of the city. The blue crystals beamed out rays into each of the lairs carved into the mountain surrounding the plateau.

Ambrielle stood captivated by the beams, trying to understand their purpose, aside from their spectacular display. "The lights . . ." Ambrielle gathered her thoughts together. "What do all these beams of light do?"

"Our greatest achievement," Maetha said. "They light our houses and buildings. Some we use to carve out the stone for lairs or to cut sheets of rock to construct buildings."

"How do they work?" Ambrielle asked.

"The white durathyst crystals refract the sunlight around the area, causing the blue vaeranite crystals nearby to glow and reflect the beams," Maetha said. "I don't know exactly how it works. We have skilled light-crafters who know the right size and shape the crystals need to be."

"They look amazing . . ." Ambrielle stood underneath the array of lights.

"Come, I will show you more about the light later. I need to introduce you to another Kavekkian." She motioned for Ambrielle to follow her into the crowd.

Many among the crowd stopped and stared at Ambrielle as she followed Maetha, then dispersed as they saw Blaez come through alongside. They passed through the crowd to a wooden table that surrounded a small doorway carved into the rock. Maetha went around the side of the table and up to the doorway.

"Welcome dawn, Corthian. Has your day been productive?" Maetha asked someone inside the room.

"Good light, Maetha. The shop has done well today," he replied from inside the opening in the rock. "How did yours go?"

"Fruit was a bit scarce out there. Hardly any dappones," she said, "but I did get one surprise."

"Oh? What's that?" he asked as he stuck his head out the doorway.

Blaez stood alert as the Kavekkian came out from the carved pathway in the rock, then relaxed after recognizing him.

"Corthian, meet Ambrielle," said Maetha.

"Ambrielle?" said Corthian.

Ambrielle curtseyed. "Hello."

"What? What is this? And it talks . . . ? I've never seen anyone like you before, Ambrielle," Corthian said.

"Likewise, until today," she replied.

"Where did you come from?" he asked.

"A place far away from here called Earth," Ambrielle explained.

"I've never heard of Earth before," said Corthian.

"She needs some shoes," Maetha said. "Could you make something that would work for her foot?"

"I can make any kind of shoe," said Corthian. "Let me measure your foot."

"Wait," said Ambrielle. "I don't have any money, or whatever you use for trade."

"I'm sure we can work something out," Corthian reassured her. "What about that crystal you wear?"

"Oh no, I can't sell this." Ambrielle rubbed the necklace between her fingers.

"What about some of the dappones that I picked today?" Maetha asked.

"That's a start," said Corthian.

"The value of dappones is going up," Maetha negotiated. "They're becoming more of a rarity lately."

"I don't like the sound of that," he said.

"What materials would you need to make them?"

"For something custom for . . . alien feet, I would say at least six balcain leaves in perfect condition. Let's say ten to be sure. Some hovanoke wood, mebri and vaspage oil. Those are what I need the most. Get that plus some extra for my labor, and I'll make some amazing shoes for you, Ambrielle."

"That would be wonderful. Thank the both of you," Ambrielle said.

"Don't thank me." Maetha grinned. "You're the one that will be picking fruit for me tomorrow."

"Okay, of course, I should help earn them myself, but . . ." Ambrielle paused. "It's just that . . . do I have to go out there in the woods again?"

"Don't worry," said Maetha. "I know how to avoid predators."

Corthian took her foot in his rough, wrinkled hand. The palms of his hands were sticky, with ridged fibers. He measured her feet. "No ridges on the bottom . . . do you cover this part of your foot?"

"Yes, that's the most sensitive part," Ambrielle said.

"Oh, how odd," Corthian said. "How were you able to climb the mountain?"

"I brought her up," said Maetha. "She was lost and had no place to go."

Maetha handed two baseball-sized fruits to Corthian. They were dark purple with some patches of red. These must be the dappones that Maetha had been referring to earlier.

"Is there anything you could throw together for her to use in the meantime?" Maetha asked.

"Let me see what I have." He stayed inside the cave for a while and then returned with something resembling sandals.

"I found some children's shoes, cut the toe part out, and made some other modifications."

Ambrielle put them on and walked around. "Yes, this will be much better, thank you." She continued walking around the street to work the stiffness out of them a little more. Maetha began walking back out into the crowded town area, while Blaez and Ambrielle followed. Walking around in these sandals was strange. She hoped that she would soon grow used to them. The sun had fallen a bit lower in the sky. Its dimmer light was more comfortable on Ambrielle's eyes, as she tried to soak it all in.

The Kavekkians all wore robes like Maetha's. Their robes were different colors, and it seemed as though groups of them were often wearing the same colors. Some of them wore shiny metallic accessories over the robes across the chest in different patterns or around the openings of their hoods.

There was one group in white robes that were sitting together talking, eating, and drinking. Occasionally they would mark something on a wooden tablet and then pass it around to the rest of the group. Perhaps drawing pictures to show a new design. Sometimes they called Kavekkians wearing other-colored robes to come over.

Still others were standing in the middle of it all under the large beams of light, holding up small crystals in their hands toward the sky. They were fascinated by light, and Ambrielle wondered if this was something of a religious experience for them. Most of them walked in and out of the shops, looking at different items, trading for some of them, and then moving on to the next shop.

Ambrielle noticed some children playing over behind some of the shops. A few of them were tossing handfuls of small objects into the air that would zigzag erratically as they fell. Another child was trying to hit them with a stick before they reached the ground. It was a type of game.

She went through the crowd nearly unnoticed at times, but some stared at her as she passed by. Some faces showed their curiosity, while others twisted with disdain. As they took a side road that left the city, they came upon a tall Kavekkian. He had some armor plating over his chest, arms, waist, and legs, with a red robe underneath, and he was holding a long staff like the one that Maetha carried as he stood on the street.

Maetha slowed down as they approached. "Raegus, it was good of you to come escort me home."

Raegus laughed. "I've been out here all day, and you know how much I hate watch duty." He eyed Ambrielle with suspicion.

"Raegus, meet Ambrielle. She is lost and can't find her way back to her homeland."

"Sorry to hear that, Ambrielle. Look to the light," he said, baring his palm toward the sky.

"Raegus is a protector," Maetha said. "They watch over us and keep us safe."

"Nice to meet you." Ambrielle curtseyed. "What sort of things do you keep everyone safe from?"

"Wild creatures, mostly," Raegus replied, "out in the fields and forests, when gatherers go out to get materials and food."

"Yeah, I saw one of those creatures earlier." Ambrielle turned to Maetha. "Why didn't you have a protector with you?"

"Maetha doesn't need protection." He laughed and pointed at Blaez. "Especially not when she has this thing around."

He reached out and gave the beast a quick pat. It growled at him, making Ambrielle nervous.

"Raegus," Maetha said, "you know he doesn't like anyone touching him."

"How many dangerous creatures are there around here?" Ambrielle asked.

"There's a few different kinds you have to worry about," he said, "like the murchas and siglas that live in the grasslands, and there's the raestrigs and harvosses that live in the forests."

"Don't let that worry you, dear," said Maetha. "You went into the forest at the worst time of day. Attacks are rare. Having protectors on gathering trips is just a precaution."

"What was it that attacked me?" Ambrielle asked.

"That was a baelgor," Maetha said. "They're scavengers, but they will aggressively attack anything smaller than them. They wait in the dark parts of the forest for animals that are walking back from drinking in the lake, trying to find one alone that strayed from the group."

"Maetha's right," said Raegus. "I haven't seen any action in a long time. We've learned a lot about their behavior over the cycles: how to avoid them, how to not provoke them, how to scare them off."

"You both seem like you have encountered a lot of strange stuff," said Ambrielle. "Have you ever heard of a place called The Hollow?"

"The Hollow?" Raegus asked. "I don't believe so."

"I have not either," said Maetha. "Why do you ask?"

"No real reason, just curious," said Ambrielle. "So, no one ever gets attacked by wild animals anymore?"

"Hardly ever, because of what we know now. A lot of that knowledge came from Maetha." Raegus nudged Maetha. "She probably wouldn't tell you, but she used to be a protector."

"Oh wow, really?" said Ambrielle.

"She was one of the first that actually cared about preserving the lives of all the creatures—even the predators," Raegus said. "For cycles, we saw predators as enemies, rather than creatures that have a purpose in the revolving system of life."

"You're giving me far too much credit, Raegus. I didn't start that." Maetha turned to Ambrielle. "It was my grandfather, and there were many others that began using his methods. I am trying to help carry on what he started."

"What were his methods?" Ambrielle asked.

"Avoiding attacks, as Raegus mentioned," Maetha said. "It was proven that if you start killing off too many predators, the plant-eater population grows, which causes a shortage of vegetables and fruits for us."

"That makes sense," said Ambrielle. "So you're always able to avoid them?"

"As much as possible," Maetha said. "We kill them when we have to, but it's minimal."

"I guess I shouldn't have been wandering in the woods, to make you have to kill one," Ambrielle said.

"Don't worry about it. We must kill them sometimes. When their population gets too large, that's when their behavior changes and they become more competitive for food," said Maetha. "When that happens, they begin attacking us more, so we have to kill a few of them to defend ourselves, and their numbers become reduced again."

"As long as we keep ourselves in check, the balance can continue on," Raegus said.

"The balance continues regardless," Maetha said. "If we become over-zealous in killing predators, the other animals eat more of the plants, and we either end up starving or we become the predators and eat the animals. Either way, the balance continues. We prefer that it be preserved in its natural state."

"There you go. She always explains it better than I can," Raegus said, nodding to Ambrielle.

"We had better get to my lair. It is beginning to get dark," Maetha said as Ambrielle turned toward the orange-and-yellow skyline. "May the dawn find you well, Raegus."

"May it find the both of you well too," he replied.

Maetha and Ambrielle proceeded through an archway onto a path that went close to the edge of the mountain, curving upward. The city crowd behind them had thinned considerably since they first started talking to Raegus, and everything had grown quieter. As they passed a group of Kavekkians that were standing on the side of the path talking, one of them paused the conversation and looked at Maetha.

"Why have you brought this outsider here? It doesn't belong here!" he shouted.

Maetha turned away from them and continued walking. Ambrielle quickened her pace enough to catch up to Maetha and Blaez. She was a little unsettled. It was the first time anyone had vocalized her being unwelcome here. She had been met with a few foul expressions, but this was different.

"Don't mind them," Maetha told Ambrielle. "All Kavekkians here are distrusting of anyone they don't know, for a variety of reasons. They all react to it in different ways."

"It's okay," said Ambrielle. "Most everyone has been kind."

They came up the steps to another street area with more houses carved into the rock. These were larger, and it was quieter up here. There were crystals here as well, on top of stands above them, with beams crisscrossing into different caves in the rocks surrounding the street plateau. With the sun setting, the beams were dimmer than the bright, focused light from earlier.

"Can the crystals work at night?" Ambrielle asked.

"No, once the sun sets, they start going out," Maetha explained. "The vaeranite crystals glow a little in the moonlight, but the durathyst crystals don't produce a strong enough light for them to reflect."

"How do you see anything at night, then?" Ambrielle asked.

"There is always at least a little moonlight from one or both of the moons," Maetha said, "but we sleep once it gets dark."

"Is Raegus going to be out there on watch duty all night?"

"Yes, but he'll be fine. They usually light some torches with the light beams before sunset and place them around the city."

They walked past a lair with intricate carvings around the open doorway in the rock. There was a design of a sun with two trees intertwined, like the one before, but this one was scratched up, like someone had tried to mark over it.

The sun had set now, and Ambrielle was reminded of the lonely desert wilderness that she had recently left. As glad as she was to be here and away from the solitude of that world, she had at times enjoyed the quiet serenity of its dimly glowing landscape by the spring, and the calm, soothing breeze.

"Here we are . . ." Maetha said in a singsong voice. "Welcome to my lair."

Ambrielle scanned the outside of Maetha's house. Above their heads, over the hollowed-out doorway, there was a smaller hole with a glowing vaeranite crystal in the middle. Blaez ran past Ambrielle and settled on a soft blanket on the floor.

Inside, the light was going from the vaeranite in the cut-out window to a decorative arrangement of smaller crystals that hung from the ceiling. This arrangement was lighting up the cavernous home and giving everything inside a blue glow. There were various stone and wood surfaces in this room, and atop those surfaces were what appeared to be various carved statues, some tools, robes, and metal trinkets.

In one corner, there was a long staff similar to what Maetha carried with her. One end of the pike had a sharp point, while the other end had a sharp edge, like a sword. Between the two ends was a textured surface for gripping.

A small fountain of water flowed from a carved stone block. It caused a dancing glow under the diming beams of light. Three cavern-like doorways led from the main room into other rooms.

"You have a lovely home," Ambrielle said as her eyes moved around the room.

"Thank you, dear," replied Maetha. "We had better go ahead and eat, and then I will make a resting place for you. I'm sure you must be hungry."

"Yes, now that you mention it." Ambrielle rubbed her stomach. "There's been so many new things to see, I barely noticed."

Maetha smiled. "It's been a long day. Feel free to sit, and I will be right back."

Maetha came back with a bowl made of stone and two wooden plates. The bowl contained fruits of various sizes, colors, and shapes. She walked over to where Maetha was setting the bowl on a stone table and sat down in one of the chairs. The chairs were slanted forward. Ambrielle slid up on the edge of the seat to find a comfortable position.

Maetha set a plate in front of her and then placed the bowl between them on the table. "Go ahead and get whatever you like."

"I'm not even sure what all of this is." Ambrielle laughed. "I don't know what to get."

"Try the apraedas. You can't go wrong there."

"Which ones are those?"

"This is one," Maetha said. "And this over here . . . and that one." Maetha pointed to a few pieces that were yellow with a blue bottom.

Ambrielle took a small one that was about the size of a golf ball and put in on her plate. She studied it for a moment and then picked it back up. The texture was smooth and rubbery. She went ahead and took a bite. It was like she had taken a bite of a plastic bag full of water. Juice from the fruit gushed everywhere, filling her mouth and spilling out of the corners of her lips. She wiped seeds and pulp from her mouth with the back of her hand, a bit embarrassed for being so sloppy when eating.

There wasn't much taste to it. It was something like a watered-down strawberry. It wasn't bad, but it didn't have a lot of flavor. *These could make good juice to drink with some sugar added*, she thought.

Maetha was eating a yellow-and-white oblong-shaped fruit.

"What is that one?" Ambrielle asked.

"These are olavas. Try one."

Ambrielle picked one up. This fruit had a firmness to it, and the texture was smooth but uneven. She took a bite. She didn't expect the results. Slightly crunchy, it broke up oddly when she chewed. It was like grinding her teeth on sand. The taste was wild and raw. She didn't like it much at first, but then it became sharp and sweet and was somewhat pleasant after she started getting used to it.

"Try one of these dappones too," Maetha said, pointing to a dark purple, baseball-sized fruit with red spots.

Ambrielle grabbed one of the firm, bumpy-textured fruits. She bit into it, not expecting how hard the surface would be, but once it began to give way from the pressure of her teeth, it opened quite easily. The inside of the fruit was a soft, paste-like substance, with several small seeds. It was odd to her at first, but the taste was heavenly! It had the right amount of sweetness and tanginess to it. As she chewed, the exterior rind had a satisfying crunch that complemented the soft interior. She could eat these all day.

"Oh, you like those, I see. You'll have to fight Corthian for them." Maetha laughed. "Those have become harder to find lately too."

"Why do you think that is?"

"Taunsin thinks the Darterrans are taking them, as you heard."

"But you don't think so?"

"They always go out to pick fruits and other plants, but they've never taken enough to cause a shortage. They believe in keeping the balance of nature too. In fact, my grandfather first learned this from them and their fables. He studied nature and animal behavior and realized that it was more than a fable. He was able to show everyone that there are repercussions for being greedy, and then he took those lessons and turned them into the basis of his methods of gathering," Maetha explained.

"Oh, so they wouldn't interfere," Ambrielle said. "What do you think it is, then?"

"I don't know. I haven't found any evidence yet," Maetha said. "I can't rule out that it could be the Darterrans, but they also pick from trees deeper in the forest, where we don't go. Aside from that, they eat escradas that live in the caves, which I find disgusting. They have no reason to take more of the fruit that we pick from, especially knowing that we would be forced to take drastic measures if they were taking our supply of food."

"Maybe there are more of them now than there used to be, so they need more," Ambrielle asserted.

"Whatever the reason, it is going to be a problem that we will have to solve," Maetha replied. "I need to talk to the vaesari tomorrow about this. I should be able to get an audience with them."

"Who are the vaesari?" Ambrielle asked.

"The vaesari are the rulers of all of Lon Kavekkia. The vaesar and the vaesara," Maetha replied, then paused for a moment. "Ambrielle, I have a confession to make."

Her change in tone caught Ambrielle off guard.

"When I first offered for you to come here, I knew the curiosity surrounding an outsider would get the attention of the vaesari. They would want to meet you." Maetha paused again and rubbed the back of her neck. "I've been trying to talk to them about the growing problem with the shortage of food for many days now, but the council won't grant me access. They haven't noticed the problem because it hasn't started affecting us yet, but with you going to meet them, I'll be right there with you and will be able to talk to them."

"So, you are using me?" Ambrielle wanted to be angry, but she was more disappointed than anything.

"I hope that is not how you see it," Maetha said, glancing down at the table. "I am not going to make you go meet the vaesari if you don't want to. I'm only saying that it would help us out if you do. If you have any interest in learning about our culture here, it may be something that you would want to experience." Maetha's gaze went back to Ambrielle. "When you first spoke, you seemed like someone like me, someone that helps others. This could be important enough that it may help save all of Lon Kavekkia."

Ambrielle felt compelled to help. She wanted to be useful again. Maetha didn't seem to have a selfish goal in wanting her to come here. She was helping her by giving her food and shelter and trying to help her fellow Kavekkians at the same time.

"Let's get some sleep, and you can make your decision in the morning," Maetha said. "I have an extra bed in my resting room that you can use."

"Okay, thank you." She followed Maetha into one of the doorway tunnels as the light beams began to vanish from the house and the glowing crystals faded out. The bright moonlight of the two moons coming through the window of the main room was all that was left. When she entered the room, Maetha was pulling a blanket from a shelf that was cut into the rock wall.

It was orange, and its material was like cotton that had been stretched out and tied together. There was one already sitting on one of the beds. The beds themselves were like stone slabs. Maetha was placing this blanket on top of the other bed.

"Here you are. This will be your bed," Maetha said.

"Perfect." Ambrielle wasn't sure this was going to be comfortable, but it was much better than sleeping out in the woods or sleeping on a pillow made of sand in solitude.

"There's one more thing I need to show you before we retire for the night," Maetha said, walking back to the main room and then entering a different doorway.

Ambrielle followed her to a small room. Their footsteps echoed as they approached amid the sound of trickling water. There was a hole in the floor with two wooden boards lying across it. Inside the hole, water flowed from the side into the darkness below.

"If you need to expend during the night, use this," Maetha said.

"Expend?" Ambrielle asked.

"I'm not sure how humans refer to it. You know when you eat and drink and then you need to expend what you don't use?" Maetha asked.

"Oh . . . yeah," said Ambrielle. "Okay, I know what you are saying now."

"Sit here on these two planks, leaving enough space between them for . . . what you need. Don't leave too much space. You do not want to fall in. Then you can use this container here to gather some of the water for cleaning your—"

"Yeah, yeah, I get it," said Ambrielle.

A flash of blue caused her eyes to close for a moment as she remembered a time back on Earth, going camping. She recalled loving it, but there were always bathrooms at the campgrounds to use. Although some of those weren't the best bathrooms in the world, it was never quite like this. Thinking back to the situation in the desert, though, she thought this was an improvement.

"Thanks for letting me know," Ambrielle said.

"Good, then let's get some sleep. I'm exhausted, and you surely must be as well."

"I *am* pretty tired."

Maetha walked into the other room and returned wearing a looser gray robe as Ambrielle got on her bed and lay down on the fluffy material that Maetha had laid over the stone bed earlier. Ambrielle tossed back and forth a bit, trying to dig into a comfortable spot. She wondered how she would ever fall asleep on this bed.

She would use this time to think, to process everything she had experienced in this new world. The moonlight made some odd shadows on the floor from the window in the main room. It was quiet except for some creature making a sound in the distance like "warrel . . . warrel . . . warrel." Probably the sound of a night bird's call somewhere on the mountain. Another called out, "Mrekkk, mrekkk, muuuurekkkk."

These strange, unfamiliar sounds were surreal and even a little frightening. There were odd creaks and grinding sounds, causing her senses to stay heightened and alert. After a while, her weary mind wandered back to the quiet spring and the carvings on her sitting stone. She hoped that Sidaire was okay and that she would find whatever she was seeking. Her thoughts went to what Sidaire had been saying about The Hollow. She was still curious as to what that was all about and what the Whisperers were. The emptiness crept near her. It was like something heading toward her on the horizon. Every day that passed brought it closer. She had to put it out of her mind. Ambrielle closed her eyes, and her thoughts began to slow as her mind wandered its way out of the waking world and into peaceful slumber.

CHAPTER 4

A VOICE CALLED OUT through the peaceful silence. The words grew louder as her senses began to return. Her mind reached for information, as if separate currents raced through her brain toward a conflux that jolted her awake. "Ambrielle . . .

"There you are, I was beginning to think you weren't going to wake up," said Maetha.

Ambrielle wanted to pretend that she was still asleep. If she could convince herself to fall back into the blissful slumber, Maetha may give up.

"Come on, now, you need to tell me your decision," Maetha said. "Will you go with me to see the vaesari?"

Ambrielle sighed. "If I say no, can I go back to sleep?"

"No," Maetha answered. "If we don't go see the vaesari, we need to go out to the forest and fetch those supplies that Corthian needs for the shoes."

"Well, we may as well go see the vaesari, then." Ambrielle began to sit up on the billowy fibers of bedding material.

"Wonderful, thank you, Ambrielle!" Maetha said excitedly.

Maetha had not been excited about anything until now. It made Ambrielle realize how important this was to her.

"I have some fruit on the table that we can eat, and there is a cave below us with a pool where we can bathe." Maetha sat down to eat. "I will let you borrow one of my daughter's old robes so you can wear something clean."

"Okay, I'll be right in there. I need to . . . use the room," Ambrielle said groggily as she stumbled across the floor.

"Need to what?"

"Expend . . ."

"Oh, go right ahead."

When she entered the main room, Maetha was sitting at the stone table with a bowl of fruit and plates for herself and Ambrielle. Ambrielle sat down and picked up one of the olavas from the bowl, taking a bite. The vaeranite crystals were glowing bright now and beaming light across the ceiling of the room.

"I made us some apraeda juice to drink, too, if you are thirsty," Maetha said.

"Oh yes, please," said Ambrielle, and Maetha stood and turned to a stone shelf and grabbed two stone cups and a larger container of juice. The stone cups had a finish like frozen liquid and were smooth to the touch.

Maetha poured a cup of juice and set it in front of Ambrielle.

"Thank you." Ambrielle smiled.

Maetha nodded as she sat back down.

The blue vortex again flashed in front of her, and she began to see a man with light brown hair making breakfast while she sat at a table drinking orange juice. She was reading over something written down in a notebook sitting in front of her.

"How many moons does Jupiter have?" she asked.

"I think it is seventy now," he replied.

"Close," she said.

"When I was in school, it was only sixteen."

"That's crazy. I bet they will find a hundred eventually."

"You sure have a lot of notes there. Is there a test today?"

"Not today, it's just interesting."

"Good to know that you have some interests besides makeup, clothes, and boys."

"Dad . . . I have plenty more interests," she said.

"Oh, so you are interested in boys. You didn't deny it."

"Dad!"

He was frying some bacon on the stove, and she remembered how good it smelled. Her dad was always frying bacon. It was about all he ever cooked. Often, he would even fry a couple of strips of bacon for an afternoon snack. Ambrielle nearly laughed out loud thinking about it and began to miss what moments ago she didn't even know she had.

"So, when we meet the vaesari"—Maetha grabbed a bowl filled with pieces of fish—"follow my lead, and everything should be fine. I will be right there with you."

"I hope I don't say anything stupid," Ambrielle said nervously.

"Oh, you'll be fine, dear." Maetha tossed a piece of fish toward the beast, which it caught in its mouth. "I'll do most of the talking. They may ask you a few questions. Answer them the best you can.

"I am a little nervous myself." Maetha laughed. "It has been a while since I have spoken at one of the meetings."

Ambrielle smiled nervously, playing with the wavy ends of her hair.

Once they finished eating, Maetha filled a container up with water from the fountain in the main room and cleaned the cups and bowls they had used.

"I'll go grab you a robe, and we can head down to the bath," Maetha said. She returned with two small, white pieces of clothing. "Here we go. Now we are ready."

Blaez perked up and sat up from his position on the floor.

"Stay . . . You can't come this time," Maetha called out, and the beast rested its head back down again. She left through the doorway into the bright outdoors.

Ambrielle was blinded by the sunlight as she followed Maetha to a cave in the mountain rock behind the house. The stairs winding down were dimly lit in blue by a chain of vaeranite.

At the bottom they came to a small, cavernous area with water flowing into a pool. Maetha lowered herself into the water and then removed her bed robe and tossed it away from the water. Ambrielle loosened her dress slightly as she climbed into the pool. She hesitantly removed it once she was immersed in the water and placed it on the rocky surface nearby as Maetha did.

"Get some of that lisper over there. You can clean yourself with it." Maetha motioned to a container with a pale-yellow jelly substance.

Ambrielle reach over to it and watched how Maetha was applying it to herself by scraping some into her hand and rubbing it on. Ambrielle reached into the container and got some on her fingers and began rubbing it on her arms and shoulders. The substance was sticky and did not spread over her skin easily. It caused a slight burning sensation after having it on for a few moments, making her wash it off quickly. It smelled nice, a fragrance that reminded her of honeysuckle. Fortunately, it washed off in the water much more easily than it went on.

She wanted to wash her hair, but this lisper was too thick and sticky for that.

"So, you have a daughter?" Ambrielle asked.

"Yes. She doesn't live here anymore, though," Maetha said.

"Oh, she's grown now?"

"Yes," Maetha explained. "I'll introduce you to her sometime."

After they were done, Ambrielle put on the white robe. The first piece of the garment was tight-fitting and had a hooded cloak at the top. The robe piece that went over it was much looser and flowing. Wearing fresh clothes again after a bath revived her soul. She picked up her soaking-wet dress from the stone floor.

"We better get going," Maetha said as she adjusted her violet robe. They walked back up to the outside of the house, and Maetha laid her night robe straight out on a slope of rock. Ambrielle did the same with her dress. Making their way past a few more lairs of hollowed rock formations, Maetha turned around the larger wall of the mountain. There were more steps here, going farther up the side.

There were some small plants growing here, where dust and dirt had settled into the grooves and cracks of the rock. They reached another plateau, where a protector stood watch at the steps. He was wearing the same kind of metal-plated red robe that Raegus had on before.

"Welcome dawn, Maetha," said the guard.

"Welcome dawn, Pathello," Maetha said in return.

"Are you sure about bringing this creature up here?" Pathello twisted the bottom of his staff into a pocket in the street.

"Yes, the vaesari may want to speak to her," Maetha said.

"I'll have to escort you, then," Pathello said.

The three of them walked up the rest of the steps until they came to an extensive open area around the mountain peak. The top of the peak itself was sloped and jagged and had no feasible ground to stand on. The open area ahead was triangular, with elegantly carved shapes of reddish-gray stone that were pieced together like a brick street. Ahead of them were several pillars and statues. It was a courtyard of sorts.

The sounds of many voices filled the area somewhere up ahead. The air smelled nice and fresh up here, coupled with an occasional rich fragrance of burning wood. There were two more protectors guarding the archways of separate paths that led out from the courtyard. The protectors didn't move but stared at them intently. A female in a gold-colored robe hurriedly approached them, staring at Ambrielle.

"Maetha . . . what brings you here today?" the female Kavekkian said in a tone that was more authoritarian than friendly.

"This is Ambrielle. I found her yesterday when I was gathering resources." Maetha met Ambrielle's glance. "Aradel is the head of the vaesari council."

The female held an expression of disdain on her face. Ambrielle gave her a curtsey, this time with a bowed head in reverence for Aradel's position, hoping to help soften the ill expression about her being there.

Maetha said, "She calls herself a human from a place called Earth, and I thought the vaesari may want to talk with her."

"Yes, we have heard rumors of this strange animal that you brought here," said the female. "You know we have rules against outsiders on Mekkinspire."

"We have rules against Darterrans being here, and she's clearly not Darterran." Maetha clasped her hands together in front of her, resting them against her robe.

"I think it goes without saying that this applies to anyone that is not Kavekkian." The female's hand settled on her hip. "Especially creatures we know nothing about."

"The rules should be clear, then. Are you going to make that decision for the vaesari based on what you think the rules imply?" Maetha's expression softened as she waited for the response.

"I am only here to serve the vaesari." Aradel sternly placed a second hand on her other side. "They do not give an audience to anyone that may pose a threat."

"I only came here today to give them the opportunity to learn of a new species from another land. I could have made that decision for them and not brought the human here. I could have gone along with what I think the rules may imply, and we could continue on having the same normal day as we always do," Maetha said. "But I trust the vaesari to make the right decision."

"Spare me the feigned virtue," Aradel said, rolling her eyes. "We both know that has nothing to do with why you are here."

"Look at her, do you see how frail her body is? She poses no threat."

Ambrielle glanced at Maetha, wondering if this was all part of the game she was playing or if she really thought Ambrielle was fragile and weak. Aradel stared off into space for a moment. "I will bring this matter to the vaesari. They can decide if they want to meet this . . . human. Wait right here."

After she turned and walked farther away from them, Maetha turned toward Ambrielle. "She has been turning me away every time I've come to tell the vaesari about the increasing shortages of food and supplies."

"What do you think she is going to do now?" asked Ambrielle, concerned.

"I don't think the vaesari will ignore you being here," Maetha replied. "It is too widely known."

Ambrielle stared off at the point where Aradel had walked away, expecting her to reappear at any moment. Her attention soon drifted to other parts of the courtyard around her. A large statue stood on a tall pedestal carved out of mekkadium. The statue of a Kavekkian was holding a vaeranite crystal in the air. There were six of these statues, each one holding a crystal. Each crystal reflecting a beam of light to another crystal. Between each statue was a durathyst crystal that refracted crossing patterns of light around the circle.

The blue beams were in a closed loop from the circular arrangement of vaeranite. Each trip around the circle strengthened them further. It caused an interesting effect where the beams would grow brighter and more solid, until they would finally dissipate and dim. The process would then start over again.

The right side of the courtyard led through an archway into an area with a large, angular building of multiple levels. It had walls of mekkadium cut into sheets and assembled together into large triangular and pentagonal shapes that stacked atop each other as the levels rose higher. It appeared to have five levels, each one with a smaller perimeter than the one below it.

There was a commotion coming from the left path again, a crowd of Kavekkians that were out of her sight. She wondered what shape her hair must be in by now, patting the top of her hair lightly to see how it was placed. It wasn't too bad. Making her fingers into a comb, she tried brushing the sides. She attempted to get all the hairs flowing in the same direction and get some of the tangles out in the process.

Aradel walked out far enough to get their attention and motioned for them to come. Ambrielle turned and glanced at Maetha. The woman gave her a slight grin. The two of them then walked over through the archway and up to where Aradel was standing. She was perturbed by the expression on her face.

"They have agreed to see the human." Aradel turned to Maetha. "But she must come alone."

"Ambrielle is new here. She shouldn't have to face the vaesari by herself," Maetha said. "Whatever problem you have with me, dear, please do not punish her for it."

"This has nothing to do with us, Maetha. Those are the conditions." Aradel turned to Ambrielle. "If you want to have an audience with the vaesari, little human, come with me now."

"At least let me talk to her first," said Maetha.

"Are you coming or not?" Aradel said to Ambrielle.

Ambrielle began walking over to her as she turned back to Maetha. Aradel quickly turned around, her robe blustered out, as if imitating her demeanor. Ambrielle followed her through the archway, past the red-robed protector standing guard. They walked through a walled pathway with carvings that contained a pattern of crystals. They reflected beams of light back and forth to each other in a crisscrossing array that was more decorative than anything practical.

She grew nervous and tried to mentally prepare for facing the vaesari as she followed Aradel. Fountains of water flowed at the sides of each wall at the end of the path. Ahead of them was a large platform where two figures sat on crooked stone seats decorated with glowing golden crystals. There were other Kavekkians sitting on benches to the left and right sides of the platform.

As Ambrielle approached, there were gasps and loud murmurings among the audience as they got their first glimpse of a human. The floor they walked on was like polished mekkadium, smooth and glassy beneath Ambrielle's sandals. Aradel walked to a place on the floor beside a circle of glowing vaeranite embedded into the marbled floor.

"Attention, everyone," said Aradel, "Our first order this day is a human visitor who wishes to speak to the vaesari of Lon Kavekkia."

She motioned for Ambrielle to stand in the circle.

"I now present to you all, the Dawnsent of the New Cycle, the vaesar and vaesara." Everyone but Ambrielle then raised their left hand to the sky while bowing their head. Ambrielle glanced around, unsure whether she should participate in this gesture or not.

"Is this the human that wanted to speak?" said a deep, calm but loud voice from somewhere ahead of them.

"Yes, Vaesar, it is she," Aradel confirmed.

"Hmm, not exactly what I expected, I must say," said the vaesar.

"The human may stand in the light," said Aradel.

Everyone in the crowd then sat down.

Ambrielle stood in the middle of the glowing crystals, unsure whether she was supposed to start talking or wait. She searched the faces in the crowd for any signs of what she was expected to do. There were about fifty or so Kavekkians in the seats around the courtyard.

"We have never seen or heard of your kind, human. How did you find your way to Lon Kavekkia?"

Now that she was here, with all eyes locked on her, she was more intimidated than she thought she would be. The mettle she had tried to psych up within herself had melted away. She had to find a way to reclaim it. She stopped twisting a strand of her hair long enough to find the jewel in her necklace as she nervously turned it back and forth between her thumb and index finger.

"Well, I arri—" Ambrielle cleared her throat. "—arrived in the lake. I don't know how exactly I got there."

Ambrielle scolded herself for giving more information than what was asked.

"How could you arrive here and not know how you did so?" questioned the vaesar.

"Well . . . I was swimming through a cavern in a spring, and when I reached the end of the tunnel, I was in the lake."

"It would seem that you do know how you arrived, then," the vaesar said as the crowd murmured with some laughter.

Ambrielle began fidgeting with the ends of her hair. "I should have said that I was surprised to have arrived here."

"We never get any visitors or new species around here, especially not ones that can speak," the vaesar said. "This is highly unusual."

"It is for me too, sir," said Ambrielle.

"What is your intent here, then?" asked the vaesar. "To find your way back to your lands, to your kind?"

"I'm lost here," Ambrielle said. "My intent is simply to survive and not be alone."

The vaesar considered her words for a moment. "You eventually intend to find your way back, do you not?"

"I wouldn't know where to start, sir," said Ambrielle. "I don't know how I would get back."

"Obviously, you would begin at the lake," the vaesar stated. "Couldn't you go back through this tunnel again?"

"I'm not sure how I would find it again in all of that water," Ambrielle replied.

"It must feed from the river. You could go back upstream and eventually find your land again."

"I don't think that would work." Ambrielle shuffled her feet. She didn't want to get too deep into this, as they would likely not believe it and end up trusting her less. "My home is really far away."

"You were able to get here, so you should be able to get back," he said. "It can't be that far away."

Even though Ambrielle was intimidated being here, the vaesar's accusatory words and tone made her defensive, but she tried to remain calm and choose her words carefully.

"Well, has anyone ever seen any humans anywhere up the river?" she asked.

"We have not," admitted the vaesar. "But we've never been far up the river. For all we know, there could be."

Ambrielle was surprised. "Really? No one has ever been over there at all?"

"We have everything we need right here. Why would we ever leave Lon Kavekkia?"

"Well, there could be new resources out there, different fruits, different trees and plants for materials."

"Doubtful," said the vaesar. "There's a reason we settled in this area hundreds of cycles ago. Lon Kavekkia is the most abundant source of resources on Anatharia. Everything we need is all right here together. There is enough of it that it is replenished well before we need it."

"Doesn't that prove my point," said Ambrielle, "that there is no civilization up the river?"

The vaesar was growing impatient. "Things can change after hundreds of cycles." He sneered. "Unless you can prove otherwise, we will assume that you came from up the river."

"Well, I don't really have any evidence," Ambrielle said.

"Good," he said flippantly.

"What is your name, human?" said the vaesara.

"Ambrielle," she said.

"Ambrielle? Where did you come by that name?" said the vaesara with surprise.

Based on her reaction, Ambrielle was unsure whether she should tell them that Maetha gave her the name. "Um, I don't . . . That's what I was given?"

"Isn't that one of the artifact names?" The vaesar turned to the vaesara and then back to Ambrielle. "Does your kind know of the tablets?"

"I've never heard of any tablets," Ambrielle said.

"Not even many Kavekkians know much of the tablets or their names. Are you someone of importance among your kind?" he asked.

"Um, no . . . not particularly . . . I'm still in high school," Ambrielle replied.

"Could you please tell us a little about your kind . . . your city . . . your way of life?" the vaesara asked.

"Well . . ." said Ambrielle, unsure where to begin.

"You've no doubt seen the crystals that project light all over the city. Does your kind have technology like this?" the vaesara prompted.

"No, we do not," Ambrielle replied. "It is impressive."

"Is there any kind of technology that your kind has that we do not?" asked the vaesara.

"Well, we do have cars, planes, mobile phones, computers . . ." said Ambrielle.

"Sounds like you are making things up now," said the vaesar. "Can you describe what any of these things do?"

Ambrielle tried to explain the inventions she could recall from Earth, but the Kavekkians did not understand. With the two worlds being so different, it made it impossible for her to explain people being so far away that they would need any kind of communication device to talk to someone, such as a telephone.

"Do you have one of these devices that you could show us?" asked the vaesar.

"Uh, well, no, I don't have mine on me," Ambrielle said. "I guess I didn't bring it with me."

"That seems perfectly convenient," said the vaesar. "Could you build one of these devices for us?"

"Well, even though I like to read about how this stuff works," Ambrielle said, "I'm not someone that can build anything like that yet."

The vaesar laughed as he glanced out at the audience. "So, we have a visitor from another species of intelligent life with all this supposed technology, and we get the one that isn't able to build anything?"

Some laughs came over the crowd, but Ambrielle was not amused. She hated when someone implied that she was less than smart or capable. The vaesar triggered a flash of the swirling vortex with the blue light. She saw Mrs. Hannington, who was her ninth grade English teacher. She seemed to enjoy any time that Ambrielle read an uncommon word improperly.

Mrs. Hannington would stop the class to point out that her pronunciation of the word was incorrect and then tell how it was supposed to be pronounced. She did this with a little chuckle at Ambrielle's expense, prompting students in the class to begin laughing as well, even though she bet that most of them had no idea how to pronounce it either, or even what the word meant.

"First of all," she replied to the vaesar, "this world is foreign to me. So, can you tell me what materials you have here that would even conduct electricity? I'd need to find out which are conductive, which are semiconductive, which ones are insulators . . . Those are the most basic things I would need to build anything electronic." Ambrielle remembered occasionally being mad enough to have the courage to speak to Mrs. Hannington like this. Not that she would ever want to be disrespectful, but more to defend herself.

She remembered girls in the class trying to get her attention whenever this happened, telling her that she may want to drop it before she got in trouble. There was no one here to do this for her now.

"Second, there's really no one person that makes a phone. Different components are made in different factories by several different companies, each composed of several humans, to be assembled into a single phone," she continued. "And lastly, have you, yourself, ever built any of your light devices here, or if you were stranded on a strange world, would you be the visitor that can't build anything?"

The crowd was silent, either not knowing how they were supposed to react or waiting for the storm that was about to come.

The vaesar chuckled. "It seems I have offended this one. Humans must be a feisty bunch, indeed. I meant no offense. It was more a joke. We understand that you are in strange surroundings, and we will try to imagine things from your perspective, as we ask that you put yourself in ours. What do you say, Vaesara? Should we allow her to stay here for now?"

"Whether you were making any of this up or not, Ambrielle, your thoughts have been perplexing but fascinating. I would like you to stay here in the city if you abide by our rules," said a vaesara. "You will also need to find a role here to trade for food and goods as you contribute to our society and maintain the cycle of balance."

"Thank you, ma'am," Ambrielle said.

"Thank you, Ambrielle. You may leave the circle," the vaesara said. "Aradel will guide you back."

"May I ask one favor, please?" Ambrielle said.

"They have other matters to address." Aradel tried to escort her away.

"Yes, we have other matters," said the vaesar, "but what favor would you ask of us?"

"My friend Maetha has something that needs to be addressed," said Ambrielle.

"And what is that?" he asked.

"Well, may I run and get her to explain?"

"I suppose so, if she is here. Aradel, please bring Maetha into the chamber," said the vaesar.

"Yes, Vaesar, but is there time for that right now?" Aradel put a hand on her hip again.

"Please, bring her here so that we can move on," the vaesar said.

Aradel glared at Ambrielle and then left the chamber area. A few moments later, she returned with Maetha. Maetha walked up to the platform smiling and put a hand on Ambrielle's shoulder.

"Welcome dawn, Vaesari," Maetha said. "I believe Ambrielle wishes that I speak on an important matter that needs your attention." Aradel breathed out an audible sigh, but Maetha continued, "For weeks now, when I have gone out to the edge of the forest on gathering excursions, there has been a noticeable lack of berries, fruits, and vegetables. The trees and plants are becoming more and more bare every time I go out. This hasn't been noticeable to the city yet because of the stores of food, but once those run out, it will be impossible to ignore."

There was a commotion among the audience members as they began to talk to each other.

"If you speak to other gatherers," Maetha said, "they will tell you the same thing."

"What is the cause of this?" asked the vaesar.

"I'm afraid I don't yet know, but something has altered the balance. It could be overpopulation of grazing animals or many other things. I'm still studying the pattern," said Maetha. "In the meantime, I propose that we open trade with the Darterrans for sharing their food stores, and we can trade clothing, crafts, crystals, and other materials like we used to. "

A visible expression of anger came over the vaesar's face. "Those insufferable milgums! We will go to war!"

What were usually thin, black lines in Maetha's eyes enlarged, and her mouth dropped open. "Vaesar? What—"

"We shall wipe them out completely this time," he roared. "They got off easy before!"

"Vaesar, it could be a great benefit to us," Maetha continued. "We used to trade with them, and it was a good partnership. We don't have to allow them back in the city again to trade."

"That is why they are doing this! So that we will trade with them again!" accused the vaesar. "I'm not going to play along with their little game!"

"I am not signing off on going to war," said the vaesara. "We would likely defeat them, but we would lose Kavekkians."

"If I may," said Maetha, "the end result of a war is either they surrender and we still have to come to some kind of agreement with them, or we eradicate them completely, which would alter the balance of nature forever. Assuming the latter is out of the question, it's either trade with them now in peace or go to war and trade lives for the food later."

"I agree with Maetha," said the vaesara. "Perhaps we should trade with them to avoid a costly conflict and then come up with a plan to prevent this from happening again."

The vaesar took a deep breath and sighed as he exhaled. "We will deliberate and reconvene at a later time for a final decision."

"You are both dismissed," said the vaesara.

Aradel motioned for them to leave the main floor as the vaesari went on to the next order of business. A group of three Kavekkians walked past them to speak before the vaesari. Ambrielle followed Maetha as she walked out through the courtyard area toward the steps leading down to the street and her house.

"How do you think that went?" Ambrielle asked, hoping for reassurance. "I hope I didn't say anything wrong."

"Oh, my dear Ambrielle." Maetha put a hand on her shoulder. "Thank you so much for getting me in there. You may have saved us all."

Ambrielle smiled. "I'm glad it worked out. So what happens next?"

"They will come back with a decision and some type of plan of action. I hope it is the right decision," said Maetha. "We may need to postpone our gathering excursion and go out for those supplies tomorrow. We're missing some of the safe time when predators would be sleeping."

"Oh, yeah, let's wait and go during the safe time."

"Will you run over and tell Corthian that we will be a day late getting those fruits and supplies? I'll head on back to the house and fix us something to eat."

❧

Ambrielle talked to Corthian and told him about everything that happened with the vaesari and about postponing their trip away from the mountain. She then headed back up toward Maetha's lair. When she came inside, Maetha was heating up some cut-up pieces of a brown plant. The plant was sitting on a crystal dish that reflected light from the vaeranite in the room. Blaez was sitting on the floor, eating some small pieces of meat.

"What was it that the Darterrans stole, anyway?" she asked.

Maetha sighed. "Our lykris."

Ambrielle narrowed her eyes in confusion.

"The lykris is a device made with some extremely rare crystals that have to be cut into a certain shape," Maetha explained, using her hands to mimic a crystal. "We use its powerful ray to carve out rock to make homes, cut sheets of rock, level out the streets, make weapons, all kinds of things."

Maetha was standing up straight now, putting a hand to her hip. "They wheeled it off the mountain and took it to the other pack that lives in the caves behind the mountain. Once we found out who had taken it, the vaesar at that time was furious and said the Darterrans could never be trusted again. He banned all of them from the mountain and eventually destroyed the stairs at the base of the mountain; therefore, they could not climb up anymore."

"Why would the Darterrans do that if they were your friends?" asked Ambrielle.

"I don't know for sure." Maetha handed Ambrielle a plate with some of the plant on it. "I was a child at the time it happened, and no one ever talks about it anymore. I heard there was some enclosure in the Darterran caves made of impenetrable rock. It was thought to be from the ancients and contain some old artifacts in there, and they wanted to use the lykris to get inside."

"Why didn't the vaesar only banish the Darterrans that stole it?"

"He and the vaesara said there were too many Darterrans involved to find all that were complicit. They felt we couldn't trust any of them. We had to build another lykris, which requires some materials that are rather difficult to come by. So they didn't want to build another and have it stolen again."

"I guess that makes sense." Ambrielle tasted the brown plant; it was a little bitter. "It's a shame that things turned out that way."

"Yes, such a shame." Maetha took a few bites. "I've always hoped that one day we could heal these old wounds between us and come together again."

"That's why you were wanting to trade with them again."

Maetha nodded. "Yes, and then maybe someday that could lead to them living with us on the mountain again. It likely will never happen in my lifetime, but I hope to see some kind of progress before I pass on."

"I hope you do get to see it one day." Ambrielle chewed on another bite. "What if—" She paused as she continued to think.

"What if what?

"I'm not Kavekkian or Darterran . . . so what if I talked to the Darterrans as like . . . a third party . . . a mediator."

"That would lead us into trouble with the vaesari. We would need their permission to do something like that, or you and I both could get banished."

Ambrielle sighed. "If they want to have peace again, they are going to have to do something . . ."

Maetha smiled. They chatted on for a bit as the sun fell toward the horizon. Ambrielle watched some birds that had landed near a cut-out window area in the house, and as it grew dark, Maetha went on to bed. Ambrielle stayed up a little longer, as she wasn't as exhausted as the night before. She had been wanting to get a view of the moons once it got dark.

Once the light beams had faded out in the streets, she walked outside. Blaez raised his head up and then returned to his resting position. There it was, Pathea, the larger of the two moons, shining even brighter than she had imagined. Even though it was not full, it lit up the whole street with its haunting glow. It was bright enough that it caused the durathyst standing above the street to glow, and the vaeranite all around cast a subtle blue onto various objects. It wasn't quite bright enough to trigger the light beams, but it was enough to create some additional light around the area.

Ambrielle stood out in the street for a while, looking up at all the stars in the sky. She reflected on the vastness of the universe, wondering where she fit into it, wondering where she even was in relation to Earth. Was she even in the same galaxy? What if it wasn't the same galaxy? There were at least billions of them.

Gazing at the stars was something she remembered doing often on Earth, dreaming what it might be like to explore other worlds one day. She never thought she would get the chance. Now she had seen new creatures, tasted new foods, and talked to another intelligent life form. She was fortunate, in a way, but she missed her dad. She wondered if she would ever get to see him again.

She began to remember the depth of how lost she was. She had experienced it in the desert wilderness. The difference was that here she was not alone. If she could never get back home, maybe she could make a life here. Ambrielle needed to have a purpose in this place. She wanted to fix this situation between the Darterrans and Kavekkians. She had to figure out a way how. Yawning as weariness began to set in, Ambrielle headed back toward the house, taking one last glimpse before turning and walking inside.

CHAPTER 5

EAMS OF LIGHT entered the room as the sunlight outside fed the
chain reaction of light crystals reflecting into nodes inside the house.
They removed most of the remaining darkness that surrounded the
sleeping girl. Ambrielle opened her eyes, happy upon realizing that she was
another day out of the deserted wilderness. She smelled something coming
from the other room and heard the sound of Maetha chopping up some
fruits or vegetables again for breakfast.

Her stomach ached it was so empty, and she hurriedly went into the
main room.

"Good morning," she greeted Maetha.

"It's already a good morning? You just woke up." said Maetha.

"Yes." Ambrielle smiled as she sat down. "We're alive, and we have
breakfast. What more could you ask for?"

Maetha chuckled. "I suppose you're right! A good morning, indeed!"

The two of them ate while talking about the plan for the day. The
most important objective was to gather food and learn more about the
decreasing food supply. They would also gather the supplies that Corthian
would use to build Ambrielle some new shoes.

After they had visited the bathing pool and cleaned up, they were set to
go. Ambrielle had found her dress hanging up, cleaned, and dried.
It was comforting to be wearing clothes that were hers again. She

wondered if anyone here could make her clothes that suited the human body better than the robes that the Kavekkians wore.

Soon they were off on the long path down the mountain, Blaez following close behind them. Maetha had talked about carrying Ambrielle and climbing down the face of the mountain, a much shorter path, but Ambrielle wasn't sure that she would be able to hold on well enough for that. On the way, they passed Corthian at his shop, letting him know that they were heading out on their quest for his supplies.

They also passed Taunsin. He was sitting on a terrace right off the path. Ambrielle wished him good morning as well.

He continued carving his wooden figurine. "What's so good about it?"

"That you got the chance to see us?" Ambrielle suggested with a grin.

Taunsin paused for a moment with a confused frown and went back to his work.

Once Ambrielle was carried down the cliff and they were all safely on the ground, they made their way behind the waterfall toward the other side of the lake. The grassy field ahead of them was so bright in the sunlight it was almost white to her eyes. The tall blue ferns tickled Ambrielle's legs as she walked through them.

"I was going to ask you about something." A breeze caught Ambrielle's hair, pulling it straight back behind her. "In the meeting with the vaesari, they mentioned something about my name."

"Oh," said Maetha, "the ancients?"

"Yes, I think that was it."

"I didn't realize they would have all of those names memorized."

"So that came from ancient Kavekkians?"

"No, we think it came from another species that lived here long ago," Maetha said. "Some stone tablets were found once. They had several names on them with their meanings. We learned a lot from studying their artifacts. A lot of our culture is influenced by them. The ancients are regarded as something close to gods by Kavekkians, so their names are reserved only for the lightborn."

"What are the lightborn?" Ambrielle asked.

Maetha turned to Ambrielle. "Once Anatharia has gone completely around Versoh, the cycle begins again. A child that is born during that first day is considered lightborn."

"If they are lightborn, they are given one of those names?" Ambrielle asked adjusting the bag she was carrying as they walked toward the forest.

"Yes, one of the names from the tablets."

"So, each cycle there's a new lightborn?"

"No, not every cycle," Maetha said. "There have been cycles when no child was born on that first day."

"Does anything else happen if someone is lightborn?"

"If you are lightborn, you are taken to live at the top of the mountain to be trained for special jobs, governance, lightcrafting, studying artifacts, and things like that," Maetha explained. "Some of them become part of the vaesari council."

"Does that mean Aradel is lightborn?" Ambrielle asked.

"Yes, she is."

"She doesn't seem so special." Ambrielle scowled. "I don't like her much."

Maetha laughed. "Why not?"

"She seems mean," Ambrielle said. "I didn't like the way she treated you."

"She's doing what she feels is best." Maetha gave Blaez a few pats on the head as he brushed up against her. "She has a difficult job."

"What about the vaesari themselves?" Ambrielle brushed away the hair blowing into her face. "I guess they are lightborn too."

"No, only the dawnsent are eligible," Maetha said. "You are marked dawnsent if you are born close to the dawn on the first day of a new cycle."

As they drew closer to the forest, Ambrielle grew nervous, thinking about the creature that attacked her a few days ago.

"What happened to the ancients? Why aren't they still around?" Ambrielle listened out for the sounds of any leaves crunching in the forest.

"That's one thing I have never heard about. To be honest, I really don't know much about them."

"How could we find out more about them?"

"You'd have to be educated with the lightborn."

"There are no books anywhere I could read?"

"Not that I know of."

"Why do they keep it so secret?"

"I don't think it's a secret. It's that the lightborn are chosen to study things like that and make decisions for our society," Maetha said. "The rest of us have other important roles to play, gathering food or protecting, making shoes, clothes, cleaning oils. The roles that the lightborn take produce nothing they could trade, but they are just as important.

"Here we are. These are the kinds of trees to look for," said Maetha.

There was a group of trees about twenty feet tall with teal-colored, triangular-shaped leaves. The bark of the tree was smooth and dark, with large, sturdy branches. The branches of these trees all had an upward curve at the ends. Ambrielle went closer to touch the bark of the tree. It had a smooth texture, almost like that of an apple, but it was hard and solid.

"This is an apraeda tree." Maetha pointed out a few. "Look through the branches and the ground around them for any fruit you can find. If it's too high for you to pick, let me know, and I'll climb up and get it."

"I can climb trees," said Ambrielle.

"Oh, you can?" Maetha asked.

"I do it all the time."

Maetha spotted one apraeda above her and went up the tree. She didn't use the branches to climb. They only got in her way.

"I may not be able to climb that fast," said Ambrielle.

Maetha jumped down to the ground with two apraedas. "Make sure they are yellow like this, not green." She placed the fruits into her pouch. Ambrielle began scanning the branches. She walked in the opposite direction from Maetha so that they could split up and hopefully finish faster. After passing a few trees and finding nothing, she eventually spotted a cluster of fruit dangling from some branches above her. The nearest branch was directly above her head.

Reaching up for the branch, she had another flash vision of the blue light coming out of the tempest. She had a memory of her brother. He was a few years younger and loved playing in the woods near their house. She would go into the woods with him a lot and even play with his friends sometimes. They would play anything from hide-and-seek to good-guys-and-bad-guys and acting out various scenes from their favorite movies.

Ambrielle wasn't always familiar with the movies and cartoons they liked, but she tried to play along. She loved the outdoors but didn't have many friends that were interested in going to the woods or the fishing pond nearby and risking getting dirty. Her friends at school always had new pictures to copy certain looks, which involved buying new clothes, new hairstyles, and new fingernail designs. She loved all those things too. But she also loved riding her bicycle, fishing, long walks through the woods, and occasionally impressing her brother's friends by climbing trees. Some of her friends knew that she had those interests but would probably cringe if they knew that she was doing these things with her newly done nails and new clothes.

Ambrielle grabbed the branch with both hands and held tight while walking her legs up the trunk until they could reach over the limb. She hung onto the branch nearly upside down and slid her legs over, making sure the skirt of her dress didn't fall. She was then able to pull the rest of her body up onto the branch. Holding on to the trunk, she stood up on the limb, positioning herself to step up to the next one.

The other limbs were much closer together from here, making it easier to get to other branches to step on and bring her closer to the fruit. She carefully moved upward, ducking and weaving through the tangle of limbs to continue climbing. At last she made it close enough for her to pick the four pieces of fruit and place them all into her pouch.

The climb down had its own set of challenges. It was easier on her muscles, but the footing was less sure. She couldn't see where her foot was going as she stretched her leg down to the closest limb. She reached the ground with a few red lines on the right side of her face and some scratches to her arms, but in one piece.

"Well done, dear," Maetha said, standing a few yards away. "Your body may not be built for climbing, but I admire your ingenuity."

They continued walking among the trees until they had checked all of them, but found nothing else that was ripe. "Did you notice that the only apraedas left were the ones high up in the trees?" Maetha said.

"What do you think that means?"

"Darterrans can't climb the trees," Maetha said. "I'm afraid the vaesari may be right."

"Oh yeah, and Taunsin too."

Maetha sighed. "Yes, Taunsin too. Let's not mention this to him, or we'll never hear the end of it."

Ambrielle chuckled. "I won't say anything."

"This way," Maetha directed as Blaez ran on up ahead. "We'll check and see if we can find any dappones."

Ambrielle ran over to where Maetha and Blaez were standing around a patch of cornflower-blue plants.

"These are dappone plants." Maetha knelt down, using her hand to check under the leaves. "See if you can find any ripe fruit; you know what they look like."

They walked all around the patches of plants, but there was not any ripened fruit.

"I was afraid of this." Maetha set her hands on her hips. "Let's go on into the forest and get some of those materials that Corthian needs."

Ambrielle had been dreading entering the woods after what happened last time, but she did enjoy exploring. As they entered the tree line and their feet began crunching on dried leaves, Ambrielle scanned for any signs of movement. She occasionally turned around to make sure nothing was sneaking up behind her.

"I don't like this forest." Ambrielle's eyes darted toward every sound. "It's beautiful, but I don't feel comfortable here."

"Neither do I, dear," Maetha confessed. "None of us do. We never go very far."

Ambrielle was only slightly at ease knowing that Blaez was with them. The sun's light penetrated the gaps in the branches and leaves as Maetha searched the tops of the trees. The forest was mostly like any other, except that many of the leaves had a bluish hue to them. There were some trees with golden, green, and red leaves as well. Deeper in the forest ahead were the balcain trees that towered over everything else, blotting out most of the sunlight.

"See? Look there." Maetha pointed up at something hanging from one of the limbs among some reddish-brown leaves. There were small insects flying around a hive that resembled crumpled paper. Maetha reached into her robe and drew out two black rods from each of her sides and brought them both together, attaching them into one longer staff like she had carried before.

She lifted the sharp-pointed end of the staff up to the nest and poked a hole in the bottom of it. A pinkish-yellow jelly fell out of it that Maetha caught and wrapped up. The insects buzzed all around the nest, intent on repairing the hole, but they did not fly down to attack them.

"This is mebri. Those zenches produce it," she said. "We use it for lots of different things. It's a great material for trading."

"Okay, I'll help find more," Ambrielle offered.

"Let's walk deeper into the forest while we look." Maetha walked forward while scanning the trees. "We need to get some balcain leaves while we are here."

Nervously, she walked farther into the woods beside Maetha. Ambrielle separated from Maetha enough to investigate trees that Maetha wasn't already near. She tried to convince herself there was no need to keep her eyes on the ground for predatory creatures. Blaez would sense something coming before she would.

The forest grew darker as they neared the balcain trees, even with the brightness of Versoh. Ambrielle spotted something in one of the trees, one of the zench nests. She alerted Maetha to it and was confirmed correct.

"Good eyes," Maetha said. "I would never have found that. I don't see as well in the dark forest." She reached up with her staff and poked a hole in this nest as well, catching the mebri that tumbled out.

There were huge, thick leaves on the ground as they came within sight of the wide, gnarled trunk of a balcain tree. Some were dead and brittle, while others were olive-green and brown, freshly fallen leaves. Maetha began to gather some of the vibrant leaves, and Ambrielle began doing the same. The leaves were thick and smooth in her hands as she put them into her pouch. Maetha gathered up several and rolled them up like a scroll, placing them in her pouch to protect them. Ambrielle took the ones she had out of her pouch so that she could roll them up the way Maetha had before putting them back in.

Deeper in the forest, Ambrielle saw some of the glowing lights in the distant darkness. "What are those lights? Is someone out there?" she asked.

"I don't know. I've never walked much farther than we are now," said Maetha. "Must be some light coming through some gaps in the trees."

"Can we go look?"

Blaez alerted to something off to their left. He growled, even though there was nothing through the trees.

"We better head back, dear. We have everything we need from the forest," Maetha said. "Let's get out of these dark woods."

They came out of the woods into some patches of turquoise ferns covering the ground. Maetha knelt and began picking some out of the dirt. "Make sure you pull these vaspages up by the roots. It's the roots that we really want." Maetha pulled one out to demonstrate. "Break off the stalks and leave them in the soil."

Ambrielle walked over to another group of vaspages and pulled one up from the soft dirt, breaking off some of the small root strands. She removed the stalks as Maetha had instructed and pushed them into the ground. Blaez began growling at something. Ambrielle turned back to where Maetha and Blaez were but didn't see anything.

She pulled on another plant but had to dig the roots out with her hand for it to come loose.

"Ambrielle!" Maetha shouted suddenly, with an unusual urgency in her tone. Maetha's eyes were wide when she turned toward her. Blaez ran to her, growling and looking back toward the forest.

Ambrielle turned back to Maetha, trying to figure out what she was yelling about. She faced the woods, but there was nothing. She turned back toward Maetha, who was motioning for Ambrielle to come toward her. Ambrielle wondered why she wouldn't say what it was she was trying to convey.

A low, vibrating growl caused her to turn in its direction. A group of large four-legged creatures was moving slowly toward her. They stood about five feet tall and eight feet in length. One had a solid reddish-brown coat with black spiked fur around its head, and another had a black coat and a dark red stripe pattern. A third one was solid brown, and the fourth was light brown with black stripes.

They all had a long snout full of teeth, somewhat like a wolf but with a larger, wider mouth. The beasts had vicious eyes that were all but closed in the bright sunlight. The animals' ribs showed through their furred skin, as if they had been starved.

Ambrielle froze. Even though every part of her being wanted to run, she couldn't get her brain to start her body. They would surely give chase as soon as she bolted. Her mind overloaded, processing any possible option for escaping death, but it repeatedly came to an impasse.

Time slowed to a crawl. Ambrielle followed Maetha's instruction and started to inch back toward her, realizing that Maetha had come over to her.

"Raestrigs . . ." Maetha positioned herself in front of her, holding her bladed staff in a guard position.

Ambrielle rubbed the blue jewel in her necklace as the black-and-red-striped beast began walking slowly to their right. The two brown-coated raestrigs circled to their left, while the red one stayed ahead.

"Get behind me and wrap your arms around," Maetha said, keeping an eye on the beasts. "I need to be sure where you are at all times."

Ambrielle did as she said as Maetha began to sidestep toward the left, in the opposite direction of the flanking red-and-black raestrig and toward the two brown ones. She let out a sharp vocalized call, pointing in the direction of the two brown-coated beasts, and Blaez charged toward them, colliding with both animals. Ambrielle held on to Maetha, moving along with her. She was attempting to keep both creatures in one straight line ahead of them, preventing them from being able to attack from two different directions.

Blaez was in a furious fight with the other two as they snarled and roared at each other. Blaez continued charging into the brown raestrig with black stripes, using his arms to swipe toward its eyes and grab it around the sides of the head. The solid-brown raestrig attacked Blaez from the side, biting at his neck while he fended it off with one of his claws. The striped beast was knocked down, and as it tried scrambling to its feet, Blaez pounced and pinned it to the ground.

The black-and-red raestrig continued circling to their right while Maetha and Ambrielle continued left. The red-coated animal left its position and began walking out of their path toward their left side, trying to outflank them. The beasts were intent on holding their attack until they had them surrounded.

"Stay calm, dear. Like Raegus said, I was once a protector." Maetha began walking straight left, disengaging from the circle pattern they had been in. This was forcing the red raestrig to separate farther from the black-and-red beast. The red one finally stopped, waiting for the other animal to come back and regroup.

"Run with me," Maetha said calmly and sprinted straight at the red beast as Ambrielle held on behind her, trying to match her speed. The red beast growled and assumed a defensive posture. Maetha lunged at it with the pointed end of her weapon, hitting it with a glancing blow. The beast yelped and bit at the staff.

A second gasping yelp went out as Blaez killed one of the two raestrigs he was fighting. The other, solid-brown animal lunged at him, knocking him on his side. The raestrig tried to hold Blaez while its jaws reached for his throat. Blaez grabbed the raestrig around the head with his paws, and the two beasts tumbled along the ground. They rolled, locked in a fierce battle of fangs and claws.

The black-and-red-striped beast charged toward them as Maetha stabbed at the red one again. The raestrig was hit in the shoulder, but not deep. It grabbed ahold of the staff with its jaws, shaking it violently and nearly yanking it from Maetha's grasp. She then detached the other end of the staff, letting go of the half the beast had. The sudden shift in leverage caused it to fall backward.

As the red-furred creature got back to its feet, she swung the bladed end down on the animal's head, slicing a deep gash down the side of its head and neck. Before she could finish it off, the black-and-red-striped beast barreled into them, knocking Maetha off her feet and sending Ambrielle tumbling away from her. It then turned its gaze on Ambrielle.

Maetha grabbed the pointed part of the staff from the ground, which lay beside the wounded red creature. She hurled it into the side of the striped beast as it lunged at Ambrielle, still dazed on the ground. Stunned, the animal got back up, furiously shaking the staff out of its side. Ambrielle got to her feet and ran toward the pointed staff, which was now bloody and on the ground. Maetha ran toward the beast as it went for Ambrielle again, but the wounded red-furred creature jumped on Maetha as she ran by.

Ambrielle turned as the beast reached her and brought up the pointed end of the staff to defend herself from the attack. As the animal went in to attack her with its powerful jaws, the blade of the staff got past the beast's teeth, stabbing it through the top of its snout. The impact jarred Ambrielle, breaking the staff and sending her backward as the animal howled in pain.

Maetha rolled over, trying to get her arm free to slash the red beast with the blade end she was holding, but it had too much weight on her arm. There was another yelp and then a whooshing sound as Blaez bore down on the red beast that was holding Maetha, easily finishing the wounded raestrig.

Ambrielle backed away from the black-and-red one as it stalked her, the top half of the broken staff still lodged in its snout. It was getting weaker as it paced along the grass. Maetha and Blaez approached the raestrig, and it turned to them, ready to defend itself. Maetha quickly slashed it with her blade as it kept its attention on Blaez.

Ambrielle unintentionally sat on the ground, her bloodstained arms shaking, still holding on to the broken piece of the staff. Her breath came in quick bursts as she stared straight ahead.

"Ambrielle, are you hurt?" Maetha asked.

Ambrielle's vision came back into focus as she looked up at Maetha. "No, I-I don't think so."

Blaez came over and sniffed her and began licking her arm. Ambrielle gave him a few pats; it was all so surreal that it was like she was in a dream.

"We need to get moving. There could be more out there hunting for food," Maetha said.

Ambrielle tried to get up, but her legs were weak. She examined them; nothing appeared wrong. Maetha pulled her up the rest of the way, and the blood rushed back into them as they began regaining their strength.

"I thought this was the safe time," Ambrielle continued, staring straight ahead.

"They normally stay in the dark forest." Maetha rubbed her chest. "They can't see well in the sunlight, lucky for us."

They began gathering up Maetha's pouches that had fallen during the fight and started walking the path back toward the mountain.

"I should have realized," Maetha said. "The balance in Lon Kavekkia is more broken than I thought. This situation with the fruit shortage is already having an effect on the animals here. The grazing animals must have already begun to move on to other areas to find food, and with them moving on, that gives the predators a shortage of food."

They began walking back as Maetha continued, "These raestrigs were starving. They normally don't attack anything as large as us."

Ambrielle continued to stare off into the distance.

"You did really well back there." Maetha turned to Ambrielle, who was lost in her own world. "I've seen protectors not do as well as you did in a real fight."

"I didn't do anything," said Ambrielle, shaking her head. "It keeps replaying in my mind, and I realize how so many little things could have gone the other way. Things I should have done differently. I shudder every time I think about it. I wish I could erase it from my mind."

Maetha nodded. "Every fight is like that. You make mistakes and hope you live to learn from them."

"Well, I hope I never have to fight anything ever again."

"You want to hear a story?" Maetha asked. "The first fight I was ever in."

"Okay . . ." Ambrielle was still holding on to the piece of staff as they walked along the path.

"One of my first excursions as a protector, probably thirty-five to forty cycles ago. I was out with my grandfather, leading a group of gatherers." Maetha turned to Ambrielle. "I took a few of them into the forest while my grandfather led the other group farther around the field. At that time, I felt invincible, being well-trained with a blade staff in both full-staff and dual half-staff forms."

Ambrielle glanced up at her, waiting for her to continue.

"I came upon a warghol that was in a charge stance, growling at me," Maetha said. "I should have backed off, but I wanted to show everyone that I was not afraid. I continued walking the same direction toward it. The warghol charged at me, closed its mouth around my side, and dragged me through the forest."

Ambrielle's eyes widened.

"That was the day I learned that I was not invincible. None of my training had prepared me for that," said Maetha. "I'm not sure exactly what happened, but I was somehow able to get a blade into the warghol as it dragged me. I had killed it, but I didn't feel like I had won a fight.

"I should have died that day," Maetha confessed. "I got lucky. When my grandfather found me, I thought he was going to ask if I was all right or congratulate me on my first kill. Instead, he scolded me."

"Why?" asked Ambrielle.

"He took me back over to where I first came upon the warghol. There was a den dug into the ground, and inside the den was a tiny warghol cub. I had killed a mother protecting its child," said Maetha. "If I had backed off at first, it probably never would have attacked me, and we could have gone around its territory."

"Oh, that's so sad," Ambrielle said, "but you didn't know."

"My grandfather had taught me to recognize behavior like that, but I was too determined to show everyone what a brave protector I was," Maetha said. "My grandfather took the cub and put it into my hands, saying that I had broken the balance. He said that in order to restore the balance, I would have to become the cub's mother and raise it myself."

"I resented the cub at first," she continued as they walked, "having to feed it and clean up after it constantly. I felt justified in killing his mother at the time—after all, the mother almost killed me. But after a while I became fond of the cub. I felt terrible every time he would look at me. It taught me that animals are not my enemy. They simply do what is instinctual to survive. Ever since, I have always tried to avoid a fight if I could, even if it looked like a sign of weakness."

"Did the cub ever accept you as its mother?" Ambrielle asked.

Maetha knelt, and Blaez ran up to her, sniffed her a few times, licked her face, and then flopped down, settling against her. "I like to think so."

"No way, are you serious?" Ambrielle put her hand over her mouth.

Maetha smiled and nodded.

"Didn't you say that was a long time ago?" Ambrielle asked.

"Thirty-eight cycles, if you want to get specific, which is a little past middle age for a warghol," said Maetha. "He thinks he's in his prime, though."

As they approached Mekkinspire, Blaez turned suddenly back toward the forest. There were two figures walking around a large outcropping of stone at the tree line.

"Darterrans," Maetha said. "They usually don't come out in the daylight."

Ambrielle wanted a glimpse of what the Darterrans were like. One of the figures had a short, brown coat of fur all over, wearing a dark brown tunic with clothing that wrapped around its waist down to its thighs. It had abnormally long legs but a small torso.

"Wait, that's not a Darterran," Maetha said. "There's another creature walking with it."

"A human!" Ambrielle said excitedly. "Whoa! Humans are living with the Darterrans?!"

"Not that I was aware of," said Maetha. "You're the only human I've ever seen."

"It's a boy," Ambrielle said. "I need to go talk to him!" She turned and began heading in his direction.

"No! Get back here!" Maetha grabbed her arm, preventing her from going any farther.

Ambrielle turned around in shock. "Why? I need to find out how he got here. He may know how I can get back home!"

"He's with the Darterrans," Maetha said. "You can't be seen associating with him; it would get you banished."

"Seriously?" Ambrielle began to grow agitated. "That's such a stupid rule! How are you ever going to make peace if you can't talk to them?"

"It's a rule that you agreed to when I brought you to Mekkinspire."

"That was before I knew they had other humans over there!"

The boy had stopped and looked at them. Ambrielle waved, and he waved back, then continued walking into the shade of the forest.

"Let me talk with the vaesari about this new development. We'll work something out," Maetha said. "They are interested in helping you get back home. If talking to this other human could help, I'm sure there is something that could be arranged."

Ambrielle sighed. "So now I'm stuck on the mountain because of some stupid argument a long time ago."

"If you want to go that badly, it's your choice. It would disappoint me as a friend, but you are free to do what you want. You would need the Darterrans to take you in, though, as you wouldn't be allowed back on Mekkinspire."

"Ughh," Ambrielle said. "Are you sure you can get the vaesari to let me talk to him?"

"I feel confident that we can," said Maetha. "I'm sure they are having to contend with Kavekkians that are displeased with them allowing an outsider to stay there. The ones that don't mind you being there don't have strong feelings about it either way. In that respect, I think the vaesari would be glad if they could help you find your way home and not have to deal with that anymore . . . and who knows, perhaps this could be what we need to start conversations with the Darterrans."

"Hmm . . . I guess you're right," said Ambrielle. "I won't go for now, but eventually I have to talk to him and find out what he knows."

"Thank you for being patient," Maetha said. "Now hold out your arm. It's bleeding."

Ambrielle searched her arm and saw a flow of dark red blood. She was a bit faint for a moment but held it out to Maetha. Maetha tore one of the straps from her bag and tied it tight around Ambrielle's arm over a piece of cloth that covered the wound. Ambrielle's arm began to hurt now—there was no pain until all the pressure from the strap woke up her nerves.

After the long walk up the path, Maetha found Raegus guarding the archway in the city and told him the story of what had happened with the raestrigs.

"Impressive. I guess you're not as fragile as you appear," Raegus said.

Ambrielle smirked at his comment.

"She can climb trees too," Maetha told him.

"Can you now?" said Raegus. "I don't think Darterrans are even capable of that."

Ambrielle rolled her eyes. She was still annoyed with Maetha and the Kavekkians' rules preventing her from talking to the human boy.

"You should have seen it," said Maetha. "She figured out a way to flip around and contort her body to get herself up."

"Will you stop calling me fragile! Why do you all feel so superior to me?" Ambrielle said. "Just because you may be bigger and stronger than me doesn't mean you are better. I should go live with the Darterrans!"

"Ambrielle . . . we were praising you," Maetha said.

"I don't need your mocking praise." Ambrielle walked away from them, unsure where to go. She walked past Corthian's shop, which was now closed for the day, to the edge of the plateau overlooking the lake, fields, and forest. There were some steps leading down to a small terrace, and she went over and sat down on a stone seat there.

She wiped tears from her eyes, not even sure why they were there. She was frustrated with Maetha but not really all that angry at her or Raegus; it was more with her own weakness. She'd almost died out there and would have if she hadn't been protected by Maetha and Blaez. She was useless, like a child that had to be cared for and looked after. Taunsin may have been right; she was just another of Maetha's pets.

She watched as the light covering the world changed to an orange glow. Raegus walked through the street above her, passing by the terrace.

"You're far from fragile, Ambrielle. There is more to strength than size." He then continued walking down the pathway.

A few moments later, Maetha walked over behind her, sharing the view with her.

"Ambrielle, we should get the healer to examine us. You may not be feeling it now, but we both likely have some bumps and bruises that need tending to," Maetha finally said.

"I'm fine . . ." Ambrielle said.

"That gash on your arm needs to be cleaned," Maetha said.

"All right, I can go myself. Don't feel like you have to look out for me." Ambrielle wanted to gain some sense of respect. She didn't always need help. As soon as she said that, though, she knew that she was dealing with this in a childish way. Whenever she had a moment of anger or hurt and said something that she regretted or acted immaturely, she never knew how to resolve it while trying to act like an adult. Her attempts usually made her look even worse.

"We all need help sometimes, but we look out for each other. We've been in battle together, and that makes us sisters. You looked out for me when they wouldn't let me into the council chamber, and I'm sure I'll need your help again," Maetha said.

They sat there quietly for a few moments. "Will you at least go to the healer with me?" Maetha asked. "I've been aching since that raestrig slammed into me."

"Oh! Yes, let's go." Ambrielle got up and followed Maetha back toward the city area.

Maetha led her into a cave in a larger side of the mountain. Once inside, they were met by a Kavekkian in a dark green robe. He was thin compared to most Kavekkians, and he had them both sit and wait while another was being helped by the healer. After they waited a bit, the thin assistant came back out, helping an older female walk out of the cave. The female was weak, as though she may be ill. Once the assistant returned, he motioned for them to come forward.

He lifted a curtain separating the healer's workspace from the main room, and they walked through. The healer was short by Kavekkian standards, and she was wearing a gray robe, which was a bit disheveled.

"Maetha, I haven't seen you in here in quite a while," the healer said.

"I've been trying to avoid you," Maetha replied.

The healer smiled. "What brings you by? And who is this with you?"

"This is Ambrielle. We were attacked by raestrigs, and Ambrielle's arm is cut. We both got banged around pretty good."

"Hello, Ambrielle, you must be the human that I have been hearing about. I am Sirendae," she said, lifting the sleeve of Ambrielle's dress to view her arm. She removed the cloth tied on with the strap of Maetha's bag.

"Ouch," Sirendae said. "Yes, I'll need to clean this and close it up."

After cleaning her arm, Sirendae brought a tiny hook toward the gash in her arm. Ambrielle closed her eyes and saw a flash of swirling blue clouds as she had another remembering. She saw her mother wiping her arm with a white piece of cloth as tears came dangerously close to overflowing and spilling down her cheek.

When she was twelve, she had been attempting to do aerial cartwheels from a movie and momentarily forgot that she wasn't invulnerable. Luckily, she hadn't broken anything and had only cut her arm on an unseen rock in the grass when she landed awkwardly.

Her mother was calm as she cleaned and bandaged the cut, talking to her as if nothing was wrong. It made her forget the sharp, biting pain and the frightening fall that still affected her pulse and quickened her breathing. Her dad often taught her to be strong, but it was her mother who gave her the courage to get there.

"I've heard that whenever someone gets hurt, they have five good things coming to them," her mother said. "So you must have some good things coming to you."

She believed it when she was younger. Sometimes those good things came in the form of chocolate-chip cookie dough ice cream that her mom or dad brought her the next day. It became silly to her as she grew older, but it gave her some comfort just to have her mom say it again. She was usually right, even though it wasn't actually a scientific rule. Even if the good things were small, everyday things, it made her realize that often little things can happen in a day that she otherwise wouldn't have acknowledged.

Ambrielle winced as Sirendae pulled the gash together and hooked the other side to close the wound. She put a second hook into her arm. Ambrielle started to yell but lost her breath in the process.

The healer wrapped some cloth around her arm. "Are your hands supposed to look like that?"

"What? Yes." Ambrielle raised her eyebrows.

"I'm not familiar with human anatomy, simply making sure there wasn't more damage," Sirendae said.

Ambrielle studied her hands, turning them over to examine both sides. "No, they're fine."

Once Sirendae finished examining them, Maetha gave her some of the fruit that they'd found on their quest.

"Let's get back home. We need some rest," Maetha said. "I'm going to meet with the vaesari again in the morning."

As things began to quiet down, Ambrielle's dread of what lay ahead returned. She stressed over something she couldn't even remember. Reviewing the day's events in her mind usually helped distract her, but this day's events were not something she wanted to focus on.

CHAPTER 6

MORNING CAME, AND Ambrielle had not slept well, her dreams filled with monsters and other nightmares during the night. She and Maetha had their typical breakfast of sliced olava and apraeda juice. Maetha was preparing for her meeting with the vaesari.

She wanted to find out what their decision was and to give the new information about the raestrig attack. This disruption of the balance had already begun to cause nature to reconfigure. The old methods no longer applied. The forest was now a dangerous place, in addition to lacking in the food they needed.

"I wish I could go with you," Ambrielle said.

"I would take you," Maetha said, "but you going to the council meeting again would start to give the impression that an outsider is meddling in our matters."

"Well, maybe I could go next time?" asked Ambrielle.

"Maybe." Maetha cleared the plates from the table. "I don't get to go that often myself."

"What should I do while you are gone?"

"Take our supply bags and get them to Corthian. That way he can get started on the shoes." Maetha tossed some pieces of fish over to Blaez.

"Oh yeah, okay, anything else?"

"I shouldn't be gone that long, but if you are done with that, go look around, talk to shopkeepers, introduce yourself," Maetha said. "Keep Taunsin company."

Ambrielle chuckled. "All right, I'll go mess with him a bit."

After Maetha left, Ambrielle bathed in the pool and put on the now-clean white robe that Maetha had loaned her before. Her white sundress with the pattern of little pink flowers was now stained with blood from the encounter with the raestrigs. Ambrielle wasn't sure that the stains would ever come out, which was a shame. She really liked that dress. This wasn't a new thing for her, as she had a habit of ruining clothes.

Ambrielle fixed herself up with what little she had to work with and headed off down the path to the city. She could already hear the bustle of activity as she approached. It was more difficult carrying all the bags and pouches of materials than she thought it would be, but fortunately it wasn't too far of a walk.

Before she made it to the archway, a female Kavekkian carrying a bag of recent purchases passed by. "You must be that outsider everyone has been talking about," she said in a less-than-friendly manner.

"Yes, it's good to meet—" Ambrielle started to reply as the Kavekkian turned and walked away from her.

That was rude, Ambrielle thought as she walked under the archway into the city.

There were already customers at Corthian's shop. As she approached, one of them was complaining to Corthian. Corthian saw her standing there with all the bags and smiled. She stood there silently as she waited for them to finish their business.

Once he had left, Ambrielle moved up to the counter.

"Ah, some Kavekkians, you just can't please . . ." he said. "I hope you are bringing good news with all the materials I need."

"I think we got everything," Ambrielle said as she placed the bags onto the counter and Corthian began digging through them.

"These balcain leaves aren't bad. Not the best, but they'll do." He rolled the leaves back up and set them aside to open another bag. "Ah, mebri, very good."

After putting that aside, he reached into the bag until he found something else.

"Ah yes, vaspage roots," he said, searching through the bags again. "Where is my hovanoke?"

"Oh, yeah . . . we never did go back and get that."

Corthian smacked his hand down on the counter. "What? That was the one thing I needed the most. How could you forget the hovanoke?"

"Well . . . we were attacked by raestrigs while we were picking the vaspages. We almost didn't even make it back."

Corthian scanned Ambrielle. "Is that why you have the bloody bandage on your arm?"

Ambrielle looked down at her arm. The bandage was half-covered in dried blood. "Yes, we honestly forgot about the wood after the attack. We were trying to get back as quickly as possible."

"Don't worry about it. You're giving me a lot of mebri. I can probably trade a portion of it for some hovanoke," Corthian said. "Where is Maetha? Is she okay?"

"She got bruised up a bit, but she's fine. She went to try to talk to the vaesari."

"Ah . . . what makes her think she's going to be able to talk to the vaesari?"

"We talked to them a couple days ago," Ambrielle said, "about the food shortage."

"Food shortage?" Corthian said. "She mentioned having trouble finding dappones lately, but I didn't know there was a food shortage."

"I think it has gotten worse."

"What are they planning to do about this shortage?"

"They are supposed to be making a decision about it soon. I guess Maetha will find out."

"Why didn't you go to the meeting with her?"

"I wanted to, but Maetha wasn't sure I should go this time," Ambrielle said. "I may have said a bit too much when I was there before."

"Oh, you spoke at the meeting?"

"Well, the vaesari wanted to ask me some questions, where I came from and how I got here. All that kind of stuff."

"Ah, that is a great honor to speak to the vaesari."

"Yeah, I guess it was nice of them to take an interest in me, being new here and all."

"I better get some hovanoke and get started on Nartere's shoes, since he'll be back tomorrow. Once those are done, I will get started on yours."

"Thanks, Corthian. I'll see you later, then."

"May the light be upon you."

"You too." Ambrielle began to wonder what was going on in the meeting. She wished there were some way to find out. She had to get close enough to hear them talking. Quickening her pace, she walked toward the archway where the steps went up to the plateau on top of the mountain.

Heading back up the path, Ambrielle hurried along the road and came to the mountain peak in the courtyard with the circle arrangement of light beams and statues. She came to the gate that led to the council area. A protector was guarding it, so she couldn't get much closer. Voices carried into the courtyard, reverberating off the walls. She recognized the voice of the vaesar.

"This attack makes the implementation of our decision even more urgent," declared the vaesar. "We have come up with a compromise solution. We are taking the council's advisement into consideration, as well as your points, Maetha."

The vaesara began to speak. "We will place five protectors out between the lake and the forest to guard the edible plants and ensure that no further food is stolen. These protectors will rotate throughout the day and night, keeping watch."

The commotion among the crowd erupted as everyone shared their thoughts with those around them.

"Then we will have an expedition team of three protectors and any gatherers willing to go beyond Lon Kavekkia to seek out other sources of food to bring back," she continued. "These gatherers will be able to trade the food they find as they normally would, to keep our economy going strong. They will also be expected to contribute some of the food they bring to our stores, as they have always done."

The nearby guard stared at Ambrielle as she stood near the gate, listening.

"The only problem I have with this plan is that it will cause issue on the opposite end," Maetha said. "We'll end up starving the Darterrans, and they will get desperate and attack the protectors and gatherers."

"We will preserve the balance," said the vaesar. "They have nearly all of this crop of food right now, which should last them a while. Once things begin to return to normal, we will lessen the protectors and allow them to take what they need, but we may never remove them entirely."

"Maetha, I would like you to lead this expedition," said the vaesara. "All your knowledge of nature and animals would be invaluable."

"I will reflect your light," Maetha said.

"I've never left Lon Kavekkia; none of us have," said another voice. "Why must we go just because we are gatherers?"

"You do not have to go, but you may run out of food to trade," the vaesara explained. "There is risk with this expedition, but we are sending protectors with you."

"Could we have more protectors come with us? Three will not be enough for all of us."

"We will consider sending more with you, but we will not leave the mountain defensively weak," said the vaesar.

"No one can climb the mountain but Kavekkians. That's all the defense we need," someone pointed out, which started a chain reaction of several voices speaking out all at once.

Aradel tried to get the meeting back in order.

"We're not willing to leave that as our only defense," said the vaesar, "especially not right now."

"Prepare whatever you need and get with Maetha if you plan to go," the vaesara continued. "The expedition will be leaving at first light tomorrow."

"This meeting is adjourned," stated the vaesar.

Ambrielle scrambled back out of the courtyard and down the path, past Maetha's district, back through the archway into the city, carefully avoiding the uneven tripping spot. She went to Corthian's shop. He was talking to another customer, but this would likely be the best place for Maetha to find her.

After standing there for a bit, she saw Maetha coming down the path. Maetha began walking straight toward Corthian's shop, greeting a few others that stopped to talk to her along the way.

"Ambrielle, I have some news," Maetha said.

Ambrielle turned to face her as though she didn't know she was there. "Oh, you're back!"

"I'm afraid I will be gone all day tomorrow," Maetha told her. "Perhaps even overnight, which I am dreading."

"Why is that?" asked Ambrielle.

"We're going on an expedition beyond Lon Kavekkia," Maetha explained, "to look for other sources of food."

"Hey, that was kind of my idea. I told them there would be resources beyond this area," Ambrielle said.

"An expedition? This food problem must really be getting serious." Corthian sounded worried.

"We're trying to solve the problem before it becomes serious," said Maetha. "I hope we can find something out there that isn't too far away."

"Me too. Can I go with you?" Ambrielle asked.

"I don't think that is a good idea," Maetha said.

"Aw, but I want to explore some unknown territory," Ambrielle begged.

"This is a surprising move for the council. How many are going?" asked Corthian.

"Any of the gatherers that are willing and three protectors." Maetha turned to Ambrielle. "I'm surprised you want to go out there this soon after the attack."

"Well, I know you can protect me, plus three more protectors, and Blaez too," Ambrielle said.

"I wonder if all of the gatherers will go?" Corthian wondered.

"I'm going to try to talk to them before nightfall and try to persuade them all to go," Maetha said. "Ambrielle, let's find out how this first trip goes, and then we can talk about you going on the next one."

"I want to be the first to explore new territory along with you, though," Ambrielle whined, "not places that you saw the time before."

Maetha laughed. "All right, dear, when you go, we'll look for places that none of us have been to."

"Our hopes are with you, Maetha," Corthian said. "I suppose we are all depending on you now."

"Thank you," she said. "How are those shoes coming along?"

❦

The sky was getting darker, as clouds had gathered, blocking out Versoh's normal brightness. Ambrielle made her way over to Sirendae's lair to get her wound cleaned while Maetha went to convince the other gatherers to join her expedition. Ambrielle saw a female Kavekkian with a swollen belly coming out of Sirendae's cave. She wondered if the Kavekkian was pregnant and what Kavekkian babies were like. Were they as helpless as human babies?

After Sirendae cleaned and redressed her wound, she headed back up the steps to Maetha's plateau. As Ambrielle got close to Maetha's house, two splashes of water hit her one after the other. Big splashes, as though she were getting hit by water balloons. She turned around, but no one was throwing anything. There was a smacking of water hitting various spots along the ground. It was raining.

Ambrielle hurried inside the house. She would be soaked in a matter of seconds if she was hit with any more of the huge raindrops. Once inside, she watched the rain out the window. The drops were large but few. Smaller drops soon came down together with the large ones, faster and steadier. Her ears were soon enveloped in the white noise of the steady rain, along with the low beating of big drops against the rocks.

She wondered if Maetha had gotten caught in it or if she had been able to get to shelter before it started. Ambrielle sat there for a while, leaning against the wall by the window frame, watching the rain, enjoying the cool splashes against her from the drops hitting the stone outside. Blaez walked up beside her to watch the rain.

She had another flash of blue with a memory of her life on Earth. It was of her running up to a small house where she once lived. A big pecan orchard that she liked to walk through was to one side of the yard. She considered it part of their yard, even though it was someone else's land.

Ambrielle recalled that she had been in the orchard once when it had started raining, but she hadn't run back to the house. She'd stood under the trees, listening to all the raindrops as they hit the natural umbrella of leaves above her. While some drops did make it through, she was sheltered from the brunt of the storm. She was in her own enchanted forest of symmetrically lined trees. As some birds gathered on one of the trees, she watched as they stood on a branch, shaking water from their feathers. There were drops that fell from the tops of the trees to the leaves below. As more gathered onto the same leaf, they weighed it down enough to bend it, spilling its collected water to the next row of branches.

The process continued from limb to limb, until some of the drops made it all the way to the ground. Others would fall hard against a surface, exploding into a multitude of tiny droplets. In that moment, she was connected to everything around her, but it was deeper than that. It was as though the universe were explaining itself to her. She understood all its mysteries for an instant before its revelation faded from her mind. It was gone without a trace, an epiphany too great for her memory to contain.

The sound of thunder made her race toward the edge of the orchard into the open clearing of her yard and then the rest of the way to the house. A woman's hand grabbed her wet hair as she entered the house.

"You were supposed to be home an hour ago. What were you doing out in the rain in your good clothes?!" she said.

"But Mom, I—it started raining, and it was too far to come home, so I stayed in the woods so I wouldn't get too wet."

"Well, that didn't work," her mother said. "Look, you're soaked . . . You're dripping water all over the floors. Go change. I'm going to quit buying you nice clothes if you're not going to take care of them."

"Mom . . ."

Her mother didn't understand her wanting to spend her time in the woods or going camping. When her dad and brother went on camping trips, Ambrielle always wanted to go with them. Her mom always hinted that she should stay home with her.

While she and her mother had several things they enjoyed doing in common, it was almost as though her mom did not like this side of Ambrielle. Her mother often reminded Ambrielle that she was sixteen now, and that was too old to be playing with her brother and his friends in the woods. She realized that her mother wanted to spend more time with her. A lot of the things her mother enjoyed doing with Ambrielle were also things that she did with her friends.

"Ambrielle . . ." a voice said. Ambrielle's physical senses came back, and she turned to find Maetha standing behind her. "Were you asleep?"

"Oh, lost in thought, I guess." Ambrielle responded.

"What were you thinking about?" Maetha asked.

Ambrielle wished that she could communicate the thoughts and feelings as she had experienced them, but trying to explain them to someone else never came out quite the same.

"Nothing, really." Ambrielle peered out the window again. "Watching the rain and thinking about how it is different from Earth."

"How is it different from Earth?" Maetha asked.

Ambrielle put her feet on the floor and sat up. "These raindrops here are huge! I almost got soaked from just two of them hitting me."

"Yeah, you don't want to be out at all when it rains. It can hurt at times," Maetha said.

"How did everything go? Were you able to convince everyone?"

"Almost," said Maetha. "All but one of them. Magraeva wouldn't come. She's probably the oldest of us and didn't think she would last walking all day. She was afraid she would slow us down."

"Do you think she would?"

"Hmm . . . she probably would," Maetha conceded, "but she still has a right to go with the rest of us gatherers."

"Well, maybe it's for the best."

"Did you get yourself something to eat?"

"No, I haven't yet. I was waiting for you."

"Ambrielle, dear . . . you should have eaten something." Maetha stood up to walk over to the bins. "You know you can get anything you want at any time, don't you?"

"I don't want to get too much, especially with this shortage."

"I have plenty for now. We'll be bringing back more soon, and besides"—Maetha sat some olavas down on the table—"a little thing like you isn't going to eat enough to cause a problem. Get yourself some fruit, and I will be in there shortly."

After Ambrielle and Maetha had both eaten, Maetha went on to bed for the evening, needing to rest up for the expedition the next day. Ambrielle went back to the window. It was raining more heavily now. It was darker than usual, as the clouds were covering the two moons. Small streams of water flowed through grooves in the rocky surface of the street, racing toward the lower areas of the mountain.

She thought of the human she'd seen the day before and wondered how things were for him during this rainstorm. Was he from Earth, or could there be humans that lived on this planet? Someday she would have to find out, but she would wait for now and give Maetha some time to work things out. Maetha had been kind to her; she had saved her twice and opened her home to her. Ambrielle was comforted just knowing there was another human in this world.

CHAPTER 7

BLUE RAYS OF light crossed through the house as a ridged hand touched Ambrielle's shoulder.

"I'm heading out, dear, and I will hopefully see you before nightfall."

Ambrielle rolled over in the bed, trying to focus.

"Hey." Ambrielle squinted her sleepy eyes. "Hope you find lots of fruit."

"Yes, I'm sure we'll find something." Maetha smiled. She turned around as she got to the doorway. "Ambrielle, if I am not back before dark, do not worry. We are prepared to camp overnight if necessary."

"Okay." Ambrielle lay her head back on the pillow, closing her eyes.

"C'mon, boy, we're going on an adventure today!"

Blaez got up and ran to Maetha. It wasn't long after she left that she came back into the doorway again. "Don't forget to talk to the workers in the city today."

Ambrielle's eyes opened again with the sudden sound of the voice.

Maetha continued, "Find something you are interested in. We need to get you on with someone as an apprentice."

Ambrielle gritted her teeth a bit and nodded. "I will."

Her eyes closed again as she drifted back to sleep.

A little while later, sunlight flooded the house, making it difficult to sleep. She got up from the bed, folding the blanket and laying it back on the stone. It appeared that before she'd left, Maetha had left out some fruit for her to eat.

After eating and bathing, she found another clean white robe hanging up that was close to her size like the others. She saw her sundress hanging up as well, cleaner now, but it still had some traces of blood on it. She decided she would take the robe. Ambrielle quickly ran her fingers through her hair to get out any tangles. She headed out the door and down the path toward the city. Everything was still wet from last night's rain. The pockets and crevasses in the rock were all filled with water, while some of it still ran down the mountain through the cracks and grooves in the street. When she got to the archway of the town, she saw a protector she did not recognize.

"Hey! What are you doing up here?" The protector lifted his blade staff from off the ground.

"What? I live here," she told him.

"Only Kavekkians are allowed to be here."

"But the vaesari said I was welcome to stay here," said Ambrielle.

"Do you want me to take you to them right now and we can sort this out?"

"Fine with me."

"If you live here, then where are you staying?"

"I've been staying with Maetha."

"Oh, *you're* the outsider. I was expecting something . . . different." He relaxed and set one end of the staff on the ground, "Go ahead. I'm not sure why we are letting outsiders up here. We don't take kindly to thieves. I'll be watching you."

"All right . . . thanks," Ambrielle said.

As she walked into the city, Corthian's shop was already drawing a crowd, so she decided to visit him later. Instead, she scanned for where she should go first. Sirendae's hut already had a line outside. There was a stone shop stand close by, and she might as well go down the line in order. The first stand had a nice, smooth countertop and some type of furnishing that stacked like shelves on display. Ambrielle walked over to shop, a bit hesitant to talk to strangers here without Maetha.

"Hello," said Ambrielle, walking up to the counter. Two Kavekkians were standing there, and they both faced her. "I'm not from around here."

She cleared her throat. "Well, I guess that's obvious, huh?" She giggled, while the two Kavekkians stared at her. "Um, I was wondering what this is. What do you do with it?" she said, motioning toward the wooden construction. One of the Kavekkians turned to the other and then back to Ambrielle.

"It's a wall ledge," said the female Kavekkian.

"Oh, it's very nice," Ambrielle replied. "What is it used for?"

The female again turned to the male Kavekkian and back to Ambrielle. "You put things on it. It stands up against the wall, and you put whatever you want on it."

"Ah, that makes sense," said Ambrielle.

There was silence for a moment. Ambrielle peered underneath the shelves, pretending to be inspecting the quality as she attempted to make this interaction less awkward. Trying to come up with something, anything, to ask so she wasn't just standing there looking stupid.

"So, you guys make these?"

They both nodded.

"Okay, nice," Ambrielle said.

The two continued staring at her, as if waiting for something to happen.

"Okay . . . thank you." Ambrielle began walking on toward the next shop.

Ugh, I feel like an idiot doing this. It went so much better with Maetha, she thought. The next shop was another shoemaker. She didn't think she wanted to be a shoemaker, and if she did, she could talk to Corthian. She walked down a bit farther and came to a table with several crystalline containers, some of white crystal, some yellow, and some blue. A male Kavekkian came over from behind the table. He was smaller than the average Kavekkian and had deep-set eyes and a thin face.

"Welcome dawn," he said.

It seemed unnatural to repeat their greeting, but she did anyway. At one point she'd thought it was their way of saying "Good morning," but they used it no matter what time of day or night it was.

"You must be the newcomer that we have been hearing about. I was hoping I would get a chance to see you."

Ambrielle smiled. "Well, yes, I am a newcomer."

"You don't look like I expected, but then, anything other than a Kavek-kian or Darterran would be unusual."

Ambrielle raised her eyebrows. "Nope, I'm human."

"Interesting. You have a nice, compact balance to your form."

"Well, at least you didn't say 'fragile.'"

"No, I wouldn't say fragile. Your skin is smooth, like polished stone," he said. "What brings you over to my shop?"

"Well, thank you. I was looking around, mostly, but these crystal bottles caught my attention."

"Ah yes, the bottles. I always say the presentation is everything."

"Oh, so it's not the bottles themselves you are selling?"

"No, no, it's what's inside them."

"Well . . . what is inside them?"

"Different things. It all depends on what you need," he replied. "We have lisper; we have vaspage oil and some new jinos cream that can make your skin smoother, though I guess you don't have much use for that."

"Kind of like an inventor?"

"Yes, I'm a plyreth. I combine substances together to make something new, and then I find a use for them."

"That sounds interesting."

"It is, it is . . . And quite profitable at times."

"The vaesari said that I need to find a profession while I am here and start an apprenticeship with someone. Do you have an apprentice?"

"I do, but there's nothing saying that I can't have another."

"Okay, well. I haven't decided on anything yet, but this is the most interesting work I've found so far."

"Good, good. I can show you plyrething, and I would love learning more about your species as well."

"Okay, great," said Ambrielle. "Well, I guess I'm going to walk around a bit more and see what else I can find."

"My name is Kinsen, by the way," he said.

"Nice to meet you. I'm Ambrielle." She curtseyed, pulling out the sides of her robe slightly.

"May the light shine with you," Kinsen replied.

Ambrielle began walking back into the crowd but stopped and turned around. "You study strange things that most people . . . well, Kavekkians, don't."

"I suppose I do," said Kinsen.

"Have you ever studied the lake or seen anything strange?"

"I suppose it depends on your definition of strange. There are plenty of water creatures that many would consider strange, but I believe it's because you don't see them every day."

"What about caves? Any caves at the bottom of the lake?"

"Not that I have any knowledge of. I'm afraid I'm not a good swimmer, but few of us are."

Ambrielle put her hand over her chin, thinking of a good way to phrase her next question. There wasn't much of a way around it other than to come out and ask. "Have you ever heard of a place called The Hollow?"

"The Hollow?" Kinsen asked. "I do not believe that I have. The Hollow in what?"

"I don't know. That's its name, I guess."

"What do you know about it?"

"Almost nothing, just that it's dark and . . . consuming. I was warned not to go there."

"Perhaps you should heed that warning. It doesn't sound like a good place. The less you know about it, the better."

"Yeah . . . I guess you're right."

Ambrielle put a hand up to wave and mouthed the word "bye" as she turned back toward the crowd. She walked through the maze of Kavekkians, scouting her next destination. There was one shop ahead on a small rise of stone. On a ramped platform behind the shop was a large object that resembled a cannon. Two Kavekkians were standing in front of it. One was slimmer and was about the average Kavekkian size, though his skin was more wrinkled than most and he had a downward slope to his eyes. The other one was broad-shouldered and younger.

The cannon-shaped machine was mekkadium combined with shiny chrome parts. It was thick toward the back, with a large, dome-shaped crystal over the top. The white, glassy crystal was different than the others on Mekkinspire. The machine had layered pieces that gradually got smaller toward the front end, which was hollow, like the barrel of a gun.

She moved closer, and the big Kavekkian motioned her back. "Please do not touch. Too much jarring could mess up the calibration."

"Oh, sorry!" said Ambrielle.

"I was expecting that you would show up here eventually," said the older, wrinkled one.

"Me?" asked Ambrielle, putting a hand to her chest.

"I figured another species, like yourself, would want to check out the technology," he said.

There was a third Kavekkian behind them that would pause to listen and then get back to pretending to be tuning some of the dials on a control panel.

"Oh. Yes, what is this?" Ambrielle asked.

"This is the lykris. You've probably heard about it."

"I think so. Is that what the Darterrans stole?"

"Uh, yeah, but let's not talk about that."

"Oh, right," she said. "So, what exactly can it do?"

"This thing projects a hot beam of focused sunlight. What good is a beam of sunlight, you may ask?" he said, almost as though he had been waiting for someone to ask that question. "We can use it for carving roads, carving out lairs for us to live in, and cutting out large sheets of rock to be used for assembling buildings. If you've seen the vaesari's citadel and courtyard, those structures are assembled out of pieces of cut rock."

"Oh yes, it was really nice," said Ambrielle.

"Yep, so if you need a home dug out or a shop built, you'll want to trade with us," said the large male.

"Well, being new here, I don't have anything to trade yet," said Ambrielle. "Right now, I'm trying to find a profession that I can join as an apprentice."

"Ah, you want to be a beamer? I've already got two learning now," he said. "I wouldn't have the time for a third."

"What about learning how to build them?" she asked.

"What?" he said. "Oh, we haven't built one in ages. The crystals inside are rare. We haven't found any of them in a long time."

"Shouldn't someone be finding more?"

"It would be nice if someone could," he said, "but if they dedicated their time to looking for crystals, they wouldn't be earning food or items to trade for all the days they searched and came up empty."

"What kind of crystals does it need?"

"Here, let me show you," he said. "Come on up here."

He took her hand as she stepped up onto the platform, and they walked behind the lykris.

"Back here on the top, you have the collection crystal—it has to be cut and rounded. This helps sunlight enter the lykris from any angle," he commented. "What if you had to move the lykris around just right to get the angle of Versoh's position all the time to be able to use it?"

"That wouldn't be very good," she said.

"That's the problem the collection crystal solves."

"Okay, makes sense."

"Let's take this off here." He pulled open a hatch, holding the collection crystal in place. "If you look down here, this is where the light from the collection crystal goes next."

Ambrielle leaned over the lykris to peer inside it.

"You see this other crystal down here," he said, pointing at a translucent, violet-tinted crystal. This crystal was also cut smooth and lens-shaped and had tiny particles trapped inside it. "This is the amplifying crystal. The light brought in by the collector passes through this crystal and is magnified, making the rays of Versoh much stronger, much hotter."

"Oh, it's pretty."

"This is the crystal that is so rare," he said. "It directs the light into this metal tube, and the coils around it. The tube ends at the focusing crystal. This is where this amplified light approaches fusion and is projected outward as a powerful beam."

"That is really interesting," Ambrielle said. "I wonder what else could be done with this."

"What else needs to be done?"

"Well, I don't know. Sometimes technology has different applications," she mentioned.

"Maybe so, but right now it does all we need it to."

"What is this for?" She pointed to a protrusion on the side near the front that pointed toward the ground.

"Oh, that's something we added a few cycles ago," he said. "The first lykris we had, the one that was stolen, always had a problem with bits of charged dust and debris being attracted to the field generated inside. It would get in the vents and eventually scatter the light. The beam would lose a lot of its power, and it would have to be turned off for a while and cleaned out before it could be used again."

"Oh, it generates an electromagnetic field?"

"It's a field. I don't know how, uh, elekrometic it is, but since we had to build another lykris anyway, we made some improvements," he said. "We put the vents back here, where most of the heat is, and put these metal prongs that attach to the metal cylinder inside. So that generates a field outside as well but attracts most of the metallic dust and debris to these prongs, keeping it away from the vents."

"Oh, that sounds pretty smart."

"It's very smart. We can leave it on much longer at a time now."

"Since you can't take another apprentice, do you know where I can find who studies the tablets and artifacts?"

"I don't know about any tablets, but that sounds like something that the lightborn would do."

"That's what Maetha said. Well, I don't know what I'm going to do."

"You'll find something. There's plenty of work to be done around here."

"Yeah, I guess. Well, thank you for showing me the lykris. I better keep looking."

"Sure, we'll see you around," he said.

Ambrielle walked back into the crowd, passing by other shops. She noticed the tool-crafting shop, another shoemaker, another healer, some tailors, a shop selling fruit. *I guess it's an easy decision after all,* she thought. *Plyrething is the only thing that is different.* She started back to Kinsen's shop, when she saw Taunsin sitting on the terrace overlooking the world below. She should say something to him. She hadn't talked to him much since the first day she arrived.

He didn't react to her approach, engrossed in a figurine that he was carving from a chunk of wood. It was a Kavekkian figure holding a bladed staff, like the one Maetha and Raegus used. She walked past him and sat down in a chair near the walled edge to get a glimpse of the lake. She glanced at Taunsin but couldn't decide if he was ignoring her or hadn't noticed that she was there. He was so focused on the carving that she hated to interrupt him.

The view from here was breathtaking. The fields below led to the forests on the other side of the lake. Ambrielle searched for the place where she first broke through the water's surface. She spotted the three inlets that she had swam toward to get up on land. From up here it was like a giant footprint, with the three inlets as toes.

"Have you ever noticed this before?" she asked. "It looks like a footprint."

Taunsin continued whittling away at the wood, oblivious to anything around him. Surely, he knew she was there by now.

"Hello! Mr. Taunsin!" she said with a bit of volume to her voice to make sure he couldn't keep ignoring her.

"Wh-What? What do you want? Can't you see I'm busy?" he replied.

"Just saying hello," Ambrielle said. "I thought you might say hello to me. I've been sitting here for the past five minutes."

"I'm working. You think I pay any mind to who comes and goes by here?"

"Well, why do you sit out here if you don't want to talk to anyone?"

"I like the fresh air, better for concentration. Everyone knows I don't want to be bothered." He moved his eyes up to her for a moment. "Everyone with any sense."

"I think you sit here because you want someone like me to come along and stop to talk to you."

"Couldn't be more wrong."

"Yep, you sit out here and carve your figurine"—she leaned over to view the carving—"which I must say is looking very good . . . and hope someone asks you about the figure you are carving."

"Hardly."

"Well, you haven't asked me to leave yet," Ambrielle said. "I guess that means you want to talk to me."

"Go ahead and leave if you want."

"All right, fine, if you're so busy."

Ambrielle turned and began walking away.

"So, you noticed the footprint down there," Taunsin said. She had taken about ten steps.

She smiled. "Yes, over there at the edge of the lake." She moved back onto the terrace. "The shape looks like a footprint."

"Versepirath."

"What?" Ambrielle asked.

"Versepirath," he repeated. "The creature that made the footprint."

"It really is a footprint?!" she asked. "But it's gigantic."

"That's what I said."

"Are you teasing me?"

"No, I'm telling you it's a footprint."

"There are giant things like this walking around? How many are there?"

"You know I'm busy. I've got carving to do."

"Taunsinnn!" she groaned.

"None—no one has ever seen one. I don't think they exist anymore."

"What did they look like?"

Taunsin's mood brightened the more her face expressed genuine interest in what he was telling her.

"No one knows," he said. "We wouldn't even know they ever existed if it weren't for that footprint."

"There must be some other signs somewhere, or some bones."

"Not that have ever been found."

"Well, how do you know about it?"

"I don't," he said. "Only the footprint."

"You know its name," she said. "Where did you learn about it?"

"Who knows? I can't remember now."

"Please, Mr. Taunsin, I want to know more."

"What's so important to you about some giant footprint?"

"I don't know. There's nothing to do, and it's the most interesting thing I've heard about today."

"I'll let you in on a secret," he said as Ambrielle's eyes widened in anticipation. "The Darterrans had some stories about times long ago. Do you know the lower caverns where the walking path begins?"

"I think so," she said. "Is that the place that you come to right after you climb the wall to the path? Where the Darterrans used to live?"

"Yeah, that's probably where Maetha takes you up. We rarely go in that area."

"Okay, what about it?"

"When they were banished, they had to leave quickly. They probably left some things behind."

"Ooh . . ."

"Most of those things were taken by looters, but looters don't care that much about stories, because they are no good for trade," he said. "I wouldn't be surprised if there was something in those dens down there."

"Oh yeah, maybe you're right."

"Of course I'm right." Taunsin was distracted by something below the mountain. "There they go again, out early today."

"Who? The Darterrans?"

"Who else? I hope they aren't doing something that is going to make this situation worse."

"What do you think this is all about?"

"No telling . . . I wanted to see the end of this mess before I passed on, but it doesn't seem like that will happen," Taunsin said. "My father was in charge of rounding up the Darterrans and forcing them to leave. He didn't want to do it, but he had his orders."

"What would have happened if he had disobeyed?"

"Probably would have been banished himself, but he hoped it might help calm the situation down if we were separated for a little while," said Taunsin. "He didn't realize that this would go on for more than sixty cycles."

"Yeah, that's crazy."

"All right, I've got work to do," he said. "Run along and see if you can find something down there."

Ambrielle grinned. "Okay, but don't worry, I'll be back to bother you again soon." She turned and walked back away from the terrace.

"Make sure you find everything you can," he said as she strolled away, heading down the sloping walkway that led to the base of the mountain. She came to the tunnel where she had first met Taunsin. She followed it as it wound around the mountain until she came to the abandoned market-place of the Darterrans. The wooden structures that must have served as a countertop and storage areas hadn't been touched in years.

Ambrielle checked through the wooden compartments of the first shops she came to but found nothing. She continued checking the shop areas until she eventually came across a small piece of wood with writing on it. Picking up the wooden object, she realized there were two wooden pieces tied together, and in between there were pages made of fabric, with well-styled text etched onto them.

It was odd that this was left behind. Why didn't the Kavekkians find value in things like books? From what Maetha told her, the lightborn did, but the general population must be too busy talking and eating fruit to care about reading these Darterran books. She read through the pages, hoping to find something about Versepirath or anything interesting about the tablets or the ancients.

The book was a story of a Darterran named Nylin who was tricked by mischievous tree spirits into losing his way in the forest. He spent days trying to find the way out so that he could get back home, but the trees kept masking the path. He was never able to return to a place with food or water. After he eventually died, his spirit left his body, but the tree spirits continued to torment him. He tried to run away, but they would not let him out of the forest. He met all the other Darterran spirits whose bodies had died long ago, and the tree spirits were tormenting them too.

One day Nylin came upon the spirit of the great tree Tirobis, who sheltered and protected him from the other spirits. Tirobis remembered that Nylin had once protected his physical embodiment from being chopped down and used for wood by the other Darterrans, recognizing the sanctity of the ancient tree. Tirobis ordered the other spirits to allow Nylin safe passage through the forest.

Nylin was free to move on but wanted to help the other Darterrans who were held prisoner in the forest by the tree spirits. When he returned home, he found that he could no longer communicate with the living, so he asked the water spirits if they would allow him to borrow their voice to speak to them. They agreed if he promised to use the voice to tell the living to no longer hold back the rivers, creeks, and streams. They must let the waters flow free and true and be allowed to cut through rock and ground as they saw fit.

Nylin agreed that he would tell them. He spoke to the living through the roar of the rivers and the babbling of the creeks, and eventually the living Darterrans listened. As cycles passed, Darterrans stopped cutting down living trees and allowed the water spirits to freely provide water to all the land and soil for the living trees, making them grow stronger than ever. When the tree spirits realized this, they forgave the Darterran spirits and stopped punishing them. Ever since then, when a Darterran died, its spirit could roam the spirit world and the forest freely and at peace.

By the time Ambrielle finished reading, Versoh had begun to set, and the market area began to grow darker. She wondered if the Darterrans really revered the trees and never cut them down. The Darterrans had more culture than she expected. She never had the impression before that they did more than live in caves and steal things, but they must value history and stories more than the Kavekkians did.

She was intrigued now, even though there had been nothing about Versepirath or the ancients that the vaesari had referenced. She searched through the rest of the market area, but nothing else of interest turned up, and she moved on to the dens where the Darterrans had lived.

She was close to the ledge where Maetha carried her up. The expedition should be getting back soon, with it getting dark, but they probably would not climb up this way. In the first den, she didn't find much other than some dusty bowls. When she picked up one of the bowls, a weird insect with a metallic, reflective body scurried to find a new hiding place. She immediately jerked her hand back and quickly left the den.

After debating whether she wanted to search any more dens and risk finding more bugs, she finally decided to go into another and continue her search. While searching the shelving, she found a crumbled-up bundle of pages that were stitched together. Wiping away the dust and dirt, she scanned the pages.

The writing in this book detailed the sun, Versoh, saying that it was a world of solid crystal and its purpose was reflecting light onto its system, which included Anatharia. The light that it reflected was referred to as Sohvius, which was regarded as the beginning of all. According to the book, Sohvius was a pure and sacred light that shone into darkness and gave form to the universe. It said that Sohvius couldn't be faced by anyone directly, or they would be consumed by the light. Therefore, surrogates such as Versoh reflected a lesser light across the universe.

As the sun began to set, it became increasingly difficult to read. The rest of the book was damaged, except a few pages near the end, which mentioned something about a whispering darkness that had once entered the world, attempting to undo everything the light had founded. It said that it nearly succeeded, until it was trapped at the edge of the forest and sealed up. It went on to say that only the light of life could keep the darkness at bay.

Whispering darkness . . . Could they mean the same whispers that she'd heard on the desert world?

A chill came over her as she thought about them. Suddenly, there was a clatter outside the den. Ambrielle stopped for a moment and then crept outside to locate what had made the sound. The sun had now set; a quiet darkness settled over the world. She listened intently for any further noises. Another sound. It was like small rocks and sediment tumbling down, and it was followed by a grunting and panting. The source was below her, at the base of the mountain, where Maetha had taken her up.

Could it be Maetha and the others getting back from the expedition? They wouldn't have any trouble climbing up here.

"Maetha?" she whispered, crouching to one knee to peek over the edge of the rocks into the darkness below. A crawling sensation crept up inside her chest.

"Maetha?" she called out with more volume.

No answer.

All sounds stopped—no pebbles falling, no grunting, no panting breath. Part of her wanted to turn and run back up the mountain path, but she wanted to know what was there. Nothing but Kavekkians and Blaez could climb anywhere up the wall of the mountain. It should be safe to find out what was there.

CHAPTER 8

AMBRIELLE STRAINED FOR any sound that might indicate that something was trying to climb the mountain. The patterns of chirping insects, night birds, and other creatures were all that remained. Whatever was there may have run off by now, startled by her voice. She stayed a few more minutes to make sure.

Then, a clunk. Ambrielle stopped, listening intently for more noise. The big moon, Pathea, now in its first-quarter phase, peeked out from behind the clouds. It began to light the world with its spectral aura. Ambrielle stared down the cliff at the ground below, not sure what she might see. Her heart was pounding as her imagination ran wild. An object moved quickly across a patch of moonlight and back into the shadows. As jarring as it was, she was almost relieved. It helped to rein her imaginings in a bit.

"Who's there?" She continued to stare out into the gloom but received no response. "I saw you out there. If you don't answer, I'll have to call the protectors."

"Very well," said a voice. "I'm leaving now. I didn't mean to cause any trouble." Then the sound of footsteps on grass and loose rock.

"Wait," said Ambrielle. "Who are you?"

The footsteps stopped. "A Darterran, gathering stones . . . I didn't mean to get so close to Mekkinspire."

Ambrielle moved closer to the edge to get a glimpse of the Darterran.

"Gathering stones for what?" She leaned over the ledge.

"It's you! the girl!" the voice exclaimed.

"What? How do you—"

"I'm here to rescue you!" he said as he stepped into a patch of moonlight, revealing himself to be not a Darterran but a young male human. He was wearing a ragged brown tunic with a dirty, off-white vest over it. A sharp-ended staff was in one hand, and he carried a satchel wrapped over his other shoulder.

"You're human! You must be who I saw near the forest the other day!" Ambrielle said.

"Yeah, that was me. I was surprised to see someone like you around here."

"So, there aren't any other humans here?"

"Humans?"

"Yeah," she said, "like you and me."

"No, you're the first person I've seen in a long time."

Ambrielle studied him as he responded. She found him decent-looking, but not the type of guy she was attracted to. His hair was disheveled, and he had a bit of a scraggly beard. Dirt and sweat were smeared across his face.

"You're from Earth, right?"

"No . . . I don't know. I don't remember much before I came here."

"I've had the same problem, but I do remember some things."

"What do you remember?"

"I was on a desert world, alone, trying to find some way back to Earth," she said, "but I went into a spring with a tunnel, and it led to the lake out there."

"I don't remember anything like that," he said. "How did you get from Earth to the desert world?"

"That's what I can't remember. What's the first thing you remember about this world?"

"I'm told they found me wandering around the Darterran caves."

"Wow, so how long have you been here?"

"I think it's been a little over three cycles now," he said. "What about you?"

"A few days," she replied, "maybe a week."

Ambrielle remembered that she hadn't been in front of a mirror in days. She could look hideous right now. Even though she didn't necessarily want this guy to be attracted to her, she hated the thought of the first impression she was presenting.

She couldn't really fault him for having messy hair or dirt on his face. Things like that might not matter here as much. The way his hair curled out behind his ears was kind of cute.

"Have you tried to find that tunnel again, in the lake?"

"Oh . . . no, I haven't. I don't know if I could find anything at the bottom of the lake."

"I suppose they wouldn't let you anyway."

"What do you mean?"

"The Kavekkians," he said. "That's why I came here . . . to rescue you."

"Rescue me?"

"Yes, I have some rope." He pulled a ring of rope from his satchel. "If you can tie it to something up there, you can lower yourself down, or I can climb up and take you down."

"I'm not climbing down there," she said. "I'm not sure that I could make it back up. Why would I want to be rescued?"

"Why wouldn't you?"

"They let me live up here. Why would I want to leave?"

"Aren't they keeping you as a servant?"

"No, what gave you that idea?"

"When I saw you the other day, you were carrying bags for the Kavekkian, and that beast was keeping watch over you to make sure you didn't run off."

Ambrielle laughed. "That's not what was going on at all. We were out gathering fruit. We were attacked by some raestrigs. Did you see that?"

"That must have been before we were out there."

"We were lucky to make it."

"Very lucky. Not many survive a raestrig attack," he said. "Is that what happened to your arm?"

"Yes, and if it weren't for Maetha and Blaez, it would have been much worse."

Perhaps it was the way the moonlight was lighting up his face, but she was captivated by his facial expressions as he talked. The way the crease in the corner of the right side of his lips curled when he said certain words. His left eyebrow twitched whenever he asked a question; she enjoyed watching him as they conversed.

"I'm glad for that," he said, "but you should know that the Kavekkians are bad."

"How so? They've done nothing but help me since I arrived in this world."

"They can't be trusted. They forced the Darterrans out of their homes. Some were even killed."

"But the Darterrans stole from them, stole their lykris," said Ambrielle, "which was really important to them. They're really hard to build or something like that."

"They didn't steal it," he said in defense. "It was loaned to them. The Kavekkians got mad about some old tablets."

"What about the tablets?

"They think the Darterrans found some and kept them for themselves. The Kavekkians think anything found using the lykris belongs to them."

"That doesn't sound like the Kavekkians. I've heard their meetings. They seem pretty fair to me."

"They are anything but fair," he said. "They have you fooled."

"Well, what about the fruit? The Darterrans are stealing all of the fruit now. How is that not bad?"

"Because you won't let us have our dens back on the mountain. You won't talk to us, so we had to do something to get your attention."

"Okay, wait, why are we arguing about this?" Ambrielle said. "We're both humans. There's no reason for us to fight with each other."

"Yeah, I suppose you're right, but I've been living with the Darterrans for a while now. They've taken me in, fed and clothed me. I consider myself one of them, but I don't want to fight with you."

"I feel the same way about the Kavekkians. Even though I haven't been here as long as you have, they have done a lot for me," she said. "But I have nothing against the Darterrans. If they took you in like that, they must have goodness in them."

"Yeah, maybe all of the Kavekkians aren't bad," he conceded, "but everything I've been told by the Darterrans . . . I don't think I could ever trust them."

"So you could never trust me?"

"Maybe," he said. "I'd like to. I'm not that trusting of others."

"That's okay," she said. "Neither am I."

She noticed the moon had made its way to the top of the sky, and the smaller moon had risen as well. If Maetha had gotten back and noticed that she was gone, there could be trouble.

"Hey, I don't mean to be rude, but it is getting pretty late," Ambrielle said. "I had better get back."

"Oh, that's right," he said. "Kavekkians sleep at night."

"That's unusual?" she replied.

"I think so," he said. "It is for us, anyway."

"Humans are supposed to sleep at night," she said. "Anyway, uh, thanks for wanting to rescue me, I guess."

"Yeah, sure," he said with a grin.

"Well, have a good night," she said, waving as she turned.

"Wait," he said. "Can I come and talk to you again sometime?"

"I can try to come back at this time tomorrow," Ambrielle said. "I'm not supposed to talk to you, though, so I can't promise anything."

"Not supposed to talk to me? I thought you weren't a prisoner."

Ambrielle sighed. "Do you want me to meet you here tomorrow or not?"

"Yes, I'll be here," he said. "Would you tell me your name?"

"Ambrielle, what is yours?" she said.

"Ambrielle . . ." he said slowly, as if he wanted to feel the form of the word in his mouth. "It was nice to meet you. I'm Gavian."

"Nice to meet you too."

He walked back around the base of the mountain, going in and out between moonlight and shadow. Ambrielle started back up the mountain path, with only moonlight to contrast the black rock and darkness. The whole way back, she was deep in thought about Earth and how she and Gavian had ended up here. She was happy to have potentially made a new friend, a human friend, that she could relate to better than anyone else around here.

By the time she made it back to Maetha's house, she was so tired she immediately collapsed on the bed. There was no sign of Maetha or Blaez. Ambrielle hoped everything was going well with the expedition, but soon her eyes closed, and she drifted off into a deep sleep.

⤞

She awakened to the sound of someone coming into the house rather noisily—footsteps on the floor, the thumping of bags clumsily hitting the walls. It was Maetha and Blaez. Ambrielle sat up, rubbing her eyes to focus. The bright light of Versoh was already filling the house up and igniting the crystals, making it difficult.

"Maetha! I'm glad you're back!" Ambrielle said.

"I'm glad to *be* back, dear." Maetha unpacked her bags of leafy yellow plants.

"What did you find out there?" Ambrielle asked with excitement.

"We found a lot of vegetables, not much fruit, but we may have to get used to that for a while."

"Well, I suppose that's good that you found food."

"Yes, very much so. I'm not complaining about that," Maetha said. "It's just that Kavekkians have more of a taste for sweet fruits than anything else. It's what we have gotten used to eating around here."

"I can understand that," said Ambrielle. "I was a picky eater, but this place doesn't have any of the foods I was used to."

"I never thought of that," Maetha said. "You must be miserable here."

"No, I love it here." Ambrielle smiled and rubbed her bandaged arm. "It's different. It's taken some getting used to, but other than the occasional monster attack, it's been great."

Maetha smiled back, her eyes a bit weary.

"What are things like out there, away from Lon Kavekkia?" Ambrielle asked.

"As one may expect. We followed the river," Maetha said, "and it was mostly more river."

"Well, that's not interesting . . ." Ambrielle said jokingly.

"We didn't find much food until we came to this place where another river joins into our river. It was nice there, lots of blue, leafy vegetables."

"Oh, that does sound nice."

"By the time we found it, it was getting too late to come back," Maetha continued. "We gathered up all we could and then started back until it got dark."

"No wonder you didn't make it back last night."

"Yes. I hope you didn't wait up for me."

"Well, I did for a little while," she said, pursing her lips together. "I was a little worried, even though I knew you had told me that there was a chance you could be gone overnight."

"I didn't mean to worry you, dear." Maetha smiled. "What all happened with you yesterday?"

Ambrielle told her about talking to the different shop vendors. Apparently, Maetha wasn't friends with Kinsen, the plyreth. She thought he was a bit strange. Ambrielle mentioned learning about the lykris and talking to Taunsin.

"So how was Taunsin?" Maetha asked.

"It's hard to tell," Ambrielle laughed, "but I think he was good."

After they ate, bathed, and changed clothes, they walked down to the town plateau and came across Raegus at the path gate, standing guard. Maetha told him all about the expedition, and they moved on to Corthian's shop.

Corthian saw them immediately, and he watched them the whole time they approached with his arms crossed.

"Maetha and Ambrielle . . ." he said. "What a pleasant surprise. How are you both doing?"

"A little tired," said Maetha, "but otherwise great."

"Oh yes, you'll have to tell me about the expedition, but first . . ."

He reached down behind the counter area and pulled up a pair of freshly made boots. They were a shiny cedar brown color, with a grainy texture from the balcain leaves showing through. The sides had a fold of juniper-colored material, and there was a triangle-shaped piece of metal at the top. The bottoms were made of wood, except for the short heel, which was mekkadium.

"Are those . . . ?" Ambrielle's eyes widened.

"Your boots. I put the finishing touches on them last night."

"They're beautiful!" she said.

"What are you waiting for? Try them on," Corthian encouraged.

"They're like . . . a work of art," she said. "It almost feels wrong to put them on my feet."

Corthian laughed. "But that is their purpose."

Ambrielle slipped off the sandals he had hastily made for her days ago and sat down on the rocky ground to place her foot inside one of the boots. The fit and weight was that of fine, expensive material, or at least, it would be expensive on Earth. It took her a little work to get the heel of her foot all the way in, but once it found its way, it was a nice fit. She put the other one on, which felt a bit easier getting into.

Ambrielle stood up and walked around, back and forth, with a somewhat unsteady walk.

"They're going to be a bit tight for the first few days, but then they will become more flexible and should be just right," Corthian told her.

"They feel incredible!"

Corthian smiled. "Your feet are smaller than Kavekkian feet, so I decided to make some boots with the extra material."

She walked to him, reaching up to give him a hug. "Thank you." He seemed surprised but put a hand on her back with a gentle squeeze. Ambrielle then turned and gave Maetha a hug as well. "Thank you, for all you've done for me."

"Of course, dear, anytime. We've helped each other out," Maetha said.

Maetha left for the council meeting, and Ambrielle spent some time wandering around the city, following the crisscrossing lights above with her eyes. After a little while, Ambrielle returned to Maetha's lair to relax. Maetha finally returned and found Ambrielle asleep by the window.

"Looks like you had the right idea," Maetha said as Ambrielle stirred from her unintentional nap.

"Yeah, I didn't think I was that tired," Ambrielle said.

"I'm pretty tired myself. I think I'm going on to bed," Maetha told her.

"What did they say at the meeting?" Ambrielle asked.

"They were pleased we found a food source out there, and they want us to bring some of the builders with us next time we go," said Maetha. "They want them to start on a more permanent campsite area, in case we have to go back to this place in the future."

"Oh, that's a good idea," said Ambrielle. "Maybe that will become a new city one day."

"I don't think there's enough resources to use all the time. There's enough to take a few trips, and then after that we'll have to wait for it to grow back," Maetha explained.

"What about starting a garden close to the mountain?"

"We could, but that risks interfering with the balance," Maetha said with concern.

"It's already interfered with," Ambrielle pointed out.

"Yes, but it will go back to how it was if we let it," Maetha said. "If we start planting more, that invites more grazing animals, and grazing animals invite predators."

Ambrielle sighed as Maetha went into the other room.

"Sleep well," Maetha said. "See you in the morning."

"Good night."

"Nothing good about the night, dear."

"Welcome dawn, then."

Maetha lay on the bed and went to sleep, while Ambrielle stayed by the window, waiting for sunset. She wondered if she should go down to the cliff to meet with Gavian. It was what she wanted to do, but Maetha had told her not to. It was perfectly natural for her to talk to another human, though. They should be able to understand that. Neither of them were involved in this conflict. It had nothing to do with them.

Finally, Ambrielle decided to go back to the cliff, at least for one more night. As she quietly snuck out of the house, Blaez lifted his ears, but fortunately didn't do much else. She walked down the path to the city. It was dark and abandoned. Pathea had not risen yet to illuminate the mountain. There was a protector at the other side of the circle, walking around with a torch.

The protector didn't turn in her direction as she passed through the deserted city. She continued down the steps, back through the cave to the old Darterran market. She knelt once she got to the cliff so that she could lean over, but this time, without the moonlight, it was too dark to tell if Gavian was there.

"Hello," she whispered, but no one answered. She whispered a little louder. Still nothing. A few minutes went by, until the sound of footsteps came from below. It had to be him. She stood up and quietly walked back toward the road, listening as he walked up to the base of the mountain.

The footsteps stopped, and a voice whispered, "Hey, are you there?"

She didn't respond, not wanting him to know that she'd gotten here first and was waiting for him.

She waited for a few more minutes and then walked back up, making sure that her boots slid across the grit over the rocks as she stepped, to make her arrival audible.

"Ambrielle?" he whispered.

"Hey! Yes, it's me," she whispered back.

"Good, I'm glad you made it."

She crouched down and crawled over to the edge of the cliff. That way she could lean over and talk to him without being too loud.

"Well, it wasn't easy," she said. "I'm not supposed to be talking to you, you know?"

"You must have really wanted to see me again," he said with a laugh.

"Well, you practically begged me to come back tonight," Ambrielle replied sarcastically.

He laughed. "Oh, so this is your kindness, allowing me to see you again?"

She smiled. "Exactly."

"What about you? Has there been much going on since last night?"

"Well . . . I had a late start this morning, but I went down to the city . . ." Ambrielle said. "Oh! I got these incredible boots!"

She stood up and posed with her right foot out to show him one of the boots on her feet.

"I can't see them really well, but I'm sure they are nice," he said.

"They're more than nice," Ambrielle said. "They are amazing!"

He leaned against the rock. "Yeah, they look really great. How did you get those?"

"Corthian made them for me. He's one of the shoemakers in the city," Ambrielle explained. "Maetha helped me get supplies to trade for them."

"You need to get me some. All I have are these sandals." He lifted a foot up to show her.

"Oh, sure, just bring some balcain leaves, some hovanoke, what else was it . . . ? I think it was mebri oil," she said.

"That wouldn't be too hard."

"Well, it's a little harder with raestrigs hunting you."

"Oh yeah. How is your arm doing?"

"It's fine. It feels a bit tight and itchy at times, but I usually forget about it."

"Glad to hear it."

"What did you do today? What do you usually do with the Darterrans?"

"Mostly slept so far today."

"Well, that seems lazy."

"Darterrans sleep during the day, and we work at night."

"Oh, they're nocturnal."

"But last night, when I got back to the cave, I mostly hauled loads of spoil out of the new tunnel we are digging into."

"Spoil?"

"Yeah, the excess dirt and rock that we don't have a use for when we are tunneling. It eventually has to be cleared out of the way."

"Oh, what are you digging for?" Ambrielle asked.

"Halacite, durathyst, esmodian, things like that," he replied.

"What do you use that for?"

"Making certain parts for weapons or armor, tools, decorations, trinkets, all kinds of stuff."

"What do you do when you aren't working?"

"Sometimes play games or sit around and talk and eat."

"That sounds nice. What kind of games do they play?"

"Mainly flakball."

"What's that?"

"It's a round ball about like that." Gavian held up his hands forming them into a round shape. "Made of clobur, so it bounces really well." He stopped leaning against the cliff and stood up. "We play in one of the chambers in the cave. So, you put a line between the two walls. One group on one side throws it and has to bounce it off the other group's side. So after it bounces off their wall, if it gets past them, you get two points." Gavian continued, "And the other group tries to catch it. If you do, then your team gets the ball.

"That sounds fun. So how does the game end?" Ambrielle asked.

"Whichever group gets to twenty points first wins," said Gavian.

"Oh, why twenty?"

He shrugged. I guess that usually makes it a good amount of time for one game."

"I bet I would be good at flakball," she said.

"What makes you think that?"

"Well, I have really good hand-eye coordination," Ambrielle boasted. "I would be able to catch the ball a lot to steal turns from the other team."

"The ball is going pretty fast," he said. "You need really good reflexes."

"I have really good reflexes."

He laughed. "Maybe you can play with us one day."

"I hope so. I want this feud to end somehow between the Kavekki-ans and the Darterrans, and then I could show you the mountain," said Ambrielle. "You could show me the caves. How great would that be?"

"I must admit that ever since I have been here, I've wanted to see the view from the mountain. Something about being above the clouds and looking down over the world . . . Yeah, if they end up having to trade with us for food, maybe that will start something."

"It's not really above the clouds, but it is a nice view," said Ambrielle. "I don't think that stealing all the food is going to accomplish any peace. They're already working around that."

"Oh, you mean the protectors guarding the fruit trees?" asked Gavian. "Medigrin predicted that. He's already working around it."

"Who's Medigrin?"

"He's the gral of the Darterrans, our leader."

"What kind of plans does he have? I hope nothing violent."

"He's not like that, but I don't know what the plans are," Gavian said. "I'm not really part of the planning. We each have our jobs to do to help the pack."

"And all these plans are to get the Kavekkians to trade with them?"

"Not all of them. He plans for everything," Gavian said. "He plans everything that we need to work on for the good of the Darterrans."

"And you trust him?" asked Ambrielle.

"He's helped all of us. Even in the time that I've been here, he's improved things a lot, and he's been right about everything."

"Well, I hope you know what you're doing," Ambrielle said as they let the sounds of the night into their conversation for a moment. She was amazed at how easy Gavian was to talk to. Normally when she talked to guys, she was guarded against giving up information about herself. She wasn't the sort of girl most of the guys in school were interested in. When they did talk to her, she was so focused on not being weird that she didn't say much. This was different; words were falling out of her mouth without her filtering them.

"So, you don't remember anything before you came to Anatharia?" Ambrielle asked.

"Very little. Vague things like grass, trees, mountains . . ."

"What about a place called The Hollow?"

He paused for a moment. "When you said that, it felt like my heart began to race. But I don't remember it."

"What about whispers?"

"You're really spooking me out with these questions. Why do you ask?"

"When I was in that desert world, I heard whispers, and there were warnings about a place called The Hollow. I met a girl there that had got lost in The Hollow and somehow escaped."

"You should have asked her."

"I did. I was just wondering if you had the same experience. Maybe if we could figure out what it means, we could both get back home."

"Whispers . . . I'm not sure . . . I remember walking through a blue tunnel, and . . . there was water pouring down on me."

"You walked through it?"

"Yes. I'm not sure where it was. I keep thinking it was in the caves, but I've never found anything like that."

"Was the tunnel like a vortex?"

"I guess you could say that. It was swirling, like wind blowing, but there wasn't any wind."

"I keep seeing the same thing. It's like it's burned into my brain."

"Yeah, I know what you mean."

"If you remember anything, let me know."

"Of course I will. Tell me about what it's like up on the mountain," he prompted.

"One day, I met with the vaesari. They wanted to ask me a lot of questions about how I got here," she said. "Lately, I've been trying to find an apprenticeship so that I can earn my way."

"What kind of work do they do up there?" Gavian asked.

"Make shoes and clothes, gather food," she said. "I think what I want to do is learn to be a plyreth."

"What's that?"

"Something to do with making new materials and substances by combining things together."

"Does that actually work?"

"You've had some chemistry in school, haven't you?" she said. "They make different oils and medicines like that."

"Not that I recall, but I guess Darterrans do that too. I never thought about it that way."

"Where is the Darterran cave at, exactly? Is it hard to find?"

"It's on the other side of the mountain," Gavian said. "There's a ravine the river and the waterfall from the mountain flow into. The caves are in the ravine."

"Oh, I guess I've never seen that side of the mountain."

A glow from the horizon signaled the rising of Pathea, illuminating the landscape and bringing long, dark shadows with it.

"Do you always plan to live with the Kavekkians on the mountain?" Gavian asked.

"I guess I haven't thought much about that," Ambrielle confessed. "I want to get back home. I miss my mom and dad and my little brother. I don't know if that will ever happen, though. If it doesn't happen, when I get older and braver, I want to explore Anatharia. I want to see what all is out there. The Kavekkians don't do much exploring. They don't care what is outside of Lon Kavekkia, but I want to know what is out there. I've only seen a small fraction of this planet. There must be incredible places, far away, that no one even knows about."

"You seem pretty brave to me. You've survived on three different worlds. How much braver do you need to get?"

Ambrielle laughed. "Brave enough to want to go into the forest again."

"It sounds like a great adventure. I would like to do that too," Gavian said. "I've been so focused on my daily routine, everything that needs to be done, that I haven't thought about that much."

In this short time, she already sensed a connection with him and was even a little attracted to him, but she wasn't sure how that would work out right now, the way things were. She was glad to have him as a friend if nothing else. It was something she needed right now more than she'd realized.

"Have you ever felt that as much as you like everyone around you, it still takes effort to fit in?" he asked.

"Yes, all the time," she agreed.

"I feel that way with the Darterrans sometimes. Even though I'm comfortable with our work crew, I still feel like an outsider sometimes," he said. "You seem different. I don't feel like that with you. Maybe it's because we're both . . . human?"

"I was thinking the same thing," she said. "I don't think it's that we're human. I didn't fit in with everyone when I was on Earth, a planet filled with humans."

"I guess it's a good thing that we met."

She smiled. "Maybe I will allow you to accompany me on my expedition."

He laughed. "I hope so. I would hate to miss out on such an adventure."

"Just as soon as we achieve world peace . . ." she said with a smirk.

They talked a little longer as the waning crescent of Pathea rose above the trees. Then they both realized it was getting late. Ambrielle needed to get back to Maetha's house to get some sleep, and Gavian mentioned that he had work duties in the cave that he had to get started on.

"Ambrielle . . ." Gavian said.

"Yes?"

"You're the most beautiful girl on Anatharia."

Ambrielle blushed. She almost thanked him before realizing how silly she was for momentarily being flattered by such a meaningless statement.

"It may be too dark to see, but I'm rolling my eyes right now," she said.

Gavian laughed as he turned and walked into the gloom. Ambrielle's head was spinning, with many thoughts to contemplate. How was this friendship going to work out if she wasn't allowed to talk to him? Was she going to sneak out here every night? She had the whole walk back to think on it.

It wasn't often that she really connected with someone, moments where she discovered she had more in common with someone than expected. It was like a new light had turned on in the darkness.

As she began walking through the old Darterran market area, a scrape on the rocks sounded behind her. She turned back, but nothing was there but moonlight and shadows. When she made it to the end of the market, another scratching sound came from the side of mountain. Something climbed up onto the path and leapt in front of her. Startled, she jumped back and lost her footing, landing in a sitting position on the rocky path. It was a Kavekkian protector, who pointed his bladed staff at her.

"Spy!" he said.

"What? No . . ." replied Ambrielle, confused.

"You were talking to that one that lives with the Darterrans! You told him things about us and the mountain!"

"No, no . . . let me explain," said Ambrielle.

Another Kavekkian walked up from behind her. It was Raegus.

"I didn't want to believe it, but I heard it myself," he said.

CHAPTER 9

AMBRIELLE SPENT THE rest of the night in a dungeon underneath the citadel. The only light she had was the moonlight coming in through some grate sections in the ceiling. She debated with herself, oscillating between how she had messed up everything and how this wasn't really her fault. Talking to Gavian had not been planned; it had merely happened. Emotionally, she careened from sad and upset to simply not caring. She knew she had disobeyed Maetha, but how much freedom was she allowed if she couldn't talk to a fellow human? Neither of them had anything to do with this squabble.

As morning came and sunlight began to pour into the room, there was a rattle, then a thud at the door as it opened. Blinding light filled the room, and then the light was partially blocked by a figure standing in the doorway. Raegus motioned for her to stand up and then took hold of her arm, leading her out of the room. Pathello stood outside the cell, and he followed as Raegus led Ambrielle up the steps.

Standing outside near the top of the steps was Maetha, who glared at Ambrielle the whole time. Ambrielle avoided eye contact.

"I told you to be patient," Maetha scolded. "Could you not have waited until this food shortage mess was over before talking to this Darterran boy?"

"He's not Darterran . . ." Ambrielle's voice trailed off as she sighed. What was the point? No one would understand.

The four of them walked through the courtyard gates. The vaesar and vaesara were sitting on their thrones, and a crowd had gathered in the audience. Raegus led her over to the platform, and he and Pathello stood beside her to face the vaesari.

"You have been charged with spying, treason, and trespassing on our mountain," said the vaesar. "Do you admit to these crimes?"

Raegus nudged Ambrielle forward to answer the question.

"No, I do not," she said.

"It's your word against Raegus and Pathello. That won't go in your favor," the vaesara pointed out.

"All I can say is that they misunderstood what they heard," said Ambrielle.

"Did you talk to this other human that has been seen with the Darterrans?" asked the vaesar.

"Yes," Ambrielle replied.

"That alone is enough for treason," said the vaesar.

"I don't care about this whole thing with the Darterrans. I was talking to a fellow human," Ambrielle said.

"Do not speak unless you are asked a question," the vaesar grumbled.

"The charge of treason stands, but how deep does your treachery go?" the vaesara said.

"How long have you been talking to this human?" asked the vaesar.

"Only two nights," said Ambrielle.

"How did he know to meet you at the pathway up the mountain? You're both humans. How long have you been planning to infiltrate our city?" the vaesara said

"I happened to be near the foot of the mountain, looking through old stuff, and he was trying to climb the mountain to rescue me," Ambrielle explained.

"Why would he come to rescue you?" the vaesara asked.

"Apparently the Darterrans think that you captured and forced me into servitude," Ambrielle said.

The vaesar laughed. "You wouldn't make a good servant."

Ambrielle sighed. "Can we get this over with?"

"Not until we are done getting answers," said the vaesara.

"How was he going to climb the mountain?" asked the vaesar.

"I don't know what he thought, but he wasn't able to," Ambrielle said.

"Were there any other Darterrans with him?" he asked.

"I didn't see anyone but him."

"Concerning the charge of spying," said the vaesara, "you were heard telling this human about the mountain, about the vaesari, things that the Darterrans could use against us."

"It was normal conversation, asking each other about what we did that day. It wasn't anything secret. I've never been told, 'don't tell anyone about this or that.'"

"You were told not to associate with the Darterrans," the vaesar said.

"What did he say about the Darterrans?" asked the vaesara.

"That they were digging in the mines," Ambrielle said. "He did say they took the fruit to force a trade."

"I knew it!" the vaesar exclaimed. "So, what are they doing now, since we have not traded with them?"

"Their leader has a plan, but he hasn't shared it with them."

"Who is their gral now?" said the vaesara.

"Meri . . . Medi . . . Medigrin! That's it," said Ambrielle.

"Medigrin, I remember him," said the vaesara. "When he was young, he would come and throw rocks up at the mountain."

"Maybe you should go and talk to him," Ambrielle suggested. "You may be able to sort all this out."

"You're in no position to give advice," the vaesar chastened. "I don't trust you any more than I do the Darterrans."

"These Darterrans aren't even the same ones that stole from you," Ambrielle said. "They are, what? The grandchildren of those involved?"

"They are the ones that stole all the fruit," said the vaesar.

"And the charge of trespassing," said the vaesara. "What do you say to that?"

"I didn't trespass. You said I could stay here," Ambrielle said.

"That was under the pretense that you would follow our rules," said the vaesar. "You didn't follow them, so now you are trespassing."

"I can't even get up here without someone bringing me," Ambrielle said.

"You are no longer welcome here," said the vaesar, "and must be removed."

Ambrielle tried to contain her surprise. She had been holding out hope that she could talk her way out of this, but she was sure that she couldn't hide it. Some Kavekkians in the audience cheered.

"Throw this Darterran spy over the edge!" yelled one.

"No!" shouted Maetha. She was standing somewhere behind Ambrielle on the platform. "That is not who we are!"

"No, we do not condone that," the vaesara agreed.

"She came from the lake, so we will cast her back," said the vaesar. "Make sure she swims back up the river. Do not allow her to come to shore until she is out of Lon Kavekkia."

"One more question," said the vaesara. "Was Maetha involved at all in your talking to this other human?"

Ambrielle glanced at Maetha for a moment and then back at the vaesara. "No, she told me not to talk to the Darterrans or anyone involved with them. I only wanted to talk to the only other human I've seen in a while, that was all."

"While that may be true," the vaesar said, "Maetha, you will be confined to the mountain indefinitely until this investigation is complete."

"Yes, Vaesar," Maetha consented.

"Good. The matter with the human is finished. You may remove her," the vaesar said to the protectors.

Raegus and Pathello grabbed each of her arms and led Ambrielle out of the arena, and Maetha followed close behind them. Once they made it past the gate, Raegus turned to Maetha and then to Pathello. "She's wearing a Kavekkian robe. We can't let her take that," he said.

"Don't you have your own clothes?" Pathello asked.

"They're at my lair," said Maetha. "Let me take her there to get them, and she can leave the robes."

They walked down the path that led to Maetha's street, and the two protectors stood outside while Maetha took Ambrielle inside.

"I hope you know better than to do anything foolish," Raegus said to Maetha.

She narrowed her eyes at him but didn't respond.

Once they were inside, Maetha told her to hurry and get her dress on and give the robe back to her. "This may be the only chance I get to talk to you, so just listen," said Maetha. "You know the place I told you about, where we found food. They are going to make sure you swim upstream. Go to where the two rivers meet. Get food before the expedition returns."

Maetha paused for a moment. "Then, consider swimming back once the sun has risen and it is bright outside. You can avoid encountering any predators from the water. Don't stay around the shallow areas near the banks that smaller animals drink from. Once you get back, head to the caves where the Darterrans live, on the back side of the mountain."

Ambrielle continued changing as she listened. "I'm not a good enough swimmer to be able to swim upstream. I'm not going to make it anyway."

"Assuming you do, the Darterrans should take you in, since they took the other human. I hate suggesting it, but it could be the best chance you have to survive," Maetha advised.

Ambrielle came out in her sundress, which was still covered in faded bloodstains on the right shoulder and sleeve. "I'm sorry, Maetha. I didn't mean for you to get in any trouble."

"Don't worry about me, dear," Maetha said. "I may be a bit angry about it, but it's short-term anger. We'll likely never see each other again, but don't think I regret any of the time we spent together. I thought it would be for much longer, but I'll always be glad I had the chance to meet you."

Tears began welling up in Ambrielle's eyes. "I didn't mean for any of this to happen. I didn't even leave the mountain," she said.

"Don't feel bad," Maetha reassured her. "If I put myself in your place, I may have done the same thing."

Raegus knocked on the wall. "We're going to need to get going. We've been here too long already."

They both walked out, and the two protectors grabbed ahold of her arms again to lead her on. "What about the shoes?" Pathello asked.

"They're human shoes. Look at them," said Maetha.

He glanced down at them again. "Yeah, you're right."

As they approached the city, there was a crowd of Kavekkians standing at different shop counters, talking to each other, walking here and there. Some of them stopped what they were doing to watch the protectors leading Ambrielle through the crowd. Many of them were too busy to notice what was going on.

Whispers rose as they worked their way through. Ambrielle saw Corthian stop talking to his customer and glance at her. There was confusion on his face, but she saw the recognition in his eyes that he knew what was happening. Some Kavekkians watched, but a few cheered and shouted their approval of her banishment. She raised her hand as much as she could with the protectors holding her to wave goodbye to Corthian, and he put a hand to his chest. She expected him to ask for the boots, but he did not.

As they walked on farther, she saw Taunsin sitting on the terrace. He was carving something from a piece of wood and didn't appear to notice what was going on. Not far past the terrace, they took her to the side of the mountain. Pathello tumbled over the side but stopped as his hands hit the cliff wall, his feet still on the mountain perch.

He then climbed down the side of the mountain headfirst, with his long legs extending and contracting. He was using them to propel and stabilize his downward climb.

"You'll have to hold on tight," said Raegus.

A warm flush of fear rushed through her as she realized what was about to take place. She had gotten somewhat used to the short climb with Maetha, but this was something different altogether. She wasn't sure how high it was from here, but a fall surely meant death.

"Be careful with her on this descent," Maetha said to him. "No acrobatics this time."

Raegus scurried down the mountain at surprising speed. Ambrielle's hair dangled over her face, sparing her most of the view of the dizzying climb down the mountain. Before she could catch her breath, they were on the ground again.

After giving her a moment, they took hold of Ambrielle again and led her toward the lake, close to one of the waterfalls.

They reached a bank of white stone about five feet above the deep pool carved out by the waterfall that flowed into the rest of the lake. There were five other protectors that were making their way down the mountain now. Once they reached the ground, they began walking toward them.

"From here, we're going to have to be a bit more forceful," said Raegus.

"What do you mean?" said Ambrielle.

"They're going to have to throw you in," Maetha explained.

"I'll jump in myself. I promise," said Ambrielle.

"The vaesar ordered it," Raegus said.

The five protectors walked past them and headed around to both sides of the lake.

Raegus grabbed both of her arms, and Pathello grabbed her by the ankles, lifting her off the ground.

"Take care of yourself, Ambrielle," said Maetha.

She wasn't sure how she was going to swim upstream once she even got to the river. This was a death sentence. Her mind began racing to think of a plan of action, as this may be the last time she would have to think without having to focus on staying afloat. She could stay in the lake and outlast the protectors and eventually have a chance to make it to land.

"I'll always remember you," Maetha said.

The two protectors swung her back, then forward, then back again. They swung her forward a second time, but this time they released her, and she went flying out over the lake. She held her breath in anticipation as time slowed down, and everything became surreal for a moment. She hit the water and sank, immersing her in a shock of cold. Lunging upward, she began the swim toward the surface and prepared to swim across the lake toward the river.

The lake was growing deeper and deeper, like she was sinking instead of rising. The underwater world she was in now grew dark and still, and she was losing balance. She could no longer tell where the surface was anymore as she tumbled over and over, as though the rotation of the planet were spinning her rapidly. She was weightless, losing the sense of the wetness of the water. Everything was quiet and peaceful as her body began to grow numb. Her need for oxygen subsided. It was pleasant, drifting into this painless, dark peace.

Ambrielle came to her senses. She tried swimming upward again to find the surface. Her senses awoke as the cold water came rushing back. She quickly held her breath again and kicked her feet while paddling her arms to move up toward the surface. There were large stones in the way above and on either side of her. She must have sunk to the bottom of the lake.

Squeezing between the rocks, her hands touched a wall of rock with indentations like a honeycomb. She used the wall to propel herself forward until she came out of the tunnel. Ambrielle expected to see the sun shining through the surface, but there was no light.

She broke through the surface of the water and took a deep breath. Ambrielle searched the area, but everything was dark. Could she have come up into a cave? Wiping the water out of her eyes, she realized it was a dark sky.

There were stars overhead and an orange glow around the horizon. The silhouettes of hanging frond trees made the realization sink in. Ambrielle was back in the oasis, the oasis in the middle of endless dunes and rock. The lonely desert wilderness she'd hoped to never see again.

CHAPTER 10

AMBRIELLE CLIMBED OUT of the cold water of the spring and walked toward a group of trees. Her old tennis shoes remained on the banks, right where she had left them before she dove into the water. She leaned against one of the weeping frond trees, allowing her soaked dress to dry.

There was a heaviness to her body again, like when she'd first got to Anatharia. Reaching for her necklace, she was relieved to find it still around her neck. She could probably get back to Anatharia by swimming through the cave again. But what was there to even go back for? She felt like Maetha had abandoned her. She could have defended her a lot more than she had in front of the vaesari.

While reflecting on Maetha, a vision of the blue light flashed in front of her, a memory of her friend Hannah. She'd regarded Hannah as her best friend. Her makeup and hair were always perfect. She had taught Ambrielle a lot about applying makeup and styling her hair, what shoes she needed and the right outfits she thought would look best on Ambrielle.

Hannah was a bit more outgoing than Ambrielle and talked to anyone and everyone at school. Most of Ambrielle's friends, she had met through Hannah. Not a weekend went by that they didn't spend most of it together, either sleeping over at one or the other's houses or spending all day at the park or the strip mall.

Ambrielle recalled that recently they had begun to grow

apart. She wasn't sure what started it, but Ambrielle remembered sitting with her at lunch and not talking to each other. There was an awkwardness between them that didn't make sense. Hannah stopped texting her after school, and they no longer did anything together on the weekend.

She'd been abandoned by two worlds now. She should stay here and not go back to Earth or Anatharia. Things were a lot simpler here, with no one around. There were no predators to worry about here, no rules to contend with. But there was nothing left for her to do. There was a tear accumulating under her eye. Ambrielle tried to wipe it before she blinked, but it was too late. The tear fell and slid down her cheek. It was official now; she was crying.

Could she really stay here alone for the rest of her life? She knew that she couldn't. She was exhausted. Her clothes were damp but dry enough to sit down. She could brush the sand off later. She would try to figure out what to do after she laid her head down for a while.

She could hear her mother's voice telling her that if someone gets hurt, they have five good things coming to them. Her dad would be telling her that she was too strong to be defeated this easily, that he knew she was going to overcome this. He always said that, no matter how difficult the situation was, and most of the time, she believed him. Ambrielle brushed the wet trail from her cheek, and soon she had drifted off to sleep.

Upon opening her eyes, Ambrielle realized that she was back in the desert again. She sat up, brushing the sand from the side of her face. *Gavian* . . . she thought. She had been so upset after her banishment that she had forgotten the choice that led to this in the first place.

Something here was different. The world around her was much clearer now. There was a sparkle to the spring that had not been there before. It was daylight now! The sun had finally risen, though it was barely visible through all the trees. She got to her feet. There were new trees here among the palms and spreading into the distance. There were blue-green-, teal-, yellow-, red-, and orange-leaved trees like the ones in Lon Kavekkia.

She recognized some in particular as apraeda trees. She couldn't believe it! How had this happened? She walked away from the spring into the new forest. Fern grass poked out of the desert sand as she wandered farther through the newly grown woods. She realized it was all Anatharian vegetation.

Everything she had known in Anatharia was here now—even some dappones grew in patches among the trees. She reached down and picked one, taking a bite. Ambrielle relished the familiar taste. It was as though part of Anatharia had come back through the spring with her.

She wandered through the new forest as though it were her first time ever seeing a tree. Eventually, she came to the end of the Anatharian plant life. The rest of the world remained barren desert. Standing at the edge of the woods, she was exposed to the sun for the first time. A large red sun, peeking just above the horizon, stained the sand and trees in its pale, red glow.

After taking in all the changes in this reformed part of the world, she began to sense that there was something out there, something to the west, unseen in the distance. She could feel its pull as it slowly moved its way toward her.

It was a familiar sensation from the last time she was here. Thoughts of the whispers creeped inside her. She decided it was time to go back. This world had become a lot more interesting now, but there was still no one to talk to but trees. There must be a connection between this world and Anatharia. At least her trip to Anatharia had resulted in something good.

The Darterrans may know something about this. They were more open with their writings and history than the Kavekkians were. She turned back toward the spring and was startled to find a figure standing there among the trees.

"You've noticed it too," said a voice. "This world is beginning to wake up."

Startled, Ambrielle turned to find Sidaire standing behind her. She had almost forgotten about Sidaire being here.

"Do you know how it happened?" Sidaire asked.

"No," said Ambrielle.

"Did your memories return yet? Do you remember who you are?"

"I remember some of it now, and I have a new name. It's Ambrielle."

"Ambrielle . . . I was afraid that you had been taken. I went back to the spring, and you were not there."

"I'm sorry about that. I wanted to see what that light was coming from the cave, and—"

"What cave?"

"The cave in the spring."

"You were down there all this time? You can breathe underwater?"

"No, I wasn't in the cave for long. There's another world at the other end of the cave. That's where I've been."

"What do you mean, another world?"

"A place with forests, a lake, and two moons. But I got attacked by a wild creature in the forest, and then—"

There was a snap in the brush among the trees behind Sidaire. It was followed by rustling leaves. Ambrielle prepared to run as the sound got closer.

A boy with dark gray skin and glowing magenta hair stepped into view from behind Sidaire. He had a similar form to hers. Like Sidaire, there were dark bruises scattered across his skin and around his eyes. The ones on Sidaire had begun to fade by comparison.

"This is my friend Kazial. I found him right after I saw you. Something pulled him out of the Hollow too."

Ambrielle was relieved as she greeted Kazial.

"I wish this place made sense. I need to figure out how I can get home," Ambrielle said.

"If it's on this world, it probably doesn't exist anymore. All I know is that it's nice to see new life here again," Sidaire said.

"What was it like before?" asked Ambrielle.

"It was all beautiful rain forests. There were some mountains and clear valleys, but mostly thick, tangled jungle forests that were hard to get through unless you stayed on the trails. Quite different from these new trees, but I'm happy to see them here," said Sidaire.

"Wow, it's hard to imagine this world being filled with a jungle. What happened to it all?" Ambrielle asked.

"It started with a place out in the forest that everyone avoided, about a day's walk from our village," Sidaire said. "It was said to be a cursed, evil place."

"It *was* evil," said Kazial.

Sidaire continued, "It had been there for a long time, well before Kazial and I were born. The trees were all withered, and the animals were dead in that area. It was all piled up together in a spiral pattern around the center. It was said that anyone that ever went there either didn't return or later died from unknown causes."

Sidaire sat down on the sand. "At some point, the evil place started growing, and as it grew, it got closer and closer to the village. It was really strange, but many of those in our village kept saying it wasn't true, that it was imagined by some."

After she paused, Kazial said, "Then one day, many more trees had turned gray, then more . . . It kept getting worse."

"Yes," said Sidaire, "until there were so many dead plants and trees that it could no longer be explained away. The animals started becoming scarce, and everyone was growing angry, blaming it on others."

"That sounds pretty bad," Ambrielle said.

"It was, and it only got worse from there," Sidaire said. "A war broke out between our village and other villages. There were many that were lost. With the growing death of plant life, leading to famine, the war eventually sputtered out.

"There were things that began to roam about in the dark. They were called Nulthereals, the Whisperers. They seemed to be helping the curse. Many of the survivors called to them," Sidaire said, "pleading with them to restore the plants. Several had simply given up hope; they were so crippled by sadness and depression that no one was doing anything practical to try to solve the problem. Everyone stopped caring. The world began to fade into the desert you see now. Then, sometime after that, villagers began to mysteriously go missing, one by one."

"Where did they all go?" Ambrielle asked.

"I don't know for sure," said Sidaire, "but when I went looking, I ended up in The Hollow."

"Is there anything else either of you can tell me about The Hollow?" asked Ambrielle.

"I'm not sure what else to say. It's . . . hard to describe," said Sidaire. "It was like death, like I no longer existed. My thoughts were drowned out by thousands of others."

"I had the same experience," Kazial said.

"Do you remember any of those thoughts?" Ambrielle asked.

"Not that makes much sense," said Sidaire. "Most of it was gibberish that I couldn't wrap my head around, but I do remember them thinking about the universe. The universe being incompatible with the rest of existence, and they wanted it to stop."

"What do you mean, the rest of existence?" Ambrielle said. "What sense does that make?"

"I don't know. They had a word for it—for everything that exists beyond the universe," said Sidaire. "If I could remember."

"The Everance," Kazial said.

"That's it! The Everance." Sidaire's eyes lit up for a moment.

"The Everance . . ." Ambrielle repeated. "That's interesting . . . but I don't . . ."

Ambrielle's thoughts began to struggle with themselves. She couldn't focus. It was as if something had tapped into her mind. Her brain began to cycle through subconscious images, as if it were playing a slideshow of her fears and insecurities at lightspeed. Images of encounters with spiders and various insects, rejection from peers, kids calling her stupid. The memories were all here if she could access them, but her mind was out of her control.

"I don't . . . I don't trust you . . ." Ambrielle said, her voice getting more agitated as she spoke. "This is my oasis! You need to leave!"

Kazial and Sidaire turned to each other. Ambrielle began to feel hot. They must think that she was stupid. She hated that, hated when others doubted her intelligence. It was one of her worst fears, that she actually *was* stupid. The few times that she had messed up on an exam or had been made fun of for misunderstanding something, she worried it might be true. Even though she did well in school, there had been some that told her it was all luck and being able to memorize things. She didn't like to think about it, but what if it was true? She recalled that recently her grades had dropped, and she began to doubt herself even more. Her teachers had noticed it and talked to her about it.

They told her she needed to talk to someone, a counselor. But if she needed help, it meant she wasn't that strong, wasn't that smart. She had stopped wanting to study anymore. It was no longer important, with everything that had happened. The emptiness in her heart was too great, and it was still there now. It stalked her no matter where she was. There was no world across the universe she could go to hide from it, but she refused to turn and face it.

"I know you're up to something!" Ambrielle shouted. "I'm not stupid!"

"Ambrielle!" Sidaire yelled. "Don't listen to them!"

"Listen to what?"

"The whispers are Nulthereals! Whatever they are telling you, don't listen!"

"What are you talking about?"

"They're in your head! Come with us to the spring!"

Sidaire's eyes darted to something in the distance.

"They're coming!" she exclaimed. "We need to get to the water!"

Its pull became stronger as it drew closer, but Ambrielle saw nothing out there.

"They're almost here! Let's go!" the girl ordered as she started running off toward the spring in the middle of the new forest.

Ambrielle stood still, unsure of her words.

Do not trust her, Ambrielle thought as the voice whispered into her mind. *She is leading you astray.*

"Go where?" Ambrielle said.

"Nulthereals! We need to get to the spring!"

Why does she keep wanting to go to the spring? Does she want to drown me?

"Come on!" Sidaire commanded.

Ambrielle stood there, staring at Sidaire and Kazial, and then looked back toward the distant rocky mounds, where the source of the approaching whispers was coming from.

"We have to go. Please meet us at the spring!" said Sidaire as they ran off through the woods. Ambrielle stood there watching the rock hills, waiting for it.

I need to see it, Ambrielle thought. *I need to know what it is. It may be a clue to what is going on here.*

She walked away from the tree line toward it, pausing occasionally to scan the area. There was a shadow on the desert sands, traveling toward her. It was constantly moving and changing shape, like a flame of pure darkness. It was coming toward the tree line.

Why would this girl be so afraid of it? Why do I feel afraid? I need to go toward it. This could be the answer, the way home. It could be something better. An end to this loneliness. Pain and sadness are no more . . . in The Hollow.

Ambrielle's mind reeled at those words. The Whisperer was in her mind again.

"Who are you?" she said out loud. She tried to make her own thoughts even more clear and focused, deliberately thinking every word slowly and surely.

Come to us and we will show you.

The slow, whispered voice was now as distinct as the one that had followed her in the desert. As she fought against the numbing in her head, the voice had become partially unbound from her mind. Ambrielle began to clearly recognize the difference between her own thoughts and the whispered ones. As she stared out across the desert, the source of the whispers became visible as it floated over the sand toward her. The shadow changed shape, like liquid smoke or black flame.

The dunes behind it warped like a lensing effect as it moved closer. A violent, scintillating outline, a thin corona of white, buzzed as though it was at odds with the air around it. Fear shot through her again like a lightning bolt. She turned and ran toward the spring as the shadow pursued at surprising speed.

Once it reached the forest, the trees in its path bent toward it, like some magnetic force was drawing them in. Limbs and branches crumpled and broke as it passed through. A treetop broke off, flying into the shadow, vanishing with a sparking light as it passed into its void. One of the trees directly in its path bent and uprooted, disappearing into the darkness.

Ambrielle ran toward the spring, but ahead of her were more branches cracking and breaking. A second shadow was coming toward her, swallowing up foliage in its path. As they consumed the trees and plant life around them, they began to slow down but still moved fast enough to catch her if she didn't keep running. She turned and ran toward the dunes, where the red sun was hanging above the horizon. She was cut off from the spring, but in this world, there were other springs.

She dashed across the sands, slowing as her feet sank into the deep sediment sifting down the side of the first dune. Ambrielle jumped as she ran, letting gravity do the work as she went down the slope. She tried to move before her feet sank too deep into the sand. It was working, until she mistimed her jump and one of her feet plunged too far into a soft pocket before she could stop.

The shift in balance caused her to tumble over, down the side of the dune. Instead of trying to stop her momentum, she let herself continue tumbling over and over down the slope until she slowed. She then rolled onto her feet and started running, checking over her shoulder to find the two shadows still moving toward her.

They continued the pursuit, never changing speed, as if they were confident they were going to eventually catch her. For now, she was outgaining them, but she wasn't sure how long she could keep this pace up. She hit the base between two dunes, passing by the honeycomb rock formation she had seen before, and began the climb up the next dune. She knew they would gain some ground on her while she was trudging up the deep sand of the slope.

Sand cascaded over her feet, burying her legs further with each step, taking a lot of her stamina. She tried to pace herself on the climb, then she would make up for it on the next descent. The shadows were getting uncomfortably close. As she reached the hard sand near the top, they had begun to glide up the side of the dune. Ambrielle sprinted across the firm surface at the top of the dune and then jumped straight out as far as she could once she reached the next slope down.

She fell for a few seconds and then hit the soft, deep sand, regaining her footing and jumping again to use gravity to speed her descent. The shadows weren't slowed down by a climb, but she had made up some distance by the speed of her fall.

The next dune wasn't as soft. It had rock that stuck out through the sand and close to the surface. She was able to climb this faster, using her arms on some of the rocks to propel herself forward. After crossing a few more dunes, she came to a rocky canyon. She had more traction here, helping her speed, but the terrain was rougher. Falling could mean being hurt, immobilized, or worse.

This terrain was familiar, an exact copy of where she had been before. It helped, since there would be no major surprises, though she didn't have the luxury of going around the cliffs this time. Her lungs were taxed, and it was getting difficult to maintain her breathing. Checking behind her, she had gained a more comfortable lead over the two shadows. She could risk taking the next climb up the cliff ahead a little more slowly.

Ambrielle scanned the rocks coming toward her, searching for the easiest path to climb up. She saw an area that wasn't too high and climbed up on the first patch of hardened dirt. She reached for a rock that she thought she could use to pull herself up to the next point, but she couldn't reach it well enough to do so. She had to climb down and find another way. She ran alongside the cliff wall, hoping to find an alternative path. She needed to stay on the move, even if she had to go around this cliff.

Ambrielle saw a place in the wall where some of the dirt had collapsed and left part of a sloped area that she might be able to climb. Lifting her leg high, she was able to get enough leverage to move herself upward. She then sidestepped across a ledge to reach a low-hanging rock that she was able to use to hoist herself up enough to get a foot onto a makeshift platform.

She had used up a lot of time on this climb and knew she had to get to the top soon. The two shadows were approaching the base of the cliff. She tried to keep her fear in check and focus. She could not afford to make any mistakes now.

It is pointless to struggle like this. There is nothing to fear. The voices entered her head again as she struggled to remain in control of her own thoughts.

"Stop chasing me, then!" she shouted.

She was fighting with the cliff physically, while mentally battling the shadows' presence in her mind. The stress was becoming too much for her, but she made it to the slope, where she could climb the rest of the way to the top.

Ambrielle darted across the hard surface, increasing the gap between her and the shadows. Her arms were a bit tired from the climb and stung from the scrapes she had acquired. There was another valley ahead as she reached the end of the cliff. Climbing down would work in her favor for speed, but she had to be more careful.

She slid to the rim of the cliff and lowered herself down to a ledge she could stand on. Holding on to jagged nooks and crannies in the wall, she searched for the next place she could stand. The shadows drifted toward her, closing the distance between them, as she methodically climbed down.

If only you could see your actions are irrational. Your fear is unfounded. We merely seek to bring you to the end of unhappiness, of everything you struggle against, anything that causes you grief and pain. If you would only give in and come with us.

It was as though her mind was being assaulted. It grew stronger the closer the shadows came. She had to get back to the ground and get farther away from these things. She took a blind step and found a ledge; her foot probed for another spot she could make it to. She found one below to her right. Holding on to the rocks, she jumped across toward it. She lost her grip and fell on the jump. The back of her head hit something hard as she tumbled to the ground.

Her head buzzed as she lay on the ground, nearly content to close her eyes and let them take her.

Beware the Hollow, she reminded herself as fear of a potential fate worse than death motivated her to get back to her feet. Her balance was shaky as she began running again.

She put her hand to the back of her head and examined her fingers. Blood. She checked again, running her fingers underneath her hair, touching a stinging gash. It hopefully wasn't as bad as it felt. The landscape ahead was mostly flat, and then the hard surface of rock gave way to more sand. She hoped there would be another copy of the spring this way.

Ambrielle tried to run through the sand. Even though it wasn't as thick as on the dunes, she could only muster a running limp. Her left knee was hurting when she put pressure on it. She went to a fast walk, trying to shift her weight off the knee as she did. The shadows had begun to gain on her again. She needed to be at full strength right now, covering the easier terrain.

Ambrielle's head throbbed as she pressed on. Noticing how close the shadows were getting, she went back into the running limp. Unfortunately, this was tiring her out quickly, but she kept running. She was attempting to ignore the pain and her lungs fighting for air, but the pain in her head and knee reminded her with every step.

At last, she saw the oasis ahead. This one was the same as the other two had been, without the new trees and plants from Anatharia. The familiar red-spined palm fronds that hung down like a broken umbrella could not have been a more welcoming sight. The sign of hope gave her renewed energy for a few moments, but her body was not cooperative for long. She slowed down to catch her breath.

As the shadows drew nearer, they connected with her mind again. *Do not attempt to go to the water. It is dangerous. Come to us. We will show you peace and safety. We will ease your pain. We will show you a place where you can find rest, the most peaceful rest you've ever known.*

Ambrielle's head throbbed even more, but she picked up the pace again, trying to ignore the voices in her head. She went from a limp to a straight run, trying as hard as she could to bear through the pain in her knee. The oasis was just ahead; she didn't have much longer to endure it. It was like being in a dream, chased by monsters but unable to move your legs.

Reaching the first tree, she used it to pull herself toward it, swinging and pushing off from it as she passed. The shadows were right behind, tearing the tree to pieces as it was pulled into them. She passed the next two trees and came into view of the spring.

You want to go back. We can show you the way. We can show you the way home. Her resistance slipped for a moment; she stopped and listened.

Home, she thought. *I must follow them.*

Ambrielle slapped the side of her cheek as her mind began to numb again.

"Get out of my head!" she yelled.

She began running again, hitting the soft rock near the lip of the spring, jumping into the water as soon as she reached it. The shock of the cold water blurred out all else as she dove under the water into the cavern. She knew the path to take this time and swam through it with purpose. The water covering her eyes made for a blurry view, but she saw a light flashing through the water. The same light she had seen the first time, but she was still unable to find the source of it.

Ambrielle got farther into the narrow tunnel, and the world tumbled again. Everything went dark, and she was weightless. She wasn't sure why this happened when she went through the cave. It was something she would try to figure out another time.

She regained her equilibrium and swam up to the light above her. Reaching the surface of the water, she scanned her surroundings to get her bearings and find the banks close to the mountain. Not only were there no banks to be found, there was no land at all. Ambrielle found herself in the middle of an ocean.

CHAPTER II

A SALTY, MISTY AIR surrounded Ambrielle as she floated in the water. A large wave crashed over her, knocking her under the surface. Coughing up water, she was able to get her head up into the breathable air again. Ambrielle frantically reached for her necklace and was relieved to find it still there.

She saw another wave coming toward her and dove into the water, swimming under it. The wound on the back of her head was stinging in the salty water as she returned to the surface. A flock of black-and-white birds flew overhead. The sky was pale yellow, with a white sun accented by thin, streaking curves of pink-and-gray clouds. A blue crescent moon hung over the ocean horizon.

It would be impossible to find this spot in the ocean again if she didn't try to find it now. She was exhausted from the shadows chasing her, but it was her only hope of getting back. She mustered up the energy to plunge back down into the water, trying to remember how far the surface had been when she entered this world. Nothing here but a blur of blue-green water, no sign of anything that could transport her back.

She reached what she thought was the right depth, but nothing happened. She swam around the area, and still nothing. She came up for air a few times and went back to try again, still unsuccessful. She needed to rest after being physically and mentally drained by the ordeal with the shadows in the desert. Ambrielle wasn't sure she would be able to swim for much longer.

Another wave began to rise under her. She swam with it and let it push her farther along in the sea. There was a strip of land out there, a row of cliffs shining bright in the sunlight above the water. Another wave passed by, and she was able to maintain her position on top of the water as it carried her forward. She was being pushed toward the island. With her body weary, she would ride in on the waves and only use her strength to keep herself in position to be pushed in the right direction.

She wasn't sure what happened, why the spring took her to this place instead of Anatharia. The only thing that happened different this time was having those things chase her. That and she went into a different copy of the spring. Was that it? Did different springs go to different worlds? If she were ever able to get back to the desert again, she would test that theory.

As Ambrielle drew closer, the mass of land stretched out farther than she'd initially thought. This was a large island, possibly too large to call an island. After riding over several waves, she was beginning to draw near to a point of land that was jutting out from the rest. The nearer she got, the higher the waves were. They were cresting now, crashing back into the sea as they rolled along.

There wasn't much of a beach. It was more of a wall of large stones. The waves crashed hard into the rocks ahead as they came in. There was a flat area to her right, still rocky, but she wouldn't be shoved into a stone wall. She began swimming in that direction, trying to make it before she hit the shore.

Another large wave rippled up beneath her, lifting her up and pushing her rapidly toward the large stones. It brought her close but crested before pushing her all the way in. As the water calmed after the wave, she realized that she could touch ground with her feet. Wading closer to shore, where she could get to shallower water and move faster, she realized that the large white stones had what appeared to be gemstones encased inside them. They were like polished opal, perhaps shaped by years of waves crashing over the rocks.

They were beautiful but jagged and dangerous. Another wave was coming in. Ambrielle ran as best she could away from the stones and made it to the flatter rocks on the shore beside them. The wave arrived and pushed her violently onto the shore. The ground here was as rough as the rocks, but with her boots on, she could walk across it.

There were shiny seashells on the wet, rocky beach. She walked over to one to investigate. It was circular in shape, with colors of pale red, white, and brown swirled together. She leaned down to pick it up, and four objects came out from under the shell. Ambrielle backed away in surprise. The objects looked like tongues. They lifted the shell up and ran off into the coming waves.

Ambrielle found a place to climb the small cliff onto higher land. Now that she was away from the sounds of the ocean, the ambience of something new filled her ears. A humming sound, coming from her left and ahead of her in different tones, almost musical, sounded here and there. Buzzing and whirring sounds traveled in different directions, as well as fleeting, high-pitched whistle sounds, unfamiliar to her ears.

She walked up the rise as the stone surface gave way to a lovely grass turf that reminded her of feathers. The tips of the grass were green, but its base had a magenta-and-black-striped pattern. Beyond the grassy field were hundreds of huge skyscrapers, pulsing and glowing with blue and violet lights. The architecture was like nothing she had ever known. The design of the building structures was extremely complex. A myriad of metal and stone archways, along with other designs and textures, filled the landscape as far as she could see. It reminded her of an insect colony but with symmetry.

The buildings themselves were alive, moving in one way or another. Some structures had layers that rotated independently from the rest. There were other structures with large moving parts on the sides of the buildings or the roof, turning constantly. In some cases, entire buildings were moving. It was like they were all parts of a giant machine.

There were red-lit streets intertwined between the buildings ahead, going in a million different directions to and from them. On each of the streets were hundreds of various objects that were being carried along from building to building in two different directions. Among the buildings were tall towers of light that resonated with energy as halos flowed down from the skies into them.

Above her there were objects flying by, entering openings in the highest floors of the tall structures and flying out the other side. She couldn't make out what they were, but they flew in symmetrical patterns. She approached the nearest pathway. The roads were made of red light, with tiny, bright glimmers like stars moving along through them. She stepped onto the road surface, and the material around her boot hummed. The impact of her step started a ripple pattern that went all the way down the path, as though she'd stepped in digital liquid.

Some of the flying objects in the sky stopped and then flew in her direction. She stepped back off the street and backed away. Before long, there were six flying objects hovering over her, making different tones and flashing lights in patterns over her body. The bottoms of these objects were like flat disks, while the tops were half spheres. They were made of a silvery metal, with a slick, highly reflective finish.

Out of nowhere, a larger winged object flew into view and landed nearby. Its humanoid body stood up on two legs. It had two arms and a feminine, humanlike face . . . although it was more like a well-sculpted statue of a human face than a real one. It was like a futuristic metallic angel, eyes glowing with light, a dark mane of long hair, and wings. Its skin was pale violet, and it had golden metallic tattoos that made sharp, sweeping lines like the pattern of a circuit board. The metal tattoos began from around its eyes and forehead and traveled down its neck, arms, and any skin that was exposed under its armor.

With a deliberately stylish sequence of animation, the wings folded up and draped around the humanoid like a long, stiff robe. The wings had an iridescent sheen that refracted light, cycling through colors of violet, magenta, blue, and cyan as they moved. The angelic being was encased in a crystalline, silver armor that shimmered with a blue glow. The armor simultaneously appeared as delicate as glass and as strong as steel. There was a small, blue diamond-shaped object glowing above its belt that was encased in the metal plate.

The being held its hand up, and the spheres stopped their sounds and lights. It was at least seven feet tall. The being knelt but did not turn to Ambrielle, instead touching its hand to the red-glowing street underneath it, waving its finger over the surface, making shapes as the street rippled with every touch.

"Hello there," it said in a soft, soothing female voice, still staring at the red-laser street. "I have come to welcome you to the planet Elyravess." It sounded close to human, with some subtle modulation oddities when it changed its inflection on the word "welcome."

The being knelt there quietly, obviously waiting for a response.

"H-Hello," said Ambrielle, unable to think of anything better to say.

The being immediately turned toward Ambrielle.

"You can speak and understand!" it exclaimed.

"Yes, I . . . I can understand you," Ambrielle said.

"At long last, the first arrivals have come!" it said. "I am Avo'Doria, and what is your name?"

"I'm Ambrielle," she replied.

"Ambrielle, I am completely at your disposal. Please tell me anything you require, and I will assist. We will build this world together!" it said.

The streets and buildings stretched far into the distance. The cylindrical towers of pulsing light energy, thousands of flying spheres flying in patterns and crossing paths in the skies.

"It looks like it's already been built," Ambrielle observed.

"What do you mean?" said Avo'Doria.

"All these buildings and streets around us."

"Yes, but there is still much to be completed. I need to show you the original landing site."

"Landing site?"

"Yes, from 343,518,887.936 revolutions ago," Avo'Doria said, "when we first landed here to prepare this world for you."

"You knew I was coming here?"

"Not you specifically," Avo'Doria said. "Our objective has always been to find inhabitable worlds and then to prepare for the first arrivals and assist in any way we can. You are the first organic intelligent life that we have found."

"What can you assist me with?"

"We can assist with everything," Avo'Doria said. "We have catalogued every life form on this world, with biological information and images. We have mapped the planet for all data groups, including topology and geology. We have full data analysis of soil, minerals, atmosphere, meteorological patterns. To summarize, any data you could possibly need, we can upload it all to the systems onboard your starcraft. I can communicate much faster with a data system than I can by speaking like this."

"Oh, well, I don't have a craft," said Ambrielle.

"What do you call your vehicle of interstellar travel?" Avo'Doria asked.

"I didn't come here in any kind of vehicle. It was a cave I swam through in a spring, and I came out in the ocean out there." Ambrielle pointed toward the sea.

"I do not understand," said Avo'Doria. "What is your species?"

"I'm human," Ambrielle told her.

"Human . . . you are unknown to us," Avo'Doria said. "What world do you come from?"

"Earth."

"That is also unknown. What is the name of your system?"

"The solar system."

"What type of star is Solar?"

"Solar? Oh . . . a yellow dwarf star, if I remember right."

"Good, that narrows it down to approximately only twenty-eight point seven six billion stars in this galaxy. What order is Earth from its star?"

"It's the third planet."

"Third planet is inhabitable, yellow dwarf star, which brings us down to approximately six hundred ninety-two point four two million," Avo'Doria said. "What is Earth's atmosphere composed of?"

"Oxygen, and I think there's nitrogen, too, maybe. I can't remember now."

"Do humans have a low memory capacity?"

"Are you trying to say I have a small brain?" Ambrielle asked. "Just because I can't retrieve every detail I've ever heard on command doesn't mean I'm stupid."

"Certainly. I was only inquiring about how human organics function," Avo'Doria stated. "That brings the number down to approximately ten point eight two one million planets with oxygen and nitrogen. For now, I'll keep data of these worlds stored for further analysis. I cannot find any analytic data to this point that would explain how you would arrive through the ocean. Is there anything further you can add to explain this?"

"Well, not really," said Ambrielle. "I need to get back home. Do you have a starship that could take me to Earth?"

"We have no need for starships. It does not serve our mission. We could build one if that is what you need, but unfortunately, we would need to narrow the search much further to find your planet."

"What else could I tell you to help you find it?"

"What part of the galaxy is it in?"

"I . . . think in the outer part somewhere."

"That's not a small enough number to find anytime soon."

"I wish I knew . . . I miss my family."

"You do know how light travel works? If we were to take you there, it would be quick for you, but your world would have aged one hundred revolutions, probably more, depending on how far it is. Your family would be extremely old. Older than most organic life can exist."

"That's not going to work. Do you think you could help me find another way?"

"Certainly. We will analyze and resolve this problem," Avo'Doria said.

"Wow, thank you."

"Can you pinpoint the location where you arrived in the ocean?"

"It was a little ways out there," said Ambrielle, pointing.

"Can you provide more specific information?"

"It's almost directly in line from where I am standing now, far enough out in the ocean where I could see a little bit of the land."

"Please indicate the spot," Avo'Doria said as she picked Ambrielle up in her arms, leaping into the air as jet thrusts came from the bottom of her feet. Her wings unfolded with the sound of a blade being unsheathed. She glided on the air as she carried Ambrielle over the ocean. Avo'Doria turned Ambrielle around so she could face the ocean. Ambrielle was still shocked at being taken to the skies so suddenly. Once the disorientation wore off, the heights, the speed, and being at the mercy of this being holding her added another disconcerting dimension.

"Do you see the location now?" Avo'Doria asked.

"It could be, but I need to be able to see the land to tell," said Ambrielle.

Avo'Doria flew upright, where Ambrielle could gauge the distance of the land.

"No, this is too far out."

Avo'Doria then began moving forward somewhat slowly.

"Wait, right there, back up a bit. Yes, right here."

Avo'Doria extended her left arm forward, and several small slots opened. Green, glowing lights flew out of the slots into the air. They went into the water, continuing to glow brightly, forming a laser grid that slowly dove deeper. The air was buzzing and vibrating as a formation of twelve robotic spheres headed toward them.

After they had finished scanning the surface area, they dove underwater. The spheres were systematically scanning the water at several depths within the grid area.

"Are you . . . like a robot?" Ambrielle asked.

"We are synthetic," Avo'Doria replied. "We each have our own roles and objectives that were coded into us, but we share common directives, such as assisting the first arrivals to this planet."

"This is so crazy . . ." Ambrielle said.

"It's not crazy at all. We have made great efforts at keeping everything organized and controlled," Avo'Doria said.

"I wasn't meaning it that way," Ambrielle said. "Why do you want to help arrivals so much?"

"It is our purpose, the reason we were made."

"Who made you?"

"Information is limited," Avo'Doria said. "The founders wished to remain anonymous. While they have transcended beyond any need of technology like we have here, they were likely once like your species. They went through the same technology progression that you are likely going through now, giving you the ability to travel between star systems and find new worlds and forge new civilizations. It is likely that as your descendants progress through the ages, your kind will cross their path."

"Well, I don't actually have the technology to travel between star systems," Ambrielle confessed.

"You have discovered a method that is unknown to us, but every intelligent species takes a similar path. Yours may be too young to comprehend the founders for now, but it is believed that all intelligences will one day come together as they reach a certain level of understanding of the universe," Avo'Doria explained.

"That's a nice thought," said Ambrielle. "I wish I could live long enough to see that."

"Living is not necessarily a requirement for observation."

"Really? What makes you say that?"

The spheres returned to the surface and hovered close to Avo'Doria. After a few moments, the drones returned to formation and flew back toward land.

"I have all of their data. Let's return to the city." Avo'Doria extended her body forward and thrust her blue jets as she sped back to land. As they got back to one of the streets, Avo'Doria hovered close to the surface. Fields of energy reached from the road surface to Avo'Doria's body as she drew close and rippled as she landed. She set Ambrielle down in front of her.

"I am more comfortable here than flying over the ocean," Avo'Doria said.

"Does water damage you?" Ambrielle asked.

"No, but I have a limited supply of power," Avo'Doria told her. "In the city, I am constantly being recharged. I prefer being here, with a limitless supply of power."

She paused for a moment; her gaze moved toward the horizon as she processed the data.

"My first-level analysis is complete," Avo'Doria said. "Foreign residue present. Microscopic particle fibers. Extremely complex shape patterns. I've yet to observe anything like this."

"What do you think it means?" asked Ambrielle.

"One of my drones has a sample and is taking it to one of the research chambers now. It can run some experiments to give us more data to analyze," said Avo'Doria.

"Okay, that sounds good," Ambrielle said.

"In the meantime, let me take you to the landing site," said Avo'Doria. She opened her arms for Ambrielle. She walked to Avo'Doria and turned around. "You have a wound on your head," Avo'Doria noted, lifting her hair and using the band on her wrist to send a warm beam to Ambrielle's head. After a few minutes, the stinging on her head was gone. "There, it's fine now," Avo'Doria said.

Ambrielle reached for the spot on her head, unable to find any sign of it. "How did you do that?"

"Closed the cut and used a regenerating beam to speed up the natural cell regeneration and healing process," she explained.

"Before I got here . . . there were these . . . shadow things chasing me. That's how I hit my head."

"Shadow things? Can you be more specific?"

"They could connect with my mind . . . and whisper things. Sometimes it felt like their whispers were my own thoughts."

"Interesting. There is nothing in the nexus that describes anything like that."

"In the nexus?"

"The central point of our data accumulation. Interconnecting data cores that reside in each region of Elyravess."

"Oh, wow. Well, there was a girl that called them Nulthereals, if that helps."

"Nulthereals . . . nothing found."

"Oh . . . I was hoping you may know something about them."

"I wish that I could be of assistance on this. Are you ready to view the landing site?"

"Sure, I guess so."

She closed her arms around Ambrielle, taking flight once again. They soared over the city. Below them was a vast network of streets and buildings. There was energy that pulsed through everything. The tall cylinder towers she had viewed from ground level glowed bright. They collected energy from the sun and toward the bottom of them fed blue and purple light into the rest of the city. In some areas, particles of light energy rained down on the buildings and streets below.

The city, while chaotic in its complexity, was systematic and controlled. Below them, synthetic humanoids were transported rapidly on the laser surface of the streets, crisscrossing multiple layers above and below each other. Drones filled the skies in formations and patterns, going from place to place.

There were some types of synthetics that were more box-shaped, with heads and arms but no legs. They flew around carrying pieces of metal or other objects in their hands. There were several of them flying back and forth to one building that appeared to be under construction—as if this city needed any more buildings in it.

Eventually they came to a square among the circuit-board patterns of the city. This square area was filled with grass and trees. It was like a huge park in the middle of the otherwise endless city. Avo'Doria landed on the feathery grass and let Ambrielle gently down onto the organic paradise below. Trees with light pink leaves dotted the landscape, which was divided by a brook that twisted and turned through it. The trees had darker pink blossoms that were bursting out into puffy petals. The combination of softness and color reminded Ambrielle of cotton candy.

She had not had cotton candy in a long time. It was not something she ate often, but every year when the fair came into town, she never missed the opportunity. It was like a tradition. Ever since middle school, she had gone with Hannah and Jessica. Hannah was afraid to get on some of the rides, usually the best ones, but fortunately it was one thing Ambrielle and Jessica had in common.

The most recent fair, neither Hannah nor Jessica had talked to her about going with them. Oddly enough, Hannah's mother, who used to take the three of them every year, had been the one to ask her. She wasn't sure what had driven this wedge between her and Hannah, or even Jessica, but it made her sad and depressed. Ambrielle hoped she would be able to get back home and find out what it was that made them turn away from her. Maybe she could fix it.

As her focus came back to the park around her, there were smaller trees with orange leaves and others with red ones. The trees were scattered but clustered together in patches, making for several mini forests spread across the landscape. There were flowers of blue and violet and some with green-and-white bulbs. Sweet, wild fragrances, unlike any Ambrielle had experienced before, filled the air.

She walked on along the edge of the brook toward a grouping of trees that gave shade to both sides of its banks. Pink leaves fell in swirling, random patterns slowly to the ground as she approached. Gathered near the brook, a group of animals drank from the water. They were four-legged creatures about the size of large sheep but had long, fine hair. They turned around as she drew closer but did not seem bothered by her presence.

One of them had black hair, while another had hair that was like her own, dark blonde. They continued drinking, occasionally turning their heads toward her to make sure she had not come any closer. They had eyes like a small dog, but a more rounded snout and a mouth like that of a monkey. The animals were strange, but they appeared to be gentle creatures. She sat and watched them drink from the brook for a bit while Avo'Doria stood back, observing.

There were birds in the trees, singing long, sustained notes as others joined in, overlapping their notes with an off-pitch harmony that was haunting. There were a few orange-colored birds up in the trees and a pale-green bird with a large wingspan that flew across the sky overhead. There was something flitting around one of the tree branches, and Ambrielle went to investigate.

When she got closer, it appeared to be tiny bugs flying around in a swarm. The bugs were blinking off and on with a bright light, like white phosphorous. They reminded Ambrielle of fireflies, but they were producing much brighter light, like stars in the night sky.

"Come, we're not far from the landing site," said Avo'Doria.

Ambrielle walked along beside her and away from the brook. She had forgotten Avo'Doria's reluctance of being away from the constant source of power that the city provided. They continued walking until they reached the center of the square patch of land left untouched by the technological monstrosity of the city.

There was a spherical-shaped metal object embedded in the land, having disturbed a patch of ground. The spherical craft had been overgrown with a web of twisting vines and orange moss.

"This is it," said Avo'Doria.

"Your spacecraft?" asked Ambrielle.

"Our probe, yes."

"I expected it to be bigger," said Ambrielle. "How did many of you fit on this?"

"Most of us were not made until after."

"After you landed here?"

"Yes, I and many others were manufactured in the first factories.

"The probe's cargo consisted of hundreds of small synthetics capable of gathering materials, building factories, creating new synthetics, improving their own design to be more efficient, building design laboratories, and so on," Avo'Doria explained. "It went on like this for many revolutions."

"Why did they build so much if you were only here to help the first arrivals?" asked Ambrielle.

"The objectives were to identify life, materials, food, and other essentials to aid any arrivals that came to the planet," said Avo'Doria. "The original synthetics did that by continually improving themselves and building more synthetics to complete the tasks more efficiently."

"Was the whole planet like this park before you started building cities all over it?" Ambrielle asked.

"No," said Avo'Doria. "There was a cataclysmic event that occurred before we ever came here. There were only small pockets of organic life that remained, plants and animals spread out in different areas."

"That's so sad. I can't believe that something ruined a world so beautiful," said Ambrielle. "So, this place was one of those areas that were left?"

"Yes. Along with some biological engineering," Avo'Doria said, "we salvaged every bit of organic life we could and cultivated this site into a sort of museum for arrivals to see what this world was once like."

"What caused it?"

"Although the data are imperfect, we concluded that it was a small asteroid impact that caused it. There was no evidence of any life capable of waging war, so that is all we had to go on."

"Are there any other places like this?" Ambrielle asked.

"No. We have some plant and animal life that we breed in research centers for study, but nothing like this place," said Avo'Doria.

"Could you cultivate more areas like this?"

"We could. What is your interest in that?"

"Look at this place . . . the trees and the grass, the flowers, the brook, the animals . . ."

"Yes, it's a mess," Avo'Doria said. "Its complexity makes it so unpredictable that even our most advanced research cannot fully simulate it. Its systems go so far into the ultramicroscopic that we do not have the storage to contain the data. The organisms living in it are at odds with each other and the environment itself, and yet it thrives. It is wholly unorganized and inefficient, but it somehow functions."

"Well, I guess that's what makes it interesting. Not knowing what could happen or the potential limits can be a beautiful thing," Ambrielle observed.

"Beautiful is open to interpretation, I suppose. I prefer systems to run as efficiently as possible," said Avo'Doria. "That's what I find beautiful about Elyravess."

"The city does have a certain beauty, but to me it is so visually complex, it's almost maddening. I wish more of the original world could be restored and that more of the original life could have been preserved," said Ambrielle.

"That is still achievable. We have learned much about the geology and agriculture of this world. We have every speck of this planet's organic life growing inside our research centers, even ones that were extinct. We have engineered and bred them to study. That is what we are here for, to assist you in building this world the way you want to see it."

"Well, that won't be the original way it was, but it would be nice to bring it back and incorporate more of the organic life along with the city. Maybe have more parks like this place."

"If that is what you want, then it is our objective."

"Just like that?"

"Certainly. You're the first arrival."

"Why did you build up so much to research the planet?"

"It started small, as I was saying before," said Avo'Doria. "Then we needed more synthetics to specialize in various tasks, we needed more power to run them, needed more systems to do analysis, more databanks to keep all the information, which in turn required more power . . .

"We then needed more synthetics to expand our study over the rest of the planet. We needed more factories, and as we researched, we made advancements. We manufactured better materials for synthetics, faster brain processors, stronger arms for builders, and better analyzing tools for seekers, and we discovered more advanced ways to generate power," she continued. "We are always improving ourselves, our facilities, our power structures . . . everything," said Avo'Doria.

"We did all this while waiting for arrivals that never came. We went dormant for much of this period, but on certain intervals we reevaluated the objective and continued on. Each time, no arrivals came. This process repeated for over three million revolutions, into what we have now."

"Okay, wow, I think I understand now," said Ambrielle. "Have you thought of sending some synthetics to other worlds?"

"We are one of hundreds of probes sent out across the galaxy to potentially inhabitable worlds. There were some that found life and many that found dead worlds. A few of them have been visited by arrivals of other intelligent life, but most have not yet," Avo'Doria said.

"That's amazing. Do you get information from those worlds too?" asked Ambrielle.

"Yes, but only small amounts over time," Avo'Doria said.

"Do you have anything showing all these discovered worlds?" Ambrielle wondered.

"Yes, in our planetary research facilities."

"Wow, I would like to see that someday."

"Certainly."

"As much as I would love to stay here and learn about all the amazing advancements that you have made and how any of this stuff works, I do need to get back, even if I can only get back to the desert world I was on. As soon as we figure out how to. There were . . . problems in the place that I left behind," said Ambrielle.

"Problems that only you can solve?"

"Problems that I can't solve," Ambrielle said. "I feel like . . . I don't know . . . that there are things left undone. There was this guy that I met, a new friend. Then there's Sidaire, and this other guy whose name I forget. I don't want them to think I abandoned them the same way my friends did me. I feel like I would need to at least say goodbye or . . . something."

"I don't know that I understand," said Avo'Doria, "but I detect that there is some confusion within you on this matter. My analysis suggests that this is regarding emotion, and I have limited data on emotion. What little information I have is difficult to understand and doesn't entirely make sense."

Ambrielle laughed. "Well, I have difficulty understanding emotions, too, but I have them, so I have to deal with them."

"Forgive me for saying, but I am glad that I am not organic. Emotions sound like a corruption in your systems, an impedance to efficient flow of information."

"No, it's not all bad. Like anything else, it has its good side and its bad. There are some feelings that I wouldn't trade for anything."

"I have no affinity for things that cannot be understood," Avo'Doria said. "We need to get back to the city, if you are ready."

Avo'Doria opened her arms to receive Ambrielle to carry her for their next flight. Ambrielle obliged and let Avo'Doria take hold of her as she launched into the sky. They left the landing site park, and the square area got smaller and smaller. Heading back over the city, with all its power sources, Ambrielle imagined that Avo'Doria felt safe again, being here.

The sun was beginning to set as they landed on the balcony of a large building overlooking the rest of the city. The beams of the sun towers began to go out as the sun disappeared behind the horizon, but the lights, power, and activity of the city did not change at all. Ambrielle decided that the towers must be storing enough energy throughout the day that the city did not need constant sunlight. These towers must have been absorbing solar energy much better than any solar panels on Earth if they could power a city such as this.

"Consider this place yours." Avo'Doria set Ambrielle down on a balcony. "There is a room behind us where you will find any accommodations that you need."

There was a large window divided in three parts and a round one in the middle, with two shaped like crescent moons on each side. "I must go to the data source and unload my silcron," said Avo'Doria.

"What's a silcron?"

"My silcron contains all the information that I acquired today. When I plug it in, it verifies my mark to ensure the data are accurate, and then they are transferred to become part of the nexus. It must be emptied at least every forty-five point three eight seven malcrums to receive new information. It ensures that everything I know, we all know. The same goes for every synthetic on Elyravess," Avo'Doria said.

"Everyone is willing to share their information?" asked Ambrielle.

"Certainly. We turn in silcrons for credit, and with credit we can trade for enhancements."

"What kind of enhancements?"

"Every kind you can imagine," Avo'Doria said. "Stronger limbs, new or better tools, new brain components, new parts for faster flight, such as wings," she said, extending her own out again, as if to show them off. "If you start out as a drone that delivers items to other synthetics, you could eventually equip yourself to do construction or maybe to do some type of research. There is always some greater purpose that you might be interested in," said Avo'Doria.

"So it really is like a society all its own."

"Certainly," said Avo'Doria. "Now, make yourself comfortable and get some rest. You look like you need a recharge."

"I guess it has been a long day." Ambrielle smiled.

"I will return at next light."

"Thank you," said Ambrielle.

Avo'Doria flew off from the balcony, extending her wings and gliding over the city below. Ambrielle missed her as soon as she left, which was strange. This was an unusual place, though, and Avo'Doria made her feel comfortable in it.

Ambrielle turned toward the three windows and walked up to what appeared to be the doorway. There was no doorknob, so she tried pressing it open. It didn't budge, so she pushed harder. Still nothing. She tried waving her hand around the outside of the doorframe, but nothing happened. Maybe it responded to voice.

"How do I open this door?" she asked.

"Would you like the door open?" said a voice.

"Yes."

The door slid upward, opening the way into the building. Ambrielle walked through a dark hallway into an octagonal-shaped room. Part of the room included the crescent-shaped windows that she had noticed from the balcony. The lights and activity of the cityscape showed through them.

"Close the door."

The door slid down and closed. Ambrielle walked around the room.

There was a big, soft mat lying on a frame rising above the floor. This must be the bed. It looked so comfortable that she flopped herself down on it. When she landed on the matting, it swung back and forth, throwing her off balance, since she was not expecting the movement. The mat was attached to the frame in such a way that it could swing freely, like a hammock. Once she realized what was going on, she rather enjoyed the swaying bed.

She got up from the bed and moved to check out a blue-lit room off the main octagon-shaped area. There was a short hallway leading to an area with walls that slowly faded from green to blue and back to green. The surfaces were soft to the touch, and there were three different-sized areas with dividers between them. Ambrielle was mesmerized by the changing colors of the walls, but the purpose of this room wasn't clear.

"What is this room for?" she asked aloud, hoping that the voice in the house would be able to answer.

"This is the cleaning room. Please enter one of the cleaning areas and give them time to adjust to your configuration."

She stepped into one of the rooms with shiny floors and walls. The room began to shrink as she stood inside. The walls and ceiling stopped when they got closer to her. Holes began to open around her in the room, making her nervous.

A voice said, "Tell your size or preferences and say, 'Turn on water.' You can adjust temperature and pressure to your liking by telling me specific numbers or by describing what you would like."

Ambrielle was excited. If this was anything like a shower, she would be so happy. It had been so long since she had a proper shower. She removed her dress, which she realized needed to be washed.

"Turn on water," she said.

"The door is currently open. Water will not engage. Would you like me to close the door now?"

"Yes."

A door slid across, closing her into the now cube-shaped area.

"Turn on water," she said again.

Water came down like rain from the ceiling, slow and soft. Then water sprayed out in several directions toward her from the walls around her, hitting her unexpectedly in the face and the back of the head and everywhere else. She turned her head away from the spray. Besides not wanting to have water shot in her face, it was too cold.

"Warmer water please," she said.

"Increasing heat to fifty percent. Is that to your liking?" said the voice.

"A little warmer," Ambrielle said.

"Increasing to fifty-five percent."

"Set it to seventy percent."

"Increasing to seventy percent."

The temperature quickly changed to warmer water. Now it was just right.

"Can you stop this water from hitting me in the face?"

"Lowering spray height. Is this to your liking?"

The water spray level moved down to where it was only below her neck, and the shower was much better now. She stood there for a while, enjoying the comfort of the warm water and steam.

"Skin type detected, and cleaning solution selected. Would you like to apply now?" said the voice.

"Um . . . sure, I guess," Ambrielle said.

"Please answer yes or no," the voice said.

"Okay . . . Yes."

The water slowed as a creamy gray foam began shooting onto her, completely covering her except for her head.

"Rinsing," said the voice.

Water began shooting from the walls again, rinsing the foamy substance off her. She took some of the remaining foam in her hands and scrubbed her face with it, as well as her neck and behind her ears. Then she ducked into the stream to rinse it off.

"Hair detected on head surface. Would you like hair cleaner applied?"

"Yes!" she said, barely containing her excitement.

This time a creamy substance poured down from overhead, and she used her hands to run it through her hair. She encountered several tangles as she ran her fingers through her hair and worked to get them all out as best she could without actually pulling any hair out. She had to tell the voice no a few times when it asked if she was ready to rinse while she worked on it.

"Okay, now I am ready to rinse," she told the voice.

"Rinsing."

After she was content and had been in long enough, she was finally ready to get out. "You can turn off the water now."

The water stopped, and then warm air started blowing out all around her, blowing her hair all over the place and blowing some of the water off her.

"Drying initiated. If you would like to end the cycle early, you can say 'stop,'" said the voice.

This was a perk that she was going to have to somehow bring back to Earth with her if she ever found a way back. Wherever she ended up, she wanted this whole setup to go with her. She stayed in the room until the drying stopped automatically.

She was so refreshed after cleaning up that she was sure it was the best shower she'd ever had, minus a few issues at the beginning.

"Are there any other clothes here?" she asked.

"What type of clothing are you looking for?" asked the voice.

"Um . . . clothing to sleep in," she said.

"Scanning for body configuration. One moment."

There were some mechanical sounds behind the wall, and then a large panel opened with several different types of clothing. She was drawn to one that was pale lavender, a one-piece like a gown with thin, smooth, and soft material. She took it from the snaps that were holding it in place and put it on. It was warm and cozy against her skin, just the perfect thing to put on after a nice shower.

Ambrielle went over to the windows to get another glimpse of the city. The lights were quite amazing at night. Metal beings and drones were still flying in organized patterns in all directions around the buildings, and the streets were glowing even brighter. The city was as busy at night as it was during the day.

She climbed into the bed, more carefully this time, still swaying slightly from her momentum.

"Turn off lights," she said.

"Darkening the room," said the voice.

The lights dimmed to almost being off but not quite. The windows went from clear to translucent, making the room dark but the outline of everything in the room still visible.

"Darker, please," she said.

Some of the lights turned off completely, while others dimmed further. The windows became even more opaque. Now it was almost totally dark.

"Would you like to swing as you sleep?" the voice asked.

"Yes, but slowly," Ambrielle said.

The bed began to swing softly back and forth. *This is kind of nice, but I'm not sure if I can go to sleep like this.* That was the last thought she had before drifting off.

CHAPTER 12

THE ROOM WAS still dark as Ambrielle rolled over in the bed. Squinting her eyes, she began to wake up. She walked over to the opaque window. "Clear the windows."

The window changed to a transparent form, and light began to shine in, displaying all the buildings in the distance. She checked for more clothes. After specifying a few times what she wanted, she found a red top. It was too long, but the voice insisted it was the correct size and was merely a style choice of its designer. According to the assistant, the room had sensed her body configuration and measurements and automatically presented only clothing that would fit her. She found some short, dark gray pants that cut off above her knee to go with them.

The voice asked if she would like any food. After it listed off a menu of things that she was unfamiliar with, Ambrielle went with its recommendation. The voice announced that the food was ready. She checked around the room, not finding anything.

"Where is the food?" she asked.

"Located here," said the voice.

"Where?" A light shone on a metal drawer in the lower part of one of the walls.

Opening the drawer, she found a container of heated food inside. She removed the container and set it on the bed. After she inquired about places to sit and eat, flexible metal squares moved out from a wall, and she found she could sit on one while using the other as a table.

Inside the container were some pieces of long, yellow leafy plants, an orange round piece of something, and two slices of some type of meat. She wondered where the meat came from. It made her a little afraid to try it, but the hesitance didn't last for long. There was a tool inside the package that pinched together like large tweezers. The utensil was useful to pick up the meat, but she needed something to cut with.

When she tried it out on the yellow vegetables, she realized that it cut when she squeezed with more pressure. She went back to the meat and used the tool to cut it, which worked surprisingly well. Then she used it to pick up the piece of meat and put it in her mouth. It chewed like a tender, juicy steak, but the taste was a little different. It had sort of a turkey-sausage taste to it.

She tried some of the orange stuff. It had a mildly sweet taste but was also oddly spicy. It must have been some type of fruit. She tried the yellow leafy vegetable, but she didn't like it as much. It wasn't bad, but it had a peculiar taste that she couldn't quite compare to anything.

After inquiring about a way to wash her white sundress, she was directed to drop it into an opening in the cleaning room.

Ambrielle asked if there were any mirrors, and after some misunderstanding, the voice finally determined that she wanted a visual representation of herself. It projected a three-dimensional image of Ambrielle into the room that moved in real time as she moved. It was like a reflection.

If the image was accurate, her hair was a mess. All her freckles were showing. The crater in her forehead was visible, and her face had some breakouts. She was appalled that she had been seen by everyone for days looking like this.

Ambrielle asked about brushes to fix her hair and makeup for her face, but there was nothing to be found in the room. Slightly annoyed, she brushed through her hair with her hand and fingers. She was able to walk around the image and view the back of her hair, which would be nice, if only she had a brush.

"Visitor approaching, identified as Avo'Doria," the voice announced.

Ambrielle commanded the door to open and went outside on the balcony to watch for Avo'Doria. Before long, the familiar blue trail of Avo'Doria's jets were seen heading toward the balcony. She landed and smiled when she saw Ambrielle there waiting for her. Ambrielle wondered what it was that prompted her facial expressions, if she didn't understand emotions.

"Good to see you, Ambrielle," said Avo'Doria, "I hope your room accommodations were suitable. Our progress on what organics would consider to be luxurious is probably well behind our other pursuits."

"No, everything has been great. Although, a few things took me some time to figure out," Ambrielle said.

"Oh, isn't there a synthetic assistant built into the room?"

"Yes, it was very helpful. This is so different from what I'm used to."

"Good, I'm glad you were taken care of."

"There is one thing, though," said Ambrielle. "There isn't anything to fix my hair with."

"Oh, use one of these." Avo'Doria pulled an oblong-shaped piece of metal from a pouch hanging off her belt and handed it to Ambrielle.

"What's this?"

"It will style your hair," said Avo'Doria "See? Like mine." She pointed to the piece hidden beneath her hair at her scalp.

"Like this?" Ambrielle asked as she placed the object into her hair.

"Not quite," said Avo'Doria. "Slide it up through the roots, and it will attach."

Ambrielle tried this a few times unsuccessfully but finally got it to stay in her hair.

Avo'Doria said, "Then you say, 'Style on.'"

The device in her hair produced a barely audible hum, and Ambrielle's hair stood straight up like it was under extreme electrostatic charge. Ambrielle wondered what her hair was doing. It was as if she could sense each individual follicle on her scalp.

"I think there are twenty-five different styles on these. Let's try style one," Avo'Doria said.

Ambrielle's hair tightened as it took a new shape. "If you don't mind, I'm going to run inside really quick to get a look."

"You don't need to go inside for that," said Avo'Doria. "Display Ambrielle."

"I do not understand 'Ambrielle,'" said the voice.

"You didn't introduce yourself?"

"Well, I—" Ambrielle started.

"Savi, this is Ambrielle."

"Hello, Ambrielle," said the voice.

"Now, display Ambrielle," Avo'Doria commanded.

The three-dimensional image of Ambrielle appeared in front of them, and her hair was now perfectly straight. It was nice, but it wasn't her style.

"Is there a style that has loose curls or waves starting about here?" she wondered.

"Probably," Avo'Doria said. "Try style seven."

Ambrielle watched as her hair in the image changed to a perfectly styled version with curly ends.

"That's a bit too curly."

"Try a lower number."

"Style four," said Ambrielle. "Ooh, that's really nice. Not exactly what I was looking for, but I like it. Now I need some makeup."

"Makeup?"

"To cover all the flaws on my face."

"Organic skin always has variations and inconsistencies. I don't see the problem."

"Well, I want it to look as perfect as possible."

"You were saying yesterday that natural organic systems were beautiful because of their unpredictable variations."

"Oh yeah . . . well, I mean . . . it's different when it's on my face."

"That seems contradictory. With all the variations you have, from the red bumps neatly clustered together to the brown spots scattered about in a nice arrangement to the grooves carved under your eyes, by your own definition, your face is beautiful. It reminds me of the moon, Sheigo. With its thin atmosphere, some meteorites make it to the surface without burning up. The impacts cause several interesting surface variations. The lines and craters on the surface are—"

"I get it, I get it. I haven't completely come to terms with my unpredictable variations yet."

"We have some graphic augmentation that may work, but you'd be better served treating your skin in some of our facilities."

"Okay, I'll try that."

"Wonderful. I came to tell you about last night," Avo'Doria said. "I plugged in my silcron, which contained a lot of interesting data, like meeting you."

"All right, is that bad?" Ambrielle played with the waves in her hair.

"No," said Avo'Doria, "but the other regional sentinels have been traveling here overnight to meet the arrival."

"They want to meet me?" Ambrielle said.

"This is an historic event," said Avo'Doria. "We've been waiting for this for over three million revolutions."

"I don't know if I want this to be a big deal," said Ambrielle. "I'm not wanting to stay for long. I got here by accident."

"It doesn't matter," said Avo'Doria. "We will have more arrivals as time goes on, but you will always be the first. Right now, you are the only one."

"Do we have to meet with them?" Ambrielle asked. "Can we try to figure out how to get me back?"

"They have come a long way and are already here waiting in the council hall," Avo'Doria said. "Once the data are confirmed by the other eight sentinels, we'll be able to open vaults. Our most advanced technology and research is kept there, saved for arrivals. There will be much more that we can use to study the sample from the ocean and find a way for you to return."

"When will they get here?" asked Ambrielle.

"They're already here," said Avo'Doria. "I came to take you to them."

"Oh . . . how should I act toward them?"

"Like you normally do. What other way would there be?"

"Well, just making sure."

Avo'Doria lifted her arms and unwrapped her wings from around her body, welcoming Ambrielle to come over again. That way she could carry her in flight. Ambrielle did so, despite some nervous hesitation at the thought of meeting a room full of strange synthetics. Flying over the city like this gave all the buildings around the apartment a new perspective.

Most of the buildings were similar in design and did not stand out, but there were a few that made recognizable landmarks because of the way they moved like machines, turning or rotating slowly. Some structures were quite close together, separated only by the red streets of light.

They flew close to one of the light towers collecting the sun's energy. Energy rippled in periodic waves, traveling down through the beams into the towers. Ambrielle wondered if this was a far more advanced version of the lykris technology the Kavekkians used or if it was something completely different.

They swooped over more buildings, some so tall that they were barely flying above them. Ambrielle saw synthetic beings below them on a fifth tier of streets, still high above the rest of the city. Energy rippled and pulsed around the feet of synthetics as they were transported to other buildings.

They approached a building with a pyramid-shaped base. The pyramid came together toward a point where a tower began. The tower traveled high into the sky to an arrow-shaped part at the top. As they got closer, the top of the tower came into view.

Steep, angular arches with several oddly shaped embrasures were cut into the walls. The embrasures started small and grew progressively larger toward the middle, then shrank as they went back toward the other side. These cutout shapes went all the way down to the balcony and served as both windows and open doorways. They were shaped in such a way that they fit together like puzzle pieces.

Avo'Doria landed on the terrace, allowing Ambrielle to get her feet on the ground. Ambrielle turned as Avo'Doria led them through doorways created with an intricate framework that was like broken bits of ceramic. Each piece was unique and jagged but fit together perfectly. They came into a large, oval-shaped room with a high ceiling filled with many arches, one overlapping another. The room was brightly lit from the large embrasures leading to the outside.

The black flooring gleamed in the light. It had the same puzzle concept of irregular shapes pieced together that the doorway and windows did. Between the separations of the black gloss pieces was a violet surface that changed to a bright magenta glow when pressure was applied. This glow highlighted everyone's position where they stood.

Ahead of them were other synthetic beings like Avo'Doria, standing behind thin stands that came up from the floor. The eight other sentinels stared at Ambrielle as they entered the room. There was an odd smell to the room that reminded Ambrielle of benzene, making her recall times in chemistry lab at school. It wasn't a smell that should be pleasant, but for some reason she liked it.

"This is Ambrielle, the first arrival." Avo'Doria rested a hand on Ambrielle's shoulder. They all greeted her at once, and then one of them gestured toward her.

"Greetings, Ambrielle. I am Nexo'Lydia. The data that Avo'Doria uploaded tell us that you arrived alone and that you did not come here by any kind of space vehicle. Is this correct?" The sentinel had a female voice and appearance. She did not have wings like Avo'Doria. Instead she had arms coming out from behind her like a spider. The arms were attached with claws and various other devices at their ends. Her silver armor shone with a red-and-magenta glow.

"That's right," Ambrielle said. "I didn't come from space. I went through a spring that led me into your ocean."

All the other sentinels turned and began talking amongst each other, but she could not make out what they were saying.

"And your species is called human?" asked Nexo'Lydia.

"Yes," Ambrielle confirmed.

"I've never heard of your kind before," said Nexo'Lydia, "and you don't appear to have come to the point in your progression to be capable of interstellar travel."

"You're right. I'm lost and am trying to get back home, to Earth. Or at least the desert world I was on before I got here."

"Why would an arrival want to go back?" Nexo'Lydia asked.

Another sentinel spoke up, this one having male features and cylinder-shaped parts on his back poking out from behind him.

"Any real arrivals would have researched the planet before landing and come to Region Seven first," he said. "We have the most suitable landing platforms to accommodate any craft."

He was using some sort of blue laser coming from the metal brace on his wrist, cutting a line into one of the two floating machines flanking each side of him. The machines were like modified versions of the drones that flew around the city.

"That is inaccurate, Tyre'Magnus. We all know that arrivals would come to Region One. We have done the most research in organic luxury, and our landing platforms are fine," said a female sentinel. She had armor partly covered by a shiny white coating that had the appearance of gel. Her hair was colored magenta, and she had fin-style wings coming from her back.

"Nova'Duriel, both of you, this is not an exposition on which region is better than another. We are here to determine whether this arrival fits within the parameters of our primary objective," said a male sentinel with long white hair, gold plating on his arms and shoulders covering the rest of his silvery reflective metal form, and a small jet engine attached to his back.

"You are correct, Sido'Varius. We must take this objective seriously above all others," Nexo'Lydia agreed. "I aim to preserve and protect Elyravess for the true arrivals. I do not believe this human meets the criteria set for the arrivals that we have been waiting for."

"How are we to be sure that she even came here from another star system?" Nova'Duriel wondered. "One does not appear in the ocean out of nowhere. We haven't explored every crevasse in the depths of the oceans. Perhaps she is a nearly extinct species living beneath the seas."

"We have taken a sample, as you are all aware," Avo'Doria reminded. "A sample of the remnant found in the ocean where Ambrielle arrived. Our analysis showed complex patterns that are subquantum, much like organic material. Its parameters are inconsistent with how matter should behave. Its mass, density, and volume are not congruent. At extreme magnification, there are details that vanish and reappear depending on changes of its location. This brings up speculation that the substance is extradimensional."

"Are you suggesting that the human entered the ocean through another dimension?" asked Tyre'Magnus, as he continued cutting out a square shape in the metal of the drone with his laser.

"I'm saying that it is a possibility, based on the evidence," Avo'Doria said.

The news surprised Ambrielle. Could this really be true? Was the desert wilderness part of some other dimension? This raised so many questions, but she turned her attention back to the meeting.

"You're right," said Sido'Varius. "We should expand our view beyond conventional interstellar travel. There is the possibility that some intelligence will discover interdimensional travel and arrive on this planet by this means. We have to change our thinking to accommodate the idea that there could be arrivals with technology well beyond our own."

"This human does not possess superior technology. If she did, I would gladly step aside and allow her to do with my region as she pleases," said a male sentinel with several dark blue armor pieces covering a silver metal body. There was no hair on him like on the other sentinels. Instead, his head was formed into a helmet, with a curved opaque golden visor that covered his eyes.

"Jerovian is correct. We cannot allow this primitive human to have control of any regions, let alone all of Elyravess," a male sentinel agreed.

"Midovius, we know each other well," said Avo'Doria. "Are you saying that you will not relinquish control to fulfill your primary objective? Has power corrupted us to the point that we've abandoned our main purpose? Synthetics do not have ambition."

"We all have desires to perform our tasks better, faster, or even to seek grander ones," Jerovian said. "Even you, Avo'Doria. We all turn in our silcrons every day for credits to better ourselves."

"Yes, but I never thought we would enter a period where those desires would turn to greed," Avo'Doria said. "The only reason for this is personal gain, not the real objective."

"This is not the promised arrival," said another female with long, curly brown hair, her silver armor etched with intricate designs. Attached to her sides were metal pockets and various tools. "We were supposed to transfer all of our information gathered to the arrival, but this arrival has no craft, no technology, no way of giving her the research and data we have worked so hard for. She's not the arrival that we are supposed to turn this world over to. This is not our objective."

Ambrielle wanted to say something, but they were talking back and forth so fast she couldn't.

"Sephyra is exactly right," said Tyre'Magnus, placing a rectangular-shaped piece inside the square hole he had cut into the drone. "She is most certainly not the arrival we are waiting for."

"I disagree," said Sido'Varius. "It doesn't matter what she came here in, what she has with her, how much she knows. That is not for us to decide. Our objective is clear, and Ambrielle is the first arrival. We should show her the respect that is due. She should be allowed all the knowledge we possess, and we should help her build her civilization for herself and other organics that may come later."

"Yes," said Avo'Doria, "Sido'Varius is correct. Finally, someone that is not obsessed with their own personal power."

"Call it obsession if you must," said a red metallic sentinel with a dark screen covering his face, "but I am not giving up control of my region for a primitive human to destroy all I have built."

"I don't normally agree with Verdax but I could not have stated it better," said Jerovian. "My silcron will bear the truth that she is not the arrival."

The rest of them all voiced their agreement. It was only Avo'Doria and Sido'Varius on the side of Ambrielle being the first arrival.

"Please reconsider," Avo'Doria said. "At least erase this information in your silcron. If Ambrielle is not proclaimed the arrival, she will be seen by all synthetics as merely a new species of animal to be tested on. She is clearly an intelligent life form."

"She *needs* to be studied and tested." Tyre'Magnus used a green laser to melt and fuse together the metal square that he had cut out of the drone "We need to find out more."

Even though Avo'Doria claimed to not have any experience with emotions, she had the mannerisms and tone of voice of someone that was angry.

"Wait, please . . ." said Ambrielle, speaking up loudly enough this time to interrupt the other sentinels. "I don't want to take your regions from you, or your world. I only want to find a way to get back where I came from."

"You see? She is no true arrival," said Nexo'Lydia, "We do need to study her and this extradimensional substance. It could provide us with another leap in technology."

"I've scanned her, and I'm detecting traces of this same substance all over her," said Jerovian, his gold visor showing red, animated lights of activity.

"Take her. We will study this further at one of the research centers," Midovius said.

Two of the sentinels left their podiums, heading for Ambrielle.

"No!" yelled Avo'Doria. She took flight, extending her wings as she grabbed Ambrielle in her arms before the two sentinels closed in. They were knocked to the ground as she rocketed past them.

"Avo'Doria, what are you doing? You are betraying Elyravess!" said Midovius.

"I am protecting the primary objective. You have all overwritten it with your own!" Avo'Doria shouted back.

"Take your silcrons to the data core. We have the overwhelming majority," said Nexo'Lydia. "Even Avo'Doria will have to comply once it reaches the nexus."

The sentinels all streaked out of the embrasures of the tower in different directions. Avo'Doria saw this and began chasing after the nearest sentinel that zoomed to the left of her. It was Sephyra. When she noticed that Avo'Doria was following, she descended, flying at high speed through the maze of buildings. Still carrying Ambrielle, Avo'Doria flew after Sephyra. The lights and prismatic shine of the buildings went by at a dizzying rate.

"Wait . . . What are we doing??" yelled Ambrielle as the sounds of large buildings continually buzzed by them.

"I have to stop them! We can't let them get to the data core," said Avo'Doria.

"What happens if they do?"

"The data will be received, but there will be a conflict," Avo'Doria said as she began to gain on the other sentinel. Sephyra did not have wings like Avo'Doria and was lacking the stability and maneuverability that came with them.

"A decision will be made based on the majority, which they have," Avo'Doria continued.

Sephyra made a sharp turn between some buildings. Avo'Doria quickly reacted and made an even more extreme turn, further closing the gap between them.

"Once the conflict is resolved, we'll all have to follow it, even me," Avo'Doria said.

The dizzying blurs of lights below made Ambrielle a bit nauseated. As Avo'Doria closed in on the sentinel, she extended her left arm. Keeping the other arm to hold on to Ambrielle, she aimed and something popped up from the armored band covering her wrist. She fired a solid stream of violet-colored laser light. Sephyra weaved to avoid it as the laser cut into buildings' stone and metal exteriors as they passed.

The other sentinel dove straight toward the lower streets. Avo'Doria followed, putting her left arm back to hold Ambrielle. Ambrielle's stomach rose into her chest as Avo'Doria held her wings back like a parachute, slowing her descent. Sephyra continued her dive toward the ground. Avo'Doria stayed above her, anticipating her having to pull up soon.

Sephyra turned upward in a steep ascent as she passed below one of the overpassing streets, coming up from under a bridged street as if she expected Avo'Doria to be right behind her. As she rose into the sky, Avo'Doria passed her at close range. Firing again, Avo'Doria severed her armored right foot, which contained one of her main thrusters. The sentinel went spiraling out of control and into the side of one of the buildings.

Avo'Doria launched into Sephyra as the sentinel fell, taking the powered silcron that was attached to the sentinel's armor. Sephyra fell until she crashed onto the street below, sending disturbed ripples through the street surface.

Searching the skies for the other sentinels, Avo'Doria flew off toward her next target. The other sentinels splitting up made it more difficult to locate them all, but it also meant they wouldn't all arrive at the data core at the same time. As Avo'Doria increased her speed, the wind began to violently whip around them.

Avo'Doria tightened her body, making herself more aerodynamic and increasing her grip on Ambrielle to an uncomfortable level. They were gaining on the other sentinel, but it was taking time. Avo'Doria ascended above the tops of the buildings. Now she could fly in a straight line instead of having to zigzag between them. It was a risk because she was now too far for power recharges to reach her.

The sentinel ahead remained at a lower altitude, flying through the tangle of buildings. Crisscrossing patterns of drones flew beneath them, going about their regular duties, oblivious to the battle going on around them. Avo'Doria was closing in on another sentinel that had not yet tried to evade them. It was Jerovian.

There was an enormous structure ahead, shaped like a dome, with large sectional pieces surrounding it. The black structure pulsed with blue energy all over. Ambrielle saw more sentinels ahead of them, flying toward the gigantic building.

Also flying toward the object were formations of drones, some going inside and some coming out of it in the opposite direction. Jerovian was flying low enough to enter the structure where the drones were going in.

This must be where the data core is located, Ambrielle thought.

As Jerovian approached the large gate, they caught up to him. Avo'Doria shifted Ambrielle to one arm and fired her laser at the dark blue sentinel. The laser went across his foot thruster, but the dark blue parts of the armor reinforced against the sustained laser stream. She moved her ray to go after the lesser-armored parts of his leg. He turned around and propelled himself toward her, grabbing her by the arm. This way, she couldn't fire on him again.

Twisting her body away from him, Avo'Doria suddenly launched back into him. She slammed her armored fist into his face and broke his golden visor in the process. He began to fall for a moment, and Avo'Doria dove into him before he could recover. The impact nearly shook Ambrielle loose in her grip. She brought her other hand to Ambrielle again to get a better hold.

Avo'Doria fired between a section of his armor and bored a hole clean through Jerovian's abdomen. He slowed, losing power.

Ambrielle saw something out of the corner of her eye and turned.

"Look out!" yelled Ambrielle. "To your left!"

Avo'Doria dodged to the right as another sentinel attempted to dive into her. It was Nexo'Lydia. She used her utility arms to grab at Avo'Doria. She grabbed her right arm, pulling it away from Ambrielle, causing her to come completely out of Avo'Doria's grasp. She fell, flipping sideways, until she stopped abruptly when she landed on one of the drones heading toward the gateway. Stunned for a moment, she looked up as Avo'Doria's laser sliced through Nexo'Lydia's utility arm.

Avo'Doria checked to make sure that Ambrielle was safe and fended off Nexo'Lydia's next attack, with her spidery arms. She severed another of the utility arms that tried to hold her. Nexo'Lydia used another arm with a green laser attached. The ray punctured Avo'Doria. Quickly wrapping her wings around herself, Avo'Doria shielded herself from the beam. The wings diffused the laser light without it doing much damage.

The drone Ambrielle was sitting on drew closer to the gateway. She saw another fight going on inside among three other sentinels. Sido'Varius faced off with them as she watched helplessly from above.

As Avo'Doria warded off the laser, Nexo'Lydia disengaged and flew off toward the data core. Avo'Doria immediately went after her. She collided with Nexo'Lydia, grabbing hold of her and flying them both away from the data core. Nexo'Lydia was unable to pry off Avo'Doria's grip as she tried to get her laser arm free.

Jerovian flew toward them to help Nexo'Lydia after a power boost from the grid below. Nexo'Lydia freed one of her clawed arms and grabbed on to one of Avo'Doria's wings. The claw broke her wing off, sending it spinning toward the surface below. As Avo'Doria spiraled out of control, she folded her remaining wing up and used her thrusters to steady herself. Nexo'Lydia ripped into Avo'Doria's armor using her free claw. Avo'Doria, still holding her, began to tighten her grip and crush Nexo'Lydia with her strength.

Riding the drone into the gateway, Ambrielle considered jumping onto the next drone in the formation, but the gap was too wide.

"Drone, can you fly away from here?" she asked, hoping the drones obeyed voice commands.

"Affirmative," it said in a strange voice, and the drone turned around, flying away from the data core.

Jerovian launched himself into Avo'Doria's side, springing Nexo'Lydia free from her grasp. Nexo'Lydia extended all her remaining arms, surrounding Avo'Doria in their deadly embrace. Avo'Doria turned off her jets and fell before the arms could clamp down on her, using her one wing to slow her drop. She caught hold of Jerovian as he was recovering from the collision. Avo'Doria quickly destroyed both of his thrusters with her cutting laser and proceeded to remove his silcron.

As she did so, she was grabbed on all sides by Nexo'Lydia's arms. She grabbed Avo'Doria's left arm to prevent her from using the laser. With both thrusters disabled, Jerovian held on to Avo'Doria's leg to prevent himself from falling. Avo'Doria kicked her leg up, using Jerovian as a shield against Nexo'Lydia's beam. Nexo'Lydia knocked Jerovian loose and cut into her with the laser.

As she cut through Avo'Doria's armor, she dragged the ray over her, leaving it in one spot long enough to burn through. Suddenly, a red blast exploded through Nexo'Lydia's chest. Avo'Doria turned towards Ambrielle as she rode the drone behind the spider-armed sentinel, using its laser that was normally used for construction work. Nexo'Lydia staggered and began to fall as she swung her claw arm toward Ambrielle. The claw smashed the drone Ambrielle was riding and sent her careening toward the surface. Nexo'Lydia dropped out of the sky but got her thrusters powered again and flew off toward the data core.

Avo'Doria rocketed toward Ambrielle as she fell, catching her in her arms. "Are you damaged?"

"No, I don't think so," Ambrielle replied.

Avo'Doria launched them toward the data core, taking out her own silcron and plugging in each of the other two glowing tokens one at a time into the socket, overwriting them with a copy of the data of her own recent experiences.

Sido'Varius fended off four sentinels as Nexo'Lydia avoided the fight and went straight to the core. She plugged in her silcron. "Silcron recognized," said a voice from the data core. "Quick analysis . . . One thousand seventy-nine point nine two credits awarded.

"Important data found, proceeding with further analysis," it said.

Nexo'Lydia was leaking a blue glowing liquid that had the appearance of mercury. She appeared to be hobbled, moving slowly as she grabbed her silcron and flew out of the data core.

As they approached, Avo'Doria opened slots in her wrist, and green lights swarmed over the area. A formation of drones arrived and fired on the green lights, covering Midovius, Verdax and Nova'Duriel. Parts of Verdax were scattered across the floor from the sustained grid of drone lasers as the rest ran for cover, knocking the green lights away from them.

Sido'Varius went on the offensive, knocking Tyre'Magnus to the ground. He turned and ignited his thrusters, slamming Nova'Duriel into the far wall of the chamber. Tyre'Magnus's drones circled Sido'Varius, firing lasers as they searched for weaknesses in his armor. He swatted one of the drones away as he turned his attention to Nova'Duriel.

Avo'Doria engaged Tyre'Magnus as he got to his feet to go after Sido'Varius, slapping him sideways with her remaining wing. She turned around in time to cut through one of his drones as it left Sido'Varius to aid its master.

"I would set you down right now, but I'm afraid they would go after you," Avo'Doria told Ambrielle.

Sido'Varius had pressed Nova'Duriel so hard into the wall that she was lodged in it. He quickly turned and flew off, removing his silcron as he charged toward the core in the center of the chamber. Despite all the damage Verdax had sustained from the drones, he launched what was left of his upper body toward the core. Propping his torso up on the console, he reached his silcron towards the opening. Midovius fired his array of wrist lasers toward Sido'Varius forcing him to take cover and preventing him from stopping Verdax.

"Silcron recognized," said the voice from the core. "Quick analysis . . . similar data recognized. One thousand five hundred two point five five credits awarded."

Avo'Doria continued swinging her remaining wing at Tyre'Magnus, giving her greater range than his arms and legs, which he was attempting to use against her. After she landed another blow, he sidestepped and flanked her as she attacked again. He ignited his thrusters to land a quick punch to Avo'Doria, knocking her to the ground. She let go of Ambrielle to get back to her feet as he came toward them again. Avo'Doria grabbed Ambrielle's hand and placed something in it, then moved toward Tyre'Magnus.

Midovius fired his lasers to drive Sido'Varius out from behind the steel columns that decorated the corners of the room. Tyre'Magnus's second drone was trying to flank him from the side. Sido'Varius fired his laser at it, trying to keep it from getting behind him.

Midovius's ravaged armor was barely containing a cluster of glowing fibers as he moved to get a different angle. He fired sustained lasers that cut through the steel columns, forcing Sido'Varius to retreat. As Sido'Varius dropped back, he charged the circling drone, punching it into the nearby wall and knocking it to the ground. Walking over to it, he crushed the drone under his foot.

Ambrielle opened her hand and realized that she was holding the three silcrons that Avo'Doria had been carrying. She moved quickly and quietly over to the core as the other four sentinels were engaged in combat. Once she reached the core, she noticed there were several input sockets in the console and plugged all three into it at once.

"Three silcrons recognized," said the core. "Quick analysis . . . conflicting data. One thousand seven hundred ninety-two point nine two credits awarded, one thousand five hundred two point five five credits awarded, one thousand two hundred sixty-five point one eight credits awarded."

Tyre'Magnus turned, eyeing Ambrielle at the console, and immediately flew over Avo'Doria to drop to the floor. He landed near the core, nearly hitting Ambrielle as she jumped out of the way. He plugged his silcron in as Avo'Doria came barreling into him.

"Silcron recognized. Quick analysis . . . data similar to original . . . one thousand two hundred sixty-five point one eight credits awarded." Avo'Doria let go of the sentinel, turning her attention back toward the one that Sido'Varius was fighting with. At the far wall, Nova'Duriel had broken loose of the wall she was pressed into and flew toward the core.

"Avo'Doria!" Ambrielle yelled, pointing at Nova'Duriel. Avo'Doria leapt toward Nova'Duriel, igniting her thrusters and speeding into the sentinel. She grabbed her, pushing her up against the ceiling. Midovius disengaged from where he had Sido'Varius pinned down and flew to the core.

"Silcron recognized. Quick analysis . . . data similar to original . . . One thousand twenty-seven point eight one credits awarded," it said.

The other two sentinels launched upward toward Avo'Doria, who had been having difficulty containing Nova'Duriel against the ceiling of the structure. The female broke her lower body free and kicked Avo'Doria hard in the face. Sido'Varius was able to grab one of the two sentinels launching toward Avo'Doria and pull him back to the ground, but the other one flew up toward Avo'Doria and sliced through both thrusters on her feet with its cutting laser.

Avo'Doria fell toward the floor trying, to use her one wing like a parachute to slow her fall. Nova'Duriel was now free and zoomed toward the core. Avo'Doria landed as the female approached the core. They all stood at a distance around the core, staring at each other and Nova'Duriel. It was too late to do anything to try and stop her now. They didn't have the speed to reach her in time and didn't have the laser range to fire at her. She stood over the core opening and smiled as she reached for her silcron.

Her smile suddenly changed to panic, as she could not find it. Her silcron was gone. She flew toward the wall she had earlier been trapped in, frantically searching. Sido'Varius landed by the core and plugged his silcron in.

"Silcron recognized. Quick analysis, data conflicting with original . . . one thousand twenty-seven point eight one credits awarded."

He then smiled as he held up a second silcron, showing it off to everyone.

"Sido'Varius has it!" shouted Tyre'Magnus.

Sido'Varius then plugged in Nova'Duriel's silcron, which he had hopefully overwritten.

"Silcron recognized . . . Quick analysis . . . data conflicting with original . . . Seven hundred ninety point four four credits awarded," it said.

"No!" yelled Nova'Duriel from across the room.

"Destroy her!" said Midovius as he fired his array of beams at Ambrielle, one of them cutting into the left side of her abdomen right before Avo'Doria shielded her with her wing. As the wing diffused the laser, he tried to get an angle around Avo'Doria where he could hit Ambrielle again. She crumpled to her knees as the searing pain hit her. The wound through the burned hole in Ambrielle's clothing created a black mark with blistering skin around it.

"All nine sentinel silcrons analyzed," said the core.

Tyre'Magnus fired toward Ambrielle, as did Nova'Duriel from behind them. Sido'Varius dashed to Ambrielle to help shield her other side, stopping the rays with his heavy gold armor. One of the lasers found a weakness in the armor and bored all the way through him, barely missing Ambrielle. All three of the other sentinels began moving toward them as they streamed their rays at them, seeking a clean shot at Ambrielle. They bored another hole into Sido'Varius as he bled blue liquid and began to weaken and slump over.

"Data conflict resolved . . . transmitting decisive data," the core said.

Avo'Doria fired her laser back at the males, hitting one of them, but he stood his ground and took it, still moving toward them. Sido'Varius was unable to stand now as another laser drilled through him. Nova'Duriel had a clean shot at Ambrielle. They were surrounded now, and there was nothing Avo'Doria could do to protect Ambrielle on all sides.

"Transmission completed," the core said.

Tyre'Magnus, Nova'Duriel, and Midovius stopped firing; their laser cutters eased back into their wrists as they stared at Ambrielle.

"My primary objective has been updated. Ambrielle is the first arrival," said Nova'Duriel.

"She is the first arrival," said Midovius and Tyre'Magnus in agreement.

Sweaty and shaking, Ambrielle exhaled a long breath that turned into an audible moan. She was exhausted, stressed to the maximum, and the wound in her side burned with fury. She had come way too close to death yet again and wasn't sure how long she was going to live, with the injury from the laser that had almost punched all the way through her body.

The three other sentinels unplugged their silcrons and socketed them back into their armored bodies. Avo'Doria put her hand under Ambrielle's arm and gently pulled her up to her feet. Slumping into a sitting position on the floor, Sido'Varius relaxed. The room was left with crushed-in walls, metal parts of sentinels scattered about, and glowing blue liquid drops and splatters all around them. The area smelled like a burning oven.

Ambrielle was still in pain from the hole in her side. Avo'Doria scanned the wound with an attachment on her left wrist piece.

"The wound is deep. One of your internal organs is damaged. We need to get you to a repair station," said Avo'Doria.

"I can't be repaired, I'm human . . ." Ambrielle said.

"We have some organic repair stations back across the other side of the city," she replied. "Don't worry. We have tested it on organic animals here and perfected it."

"All right, I guess we can try it," said Ambrielle.

"The only problem is that I'm no longer able to fly. I'll have to travel back on the streets, and I don't think Sido'Varius is going to be able to take you either," Avo'Doria said. "We need to get you there quickly."

"I will take her," said Nova'Duriel.

"No," said Ambrielle. "I don't think so."

"It's all right, Ambrielle," she reassured. "You're the first arrival. I'll do anything to protect you."

"No, I could never trust you," Ambrielle said.

"It's fine now, Ambrielle. The decision has been made and our objective is clear. You are now defined as the first arrival, and everyone in Elyravess is at your service," Avo'Doria said.

CHAPTER 13

AVO'DORIA WAS HEAVILY damaged. One of her wings was completely broken off, her abdominal armor torn open, with ribbons of fibers hanging loose; thick, glowing blue liquid spilling out; and her feet cut through, rendering her unable to fly. She turned to Sido'Varius, who was still crumpled on the floor, three large holes drilled through his body and leaking the same blue liquid all over the floor.

Ambrielle looked at the three sentinels that had, moments ago, tried to kill her. Ambrielle had nothing but utter contempt for them. She despised them. She wished she had a weapon so that she could finish them off right now, even as she knew she shouldn't be having such thoughts.

"I . . . I don't know." She twisted the jewel in her necklace back and forth, thankful that it remained on the chain around her neck.

"I hate to do this, Ambrielle, but if you won't come willingly," Nova'Duriel said, "I will have to take you by force."

She engaged her thrusters, scooping Ambrielle up in her arms and taking flight. They passed through the gateway into the rest of the city. Work in the city continued as if nothing had happened, as if all were oblivious to the battle that had taken place among the sentinels.

"I know that you aren't happy with this," said Nova'Duriel, "but I must protect you. We need to get you to a repair station as soon as possible."

Ambrielle didn't respond. She owed Avo'Doria and Sido'Varius her life but had nothing to say to Nova'Duriel or the others.

Nova'Duriel's body hummed with recharging power as they flew close to the street grid. Ambrielle wondered if Sido'Varius would be all right, if both he and Avo'Doria would be able to fully repair.

Nova'Duriel took her to another one of the tall buildings in the city and set her gently on a table, where a device with different types of laser lights worked on her. Ambrielle thought of her mother saying that whenever someone is hurt, they have five good things coming to them. She wished her mom were here right now.

Once the light beams had numbed the area, a tube was placed against the wound. There were tiny metallic objects slowly moving through the tube into the wound in her side.

"Nano drones . . ." said Nova'Duriel. "They will go in and repair your liver. Hyper cell regeneration."

Once the nano drones were done, they exited the wound, and another light beam made the tissue around the hole in her side grow back together.

"That is amazing . . ." said Ambrielle.

"It works quite well," Nova'Duriel said. "Are you comfortable? Would you like to go back to the housing area you stayed in the other evening?"

"Yes, that would be fine."

"Are you going to come with me willingly this time?"

Ambrielle nodded.

The sun was beginning to set as they came outside. Ambrielle held her arms out as Nova'Duriel came around behind to wrap her arms around. They lifted off, flying toward the apartment balcony.

Once they reached the apartment building, Nova'Duriel set Ambrielle down gently on the balcony.

"Would you like me to stay here, or would you rather be alone?"

"Alone . . ." said Ambrielle. "I'll probably sleep soon."

"As you request." She flew off from the balcony out into the city.

Ambrielle breathed a sigh full of relief and a little bit of exhaustion as she entered the apartment again. The room was such a welcome sight that for a moment it almost felt like home. She went in and showered, checking her new skin where both wounds used to be, touching it to make sure it was real. It was just like any other skin—the same texture, elasticity, and sensation.

Ambrielle changed into something more comfortable to sleep in. Before climbing into bed, she took the hair styler clip out of her hair. Her dark blonde waves fell free from their tightly shaped, static-induced styling. She put the bed into a slow rocking swing. Intending to lie back and try other settings, she instead fell fast asleep before having time to try the next one.

❦

When the sun came up, she was awakened by the light. She realized she had forgotten to turn up the opacity on the windows. After showering, she got dressed, this time going with a burgundy top and some dark blue pants that were cut short. Each pant leg was a different length. The left leg was barely longer than shorts, and the cuff was angled, with the inside seam being longer than the outside. The right leg was longer, and its angle continued from the other pant leg.

These had to be the strangest pants she'd ever worn, and she laughed as she imagined what it would be like if she went to school in these. She began to wonder if there were synthetic clothing designers that tried to design clothes that organic beings would like or if they had replicated things like this from other beings. With all the angular architecture to the buildings, perhaps it was what synthetics would like if they wore clothes.

She tried to describe the kind of food she wanted for breakfast: eggs, pancakes with maple syrup, and some bacon on the side. What she ended up getting was more like a few large, crispy crackers with something like thick tree sap on top. Two pieces of some unknown kind of meat rested beside them. There were real eggs, but they weren't nearly as appetizing in appearance as what she had been used to.

The sap on the large crackers was thicker and harder than any syrup, but it was sweet. The eggs were pretty good if she didn't look at them. The meat was decent, but nothing like bacon. Overall, though, it was still one of the best breakfasts she'd had in a while.

Shortly after breakfast, Savi, the apartment assistant, notified Ambrielle that Avo'Doria was on her way. She hurried outside onto the balcony to meet her. Avo'Doria flew toward the apartment. Ambrielle smiled. Avo'Doria had been repaired. Once Avo'Doria landed, it was apparent that she was still missing a wing, but her armor was all intact now and more polished than ever.

"Your wing isn't repaired?" Ambrielle asked.

"I'll have to buy another once I get enough credits," Avo'Doria said.

"Oh, I'm sorry . . ."

"It won't take that long, don't worry."

"How is Sido'Varius?"

"He's fine now. He's repaired enough to resume his duties," Avo'Doria said. "He had to get back to Region Nine."

"I'm glad. Though I wish I could have thanked him before he left," Ambrielle said. "What about all the other sentinels?"

"Most of them are repaired. Two of them are in for extensive repairs, but they will eventually be fine," she said. "Nexo'Lydia is repaired but like me will have to wait to buy some of her more expensive parts."

"She deserves it, as far as I'm concerned."

"I came by to show you what we found at the newly unlocked research center."

"Oh! You found a way to get me back?" Ambrielle found it ironic that she was now almost excited about getting back to the desert world, even though it was only a bridge to get to Anatharia.

"Nothing for certain, but I have some theories."

"Oh, good, that sounds promising."

"I have been working on it for so long that I haven't uploaded the data to my silcron since we were there yesterday, so I will need to do that once we finish this. There are some interesting new data that need to be in the nexus."

Avo'Doria flew the two of them across the city. They came to a structure with an outer layer that spread into four top-corner arches. There was an inner layer that climbed straight up and tapered off into a round-edged plateau. It appeared the sentinels never wanted to enter a building from ground level, since they always landed on the inner platform.

Avo'Doria led Ambrielle to an elevator room, and they descended into the lower levels of the facility. Beams of light crisscrossed all around the walls, some going into a metal chamber in the middle and coming out as even larger and brighter beams.

They reached a large chamber with shells of synthetics standing in place along the walls. The walking worker ones, the drones, a crawling bot that she hadn't noticed before, and one that was more like a sentinel. In one area was a projected image of a star system with planets circling around it.

There were two cubes of light hovering over the floor.

"This is the substance that was found in the ocean." Avo'Doria walked over to one of the cubes. "It's invisible without extreme magnification, but it has some unusual properties. It seeks to bond with anything that interacts with it, and while bonding with most material fails, it is successful with water particles. Once the bond with water has been achieved, it reacts to everything quite normally." She walked over to the other cube. "We isolated these particles from a portion of the substance and removed them to get a clearer picture of its original state.

"It reacted violently when attempted to bond with other material; both the material and the substance were destroyed. Fortunately, there was no chain reaction, or this world may have disintegrated."

"If that part is destroyed, why do you still have it in that cube?"

"I'm getting to that." She turned off the light that was surrounding the invisible object, leaving only a glowing outline of the cube. "When I say destroyed, I mean it left a void in matter itself, which should not be possible. Observe." She took a square metal container and held it near the cube outline. "This is strong metal. My laser would take 14,486.2873 digimecs to penetrate this."

"What's a digimec?"

"You're interrupting my presentation," Avo'Doria said. "It is a unit of time measurement."

"I figured that, but, like . . . sorry. Never mind. Go ahead."

Avo'Doria then moved the metal through the outline of the cube. A thin line began to appear in the metal as she passed it through the cube outline. Eventually, the metal was divided in half and the bottom piece fell onto the floor.

"Wow . . ." said Ambrielle.

"Indeed." Avo'Doria reactivated the shield over the invisible dead spot.

"So, what is going on here, exactly?" Ambrielle asked.

"All we really know so far is that as long as this substance has bonded with water, it is like any other physical material, but if not? The substance and matter cancel each other out, leaving a spot devoid of either. Nothing material can pass through the zone, and we expect that this substance cannot either."

"Wait, don't I have this stuff all over me?" Ambrielle asked. "That's what Jerovian was saying before?"

"Yes, but it was already bonded from the ocean or the spring you mentioned, so you don't even notice the difference."

"What if it dries out? I don't want to wake up one day with holes all in me."

"It's not as simple as drying it out. Additionally, your body is made mostly of water."

"How does all this help me get back?"

"It doesn't. I thought you might find it interesting," Avo'Doria said.

Ambrielle huffed out a sigh.

"I think water has something to do with it, though," Avo'Doria said. "Tell me about the times that you have traveled to another world."

Ambrielle went through the story, detailing the parts with the two different springs in the desert world that led her to Anatharia and Elyravess and how she ended up in the desert world again after being thrown in the lake by the Kavekkians.

"So, the times that you left your desert planet, you went through a spring, an underwater cave," Avo'Doria said. "What brought you back was through a lake, more specifically being tossed into a lake. Water is the key component of this. I can't really make sense of it yet, but my hypothesis is that your whole body needs to be immersed in water almost instantaneously."

"Okay, let's try it."

"We will, but first I need to upload to the data core, or I will not be able to collect new data. Having this information in the nexus could also be useful if the other sentinels have some ideas."

Avo'Doria flew Ambrielle with her to the data core. It had been cleaned up since the battle the day before. It was so spotless that you couldn't tell anything had ever happened there.

"Silcron recognized . . . Quick analysis . . . three thousand seventy-seven point one two credits awarded."

"Whoa, that was a lot more than last time."

"Yes, it has been a longer amount of time in between uploads, so there is more data memory."

Suddenly, lights in the room began to flash. Avo'Doria's face became blank, as if she were deep in thought.

"Protocol change in progress . . . Founder data reservoirs one through nine have been decrypted. Flowing new data into the nexus," said the voice of the data core.

"What is happening?" Ambrielle asked.

"I've never seen this before. There's new information coming in, with new protocols," Avo'Doria explained.

"What kind of information?"

"It's about the substance, but it's too much to explain quickly in words, and much of it seems irrelevant to our needs."

"Can you summarize?"

"The founders encountered this substance long ago. Apparently, once my data went into the nexus, it triggered a security event. There were protocols making sure there has been no breach. The collected data showed this substance had come from a contaminated source . . . you. The substance is neutralized and not an immediate threat, but the fact that it was acquired in the universe was enough to trigger the alert.

"Furthermore, the data state that the substance is from a space beyond the universe that is immeasurable; it is a space between all universes. The name it gives to this space is Nulvare, but it is more commonly known as The Hollow."

Ambrielle's eyes grew big. "The Hollow??"

"According to this new information, there were beings from The Hollow that have entered this universe before. The cataclysm that Elyravess suffered was not natural. It was caused by these Nulvarians. The founders worked to drive them back and seal the breach so they can never enter Elyravess again. Our true primary mission is to watch over Elyravess and alert if they find a way to return. The founders themselves were likely alerted that this substance was collected, but my data were enough to show that there is containment."

"That's incredible . . . and frightening. The Nulthereals on the desert world must be part of that."

"Possibly. They must have found a way into another world."

"How did the founders stop them?"

"I do not understand the data. It says that they were weakened by vibrations, energy generated by living matter. Perhaps a large concentration of living things in an area may be enough to keep them at bay."

"I guess that is something, at least."

"Do you still want to return to the desert planet?"

"Well, even though I know more now, it's no more dangerous than it was before. I need to try. Hopefully the Nulthereals that were after me have moved on elsewhere by now."

"Before we attempt to send you back, since we went to great lengths to make sure you were dubbed the first arrival," she said, "show me how you would build this world."

"Oh . . . okay, I'll try."

Avo'Doria made some gestures. The star system model that was floating in the room became larger, and she zoomed in on the second planet in the system, zooming in farther until she saw a city that was spread over the entire planet. Ambrielle realized it was a model of Elyravess.

"You wanted more of the organic world incorporated among the synthetic city?" Avo'Doria said.

"Oh yeah, I'd like to see more of the plants and trees brought back from the destruction. Something closer to the natural state that the world was in, while keeping the city that you built also."

"Underneath this current planetary model layer is the surface of the original planet. I'll show you what it was like when we landed here."

Ambrielle watched as the cityscape of the planet faded to a world of black, gray, and white. A few large rocks dotted the surface, and dust and debris settled in windswept patterns. There were only a few small patches of green and magenta scattered about.

"I wasn't expecting it to have been this bad."

"Yes, you can see why we concluded that it was caused by asteroid impact. I'm not certain how the founders and Nulvarians fought here, with no evidence left behind."

Sadness washed over Ambrielle, imagining this once beautiful world and most of its creatures destroyed by these beings from The Hollow. But her sadness went beyond that. There was something bothering her in the depths of her soul. The emptiness that stalked her. A dread of a darkness that lay ahead.

The dark spot on her soul was just outside her memory's reach. It was like something that her brain had forgotten, but her heart had not. Going through the memories that she knew, the only thing she could think of was the abandonment by her friends. As bad as that was, there was more there. It was like there was a cataclysmic event of her own personal world at the root of this, but she could not deal with it right now.

Avo'Doria brought the present-time layer back up.

"Touch where you would like the organic part to be, and we can begin engineering," Avo'Doria said.

Ambrielle traced out around some of the buildings, leaving a green trail where she had traced. She lined the sides of the streets and small patches surrounding some of the buildings, drawing out a few large areas where the world could return to its former glory while maintaining most of the city and its functionality.

"Why don't you stay here, and we could work on this together?" said Avo'Doria. "You would never want for anything here."

"It's tempting, very tempting, but I feel like my place is to return to my new friends. I haven't felt like I had 'a place' in a long time."

"You'll always have a place here," Avo'Doria said.

"Thank you," Ambrielle said. "I would love to return here one day."

"Since you are the first arrival, you also have access to the vaults, our most advanced technology research for this region, which was designed to assist your kind with the development of this world going forward," Avo'Doria said.

"Well, if this works out, I won't be staying long enough to use any of it," Ambrielle said.

"Use it to help you in your return to the other world. You said there were problems that needed fixing," Avo'Doria said.

"What sort of things are in there?" asked Ambrielle.

"I'm not even sure myself," said Avo'Doria. "It would be things that right now cost the most credits. I haven't seen the items that far up the scale."

"That sounds kind of exciting. Let's go look."

CHAPTER 14

MBRIELLE WALKED UP the stone steps to the huge, black, metal door that Avo'Doria had brought her to. The door was oddly textured, quite different from the precision designs that the synthetics normally made. Ambrielle wondered if part of the process of making this metal added the random texturing. Red lights came on that projected a rectangular cube around Ambrielle and then disappeared. The door began to slide open, sounding incredibly heavy, judging by the slow groaning as it lifted open.

By the sound of the door opening, Ambrielle expected everything inside to be old and dusty, but it was immaculate. The room smelled fresh, like everything was placed inside yesterday. There were display cases and items hung up all over the walls: suits of armor that had a similar style to the sentinels', various tools of unknown uses, clothing, even pairs of wings.

Ambrielle walked over to a pair of wings that were different from anything the sentinels had. These had golden stems that were projecting wings that seemed to be made of a solid state of blue-violet light. The outside edges glowed, and their diaphanous interior rippled when something was close.

"Wow!" said Ambrielle. "I wish I could use these."

"You can . . . They are made for organics too. You need a power station to wear on your back for them to attach to," Avo'Doria said.

"Hmm . . . are the power stations heavy?" asked Ambrielle.

"Not to me," Avo'Doria said. "You'd also need thrust boots or some other device fitted to propel you in order to fly. You could glide with them, though, if you jumped from something high enough."

"And I can take whatever I need?" Ambrielle asked.

"Certainly. This is here for you," Avo'Doria said. "I should warn you, though. They would be extremely dangerous for you to use without approximately ninety rotations of training. That is how long it will take before it will be safe for you to fly with them."

"Oh, I guess that's out for now, then," Ambrielle said. "Maybe when I come back."

"Yes, with the time to train," Avo'Doria said, "you definitely could."

"Why don't you take them?"

"I can't. Everything in here is designated for the arrivals."

Ambrielle grabbed the wing stems from the display; the generated light wings turned off. Ambrielle then handed the golden stems to Avo'Doria. "I'm taking these, and now I'm giving them to you."

"What? Giving them to me?"

"Yes, is that allowed?"

"I suppose it is."

"Well, put them on."

Avo'Doria loosened her remaining wing from the attachment on her back and removed it. She then attached the golden stems into the sockets, and the laser wings projected again. Avo'Doria stretched her new wings out with an almost giddy smile on her face.

"These feel great. It is even better than what I had before," said Avo'Doria. "This would have surely cost in the billions of credits. I . . . appreciate this."

"You're welcome," Ambrielle said. "I'm happy to see you complete again."

Walking around the room, Ambrielle scanned around to see what else there may be inside. There were so many things that she had no idea what she was looking at.

"Avo'Doria, could you tell me what all is in here?" she said. "I don't know what most of this stuff is."

"That may take a while," Avo'Doria said. "What sort of things are you looking for?"

"Well, I'm not sure what I would really need."

"What would solve the problems you were talking about?"

"It would take mind control to solve these problems."

"We have something like that," Avo'Doria said, "but it would only work on nonintelligent organics."

"Oh, I was only kidding."

"Are there any problems you had there that affect you personally?"

"Hmm, let me think," Ambrielle said. "Oh! Sunglasses . . . the sun is so bright there."

"Sun what?"

"Something to make the sunlight not so strong where it hurts my eyes."

"There are optical upgrades for synthetics, but that wouldn't work for you," Avo'Doria said. "That's something that we will have to work on for organics. We thought organic eyes adjusted automatically to light."

"Well, they do, but only to a certain extent."

"So you need something for the extremes."

"Yes, to make it comfortable, at least."

"Perhaps when you return," said Avo'Doria, "we'll have something for you."

"Okay, what else . . . ?" Ambrielle said.

"Take an armor suit," Avo'Doria said, "to protect you from any kind of damage."

Ambrielle checked the armor displays. "No, I don't think so. They look heavy."

"They shouldn't be. They are powered and adjust to your stance, movements, whatever you are doing," Avo'Doria said. "They almost do the moving for you."

"They don't look like they would fit me. The arms are way too long on that one, and the other one has three legs."

"These can change shape to whatever species or size you are, within . . . certain parameters. Don't let that concern you."

"It would be kind of awesome. I just don't think I want to go back looking like I'm going into battle or something," said Ambrielle. "I could use some more suitable clothing, though."

"According to my information, there is some clothing toward the back of the chamber," Avo'Doria said. "What are you looking for?"

"Well, something that looks nice . . . I like my sundress, but it's not practical for climbing trees or going in caves," Ambrielle said. "Speaking of which, I need to get that dress from the apartment before I leave."

"So, a sundress that is practical for climbing trees . . ." Avo'Doria said.

Ambrielle laughed. "I'm thinking out loud. You're not going to find that."

"What about something like this?" Avo'Doria closed her glowing eyes for a moment. "It's categorized as an operations commander dress, female formal."

She waved her hand over a sectional wall, and it opened into a wardrobe-style area, like the one in the apartment but much bigger. Avo'Doria called up a projection of Ambrielle and asked for the operations commander dress to be displayed on the projection. Azure-blue clothing appeared on Ambrielle's image. The right shoulder was open like a cold shoulder. The left shoulder had a silver metal cuff with cloth material that wrapped over diagonally to the lower-right side. The wrap had golden symbols embroidered down the crease. It came down to a brown V-shaped belt made of thick material. The top formed a dress skirt on the right side below the belt and fell over the right-side hip and back side. The upper part of the pants was dark gray, coming down to a black, leathery material that started in a slant at the knee.

"Nah." Ambrielle shook her head. "Well . . . it may be perfect, actually."

"Great for climbing trees, right?" Avo'Doria said.

Ambrielle laughed again. "That was just an example."

"Try it on and see how it feels."

Ambrielle changed what she had on into the blue dress suit, checking herself in the live projection, patting the dress down to stretch out the folds. The suit adjusted itself to Ambrielle for a perfect fit.

"Ambrielle, operations commander . . ." Avo'Doria said.

Ambrielle laughed. "This is more like battle princess."

"Princess?" Avo'Doria asked.

"It's a title of royalty on Earth, and something that my friends used to say when we were kids dressing up really fancy and pretty."

"That's why you like the sundress, even though it is not practical?" Avo'Doria asked.

"Well, not exactly . . ." Ambrielle said. "I guess it is. But, come on, with the way your armor is styled, and the wings, you can't tell me you don't care about how you look."

"Certainly aesthetics are part of the appeal of acquiring new upgrades, but it's mostly about results," Avo'Doria said.

"Don't you ever wish you could change into some new look every day?"

"Perhaps . . . there would be some enjoyment in changing aesthetics more often."

"Exactly. That's what is so great about buying new clothes . . . I'm sure that armor is too expensive to change like that."

"That is true, but I don't understand the appeal of clothes. They aren't solid or shiny. I prefer something with glow, polished sheen, and intricate inlay designs."

"Try something on," Ambrielle said. "Look, there's even some clothes that have cutouts for power stations on your back."

"Yes, that is for organics that are using power stations," Avo'Doria said. "They can change between clothing and armor easily."

"Try this one." Ambrielle held up a long, black dress.

After turning off the laser wings, Avo'Doria had a difficult time slipping herself into the dress, accidently tearing it under one of the sleeves a little. Ambrielle assisted in finally getting it on as it auto-adjusted to fit.

Ambrielle stepped back to get a view as Avo'Doria powered her wings back on.

"Oh no . . ." Ambrielle burst out laughing. "That looks frightening!"

Avo'Doria turned on an image of herself so that she could look. "I don't see how it's frightening . . ."

"You look like the angel of death," Ambrielle said, still laughing.

Avo'Doria lifted her arms up to view the top, turning herself side to side.

"It's not bad, but it covers up the polished armor too much."

"Oh, can we get Sido'Varius something?" Ambrielle asked.

"Yes, I suppose we could," Avo'Doria said.

"What would he like?" Ambrielle asked.

"He's been saving up for some new armor, but the armor in here is beyond what he was planning to get. I'd almost hate to rob him of the satisfaction of getting it himself. I keep telling him he should get some wings, but he keeps buying larger jets to go faster and higher for work in the upper atmosphere," Avo'Doria said.

Avo'Doria searched the chamber as she walked over to check a display panel.

"He would probably like these," Avo'Doria said, turning a display on.

The power pack attachments morphed into silver wings and then changed into spiderlike arms with hooks, claws, and laser cutters, like the ones that Nexo'Lydia had. They transformed into other shapes as well that didn't have any apparent use.

"Okay, good, I'll get that, too, so that you can give them to him," Ambrielle said.

She took one last look around the room. There were so many things that would probably be useful, but she had no idea what most of it was for. She wouldn't be able to carry everything with her anyway.

"Well, I guess I'm done here. I can only hope that your idea works to get me back," Ambrielle said.

"One more thing before we leave. Take one of these," said Avo'Doria.

She handed Ambrielle a silver cylindrical piece with a few glowing blue lights on it.

"What is it?" asked Ambrielle.

"A silbrace like mine." She showed Ambrielle the raised metal piece that she used to communicate with drones and control certain areas of the city, as well as the cutting laser that she had used as a weapon in the battle at the data core.

"I don't think I need that."

"I insist you take one. This will be the most useful tool you have, and this one is even more advanced than anything any of us sentinels have."

"All right, I'll put it on." Ambrielle reluctantly slipped her wrist into it, and it closed around her arm to fit.

"Very well, we can head back to the ocean and attempt to get you back."

"Thank you. Could you please first take me back to the apartment to get my other dress?" Ambrielle asked.

"Certainly."

They flew back to the apartment, and Ambrielle went into the cleaning room and retrieved her white sundress from where she had left it to wash. She was surprised to find the dress bright white, with no bloodstains on the sleeve at all.

"Wow, aside from the laser hole, it looks like its brand-new!" Ambrielle said.

"Yes, it's a cleaning device." Avo'Doria seemed a bit confused.

Ambrielle stuffed the folded sundress under her clothing, held secure by her belt. "Well, I guess I'm ready to go now."

"This will be an interesting experiment."

Ambrielle stood on her tiptoes to compensate for their height difference and hugged Avo'Doria around the waist. Avo'Doria, apparently not understanding at first, returned it by putting a hand on her back.

"These last few planetary rotations have been eventful," said Avo'Doria. "I look forward to doing this again."

Ambrielle chuckled. "I'll miss you too." She moved her hand up across the hair above her own forehead out of nervous habit, striking something stuck in her hair.

"Oh, this hair thing, do you need it back?" Ambrielle asked.

"No, please . . . keep it."

"I hope it doesn't get damaged from the ocean."

"It won't, but the impact could dislodge it," said Avo'Doria. "Keep it attached to something like your silbrace."

"How would that work?" she asked.

Avo'Doria stood back a bit from Ambrielle. "Styler, secure," she commanded, and the hair styler flew out of Ambrielle's hand, hitting her metal silbrace and sticking to it.

"That will hold it. It can use its electromagnetic charge to attach to some metal objects," Avo'Doria said.

"Oh, thanks, that will come in handy."

"Ready?" Avo'Doria asked.

"Yes, I think so."

They flew up and out away from the city, headed toward the vast ocean. Avo'Doria tested how much stability she could maintain at faster speeds with her new wings. At times it put a bit too much stress on Ambrielle, but she tried not to complain. As they reached the spot of ocean where the substance had been found, Avo'Doria stopped and hovered over the water.

"I'm not certain that it matters whether you go back to the same spot," Avo'Doria said, "but the fewer variables, the better."

"Okay, so you're going to drop me in?"

"Yes, I think that you need to rapidly submerge completely to trigger this phenomenon. I still have no theory on how this works, but it's the best we have based on what worked before."

"Okay, ready when you are."

"Tighten your body before you hit the water."

"Okay."

"Here we go . . ." Avo'Doria dropped Ambrielle so that she would hit feet first into the waves below.

Time stopped for Ambrielle as she went through her planned thought process: hold your breath, tighten up, go under . . . and hopefully be transported back. She tightened her feet and legs, imagining herself as a spear piercing the surface and through the waters.

Once she hit the water, everything rushed so quickly that it took her a moment for her thoughts to catch up with what was happening. She was sinking under, rapidly at first, but her momentum began to slow. She let herself slowly continue drifting, until she finally came to a stop. Nothing was happening.

Time slowed again, and then it hit, that chaotic equilibrium she'd experienced before, and then there was a calm weightlessness, like she was drifting out into space. A sudden rush of cold water awakened her senses from their respite.

She was surrounded by honeycomb rock formations back in the cave of the spring. She swam through the tunnel as quickly as she could and out into the open spring. She reached the surface and scanned the area, making sure this was where she was supposed to be.

CHAPTER 15

AMBRIELLE CLIMBED OUT of the spring, her clothes and hair dripping wet and her body shivering from the icy water. The red sunlight sparkled in the water. Since the last time she was here, the sun had risen higher in the bluish-gray sky. As she walked toward the edge of the oasis, her clothes began to dry.

That sense of heaviness that she had every time she traveled between worlds came again, and it was more intense now than the previous times. Trapped water sloshed in her boots with every step, and the sand stuck all over them. It was annoying, but she did not want to wait to finish drying before heading toward the Anatharian oasis.

Goose bumps formed on her arm as she remembered her encounter with the shadows chasing her. They were out there, somewhere, across the dunes or waiting for her among the hardened, rocky hills. She tried to put those thoughts aside as she left the oasis.

There were small plants here, growing through the sand, that were not there before. She knelt to get closer and saw a tiny magenta base with green tips and black-striped feather grass. The same natural grass from Elyravess was beginning to sprout here. She couldn't help but smile, picturing the lovely meadow forest in the park becoming part of this world.

Realizing she'd better not linger for long, she stood up and began walking again. She wanted to stay on the move, and ran as much as she could to avoid any further confrontation. The rock-covered landscape came into view, putting her at ease that she was generally heading in the right direction. Climbing down the banks, she took a little more care this time in and with the cliffs and drops of this rough terrain.

Arriving on a stretch of flat rock, she surveyed the landscape, watching for any moving shadows. She came upon the sloping sand dunes. Trudging through the thick, silting sand robbed her of stamina. She had crossed two of the larger dunes when its presence surrounded her.

The eyes of something out there, watching her. She couldn't tell which direction it was coming from or how far away it was, but it made her feel uneasy, uncomfortable, and endangered. Ambrielle quickened her pace, using gravity and momentum when descending the dunes. The Anatharian forest lay ahead toward the horizon on her left. As she approached, the presence that Ambrielle sensed began to dissipate.

Among the trees there were intersecting pathways that cut through the forest, dead spots made by the shadows that consumed anything in their way. The trees near the pathways were cut clean and precise, down to grass being removed from the desert sand. The edges of the trees that were touched by the shadows had begun to turn gray with decay.

"Ambrielle!" said a familiar voice. "I'm so glad you weren't taken!" Sidaire ran over to her, with Kazial beside her. The bruises on their faces had mostly healed.

"Hey! Yeah, I was able to get to another spring," Ambrielle said.

"There's another spring?" asked Sidaire. "You could have met us at the spring here."

"I know, but I kept picturing in my head that you were going to drown me in the spring," Ambrielle said. "That probably doesn't make any sense."

"They spoke to you," said Sidaire. "Nulthereals can enter your mind if they get close enough."

"Yeah, I found that out."

"So you believe us now?"

"Yes, I mostly believed you, really, and I found out there was another world that this happened to a long time ago. The Nulthereals were driven back, and the place where they entered was sealed shut."

"How do you know this?" Kazial asked.

"I went through the spring out there." Ambrielle pointed at the horizon. "It led me to this other world called Elyravess, where these robots are guarding it, making sure the Nulthereals don't return."

"What's a robot?" said Kazial.

"How do you keep finding other worlds in the springs?" Sidaire said.

"There's a cave down there," Ambrielle replied.

"I know, but . . ." Sidaire started.

"When I came back to this world, the plant life that was on Elyravess had started growing around the oasis over there."

"Really? How is this happening?" Sidaire asked.

"I don't know. I wish I knew," said Ambrielle.

"We need to go there and see," Sidaire said excitedly.

"There's one more thing I need to do," said Ambrielle. "I'm glad you both are safe, but I need to go back to the other world."

"You just got back," said Sidaire.

"How did they drive the Nulthereals away?" Kazial said.

"That wasn't clear. It was a long time ago," Ambrielle said. "I think life somehow disrupts them."

"When I was part of their thoughts, they were thinking about something like an energy that living organics produce that prevents them from growing," said Sidaire. "But they swallowed up the trees when they went through, so I don't know how that makes sense."

"Yeah, I don't know. They were slowed down once they consumed the trees," Ambrielle said.

Ambrielle walked toward the spring and waded in. "I need to see another friend on Anatharia."

"You'll be back, won't you? Don't forget about us."

Ambrielle grabbed hold of the stones near the edge of the spring to keep herself afloat easier.

"I won't . . . I promise," Ambrielle said.

Underneath the surface she went, heading into the tunnel. Navigating her way through the system of tunnels, she reached the end of reality, floating in the nothingness outside her body. She was beginning to get used to this process of traveling between worlds.

She began her ascent to the surface, sunlight beaming through the rippling surface above. As soon as her head broke through into the dry air, the roar of wind and melodies of birds filled her ears. The musty smells of the nearby forest met her on the breeze. Back in Anatharia, it was like returning to an old friend after being away for a while.

The sight of Mekkinspire towering over her again gave Ambrielle a warmth in her heart, until she remembered her banishment. She swam toward the same edge of the lake and came upon a shallow area near the banks where she had first come ashore. She passed by the three inlets that, according to Taunsin, were made by the foot of some extremely large creature called Versepirath. Dripping wet, she stepped up on the white rocks at the shoreline and onto the blue-and-green grassland.

That cumbersome weight hit her again, the heaviness. It was getting worse with each trip through the spring tunnel. It was coursing through her. She rested against a rock to recover before moving on.

Drawing closer to the mountain, she left the path and tried to remain as close to the water as possible, in case there were any more raestrigs or other predators around. Once she made it to the foot of the mountain, she took the path that Gavian had used to come back and forth to the mountain ledge. It should lead her around to the side of Mekkinspire she had not seen before.

As the path curved around the base of the mountain, the sound of roaring waterfalls began to get louder. She needed to find the caves of the Darterrans and hopefully locate Gavian. The soft, grassy path gave way to hard stone. She caught a glimpse of the waterfall around the back of the mountain. This waterfall was much bigger than the other two she knew from the other side of the mountain. Ahead of her was a large chasm, with the waterfall roaring down into it. There was a river that flowed from the lake around the other side of the mountain that created its own set of falls into the canyon.

In the middle of the chasm was a lone formation of rock that rose nearly even with her position as she stood at the edge. It was a mesa-like formation that had a large tree growing on top of it with roots that peeked out through cracks in the rock. The tree appeared to be quite old, its limbs crookedly branching out with great width.

The path ended here. There must be some way around, but the rocky terrain at the edge would make that difficult. She got a little closer to the edge to try and get a view of the bottom of the ravine. There was a cave in the side of its walls above the river in the canyon. There was a path leading from the cave onto a ledge that wrapped around the side.

She traced the path with her eyes. Some places of the path ended and began again as she followed it to find its origin. She lay on the ground on her stomach to peer over the edge without having to lean her body over it. Ambrielle realized the path led under where she was standing.

There were small steps below where the path ended. She didn't like the idea of stepping down onto them, especially since they were invisible from her position. She took a leap of faith, dropping her foot onto the unseen steps beneath her. Pressing her body toward the rock side of the ledge, she slowly moved around the path.

Gravel and rocks fell with her steps, echoing with every hit against the walls and the river below. As she reached the cave, she hoped this was the one that Gavian was talking about. Ambrielle took a step inside the mossy entrance and started forward. It was dark in the tunnel. She couldn't see a thing.

Holding on to the sides of the walls, she slowly inched her way through the caverns. There was a vibration on her left arm, which was against the rocky wall of the cave. Perhaps it was coming from elsewhere in the cave? Somewhere the Darterrans were located. After she had spent a while maneuvering through the tunnel, she sat down to rest. This was not going to work. The vibration came again, even though her arm was not touching the walls anymore. It was coming from the silbrace on her wrist.

"Can you do anything about the darkness in this cave?" she said.

Nothing happened. "Power on," she said. Still nothing. "Silbrace, power on."

The silbrace vibrated again. "Can you turn a light on?"

Still in the dark.

"Activate laser or something."

Nothing happened.

She wondered why Avo'Doria never showed her how to use this if it didn't take commands. She had been in too much of a hurry to get back here, and now here she was, stuck in a cave in total darkness, without much left to do but turn around and walk back out. She lamented her need to rush into situations without preparation. She never had patience when it came to stuff like this.

She sat down on the floor of the cave, tempted to turn around and go back, but that was the old version of herself. The new one had taken risks and overcome dangerous situations to get here. She needed to prove to herself that she was braver now, that she could find ways to overcome obstacles. Thinking back to when Avo'Doria had used her own silbrace, she remembered that she used the buttons sometimes, but usually there was nothing apparent that she did at all. It was like she willed it to do what she wanted. She never spoke any commands to it. Ambrielle pressed both glowing buttons on the side, and the compartment holding her white dress opened, but nothing else.

Ambrielle tried to imagine how Avo'Doria might use the silbrace to light the cave up. Would she use a gesture or something else? Suddenly, a bright light came from the silbrace, shining onto the cave floor, reflecting on the ceiling. Pointing her arm ahead, she cast the light out into the darkness. She could now see at least fifty feet ahead of her. Unsure of what it was that had turned the light on, she knew she'd better take advantage while it was here.

Getting up from the floor and dusting her suit off, she noticed the hair styler attached to her silbrace. She tried to grab it, but it didn't budge. "Styler, detach." The styler device dropped to the ground. Ambrielle picked it up, cleaned it off, and placed it back into her hair. "Style four," she said, and her hair tightened into place. Farther into the tunnel, she noticed the wall to her right had opened into a wide space. The winding path was leading downward into a large chamber that was too immense for her light to cast on anything when she pointed the silbrace toward it.

The mekkadium heels of her boots produced a clatter as she reached some stone steps that led her down to the bottom of the chamber. She walked around the chamber, shining her silbrace light throughout the area, trying to figure out where to go next. There was a lot of old junk scattered about among large piles of rocks and dirt. She examined the perimeter of the room. There was an archway ahead, opening onto a hallway that was carved through the rock.

Before she made it to the hall, she stumbled over a metal container with wheels attached to it. Her head buzzed as electricity passed through her hair and the hair styler readjusted it. Entering the hallway, she shone the light along the walls. Pointing the light upward along the wall, Ambrielle saw the arched ceiling high above her. There were columns with carvings running along the walls. Carvings of lines, squares, and various other shapes all ran vertically up the columns.

On the wall behind the row of columns, there was an engraving of two trees intertwined. It was like the one in the abandoned Darterran dwellings on the mountain. As she moved farther on, she found another carving of a figure standing underneath a large tree, with lines of radiance emanating from both. The intricate etching depicted water rushing past them on either side and portrayed faces in the rushing currents, along with arms that were digging into and breaking the rocks around them.

While studying the carving, she heard a skittering noise coming down the hall. She turned the light toward it and saw two pairs of glowing green eyes. The creatures shrieked at the light and turned away, but one of them was able to get behind her and grab her right arm. Ambrielle's heart pounded as she swung at it with the silbrace on her left arm, hitting it on the head.

The other one grabbed her left arm. She thrust the back of her shoulder into the creature's face, knocking it into the wall and freeing herself from its grip. Ambrielle ran back toward the steps, but a clawed hand grabbed her leg, tripping her. She got back to her feet, swinging her arms to hit anything nearby. Turning the light on them again, she made them stop and cover their eyes.

The sound of more skittering echoed through the caves as she saw more pairs of eyes glowing in the light. They slowly moved toward her, shielding their eyes. Ambrielle backed up; there were too many of them now. One of them lunged at her, and she swung and missed. It grabbed her left arm with the silbrace, preventing her from shining her light toward them. She struggled to get the arm free, but more of them grabbed her.

No longer able to move against them, she stopped fighting and let them take her into the shadowy hall. The only thing that she could see now was the floor of the hallway and the furry legs of her captors as her light was aimed beneath her. As they were walking her along, she occasionally tested their grip, but they had not relaxed at all since they had first taken her.

They led her into another open chamber. This one had a flaming torch up high on the wall. There were more creatures filing into the round room as they brought her in.

A commotion echoed toward them from the chambers ahead. Many creatures were running toward them.

"Ambrielle!" shouted a male voice. "Please, let her go!"

"Gavian!" she said.

"I'm not letting her go. She hit me!" said one of the creatures holding her.

Gavian chuckled. "You probably deserved it."

"He did deserve it. He attacked me. They all did," Ambrielle said.

"Let her go. She's a friend," Gavian said.

They slowly released their grip on her as she shrugged away from them.

"She's an intruder!" someone said.

"Who comes into someone's home in the middle of the day, when everyone is sleeping?" said another.

"I wasn't trying to disturb anyone," Ambrielle said. "I came to see Gavian."

"Is this the one you rescued from the Kavekkians?" someone asked.

"Yes," Gavian said. "Well, no . . . I mean, she's the one I was talking about, but I didn't rescue her."

"I reckon she didn't need you anyway," one of them said, laughing. "She escaped on her own."

"I didn't escape. They weren't holding me prisoner," Ambrielle said.

"Where have you been, Ambrielle?" asked Gavian. "I've been going back to the cliff every night to see you."

"They wouldn't let you on the mountain if they weren't using you for something," said someone in the group.

"Yes, I'm sorry about that, Gavian," said Ambrielle. "They caught me talking to you and—"

There was a sound coming down the hall behind Gavian and the others, footsteps with claws scratching on stone. They all turned and fell silent.

A voice came out of the dark. "What's all this ruckus? I'm trying to get some sleep."

"Sorry, Gral Medigrin. This girl was intruding on our cave," one of the Darterrans said.

"Is that so?" Medigrin said as he appeared from the shadows. He was larger than the other Darterrans, wearing a balcain tunic. He wore a metal helmet on his head and a gold metal piece around his neck. He had clawed hands like the others, but one of the claws on his right hand was golden.

"Who are you to trespass in my city?" he asked as some armor-clad guards with crystal-tipped staves filed in behind him.

"This is the girl that was taken by the Kavekkians," Gavian said.

"Quiet, boy," Medigrin said. "I'm asking *her*."

"My name is Ambrielle." She curtseyed and then bowed, only having a skirt on one side to hold out on her new outfit.

"And what makes you think you are welcome to enter our city in the middle of daylight?" he said.

"I-I came to see Gavian," she said. "I didn't know it would be a problem."

"Now you've seen him, you can go back out the way you came," Medigrin said.

"Well, okay . . ." she said as she started to slowly turn away, but then turned back. "I don't really have anywhere else to go . . . and there might be predators out there."

Medigrin laughed. "If you were staying with the Kavekkians," he said with some measure of contempt, "why don't you go back with them?"

"You said she could come here," said Gavian.

"I said, quiet!" Medigrin said.

"They banished me from the mountain," Ambrielle said.

He chuckled. "You made a poor choice in friends, but that is no concern of ours."

"I was a stranger in this world," she said, "and they were willing to take me in, but I did break their rules, I suppose."

"They've got a rule for everything," Medigrin said. "And what rule did you break?"

"I wasn't supposed to talk to any Darterrans," Ambrielle said.

"I assume that it was Gavian here that you talked to . . ." Medigrin said.

"Correct."

"Well, Gavian, I guess you did liberate her after all," Medigrin said with a laugh. "You should have joined us when Gavian first tried to get you. They were going to kick you out sooner or later. That's how they treat everyone that isn't Kavekkian."

"They may be set in their ways, but they were never unkind to me," Ambrielle said. "Well, except for throwing me into the lake . . . that was a bit uncalled for."

"They threw you into the lake?" Gavian asked.

Medigrin glared at Gavian.

"Sorry, Gral," Gavian whispered.

"That's nothing compared to what they did to us," Medigrin said. "They cast us out of our homes and our market. They even threw some of us off the mountain to our deaths."

"That sounds horrible," Ambrielle said. "None of the Kavekkians that I met seemed like they would do anything like that."

"Don't let their hospitality fool you. There was a time when they welcomed us in as well," Medigrin said. "We have all realized what they really are. I was a child when they forced us to leave, but I still remember finding my father at the foot of the mountain, breathing his last breath after the vaesar threw him over the edge."

"Wow, is that the same vaesar that is there now?" Ambrielle asked.

"No, that generation has all passed into the spirit world now. I can only hope the elemental spirits are tormenting them as we speak," Medigrin said.

Ambrielle wasn't sure what to say to that. Medigrin was harboring a lot of anger over his father's death. She wasn't sure what had happened, and there were always two sides to every story. She couldn't imagine the Kavekkian leadership killing him for no reason.

Even though Maetha had not done as much as she thought she could have to defend her, she decided she should be careful what she said about the Kavekkians. She did not want to inflame what was already a delicate situation.

"Here's what I'll do," Medigrin said. "As long as you will work and earn your stay here, you can join us."

"Of course," Ambrielle said. "I'll do my part."

"I need you to answer one question for us," he said. "Are they desecrating our old dens? How many Kavekkians are living there now?

"None. No one is ever there," said Ambrielle.

"Interesting . . . All right, then, welcome to the pack," Medigrin said. "Now, let's all get back to sleep while we still have some daylight left."

CHAPTER 16

DARKNESS BEGAN TO settle over Lon Kavekkia as the rays of light
that shone through vents in the cavern began to fade. Ambrielle had
hardly slept at all, and the female Darterrans were getting out of their
beds to line up. The line moved in single file as they were led into a hallway.
Ambrielle tried to get her silbrace light turned on but was unsuccessful.
She could do little more than follow their sound as they walked through
the dim hall to another location.

Ambrielle tried to figure out what she'd done before to get the light
on. She tried to picture what position her arm was in, if that had anything
to do with it. As soon as she pictured the light coming on, the silbrace
light activated. She aimed it at the stony floor to keep the light out of the
Darterrans' eyes.

The hall led into an enormous chamber with long stone tables and
chairs lined up around them. It was black as night, except for a few candles
and torches in the room. The group of females dispersed and began sitting
at random tables. The males were entering from another hall, and the
chairs began to fill as more of them came into the room.

Ambrielle searched for Gavian, but there was no sign of him. In the
darkness of the caves, she could have easily missed him. She passed through
the rows of tables to look for him. Some of the Darterrans did not
appreciate the light on her silbrace. At last, she spotted him sitting
at the end of a table with a group of Darterrans.

Ambrielle found an empty chair next to a Darterran that was sitting across from him.

"Ambrielle! Hey, you need to join our crew," Gavian said as she sat on the stone bench.

"What crew?" Ambrielle asked.

"All of us over here, Fegrin, Taragris, Eregrin, and Segrit. Our work crew," he said.

"Good to meet you," Ambrielle said. "What kind of work do you do?"

"Tonight we're digging tunnels," said Fegrin. "How are you at digging? Let me see your hands."

Ambrielle held up her hands, turning them to show the outside and then her palms.

"Those are even worse than Gavian's," he said. "How are you going to dig with those?"

Fegrin showed her his own hands, covered in a coat of fur, with dark padded areas on his palms, some webbing between each finger, and thick, black claws protruding from each of them.

"Look at these beauties. I could outdig you in seconds."

Ambrielle turned to Gavian to read his face, but he didn't react, as though this were an unusual thing to brag about. She turned back to Fegrin.

"Impressive," she said with a hint of sarcasm.

"Fegrin is the head of our crew," said Gavian.

"She can replace me on haul duty," Eregrin said. "I'll dig in one of the tunnels."

"What is that you are wearing?" asked Gavian, turning to Ambrielle.

Ambrielle looked down, unsure what he meant, until she noticed she was still wearing the blue Elyravess operations outfit.

"Oh . . . I got this from another world. There's a lot that's happened since the last time I saw you," Ambrielle replied.

"What are we doing after our work is done, Gavian?" asked Taragris, a female Darterran with a short braid of hair falling over to one side. All the females seemed to have braided the tufts of longer hair that grew on the tops of their heads.

"You'll have to tell me about what happened sometime, Ambrielle," Gavian said.

"Gavian . . ." Taragris had her chin resting on her curled hand, and she patted a finger back and forth on her face to show her impatience.

"I don't know, maybe play some flakball," Gavian said.

"We do that every night," she said.

He turned to Ambrielle.

"She thinks we're a couple," Gavian told Ambrielle.

Taragris laughed and leaned on his shoulder.

Ambrielle wondered if he was joking or if she really was trying to be a couple with Gavian. Surely, he wasn't attracted to one of these creatures. Even still, she was a little bit jealous.

"You want to play, too, Ambrielle?" Gavian said.

"Yeah, sure, I'll play," she said.

"Ambrielle, you and I are going to be best friends," said Taragris. "I'll show you everything there is to know about being a Darterran."

"Oh . . . okay," said Ambrielle hesitantly.

Some other Darterrans entered the room carrying fruits, vegetables, and other foods in bowls that were sitting on stone trays. They went row by row, setting the trays of food in front of each Darterran seated at the tables. As more containers were brought in, the room filled with the scent of cooked meat. A simple thin metal bowl was set down in front of Ambrielle with some mashed-together fruits consisting of apraedas, olavas, and dappones. She wasn't sure why they mashed them together like this, but at least it wasn't food that was foreign to her anymore.

Darterran servers were coming around pouring liquid into everyone's bowl. There was something coming out with the liquid. She tilted her head, peering through the crowd as they came down the table closer to her.

"Wait, no . . . hold on . . . are those . . . bugs?" Ambrielle asked.

"What's bugs?" asked Taragris.

"Insects," said Ambrielle.

Gavian laughed. "No, those are escradas. They live in the pools and lakes of the deep caverns."

"Oh, so they are like crawfish, maybe? Or shrimp?" Ambrielle asked as they poured some into her bowl.

"I couldn't say," Gavian said. "I don't know what those are, but they are good. Try one."

"All right, if they aren't insects, I'll try one," she said.

Ambrielle searched the table for some utensils and noticed the rest of them were eating with what looked to be some small, handheld tongs. She found one behind her bowl. She picked up the tongs and grabbed an escrada with them. She took a tentative bite and slowly chewed, bracing herself for a potentially bad taste.

The texture and consistency were not bad. She turned her focus toward the taste. As the flavor began to fully register, she decided they were pretty good. She was expecting a taste like shrimp, but the flavor was more like pork than any kind of seafood.

"You know, Maetha had told me these were disgusting, but they are good," Ambrielle said.

"That sounds like a Kavekkian name," said Segrit.

"Yes, she's a friend I met when I first came here," Ambrielle said.

"How could you be friends with them?" Taragris said.

Gavian continued eating but was listening intently.

"Well, they took me in when I first came to this world. They fed me, gave me a place to sleep . . ." Ambrielle said.

"And then kicked you out," Fegrin said.

"Yes, although I did go against their rules," Ambrielle said.

"It's all about rules with them," Fegrin said.

"So, you have no rules here?" Ambrielle asked.

"We can live by our own rules, not according to how their vaesar thinks we should," said Fegrin.

"What if I stood up on the table right now and kicked everyone's bowls over, what would happen to me?" Ambrielle asked, and Gavian's eyes widened a bit.

Fegrin laughed. "You'd be . . . you would . . . be punished. There's no rule against it, but you can't be causing a mess for the rest of us."

"They're unwritten rules," Ambrielle responded. "Well, you could make the argument that this is the reason for the Kavekkians' rules. They are untrusting of outsiders or anyone that interrupts the way they want their society to function. So they have rules that deal with these problems, even if it means casting out those that cause dysfunction."

"You're defending them for throwing us out?" Taragris asked.

"I think they are wrong about all of us," Ambrielle said. "But ultimately I went against their wishes. From their point of view, I brought potential mistrust and dysfunction to their society."

"But you're still saying they did the wrong thing, so in the end, their rules are too rigid," said Taragris.

"Maybe. I don't agree with being thrown out, but I understand it," Ambrielle said. "I knew the rules beforehand."

"You are lucky they didn't toss you over the side of the mountain," said Fegrin. "I bet you wouldn't be so understanding then."

"No, probably not, but then I wouldn't be here," Ambrielle replied.

"It happened to Medigrin's father," said Eregrin.

"Yeah, and if that's true, there's no excuse for that," Ambrielle said. "But I don't think the Kavekkians that are around today are like that."

"They all come from the same bloodlines. I doubt anything has changed," Taragris said.

"The Kavekkians I was friends with told me they wished things could be mended between the Darterrans and Kavekkians," Ambrielle said. "They've heard stories from their grandparents of how things used to be."

"They were lying to you, trying to make themselves out to be the victims in all this," Taragris said.

"When I was first brought to the mountain . . ." Ambrielle shifted her gaze between all of them, as well as others seated farther down who were pretending not to listen. "I walked through the old Darterran dwellings and past the Darterran market on the way up the mountain. They are still there, basically untouched. You know what that says to me? They still have hope. Hope that one day things will be as they used to, that those parts of the mountain will be filled with Darterrans again. Even if for some of them it is a subconscious thing."

They sat there quietly for a moment.

"It's really all there like it used to be?" Fegrin asked.

"Yes," said Ambrielle. "I talked to one of the older Kavekkians, and he told me that his father was one of those that had to gather up Darterrans and make them move out of the market and out of their homes. He said that he didn't want to do it, but his vaesar demanded it. Tempers were flaring, and he felt that once everyone separated for a few days, everything would calm down and they could all come back. Obviously, that never happened."

"He should have refused," Fegrin said. "Actions matter more than intentions."

"I agree. That is a good point," Ambrielle said. "It's up for debate whether his actions prevented more violence or did more to further the animosity. But it makes me think that most of this conflict was between the vaesar and whoever he thinks took their lykris and not with the Kavekkians and Darterrans."

"No one stole their lykris," Fegrin said.

"So what was the issue, then?" Ambrielle asked.

"The tablets of the ancients," Fegrin said. "A long time ago, our ancestors found the tablets in front of this hard stone that they never could dig through. Many cycles later, after the lykris was created, the Kavekkians wanted us to use it to break through the impenetrable stone, thinking that there could be more tablets or information about the ancients. But even the lykris couldn't crack it. Their vaesar didn't believe it. He accused us of taking the tablets for ourselves, but Kavekkians don't like the caves, so he wouldn't come down here to see it for himself."

"Why couldn't they dig around it?" Ambrielle asked.

"It's a cube-shaped chamber. There's no digging around it," said Fegrin.

"I wonder what could be inside . . ." said Ambrielle.

"I've often wondered that, but it is probably best left alone," Fegrin said.

"What all do you know about the ancients?" Ambrielle inquired.

"I know they lived in this area a long time ago, before Darterrans or Kavekkians ever did. They lived in these caves and built some of the halls here. They used technology that neither us nor the Kavekkians completely understand yet. It's the technology that was used to build the lykris. All of what the Kavekkians learned about their crystals, they got from the ancients," said Fegrin.

"What happened to them, then? Where did they all go?" Ambrielle asked.

"According to some of their tablets, a dark spirit was able to influence the ancients, turning them against each other. There was a great war between them, and many were killed. They say that there were a few among them that resisted the influence. Those that resisted found a place in the forest where the spirits were being removed from the trees. They were using the war to keep the ancients occupied while they removed all the spirits from the land. The rock spirits, tree spirits, and water spirits were all being removed from the world."

"What did they do?" Ambrielle asked.

"With the spirits' help, the ancients were able to send the dark spirit back into the shadow realm, where it belongs."

"How did they send it back?" said Ambrielle.

"The dark spirit? Something that the tree spirits and water spirits did. I don't know."

"Do you think the spirit is in that chamber that couldn't be broken by the lykris?"

"What? Why would you say a thing like that? No, the dark spirit went back to the shadow realm."

"Now I'm spooked a bit. I hadn't heard that whole story before," Taragris said.

"It's time to get to work. Clean up your messes, and move out," Fegrin said.

Ambrielle finished up the last bit of the fruit mash, grabbed her bowl, and got in line with the rest of the group. Everyone stacked their bowls onto a stone table near the hall they had begun entering. She followed Taragris into the hall, with Gavian ahead of her. They turned down another corridor as others continued walking straight on.

As they came to the end of the smoothly carved-out hall, they entered a rugged tunnel. Taragris went into a small, tight shaft and began clawing into the rock and dirt, throwing dirt everywhere behind her. The webbing between her fingers acted as a shovel, scooping and throwing out debris as soon as her claws cut through the rock. Fegrin went into another shaft, as did Eregrin and Segrit, to begin digging.

Gavian grabbed two carts and left one beside Ambrielle, then handed her a shovel. "Check this out. I invented these tools so that those of us without claws are able to dig and scoop the debris piles into these carts."

"Invented?" Ambrielle said. "I don't think you're using that word properly. You made them?"

"Yeah, but I came up with the design," he said.

Ambrielle laughed. "I think you may have been heavily inspired by your past life. These have been around forever on Earth."

"Have they? Oh, well, I made them, at least."

She inspected the shovel. The sturdy, smoothed wooden handle, the metal blade, were nothing fancy, but it was well put together. "Yes, they are nicely made."

He smiled as he wheeled a cart into Taragris's shaft and began to shovel the debris that she had dug out. Ambrielle grabbed the cart close to her and wheeled it into the next shaft, which happened to be Fegrin's.

Once far enough into the shaft, she took the shovel and began scooping up the debris and tossing it into the cart. After she had thrown a few shovelfuls of sediment into the cart, she was surprised at how heavy some of the piles of dirt were. A lot of the debris consisted of small rocks.

"So what are we looking for?" Ambrielle asked.

"Crystals," Fegrin said, "and certain kinds of rock."

He continued digging and throwing rubbish out toward her. She backed up, brushing the dust off her clothes.

"When you drop the load off in the sifting chamber, they will go through it. You don't have to worry about picking it out. Just carry the loads to them," he said.

She had filled up half the cart, and Fegrin took a short break to rest.

"My parents used to tell me stories that they heard from their parents about living on the mountain," Fegrin said. "They, my grandparents, talked like it was some paradise and about all the Kavekkian friends they missed."

He continued digging again, slowing down occasionally as he spoke. "They told me they thought things would eventually blow over and they would move back to the mountain."

Ambrielle began to shovel the new piles into the cart, which fortunately was lighter sediment than before.

He continued, "My parents weren't as optimistic as my grandparents were. To them it was a dream. They were neutral-minded to Kavekkians in

general, but I always despised them. Most of the Darterrans in my generation despise them. They think they are better than us."

"They really don't." Ambrielle struggled with a heavy load of some
larger rocks buried in the dirt.

Fegrin stopped digging for a moment. "If they really want to make
amends, why haven't they come, in all this time, to talk to us, despite what
their vaesar, then and now, says?" Fegrin said.

"I don't know. Maybe for the same reason none of the Darterrans have
come to talk to them," said Ambrielle.

"They killed our gral. They drove us out of our homes. We won't go
groveling to them to let us back in," he said.

Ambrielle grunted as she lifted another heavy shovelful. "I mean that
they have to deal with their leadership as you would. They have to convince
both them and you. It's a complicated situation. To get everyone on board
with this all at the same time, it probably seems impossible."

Fegrin dug out enough for another pile and then paused. "It *is*
impossible."

Ambrielle tightened her lips together and stuck her shovel back into
the pile of dirt, shoveling the rest of it into the cart. The cart was full now,
and Ambrielle walked it backward out of the shaft. It was quite heavy with
a full load.

"I hope you are right that they want the same things we do and don't
think of us as inferior." Fegrin turned around. "I suppose I don't hate all
of them."

Ambrielle grinned. "Well, that's progress."

After backing out of the shaft, she ran into Gavian pushing his empty
cart back to Eregrin's tunnel on the other side of her.

"Hey, how's this work going for you so far?" he asked.

"It's going okay," Ambrielle said. "So where is this sifting chamber?"

"Oh, it's at the end of this tunnel," he said, pointing her in the direction.

"Thanks."

"So, what all happened while you were away? You seem . . . different."

"I don't even know where to begin."

"Start at the beginning, when you were banished from the mountain.
Why didn't you come find me then?"

"They threw me into the lake," Ambrielle said. "I ended up back in the desert world, but there are trees growing there now. I got chased by these mind-controlling shadows. I went into a different spring and was in this cyborg city world. I got in the middle of a robot war. One of them helped me get back, and then I came to find you."

"Oh . . ." said Gavian. "You don't think I've heard that excuse before?" he said with a grin.

She smiled back, rolled her eyes, and walked toward the sifting chamber to dump the load she was hauling. There was a large grate over the floor, with tiny holes. One of the Darterrans in the chamber motioned for her to deposit the load onto it. The cart was too heavy for her to turn over, but one of the Darterrans in the room came over to help. When she returned, she entered the fourth shaft, where Segrit had been digging. He watched her as she dug into the pile, starting a new load in the cart.

Lifting these heavy shovel loads was beginning to put a strain on her back. She tried to shift more of the weight to her arms as she shoveled more loads into the cart. After a few more shovelfuls, her arms began to tire out, and she paused to rest them.

Segrit stopped digging when he noticed her resting. "Don't tell the others that I said this, but I've always wanted to meet a Kavekkian. My grandparents' stories always contradicted what we are usually told."

"I wish there was a way that could happen. I think if they could meet you, this could be resolved," Ambrielle said.

"I like to think that," he said, and then resumed his digging.

Ambrielle went back to shoveling. Once she filled up the cart again, she began hauling it back out of the shaft and into the tunnel. She pushed the heavy cart through to the end of the tunnel into the sifting room. Gavian was there, talking to a Darterran.

"Oh, I see," Ambrielle said, "the rest of us are out here working hard, and you're in here taking a break."

Gavian laughed. "They are digging fast now, but they slow down a lot as the night goes on, so I try to pace myself."

"I hope they do slow down." Ambrielle rubbed the blisters on the palms of her hands.

"Yeah, you look like you need a break," Gavian said. "Actually, why don't you take a long break, then start back in a few hours?"

"You don't think I can do this?"

"I'm sure you can," Gavian said. "But it's tough when you aren't used to it. When I hauled on my first night, I thought I was going to die."

"How did you get through it?"

"I took some long breaks. Fortunately, Fegrin was okay with it."

"Okay, I'll take a break." Ambrielle smiled. "If you're sure it's all right."

"It's fine."

"Thanks for understanding."

"Hang around this chamber on your break, and I'll talk to you when I bring another load back." He grabbed his cart and started heading out of the chamber, then paused and turned his head toward her.

"Ambrielle." He grinned as her eyes met his. "You're still the most beautiful human on Anatharia."

"Well, what does that make you? The ugliest?" She smiled, waiting to hear what he came back with.

He exhaled loudly into a chuckle. "Yeah, I guess it does."

He continued pulling the cart out of the chamber. Ambrielle found a place to sit on a smoothed stone in the corner. She stretched her back, trying to prop it in a straight line as she sat against the stone. She rubbed her forearms, trying to get more blood circulating to help ease the fatigue in her muscles.

After sitting there for a bit, she began to get restless. She walked over to where a few Darterrans were sifting through the rubble. They were using long-handled tools to push the piles into the grated floor. They kept working it in until there were only bigger objects that remained.

Ambrielle walked over, wondering what they were finding in the piles. It was mostly uninteresting gray pieces of rock, but there were a few blue crystal pieces. The same vaeranite crystals that the Kavekkians used to light up their dwellings in the mountain. One of the Darterrans nodded as she gestured that she wanted to pick one up.

She examined the crystal as she held it. It was uncut but had smooth sides that were shiny. When she held it up in the light of the nearby torches, it contained a tunnel of light in the center of it. She wanted to keep it but recognized that she should place it back on the sifter floor with the Darter-ran, who was watching her intently. Farther over was a larger white crystal that was cloudy but gave off a faint glow.

The Darterran beside her stared at her when she got close to it, so she didn't pick it up. Ambrielle walked around the chamber. There were two more tunnels like the one she had come through. Peering in, she saw other mineshafts, and there was a Darterran wheeling a cart toward the chamber to drop their haul.

A fourth pathway was a hall with carved decorative columns like the first hallway near the cave entrance. She wandered down the hall. There were more carvings on the walls here. She passed a sculpture of a Darterran face that was quite eerie in the light of the torches flickering above.

Ambrielle continued until she reached an intersection, deciding to maintain her course and go straight. As she progressed farther down the hall, the air changed, producing an older, mustier smell. Her footsteps echoed longer through the corridors. At the end of the hall was another immense cavern chamber, but this one was different.

Waterfalls cascaded down from somewhere in the darkness above her, creating a small river that flowed into a natural tunnel to exit the chamber. There was a large blue pool in the middle of the chamber, and stalactites hung above it, water dripping off them into the water below, producing haunting melodic echoes as they hit the pool's surface.

There were a few large stalagmites rising out of the water of the pool, its water perfectly clear in the shallow areas near the edges but becoming an opaque blue toward the middle. Even with the constant drops hitting it, the water was so still that it looked like a picture. She watched some small, shiny creatures that walked through the shallowest areas of the water.

The walls of the chamber sparkled like tiny stars embedded in the rock, tapering off as they neared the floor. Some of the stalactites and stalagmites had merged to form several natural columns of smooth, swirled colors of rock. There were stalagmites along the cavern floor, irregularly shaped but smooth, like melted candle wax. This was the most beautiful part of the caverns by far. She stood in awe of the beauty of these natural formations.

Ambrielle headed back toward the intersection. She decided to explore the left path this time. The hall led into another chamber with walls of white stone. There was a faint circle of light on the floor. High above her was a hole that went up to the starry sky outside.

She turned on the light on her silbrace. The walls in this area were unnatural. Judging by the claw marks, the area had been dug by Darterrans. Dark, shadowy creatures flew away from her light. They had leathery wings like bats, but with long twin tails. They landed on a group of rock formations protruding from the ceiling. A small waterfall spilled from the rocks and disappeared into a fissure in the cave floor. The thin sheet of flowing water formed an animated mirror as her light reflected off it.

Moving farther into the room, she saw a large, cube-shaped structure ahead. As she walked around the structure, she found no doorway of any kind. The walls were smooth and not naturally formed. She put her hand on the side, and a tingling sensation went through her. There were a few burn spots along the wall and several claw marks.

As she moved her light around the chamber, she noticed an object in the corner. As her light shone toward it, a large, white crystal began to give off a faint glow. Moving her light across the object, she finally could tell what the object was.

A lykris, like the one on Mekkinspire. There were a few small differences. At the bottom, there were shiny white panels that looked like a broken window that had been reassembled. Six wooden staves were stuck into some metal housing that held the crystal panels in place. Ambrielle realized that this must be the original lykris that Maetha had said was stolen from them.

Whether it was borrowed or stolen, this was the object that had caused so much trouble between the Darterrans and Kavekkians. The hole in the ceiling of the chamber must have allowed sunlight into the cave for them to use the lykris. She wondered what they used to dig for in this room. Then she remembered that they were trying to break up a chamber of the ancients.

Ambrielle quickly went back over to the cubed structure. She focused her light on the burn marks. This must be the chamber they were trying to break into. It looked as though several attempts had been made in various parts of the smooth stone, perhaps trying to find a weakness.

One part of the stone had fewer burns, revealing strange symbols carved into it. She wished she could understand what the symbols meant. Ambrielle put her hands on the sides again, unsure what was causing the tingling sensation. It was subtle, but the whole structure was rapidly vibrating against her skin.

Was the dark spirit they talked about inside? Was it a Nulthereal?

"Ambrielle!" shouted a voice that echoed through the halls.

She turned, startled by the sound, quickly moving back into the hallway.

CHAPTER 17

"AMBRIELLE?" CALLED THE voice again. It was Gavian.

"I'm coming back!" she yelled.

"Okay, good," he said.

She reached the hall he was standing in, his hands on his hips, as though she had done something wrong. She rolled her eyes. Rather than stop when she made it to him, she walked on past.

"Hey, where did you go?" He turned, following behind her.

"What happened to the Darterran freedom you kept going on about?"

"What? I was wondering what happened to you."

"I'm fine. I don't need someone to watch over me all the time."

"I thought you were staying in the sifting room. I thought you were resting."

"I was resting my arms, not my legs."

"All right, so you were looking around? There are some places I wanted to show you anyway."

"I got bored. I can't sit still for too long."

"I'd show you around now, but I have to finish up some more work first."

She warmed her tone when she realized that he wasn't mad at her for walking off. "Okay, I'll come back and help."

"Are you sure? You don't have to."

"Yes, I'm good now."

"It won't be that much longer, and then we'll eat again, and after that we'll have the rest of the night."

Ambrielle and Gavian went back to hauling, and after a few more loads, it was quitting time. They all filed into the dining hall with the rest of the Darterran workers. The meal was escradas again, but with a thick, sour-tasting topping. It was served as a sauce, but the consistency was more like butter. The escradas were piled on top of a grainy substance that reminded Ambrielle of creamed corn, with a saltier taste.

Once they finished and cleaned their area, Ambrielle followed Gavian and the rest of their crew into the nearby hall.

"Do you want to go explore the cave some more or play flakball?" Gavian asked her.

"Well, I know you were wanting to play," said Ambrielle. "We can go do that."

"Are you sure?" he said. "I'm fine either way."

"Yes, I want to play too," Ambrielle said.

They walked with some other Darterrans back into the chamber where she had first met Medigrin. There was a small opening in a corner of the room that led to an equally small tunnel. Ambrielle followed the rest of them as the tunnel sloped down into a lower part of the caverns. In the next chamber, signs of Darterran claw marks branded the walls, and piles of hardened dirt lined the edges of the floor.

Four torches lit the area, making it one of the brighter rooms in the caverns. There were white lines marking a large square on the floor and across the center. In the middle of each wall was a small hole. There were two sides already getting ready to start playing. Fegrin, Taragris, and the two other members of their work crew showed up as well.

"Hey, Ambrielle wants to try playing. We already have four. Do any of you mind if she plays?" Gavian asked.

"She can take my spot," Eregrin said. "That will work out well, since my brother's crew usually are down one."

"Okay, thank you," Gavian said.

"We'll play winners!" Taragris shouted at the two teams about to begin.

The two sides of four separated between the line in the middle. A female Darterran took the ball first and threw it against the wall. It bounced off hard and hit the floor, traveling past the reach of the other team trying to grab it.

Most of the Darterrans in the room cheered, while others shook their heads.

"You remember the rules?" Gavian asked.

"Well, somewhat, but you'll probably have to refresh me," Ambrielle said.

"That was two points for Canlin's crew. They got the ball past the other team. It must hit the wall and bounce on the other team's side of the floor at least once. Since it wasn't caught, they get to throw again."

The same female Darterran launched the flakball into the wall. It bounced off and hit the ground, but it took a low, sideways bounce, fooling the other Darterran team, who were anticipating it to go high.

"See that?" Gavian pointed. "You want to try to get different spins on the ball. Fegrin is good at that backspin bounce. You have to hit the wall at the right level from the floor too."

"How do you get spin?" Ambrielle asked

"You want to grip the ball like this," he said motioning for her to hold out her hand. He took her hand and rolled it into a fist. He positioned his fingers around her balled hand, showing her the grip. "Then you want the ball to roll off your fingers as you throw it, like this."

Part of his hand was smooth, while other parts had a rougher texture. All the tiny grooves in his skin seemed to fit into the ones in hers. The physical connection with him in this simple touch caught her off guard. She could barely focus on what he was saying.

"Okay, and that will give it backspin?" she asked.

"Yeah, there's some different grips you can use. You have to find what feels natural for you." When he let go of her hand, the tingling sensation remained, as though he were still holding it. There was more cheering as the other team caught her throw this time. "So now the other team gets to throw and a chance to score points."

"Okay, so it's four–zero, right?" she asked

"Right, four–zero."

"When is the game over?"

"Whenever someone reaches twenty points."

One of the males on the other team threw and got one past Canlin's team. Shouts of "Four–two!" went up among the mix of cheers and moans. The same Darterran got the ball again and threw it toward the wall, but it hit the edge of the hole in the middle of the wall and bounced off to the side, out of bounds.

"Oh! He almost made the notch!" Gavian said.

"What's the notch?"

"That hole in the middle of the wall. If you happen to get the ball inside that hole, it will stick in the wall, and you get five points."

"Oh wow, that would have put them ahead."

Canlin's team got the ball back and promptly got another throw past the other team for a six–two lead. As the game went on, Canlin's crew quickly beat the other team twenty to eight. Everyone took a break for a short while, and then Gavian and the others began walking out onto the game court. Fegrin began placing everyone into defensive positions.

"For defense, Gavian on the front left. I'll take the back left. Taragris will be on the back right, and Ambrielle, you have the front right. So this whole square is your zone." Fegrin traced an area with his foot. "We'll stick to a simple zone scheme for this game."

Ambrielle stretched out her legs while waiting for the game to start.

"Don't let anything get by you, Ambrielle," Gavian said.

"I won't," she said, smiling. "I can catch pretty well, actually."

"You ready over there?" someone from the other team asked.

"We're ready," said Fegrin.

"All right, you get first throw," said Canlin.

"Okay, Gavian, you throw first, and we'll go to Ambrielle next, and then Taragris and me," Fegrin said.

Gavian wound up and threw the ball hard and fast against the wall. It hit the ground and skipped rapidly through the other team's defense. He pumped his fist, and the rest of the team cheered.

"Good one," Ambrielle told him. "Do it again."

"That was the topspin fastball," he said.

He tossed another, but it was too much like his first throw, and the other team anticipated it. Two of them broke toward the middle, and one of them caught it on the bounce.

"I didn't mean do exactly the same thing again," Ambrielle said.

"Ha ha," he said sarcastically. "I was trying to get it to skip harder on the bounce that time."

"Didn't work," she said.

"Is that how it's going to be?" Gavian said, smiling. "Where's the support for your teammate?"

The back-left player on Canlin's team threw the ball, which whizzed past Ambrielle's head as it went by. They turned for the bounce. It was too high for Gavian to reach, but Fegrin backstepped as it arched and began to fall, catching it before he crossed the boundary line.

"Feggy!" Taragris said amid the cheers of those watching.

Fegrin tossed the ball to Ambrielle. She caught it and moved the ball around in her palm. It was like a hard rubber material. It had a small, bumpy texture to it and was about the size of a baseball.

"Let's make it four–oh, Ambrielle," Taragris said.

"I set you up for a backspin throw," Gavian whispered.

Ambrielle kicked her leg out, setting it down wide ahead of her as she followed through. Instead of throwing straight, the ball went up in an arc before hitting the wall above the notch and bouncing down into the hands of the other team for an easy catch.

"Aww!" said Fegrin. "You have to throw it harder than that."

"Sorry, I messed up," Ambrielle said.

"Okay, don't worry about the backspin," Gavian said. "Just get a good throw off next time."

A player on the other team launched a shot that Fegrin got a hand on but couldn't catch, making the score two–two. He threw another that hit the wall high but died when it hit the ground. It was a low bounce that didn't go far, and Ambrielle got it on the ground.

"It wasn't on the first bounce! Doesn't count!" Canlin shouted.

"Drag! Good catch, though, Ambrielle," said Taragris.

The next throw went past Ambrielle, out of her reach, but Taragris caught it, giving them the ball back. Taragris kept the ball, as it was her turn to throw. She launched the ball into the wall low, causing it to bounce near the wall, thanks to the topspin she put on it. The ball bounced high over the heads of the closer defenders, but one of the tall defenders in the back was barely able to reach it while staying inbounds.

"That was nearly a perfect throw. If you could do that every time, we would be unbeatable," Gavian said.

The other team had the ball again, and one of their players used a sidearm delivery that gave the ball some crazy spin. It hit in front of Gavian, then bounced way off to the side, where he was now out of position to make the catch. The ball then went out of bounds before Fegrin could come up and get an angle on it before it went out, making it six–two.

"Isn't that out of bounds?" Ambrielle asked.

"The first bounce was in bounds, so it counts," Fegrin said.

The other team threw again, and the ball went past Ambrielle before she could get her hands up, making it eight–two.

"I thought you were going to have that. You said you could catch really well," Gavian said.

"This is faster than I thought it was going to be. I'll adjust," she said.

"Keep your hands ready so you can react," Gavian said.

"Okay," she said as the next throw came through between Ambrielle and Gavian. Taragris was able to get over behind them and grab it, tossing it to Fegrin. Fegrin launched the ball hard into the wall for maximum speed. The first line of defenders backed up for the speeding line drive they were expecting, but the backspin killed the momentum, and it bounced upward instead of at them. They were unable to run forward to get to it in time. Eight–four.

His next throw was caught, giving the ball back to Canlin's team. The player threw another rocket into the wall, careering toward Ambrielle, with Fegrin backing her up. She got her hands on it but couldn't grab it, knocking it away from Fegrin and out of bounds. Ten–four.

"Ambrielle . . ." said Gavian. His expression changed when she glared at him with narrowed eyes. "Don't worry, it's your first time playing. Takes some time to get used to the speed."

The next throw also came into Ambrielle's zone but out of her reach, and Fegrin couldn't get to it either. Twelve–four. Fegrin was growing frustrated, as were the rest of the crew. The throw and bounce again came toward Ambrielle. Fegrin called her off and made the catch.

It was Gavian's turn, and he made his throw low into the wall with backspin. The ball got an early bounce with little height, but one of Canlin's crew dove for it and made the catch, getting a huge reaction from everyone watching.

"They're targeting Ambrielle right now, so cheat toward her side," Fegrin whispered.

The next throw came in, and they all moved toward Ambrielle's zone. The ball came through fast, and no one was able to nab it in time. Fourteen–four.

The next one got through as well, as this one went away from Ambrielle just as they were all breaking toward her side. Sixteen–four.

"We're going to lose worse than the other team did," Gavian said.

The throw came in, and Gavian caught it on a low bounce, passing it to Ambrielle for her turn to throw. "Remember, don't worry about the spin. Get a good, hard bounce."

Ambrielle wound up and stepped as she released another slow, arching throw. The ball fluttered with a downward spin toward the wall and then stopped, stuck inside the notch in the wall.

"Notch!" came from the crowd as cheering rose around her.

"Ambrielle!" said Gavian.

Taragris came over to hug her.

"Five points!" said Fegrin as he gave her a pat on the back.

Someone retrieved the ball from the hole and threw it back over to her.

"That wasn't a great throw, but it worked out," said Gavian. The score was now sixteen–nine as Ambrielle wound up again, releasing another slow, arching throw, spinning downward and sticking into the notch again.

There were even more cheers, though this time there was a lot more discontent on the other team.

"Are you kidding me?" said someone as the score went to sixteen–fourteen.

"AM-BRI-ELLE!" shouted Gavian as the other team began to pace, staring down at the rocks in disbelief. Taragris and Fegrin also stared in disbelief.

"We gotta change these rules. This is ridiculous. That should *not* be five points," said a player on the other team.

"Do it again, Ambrielle!" Taragris said.

Ambrielle wound up, keeping her throwing mechanics the same, and launched another slow, spinning throw. The ball hit slightly off the curved edge of the hole, taking an odd bounce and landing out of bounds.

The throw from the other team was caught by Gavian, and it was Taragris's turn to throw. Her throw was caught, though, turning it back over to the other side. The next throw came in near the corner that neither Gavian nor Fegrin could reach, to make it eighteen–fourteen.

"We can't let another one through," Gavian said.

"Next point for them wins," said Taragris.

The player launched a quick, hard throw into the wall that bounced hard at the line. Ambrielle reached as far as she could for it and snagged it as she fell onto the dirt. Her team cheered, and Gavian came over to help her up. All the sounds in the cavern muted as his hand touched hers while he gently pulled her back onto her feet. She used his shoulder to steady herself as her eyes went up to him.

"Good catch!" he said with a big smile on his face.

"Thanks," she responded, her face getting warm and red as she smiled back.

Being close to him was like having an electric current running through her, and she wondered if he felt the same thing.

"Let's get back into position," Fegrin said, and Ambrielle became aware of her surroundings again.

Taragris tossed the ball over to Fegrin for his turn. He wound up and fired a side-spinning throw that changed course on the hop and flew out of the reach of the other team's back row. It was now eighteen-sixteen.

Fegrin's next throw was caught, giving the other team the ball. It was Canlin's turn. He launched a throw into the wall, and the ball headed toward the middle of the court. They all eased toward the middle, and the ball landed on a small rock, causing it to bounce back toward the wall again, making it impossible to catch.

The other team cheered as the score reached twenty-sixteen, making them the winners.

"Aw, who put that rock on the court? That doesn't count!" Fegrin said.

"It counts. There's no rule saying it can't hit a rock," said Canlin.

"That's pure luck. There's no skill in that," Taragris added.

"Doesn't matter. We win!" said one of the other team's members.

"You need to sweep the court off better next time. We would have beat them easily if not for that," said Fegrin.

"You did great," Gavian said to Ambrielle. He smiled as though the loss didn't bother him at all.

"I messed up a bit at first."

"That's fine. It was your first time playing, and you more than made up for it."

After the commotion had died down, the crew went back to the dining hall for water. When Gavian returned to hand Ambrielle a cup, he told her that they should probably get some sleep soon.

"They're asking you and me to go out during the day tomorrow before sunset. They want us to check on the vecilators," Gavian said.

"Vecilators? Okay," she replied.

"Yeah, I'll show you tomorrow," he said. "Meet me here in the dining hall as soon as you wake up."

"How will I know what time it is?" she asked.

"The vents in the grottos . . . If the shape on the floor is round, it is noon. When the shape is a crescent going this way," he said, drawing it on the floor, "that means it's afternoon before sunset."

"Okay, got it."

"All right, I'll see you then."

"Okay, well . . . good night," she said, hoping that he would hold her hand again. She almost asked him to show her again how to grip the flakball, but that was too obvious.

"Yeah, it has been a good night."

They both stood there for a moment, as if waiting for something to happen. After a long, awkward moment, he reached over and rested his hand on her shoulder.

"Sleep well," he said.

Once he initiated it, she was comfortable putting her arms around him and giving a hug. He returned it, moving his hand from her shoulder to wrap it around her. The corners of her mouth felt stretched, as if she had not smiled so much or this wide in a long time. They held the embrace, and Ambrielle wondered how long was appropriate for a hug. She wanted this to last forever but did not want it to be awkward to him.

Gavian began to release, and she took the cue to let go of him as well.

"See you tomorrow," she said, trying to contain what must surely be a stupid-looking grin on her face.

CHAPTER 18

AVIAN HANDED AMBRIELLE a spear as they prepared to leave the caverns.

"Is this another one of your inventions?" she asked, trying to stifle a giggle.

"Shut up," he said, laughing, making Ambrielle laugh even more. He handed her a satchel like the one he was wearing over his shoulder.

They emerged from the cave entrance, the light blinding them as they climbed the steps that circled the inside of the chasm. The roaring of waterfalls, the smell of wet stone, and the sweet sounds of the birds greeted them. As interesting as parts of the caverns were, there was nothing quite like the plethora of sensations of the outdoors.

As her eyes began to adjust to the light, the large tree atop the stone pillar in the middle of the chasm came into focus.

"It's amazing how that tree is still there, with the falls and this canyon all around it," Ambrielle said.

"That's Tirobis, one of the oldest trees in Lon Kavekkia," said Gavian.

"Tirobis . . ." Ambrielle said. "I read a Darterran book about that tree. I didn't know it was still around."

"I think nearly all of the Darterrans' stories are about that tree," said Gavian.

"What about the story of the dark spirit?"

"I had not heard that one until Fegrin mentioned it the other night."

"You said that you remembered the Whisperers too . . ."

"Yes, but not much."

"Do you think they are the same as the dark spirit?"

"Why would you think that?"

"I saw some of the Whisperers in the desert. They look like shadows, like black, fiery ghosts. Dark spirit seems appropriate."

"I wish I could remember something that would help you. I remember faces of people I guess I knew before, but . . . it's frustrating. I gave up trying to remember anything before I got here."

"Sorry, I'm just trying to figure all this out. We need to find a way back to Earth eventually. Maybe once you get back, you will remember."

Reaching the top of the steps, they walked along the path around Mekkinspire, then headed toward the forest.

"Do we really have to go into the forest?" Ambrielle said. "Every time I do, I get attacked."

"Don't worry, I've walked this path for over a cycle," said Gavian. "There's no predator territory along here."

"Right . . . "Ambrielle said. "I've heard *that* before."

They walked along the edge of the forest, Ambrielle's senses keen to any sound or movement.

"This is where I was walking when I first saw you that day," Gavian said.

"Oh yes, it is. Is this what you were doing that day?"

"Yeah, the Darterrans don't like to come out here in the light. So I always have to go check on these."

Gavian entered the woods, and Ambrielle hesitantly followed. The crunching of dead leaves sounded under their feet as they zigzagged between trees and brush.

As they traveled farther into the forest, they came under the shadows of the great balcain trees. This part of the forest was thick with underbrush. The ground was covered with huge dried balcain leaves. Among the leaves, there was moss-covered stone, and the air smelled musty and old. As they moved farther, there were large webbings covering the path between the trees.

"Wait . . . let's go back!" said Ambrielle.

"What? Why?" Gavian said.

"I can't deal with huge spiders!"

"What are you talking about?"

"Those big spiderwebs."

"I don't know what that is, but those are vines."

He walked over and cut through some of them with his staff blade.

"How are you from Earth but don't remember spiders?" Ambrielle said.

"I don't know," Gavian said. "I don't remember Earth that well."

"Well, I don't remember everything either," said Ambrielle, "but I remember spiders, because they are the worst things in the world."

"Okay, so what's a spider?" Gavian asked.

"Creepy, eight-legged, little crawly things," she said. "They have a bunch of eyes too."

"What do they do that's so terrible?" asked Gavian.

"Exist," Ambrielle stated.

"Yeah, I don't really get it," Gavian said. "There's lots of crazy stuff like that."

"Don't tell me you are one of those guys that has a pet tarantula," Ambrielle said half-jokingly. "Because if you are, we are going to have to stop being friends."

Gavian laughed. "I have no idea what you are talking about."

Moving through the tangled maze of the forest, they came to the end of the shadow of one of the balcain trees. There was a small clearing ahead between two of the huge trees, and sunlight beamed through, bathing the glade in its golden-blue light. Gavian walked over and knelt near two glowing disks on the ground.

"These are the vecilators. They seem to be working fine," said Gavian. "It looks like they are at full charge, so we can go ahead and take them back."

The glowing crystalline disks were about the size of a hubcap, with thin metal strands wrapped around it. They each had four holes in them around the outside edge.

"What do they do?" Ambrielle asked.

"They absorb sunlight and store the energy for a while," Gavian said.

He removed his satchel, taking two of the same disks out and putting one of the charged disks inside. He then set each of the two uncharged disks onto the sunny grass.

"I'll take one of them," he said. "You take the other. It's not good for them to be touching each other; they could overheat."

"What happens if they overheat?"

Gavian laughed. "You never accept what someone tells you. You always have to know the reason."

"Well, what happens?"

"They can explode," he said, "but don't worry about it. That never happens."

"Oh yeah, I'll just carry this bomb around, no big deal."

"You can carry it in your hands if you prefer, but they get pretty heavy."

"Okay, fine, but if I see a spider or anything creepy in these woods, you have to deal with it."

They headed back the way they came, and the purple light of the setting sun peeked through the mass of trees ahead.

"Why do they put these all the way out here, if they need sunlight?" Ambrielle asked.

"To keep them hidden. They don't want the Kavekkians getting them."

"I guess that *is* a good hiding place. The Kavekkians don't go this deep in the forest."

They walked near enough to the edge of the forest that they could see the Kavekkian protector guarding the apraeda trees. Remaining in the cover of the forest, they avoided the protector as much as possible. Although their footprints had likely told of their presence, the protector stayed at his post.

Ambrielle followed Gavian through a corridor to the left, which angled its way into another chamber that she hadn't visited before. There were cubbyholes all over the walls, with white, blue, and some yellow crystals in them. Gavian handed his satchel over to one of the Darterrans in the room, and Ambrielle followed suit. The vecilators were taken out and placed separately into storage slots in the wall.

They walked back into the dining hall as they were serving more mushy fruit and escradas. Ambrielle and Gavian sat down with the crew as Darterrans came by and congratulated her for hitting two notches in a row in the game of flakball the night before. After all the patting on her shoulders and head, her hair styler came loose, and her hair fell flat, messily covering her face.

She put the styler back in her hair and whispered, "Style on, style four," and the static charge went through her hair as it fell back into place.

"Wait, what was that?" Gavian asked.

"It's . . . nothing," Ambrielle said.

"What's style four?" Taragris asked.

"It's just something I say sometimes," Ambrielle said.

"Is there a style five?" Gavian asked.

The ends of Ambrielle's hair became wavier with the style change command for style five.

"How is that happening?" Taragris asked.

"Style fourteen," said Gavian.

The charge went through Ambrielle's hair again, changing her hair into tight curls all over.

Gavian and Taragris laughed. "This is amazing!" he said. "But I don't think that's your look."

"Style ten," Taragris said.

Ambrielle's hair changed to large, loose curls.

"That's kinda nice," said Taragris.

"Guys . . . stop," Ambrielle said.

"Style twenty-one," said Gavian, and Ambrielle's hair spiked up all over.

Now Taragris and Gavian were really laughing.

"Style four, and do not change," Ambrielle said.

"No, change to style twenty-two," said Gavian.

Ambrielle's hair changed to a style that was spiked down the middle, and Taragris and Gavian started laughing again. Even Fegrin began to laugh now.

"Stop!" Ambrielle said.

"But we have to see all the styles first," Gavian said.

Ambrielle took the styler off, and her hair fell back down again. "Styler secure." It locked back onto her silbrace.

"I can't have anything nice with you two around," Ambrielle said.

"Sorry, Ambrielle," said Taragris. "We thought it was fascinating and fun."

Ambrielle didn't say anything as the servers placed the bowls of fruit mash in front of them.

"Since you are a Darterran now, I need to give you a braid like mine. You may have noticed that all the females put our patch of hair on the right side in a braid," said Taragris.

"Yeah, we didn't mean to annoy you, Ambrielle. We got a little carried away," Gavian said.

"Do you mind if I come over there and braid the right side of your hair?" Taragris asked.

"You're not going to eat?" Ambrielle asked.

"I'll wait until they bring the escradas out," Taragris said.

"Okay, I guess it's fine," Ambrielle said.

Taragris walked over behind Ambrielle and took some of her hair in her hands, smoothing the strands out.

"You have so many long hairs. They're lovely," said Taragris.

"Thanks," Ambrielle said.

"We have smaller braids, so I'll take a little of the hair on this side, to be more like a Darterran," said Taragris.

Taragris took a handful of hair and started the braid near the top of Ambrielle's ear. Blinking as another blue light flashed before her, Ambrielle had another memory. Her friend Kaitlyn had used to like to braid her hair while she sat behind her in algebra. It was somehow calming and got her to focus on the teacher instead of daydreaming. Ambrielle enjoyed mathematics, but watching someone draw Xs and Ys on the chalkboard for an hour wasn't interesting enough to hold her attention.

Kaitlyn was the math nerd, and Ambrielle found listening to her talk about what algebra is used for in the real world made it far more interesting than the teacher did. Like her other friends, she had changed. Kaitlyn had stopped braiding her hair during class and didn't offer to help her with homework either. Ambrielle wondered what she had done that was so wrong, that all her friends would turn away from her.

When Taragris had finished, the braid came down to Ambrielle's chin, lying over the rest of her long hair.

"There, now you are one of us," Taragris said.

Ambrielle smiled. "Thank you."

"That looks really good," Gavian said.

The sound of many footsteps came down one of the halls, and Darterrans began to stop what they were doing and stand up. Several Darterran soldiers with metal-and-balcain armor entered the room. They carried staves with white crystal points on the end, and Medigrin followed them. Gavian, Taragris, and everyone else at the table stood up. Ambrielle imitated their actions and stood up too.

"You have all been working hard in the mines, gathering crystals for our cause. It is time now to enter the next phase of our work," Medigrin said as he propped one leg up on a nearby formation of rock protruding from the floor.

"Tomorrow we will be gathering before sunset and going to the foot of Mekkinspire, where the stairs once stood. There we will use the lykris to carve out new steps, and we will take back our part of the mountain."

Many cheered. Ambrielle turned to Gavian, and he met her gaze with a look of uncertainty.

"It has come to my attention that a new one among us has been talking about the decency of many Kavekkians and how they have largely preserved our city there and our dens. I don't have a way of knowing whether that is true or false, but it seems to be enough to convince some of you that it is worth giving them a chance to allow us to occupy our part of the mountain peacefully," Medigrin said.

A warm flush spread across Ambrielle, as she knew he was referring to her, unsure of what that would mean.

"Apparently, Darterrans have been talking about this, and it has spread around enough that I must address it and hear it from the source," said Medigrin.

Ambrielle began fidgeting in her seat. She tried reminding herself of all the conflicts she had been in and that she could handle this. It wasn't helping, though.

"Where is the human girl?" asked Medigrin.

Many began pointing toward where Ambrielle was standing.

Medigrin walked over, stroking the long hair on his chin with his gold claw.

"Tell us why you believe we should give these betrayers a chance, the murderers of my father. Why do we owe them anything?" he said.

Ambrielle cleared her throat, her mind scrambling for something to say.

"Well . . ." She cleared her throat again. "It's like the story of Nylin."

The murmuring of the crowd filled the chamber.

"He recognized that every part of this world is important, that we all have a purpose. The trees, the stone, the water, Darterrans, even the Kavekkians . . . I believe the story is telling us that if we don't recognize that we are all necessary for making this world work, we are doomed to break it." She rubbed her new braid in between her fingers. "If the Kavekkians are cursed for what they did to the Darterrans, we should not make the same mistake and join them in their fate."

The murmurs grew louder.

"We should give them one chance to start making it right," someone said. "I'm not willing to let it all go, but it could be a start we could build on."

"That takes away our element of surprise," said another. "If we go out there and try to talk to them after all this time, they are going to be suspicious for a while."

"We can't risk undoing Nylin's bargain," another said. "Let's put it on them to make that choice."

After many in the crowd had spoken, it was clear that most of them wanted to give the Kavekkians a chance to allow the Darterrans to come back to the mountain peacefully.

"As much as I don't want to," Medigrin said, "you have spoken. I will give them that last chance. Tomorrow at sunset, we will all go to the base of the mountain and call to them. We will bring the lykris as planned, but I will only offer it back to them if they allow us to move back to Mekkinspire. It will be low light, so we won't have to fear them using their lykris against us, and they won't have to fear ours."

"As some of you know," said Medigrin, moving his propped foot back to the floor, "there is an event tomorrow night that only occurs every eighty-seven cycles, The Night of Absence. Both moons will be in their dark phase on the same night, so there will be complete darkness. The Kavekkians once feared this night, but it has always been a celebration for our kind. Eventually, they adopted some of our celebration, no longer viewing it as the cursed night that they had in the past. It was one of the ways that our cultures came together. It would be a fitting night for us to settle our differences."

After they had all sat back in their seats, Ambrielle couldn't help her heart bursting with pride for playing a part in this. She hoped the Kavekkians would agree to this deal. It was like it was meant to be. Perhaps this was the reason she was brought to this world in the first place, to be an outside mediator and bring these two sides together again.

Medigrin spoke to Ambrielle again. "If I am going to risk my pack for this, I need to ensure there are no surprises. When I call out to the Kavekkians, what would be the best side of the mountain to be on? Where is their city?"

"The city is overlooking the field in front of the forest," Ambrielle said. "I think it is a little more than halfway up the mountain."

"I've heard there is a large cavern inside the mountain. Have you seen it?" Medigrin asked.

"Yes, the main path goes through there."

"What part of the mountain?"

"It's below the city, where the waterfalls come from."

"There are no secret passageways from the cave, are there? Other ways to come down from the mountain and attack us?"

"No, they always climb down the mountain."

"There is one who walks with a warghol," Medigrin said. "We have seen her leave with a group, up the river."

"Maetha, she goes to the new camp for food, since you . . . since all the fruit was taken," Ambrielle said.

"So, she should be up the river?" said Medigrin. "That beast could pose a threat and ruin any chance of peace."

"Yes, she should be," Ambrielle said, unsure whether it was true.

Maetha had been confined to her home when the Kavekkians had accused Ambrielle of being a spy, but that could have changed by now. She knew that Maetha wouldn't attack the Darterrans while they were trying to negotiate for peace, so it was largely irrelevant.

"Good, that will help a lot," Medigrin said. "Thank you, Ambrielle."

After he walked away, with his troops behind him, Ambrielle and the rest of the crew finished eating and started clearing their bowls from the table. Ambrielle marched with them back into the mines and grabbed one of the carts from Gavian. As they were hauling loads into the sifting chamber, they kept passing Darterrans carrying metal parts through the mines.

They were parts of the lykris. It could be a good move to disassemble it when they offered it to the Kavekkians. Perhaps it would help keep the level of threat down a bit.

Later during the night, one of the armored troops visited with Fegrin for a while and then let him get back to work.

"What was that about?" Gavian asked Fegrin.

"Our orders," said Fegrin. "They want our crew positioned behind the front line of the formation, behind the soldiers."

"Why there?" Eregrin asked.

"He doesn't want us on the back end, because most of their protectors are guarding the fruit trees, behind us. If the Kavekkians attack, those protectors will be coming from behind."

"They're not going to attack," Ambrielle said.

"If they do, we will have to be ready to support the front line. We'll have to fight them if necessary. Are you going to be willing to do that?" Fegrin asked.

"If they actually attack us while we are asking for peace, then yes, I will help defend us," said Ambrielle.

"Do you know how to fight?" Gavian asked.

"Well," said Ambrielle, "I haven't had a class, if that's what you mean."

"I can show you," Gavian said. "I haven't used a staff a lot, but I do remember using a sword."

"A sword?" Ambrielle said. "A plastic sword, maybe."

Gavian laughed. "I don't know what that is, but it sounds like you are making fun of me."

"No," Ambrielle said, smiling. "I'm picturing mighty Gavian with his pet tarantula and his plastic knight armor and sword."

"I'm hurt without even knowing what you are talking about," Gavian said in a facetious tone. "Fortunately, whenever I need to feel better, there's one memory that always helps."

"Oh? What's that?" Ambrielle asked.

"Style twenty-two," said Gavian, laughing as Ambrielle rolled her eyes, smirking at him.

Taragris chuckled from one of the mineshafts.

After the rest of the work shift was over, Ambrielle and Gavian made their way out of the caves to enjoy the late-night air. The moons had risen over the horizon, both thin crescents, positioned close together, with Miraeda, the smaller moon, partially obscured by the dark side of Pathea. The soft roar of the waterfalls and the cool breeze were a welcome respite from the work in the caverns, but it wasn't enough to quiet the looming tension in her mind about the coming events.

It was one of the rare chances they had to be alone together. She wondered if he might take the opportunity to kiss her. The thought made her excited and nervous. She tried to keep from shivering as goose bumps rose on her arms.

Even though tomorrow night could be exactly what she and many Darterrans and Kavekkians had been hoping for, there were risks. What if the Kavekkians refused their offer—what would happen then? Would the Darterrans make a new plan? She reminded herself of the spring and how any potential change for the better involved the risk of making things worse.

It was something that needed to happen. All that it would take was for both sides to acknowledge that they could no longer give credence to the actions of their leaders in the past. The current generations could forge their own bonds based on their own actions in the present.

An odd call sounded out in the dark, surprising her. An eerie, deep warbling sound of a night bird.

"Are you worried at all? About tomorrow night?" she asked.

"A little, but I think it will be fine," he said, placing his hand on her shoulder. "Stay close. I won't let anything happen to you."

"I will so I can make sure you don't do anything stupid," she said as she turned around, grinning at him.

"When have I ever done anything stupid?" He laughed.

"I don't know, but I'm going to make sure you don't start. When this is over, will you come to the desert world with me so that we can try to find a way home?"

"The thought of traveling to another world scares me a bit, but if you are going, then I will too."

He gently held both of her shoulders, nudging her to turn to face him. Her nerves could barely take this. She started shivering again, though it wasn't cold. She hoped that he didn't notice.

As she turned around, she leaned her head back, expecting him to lean in and kiss her.

Nothing was happening. Perhaps she was wrong; maybe it was better that he didn't kiss her. Her nerves were going crazy enough already. The moment lingered awkwardly, with their faces this close together. Ambrielle shyly peered up into his eyes, and he was looking into hers.

He quickly moved his eyes away and then slowly came back to hers again. Before realizing what she was doing, she leaned forward and kissed him. Mostly missing his mouth, she kissed his upper lip and nose. Her nervousness changed to embarrassment as she pulled away. When she glanced back at him, his eyes were wide with surprise. Before she could say anything, he leaned in and kissed her back. Unlike her, he hit the mark. As their lips met, the world around them melted away. Ambrielle's feet were numb to the ground underneath her.

Droplets of water danced across her face as another breeze passed by. When the world reappeared around them, it had changed. Kissing him by the misty waterfall in the gleaming moonlight was so surreal, she was certain they had fallen into a dream. The most beautiful dream she could imagine. The Darterrans, Kavekkians, the whispering shadows, The Hollow, trying to find a way home, none of that mattered right now.

He reached for her hand as they stood watching the waterfall. A symphony of emotions played in her head. It was as though they had unleashed a power that could change the universe. Even as that familiar emptiness in her heart reminded her of its presence, this newfound magic was enough to dispel it, at least for now.

CHAPTER 19

AMBRIELLE WOKE TO the sound of commotion coming through the halls. Quickly remembering what night this was, she grew anxious. It was earlier than they normally woke, with sunlight still coming through the vents onto the floor. After she bathed in the female chamber pools, they all moved into the dining hall and had their meals. They served a smaller portion today than usual, but it was enough to make her stomach content.

After the meal, they all marched through the halls. They were grouped into their crews, and their crews became parts of a unit. Gavian, Ambrielle, Taragris, Fegrin, Eregrin, and Segrit filed in with the second unit. They followed the first, which comprised Medigrin's soldiers and a few others. It was quite a sight as they all walked up the steps around the walls of the canyon. She turned to get a look at all the Darterrans behind them, some beginning to step out of the caves.

The sunlight was too much for the Darterrans, but they could get around well enough to walk where they needed to go. The soldiers ahead of them were taking position on the front lines of the grassy field facing the forest side of the mountain. Ambrielle and the rest of Fegrin's crew moved in behind them. Other units continued to move in as they gathered in formation. Finally, Medigrin entered the field and walked toward the front line, talking to his soldiers.

The soldiers moved back and forth, working on something. There were no soldiers guarding the rear formation, which was odd, since they were concerned about the protectors that guarded the trees being behind them.

"Do you think they've noticed us yet?" Gavian asked.

"I don't know. It's awfully quiet," said Ambrielle.

Some of the soldiers followed Medigrin as he walked off from the line. The lykris was brought to the front, fully assembled. Ambrielle began to worry that Medigrin was not going to stay true to his word. She wasn't sure what she was going to do if they used the lykris to reach the mountain.

"I thought they took it apart," Ambrielle said.

"They may have taken it apart to carry it up the stairs in the canyon," Gavian said.

"I was hoping they would leave it like that. It would be less threatening," Ambrielle said.

"Yeah, but they probably don't want to offer it back to the Kavekkians in pieces," said Taragris.

"I guess you're right," Ambrielle said. "They can't use it once the sun goes down anyway."

Ambrielle scanned the field as all the Darterrans lined up behind them. It was amazing to be part of something like this. It had an epic feeling to it, but it also made her nervous. If things went badly, she would be caught in the middle of a war. The sun was rapidly setting behind the trees. She wished she could slow it down a little as she grew more apprehensive. She was never much for confrontation. Even a confrontation between other people made her want to leave.

As the sun set and the light faded, Ambrielle anxiously glanced at Gavian, then Taragris and Fegrin and back to the lykris, then toward the forest. A group of soldiers walked up from the rear to where Medigrin was standing. Medigrin and the soldiers moved over to join the rest of them on the front.

"Everything is good. They've been taken care of," said one of the soldiers.

Ambrielle's restlessness grew with all the waiting. They were losing the last bit of light, as the sun had now set and dusk settled over Lon Kavekkia. She played with her necklace as her hands began to shake in anticipation, and then a voice called out.

"Why have you assembled out here under the mountain? I see that you have brought the lykris with you, and the human spy as well. Come to display the spoils of your treachery?" said the voice, amplified by something that he was holding as he stood high above on one of the terraces.

It was the vaesar.

Medigrin walked out from the group holding some sort of horn as he called back. "We all know what was truly stolen—our homes, in some cases our lives."

The Darterran soldiers placed their crystal-tipped staves into the sockets of one of the glowing vecilators sitting on the ground. Another group of soldiers carried a second vecilator, which was inserted into the lykris. She noticed there were two more vecilators up at the front that soldiers were inserting their staves into.

As it grew darker, some of the soldiers lit torches and stuck them into the ground on the left and right of the assembled lines of the pack.

"We can go back and forth all night, but after what happened with the lykris, we could no longer trust you," said the vaesar.

"You have the events wrong, as always. You speak of trust. How could we trust you after the murder of my father?" Medigrin said.

With no light from the moons, the world was now covered in complete darkness. Nothing but black, except the dancing light on Medigrin from a torch at the left side of the formation. This wasn't going the way Ambrielle had hoped. Medigrin was too hung up on avenging his father to make peace with the Kavekkians.

"Your father tried to kill the former vaesar. They fought, and your father was thrown from the mountain in the process," said the vaesar.

The unit lines began moving toward their right, lightly pushing on Fegrin, Taragris, then Gavian, and then Ambrielle. She started walking with the group, careful not to trip on anything in the dark. The blunt sounds of the large crowd stomping on grass and dirt made it harder to hear the vaesar. Perhaps it was necessary for them to air these grievances to get past them and start a negotiation.

"My father wouldn't have lost a real fight against your pathetic vaesar," Medigrin growled.

The glow from the vecilators cast on some of the soldiers as they removed their staves from the disks. The crystal tips of the staves now shone brightly. One of the vecilators was moving toward the right as well. It was the one attached to the lykris.

"Is this what you have come for? To fight old arguments?" asked the vaesar.

The formation stopped moving once they had all passed the torches on the ground. Only the soldiers and the first unit remained inside them. Ambrielle was wondering why they'd moved out. She wondered if the Kavekkians on the mountain knew they had shifted position in the darkness. They might believe they were all still in between the torches, where they had seen them with the last glimpse of sunlight.

"No . . . I have come to end them," Medigrin said.

"How do you propose we do that?" said the vaesar.

"By doing the same thing you did to us, removing you from the mountain!" Medigrin raised his hand.

The ground lit up as a powerful beam of light sliced through the darkness. The lykris sent a solid beam of energy up into the mountain, drawing power from the energy stored in the vecilator. The figure of the vaesar staggered back as the terrace beneath him began to crumble. The sheer power of the lykris was shocking, far stronger than the reflected beams of the crystals in the city.

Several Kavekkians climbed down the side of the mountain in the reflected glow of the lykris beam. The Darterran soldiers pointed their staves, firing bursts of energy from the crystals that were attached to them. Some Kavekkians descending the mountain were hit by the blasts, while others were knocked from the mountain as the blasts loosened stones. A few made it to the ground as they charged toward the lykris.

Ambrielle stood there, stunned amid the chaos.

The Darterran soldiers stabbed their crystal spears back into the vecilators nearby, recharging them with new energy and causing the crystal to shine again. Three Kavekkians running toward the lykris were gunned down by energy blasts from the soldiers. Crystal spears were placed back into the vecilators again, recharging after each burst they fired.

The lykris stopped firing, and the area fell dark once again. A few moments later, the blinding energy returned, this time aimed at the city plateau. The stone underneath the city began to melt and crumble as the energy tore into it. Ambrielle didn't want to take sides in this, but she couldn't stand by while Medigrin destroyed Mekkinspire and killed innocent Kavekkians.

"No!" cried Ambrielle as she ran full speed toward the lykris.

Gavian ran after her, as did Taragris and Fegrin. Some of the soldiers turned to block her from reaching the lykris. She raised her spear as a soldier rushed forward to stop her. The soldier swung his staff and broke the spear she was holding, sending Ambrielle tumbling to the ground with the back of his fist.

"Come no closer, or we'll be forced to kill you!" the soldier said as a few of them lined up beside him.

A group of Kavekkians with torches strapped to their backs had climbed down another part of the mountain, unseen. They charged toward the lykris. Many of the soldiers directed their attention toward the oncoming Kavekkian rush, while others formed a circle around the lykris, keeping their attention on Ambrielle and Gavian. Many Kavekkians were mowed down by the range advantage the Darterran soldiers had. The darkness also favored the Darterrans.

After having moved from the bracket of torches on the ground, the remainder of the Darterran units remained hidden in the dark. The order was given for them to flank the Kavekkian assault as they began to get closer to the lykris. Some of the Darterran units began their attack, but many of them did not. Some of them threw down their spears and stood back, not wanting any part of this, while there were a few that ran to where Fegrin's crew were facing off with the soldiers.

"Medigrin, you lying milgum! It wasn't supposed to be like this!" Fegrin said.

"Shut down the lykris!" shouted Gavian.

The air was filled with bursts of light, shouts, and screams as a new squad of Kavekkians led by Pathello stormed into the Darterran formations that were trying to outflank the main Kavekkian assault. Pathello's forces cut a path through the formation, effectively surrounding part of the Darterrans' flanking attack.

With the chaos of the battle all around her, Ambrielle tried to focus.

She activated the laser cutter in her silbrace, and a violet beam shot out from it as she pointed it past the wall of Darterran soldiers, toward the lykris. The laser couldn't reach it from this distance. The nearby soldiers came for Ambrielle, and she turned the laser on them. She hit two of them before a volley of light bursts came toward them.

They all scattered in different directions as the energy blasts hit the ground around them, starting small fires in the grass. Taragris was hit by an energy blast and fell in front of Fegrin. Ambrielle and Gavian found a group of stones to use for cover, when they saw Fegrin in the distance kneeling to check on Taragris, who was on the ground.

"Taragris!" Gavian yelled.

"Protect the lykris!" Medigrin said. "Kill anyone that gets close."

Another squad of Kavekkians had circled around the lykris and began attacking from another side as Raegus led the charge. They separated their staves, throwing the spear end toward the wall of soldiers protecting the lykris.

Fegrin growled at Medigrin, grabbing a glowing crystal staff from one of the fallen soldiers. He aimed at Medigrin as the soldiers fired another volley toward him. As their blasts missed him, Fegrin fired at the vecilator nearby, causing it to explode. The blast took out two of the Darterran soldiers. Fegrin dashed toward Medigrin and the other soldiers in the area. With no vecilator nearby to charge their crystals, they couldn't stop him in time.

Fegrin bored into Medigrin before he even saw him coming, clawing at his face. Suddenly, a large piece of rock from the mountain broke loose, causing a large chunk of the city plateau to fall in the avalanche.

Ambrielle and Gavian were pinned down behind the stones as the soldiers continued blasting the area with periodic light bursts.

"There was something about the old lykris not having vents . . ." Ambrielle said.

Raegus had lost half of his forces, being outgunned by the energy blasts from the soldiers. Pathello's squad was now mixed up in a melee battle, squeezed between the frontal assault and the flanking Darterran formations. The Kavekkians were winning the push on the front, but progress was slow.

"I wish I had something that could spark electricity. I don't guess you have anything?" Ambrielle asked.

"Uh, no . . . I don't think so," Gavian said.

As the battle ensued from two opposite fronts, the lykris continued blasting into the mountain under the city, sending more chunks of the city street plummeting down as molten mekkadium oozed through the cracks in the mountainside.

"Oh, wait a minute . . ." said Ambrielle, reaching to her silbrace. "Styler, detach."

She grabbed the styler and threw it in an arc over the soldiers. It landed right on top of the lykris, then bounced off it onto the ground.

"You hit it, at least," said Gavian.

"Styler, secure!" shouted Ambrielle.

The hair styler launched toward the lykris and stuck to it. Clouds of tiny rocks and metallic debris were drawn around the styler, adding to what was already attracted to the lykris's electromagnetic field.

"Style twenty-two!" said Ambrielle. From experience she knew it was a style that used a larger amount of electricity.

The static charge of the styler sparked and reacted with the dust. The lykris sparked furiously, and its beam went out. With the lykris disabled, darkness fell over the field again. The only light left was from the many small fires in the grass. Gavian and Ambrielle moved from their cover of stones as the Kavekkian attack drew nearer.

Mekkinspire was safe from the lykris's destruction. But with no need to protect the lykris, the Darterran soldiers changed their strategy. Some left their posts to ensnare Raegus's squad. A few lykris operators ran to it, trying to clean out the dust and get it functioning again.

Some of the Darterran soldiers ran by them in the darkness as they moved to outflank Raegus. They didn't have their spears charged and glowing, obviously intending to use the shadows to ambush them. Ambrielle turned on her silbrace light and shone it on the Darterran soldiers as the Kavekkians turned to fight off the attack. She had another idea, as she remembered Avo'Doria using her silbrace to send green lights to mark targets for the drones to scan or shoot. As she imagined it, the green lights launched out of the sides of her silbrace onto the battlefield. There were no drones here, but her intent was to illuminate the battlefield for the Kavekkians.

Raegus grabbed the spear of a Darterran solider, stabbing him with it. He leapt in the air to land on another, turned, and ducked the swing of another attack, slicing its source as he came up.

"Ambrielle!" he said. "You saved us!"

A group of Darterrans rushed toward Ambrielle to prevent her from shining her light on their positions. Gavian moved in front of her, trying to fight them off to keep them at bay. He was doing surprisingly well, parrying their attacks and pushing them back.

The ranged Darterran soldiers began firing beams at Ambrielle as she continued shining light on them. Raegus rushed their position but was only able to take one of them down before being hit by a barrage of energy. Gavian fought off a group of Darterrans trying to stab at Ambrielle with their spears. Ambrielle was able to use her laser and take out a few of the Darterrans that closed in from behind.

Three soldiers came over with charged crystal weapons aimed at Ambrielle. They turned as a growling roar signaled the approach of a newcomer. It was followed by the sound of swift wind launching past Ambrielle and Gavian into the three Darterrans. There was a large commotion among the group of soldiers, as many of them were now preoccupied with Blaez. Realizing that Ambrielle was safe for the time being, Gavian seized the opportunity to take one of their nearby vecilators. When the soldiers returned to recharge their crystals to deal with Blaez, they found nothing there. Ambrielle realized what Gavian was doing and ran toward another vecilator, grabbing it from its position on the ground.

Darterran operators continued to work on the lykris to get it firing again. With the Darterrans having ambushed the Kavekkian squads in the dark, the numbers were turned in the Darterrans' favor. Gavian ran toward the lykris, carrying the vecilator with him. As soldiers began closing in on him, Ambrielle was able to hit one with her laser as she ran after the group.

"Silbrace needs recharging. Power at fifteen percent," said a voice from Ambrielle's wrist.

The numbers of Pathello's squad were dwindling as they were pressed together into a fight on both sides. Energy blasts rained down on them.

Many Darterran and Kavekkian bodies lay motionless nearby from where the frontal assault had begun. That group had become scattered after the lykris went down and the Darterrans broke their circle around it to ambush the Kavekkians' attack.

With his vecilator in hand, Gavian ran toward the lykris operators. They jumped down to block him. Before they could do anything, he tossed the vecilator he was carrying onto the one that was powering the lykris. Gavian turned to run as both vecilators exploded, which sent parts of the lykris flying and threw Gavian onto the field. The explosion took out the operators and a few soldiers.

Ambrielle ran over to him. There were growing spots of blood coming through his shirt.

"Gavian!" she said, shaking him.

He groaned. "I'm okay."

"You don't look okay to me."

The fire from the damaged lykris lit up the area, adding light for the Kavekkians as they fought against the Darterrans. Medigrin had his claws around Fegrin's throat. He had Fegrin pinned to the ground as the battle ensued around them. Ambrielle knelt beside Gavian, exhausted and unable to help Fegrin.

As Medigrin was about to finish him off, a whooshing sound went by, and before he could turn, his arm was bound in the jaws of a beast. He let go of Fegrin and tried to swipe his other hand at Blaez as he bit down harder on Medigrin's arm.

Maetha walked out of the shadows toward him.

"Order your pack to retreat!" she said.

"No," said Medigrin. "We still hold the advantage. We'll wipe out the remaining Kavekkians on this field, and Mekkinspire will be left unprotected."

"Order the retreat, or I will give my pet a kill command."

Ambrielle almost hoped that Maetha would do it. Medigrin was the cause of all this. He never had any intention of making peace, using the Darterrans for his own personal vendetta. At the same time, she empathized with him. What it must have been like for him as a child to watch his father die. A memory like that can scar your mind forever.

There must have been no one that helped him through that growing up. Things could have been different for him if someone had been there for him. She wondered if everyone had abandoned him as her friends had done to her. Either way, the responsibility for his actions was his to bear. His experiences may have given his hateful thoughts something to focus on, but he was not the only one with tragedies like this.

"If it weren't for a portion of my forces' unwillingness to do their jobs, Mekkinspire would be a pile of rubble right now."

Fegrin's eyes widened as he got up on his feet and rushed in Maetha's direction.

Ambrielle turned her light back on. Maetha drew her spear to defend herself, as Fegrin cut down a Darterran sneaking up behind her.

Maetha nodded at Fegrin and turned her attention back to Medigrin. "Order. The. Retreat." She raised her hand, and Blaez increased the pressure on Medigrin's arm until he finally gave in.

"Retreat! Back to the caves!" he yelled in anguish.

The soldiers and other Darterrans that remained loyal to Medigrin disengaged and began to run back to the caves, calling out his retreat order to everyone. Maetha ordered Blaez to release, and she allowed Medigrin to get up.

"Remember this decision today. I chose to let you live. Take this choice and do something productive with your life. Lead your pack toward harmony with the world around it, or turn it over to someone else."

He gave her one last glare before running off into the night.

Ambrielle surveyed the battlefield. Fegrin lay wounded on the ground. Raegus had a burn blast in his chest. Taragris lay in the grass, motionless, and Gavian bled in front of Ambrielle on the ground. She knew her silbrace might be able to help, but the power was nearly drained. She might not be able to heal them all.

She wasn't sure who needed it the soonest or who was too far gone. She had already made her decision, but she was nauseated by having to make this choice. She pointed her silbrace at Gavian. The beam began to slow and stop the bleeding. Cells around multiple wounds began regenerating as they closed. The beam on the silbrace came to a stop as the power became drained.

The wounds healed around bits of metal shrapnel stuck in Gavian's chest. That might not be a good thing, but at least temporarily it may be all right. She ran over to Taragris and got the beam to stay on for a few seconds before it dissipated, but it was not regenerating cells at all. Her burn marks were not healing. Tears began to blur her eyes as she went to Raegus, trying to get any power she could from the silbrace to his awful wound. It began to regenerate tissue, but the power quickly died.

"We were wrong about you," Raegus told her.

Ambrielle continued trying to start the silbrace, whacking it with her other hand, but the power was all gone now.

"We'll try to help him, but it doesn't look good," said a familiar voice behind Ambrielle.

"Your human friend has internal injuries," Maetha said as Ambrielle went back to Gavian. He groaned from the pain.

"Unless that device of yours can pull shrapnel out of him properly and mend organs, he's still in trouble. It's going to get infected," Maetha said as she went over to tend to Raegus.

"I know who can help him," Ambrielle said. "Can you walk, Gavian?"

Gavian tried to get up, but the pain was too much. Ambrielle began dragging him toward the lake.

"Ambrielle, where are you taking him?" Pathello said as he walked over.

"I'm trying to get him to the lake," Ambrielle said as Gavian's shirt slipped out of her hand, causing her to fall back.

"After what both of you did, I will help you any way I can," Pathello said. "I'm not sure what good the lake will do, but if that is what you want." He came over and picked Gavian up and carried him, following Ambrielle toward the lake. Once they got to the pool at the base of the waterfall, they stopped.

"Can you throw him into the lake?" Ambrielle asked.

"I already regret doing that once," said Pathello. "Why do you want me to do this?"

"I don't have time to explain. Please?" Ambrielle said.

"If that is what you want."

"I'm not sure if this is going to work or not, but I have to try," Ambrielle said. "I'm hoping that if my clothes and anything I'm wearing is transported, then anything I'm touching will work too."

"Then what will work?"

"Throw him in, and then I'll dive in while he's underwater."

"All right, if that's what you want."

"What are we doing, Ambrielle?" Gavian asked.

"You'll see. Now hold your breath and hold on to me when I jump in," Ambrielle said.

Pathello tossed Gavian out over the water. Ambrielle dove after him, hardening her muscles to sink as fast as possible. As the bubbles subsided, she found Gavian and grabbed hold. Their momentum slowed, and gravity shifted, tumbling them through a liquid space. Then weightlessness came over her, and she could no longer feel Gavian's tunic in her hand.

After regaining sensation, she pulled Gavian through the tunnel. He was fortunately able to help push himself along with his legs on the bottom, and Ambrielle led up to the surface. They both gasped for air, coughing up some water, but it worked. They were in the desert world. She tugged Gavian's shirt to get him out of the water and onto the sand. He had started bleeding again from the shrapnel stuck in him, and blood trailed where she had dragged him onto the sand.

"I'm going to leave you here for a bit. I need to get help," she told him.

"Where are we?" he asked.

"Hang on, I'll be back!" she said as she ran out of the oasis into the Anatharian forest. Some of the trees had grown even larger, while the gray disease had also spread to more of the trees near the trails made by the Nulthereals.

Ambrielle reached the edge and ran out to the desert. Sprinting across the sand, she went down the first dune. She halted immediately as two Nulthereals came toward her from below. She slid down toward them, barely able to get enough footing to stop.

Come down to us. Free yourself from this corporeal reality of suffering, the shadow whispered through her mind. Intense fear gripped her as she turned around and ran back up the hill to find another way around them.

Not now! This is the worst time for this! As she reached the top of the dune, a third Nulthereal appeared. Ambrielle jumped back, but there was a force pulling her toward it. She tried to turn and run, but she could not. She couldn't move at all. She began to scream, hoping someone would come to help her, but no sound came out.

She tried to resist with all her might, her boots dragging across the sand as she was pulled toward it. Ambrielle's heart was racing, faster and faster the closer she was brought to the dark shadow. Her breath left her as she struggled for air and its shadowy form billowed out like a cloak in the wind.

She triggered the silbrace with her mind, causing the laser to ignite, but she could not move the silbrace up to aim at it. The force became too great as she stretched toward it. As her silbrace hand passed into the shadow, the laser hit nothing, only reaching into the endless void as she was consumed.

CHAPTER 20

MBRIELLE'S MATERIAL BODY became evanescent as she fell through the darkness. Her senses faded as her conscious mind raced to catch up with what was happening to her. Her reeling consciousness attempted to fathom the vast sea of emptiness around her.

Was this death? Had she been destroyed by the Nulthereal? Was she going to spend eternity like this? Shouldn't there be a bright light at the end of a tunnel? The thought of this conscious oblivion was unbearable. It was painless, but she was left to reflect on events from when she was alive, with feelings and senses.

As foreign as this was, it had a certain familiarity. She remembered this dark emptiness. That emptiness that followed her wherever she went. She couldn't remember what it was, but she knew the way it felt. It was the feeling that nothing would ever be the same again. That there would never be joy in life again. It was like her heart had collapsed into a black hole and nothing could escape. Whatever it was, she could not bear to face it.

As she began to face her new reality, she thought of so many things in life she had left to do. How could this be her purpose? So many problems left to solve, so many mistakes to rectify, so much left undone.

Ambrielle longed to be able to stretch her legs again, to make contact with the ground, to wiggle her fingers and stroke them through her hair. To pick up an object and manipulate it in her hand. How could there be nothing after death? If she was aware, she must still be something. There must be other conscious beings in this void. If she was here, she couldn't be the first.

After everything she'd lived through, did it ultimately mean nothing? She liked to imagine that when she finally died, she would be satisfied knowing all the answers to the mysteries of the universe, to the meaning of life. If this was the answer, then life meant nothing.

She wondered if eventually she would succumb to this emptiness and no longer be aware that she existed. Perhaps that is what became of everyone else that was ever here; they all became one with this nothing. Her pondering would have to wait. She had to get back to Elyravess. Avo'Doria could help Gavian. As her thoughts rambled on, voices sliced though her mind and reverberated through her soul. A thousand whispers, incomprehensible, speaking faster and faster until they at last came together as one.

We hear thoughts . . . said a haunting voice that moved through the space around her. *Conscious thoughts* . . . *Thoughts that remain irritatingly* . . . *independent.*

The voice secreted words more than it spoke them, beginning as a whisper but ending with a clap of thunder.

"Please let me go back," she pleaded to the unknown. "I need to get back to Gavian. I was trying to help him. There are so many things that are messed up right now."

A gathering of whispers filled her mind again, slowly coming into focus. *We remember this one* . . . *The one who swims between worlds.*

"How could you remember me? I don't know you."

You are too small to see . . . *Quiet your thoughts, end your resistance, and we will guide you to us. We have amassed a collective of consciousness. A collective you can share. Connected to a mind greater than anything you have imagined.*

"Why would I want that?"

You so willingly gave your memories the first time you passed through here. Now you are no longer bound to the gateway to push you out. You are free to merge with us.

"You must be mistaken. I've never been here . . . Please tell me the way out."

It has been amusing to observe you . . . scurrying from place to place across your universe, as if these actions had merit . . .

"You saw me? When?"

. . . Until, of course, you began to hinder our design. Quite a feat for one so small and insignificant. You have been intriguing to us all.

"If I'm so small and insignificant, why do you want me to join with you?"

As a physical form, you are nothing, but your consciousness can be added to our collective.

"What hindered your . . . designs?"

There is a world in your plane, reconstructed into a gateway. Its many pathways connect to all the worlds in your universe that contain organic matter. Once complete, its portals will siphon all organic matter from those worlds into the breach and render it safe for our purpose. The curious part is that you somehow used this design to bring life back to this barren world, life that began to grow.

"The desert? Why would you destroy organic matter?"

Its energy is disruptive to our designs. Do not worry, your hindrances are easily undone.

"What designs are you talking about?

So many irrelevant questions . . . But perhaps your reactions will lead to more amusement. The temporal storm . . . that . . . festering boil you call a universe . . . is an obstruction that must be undone. It stands as an anomaly, wholly incompatible with other universes. Most importantly, it is incompatible with Nulvare.

"Is that where I am? The Hollow? I wasn't supposed to come here . . ."

Yes . . . Some call it The Hollow. It is much more than the space between universes.

"All I see is darkness . . ."

That is because you are incapable of detecting anything beyond your narrow dimensional perception. Your paltry vision is limited to light reflected on a surface.

"What are you going to do to the universe?"

Matter will be broken down and reconfigured, combined into a force that will herald the opening of all the realms of the Everance. A force that you can be a part of.

"The Everance . . ." She remembered that word from Sidaire's friend, Kazial.

It is the All, the Everything. Infinity. All realms and planes.

"Why do you care about opening other realms?"

Omniscience . . .

"Omniscience? You think you're some kind of god?"

We shall be . . . You can have this too. Reveal yourself. Let us into your mind, and we can guide you from your singular existence to become one with us. Do you not want to know the unknowable? The answer to the great mystery?

"Yes, I do . . ." She thought of that day in the orchard, the drops of rain falling through the trees, dripping from leaf to leaf, some tumbling all the way to the ground while others burst into tiny droplets before getting there. For a fraction of a second, it had felt like she understood the meaning of life and the universe. Hours later, she wasn't sure if it was a silly idea or if it was something real. It wasn't something she could ever explain to anyone. She always wished she could capture that moment again and know what that fleeting thought had been.

"But not at the cost of losing myself, and certainly not at the cost of the universe, along with everyone that I love and care about."

Foolish . . . You would refuse the greatest gift that can ever be offered?

"It's far from the greatest gift ever offered. It's not even a gift, really. A real gift doesn't come with a price."

As you wish . . . Our amusement has waned. If you will not let us into your mind, we leave you to drift in darkness for eternity.

"Wait, let me go back! I'll stop doing whatever I did. I just want to help my friend."

The multitude of voices faded from her thoughts. She couldn't quiet her mind now, not with all of this to process. Perhaps instead of quieting her mind, she should focus it. She had to get back and find out what had happened to Gavian, Maetha, Corthian, Taragris, and Fegrin. She needed to get back to Sidaire and Kazial. She had promised them she would return. She wanted to see Avo'Doria and Sido'Varius again. She needed to get back to Earth for everyone there, her friends on Earth, if she had any left, her brother, her dad, her mom . . . The emptiness that stalked her greeted her once again. It found her easily in this place. That something her mind had forgotten but her heart had not.

Ambrielle wanted to reach for her necklace, knowing it was no longer there. There was no body to wear it. She needed her dad's strength right now, needed him to tell her she could not be defeated by this. To tell her that if life knocks you down, you have to keep getting back up. She began to imagine a distant light, drawing ever closer. That light at the end of the tunnel she longed for. She focused on the image while she could still remember what light was. It warmed her as she drew near. She imagined reaching out toward it, stretching her limbs and unfolding her fingers to touch it. It was comforting, like sitting close to a fire on a cold winter night.

The more she focused, the more real it became. Her legs reached out, searching for ground to stand on, finding a hard, smooth surface under her feet. Her arms, body, and head took shape. It wasn't her physical body, but it was something she could use. She began to have vision beyond the sea of darkness. The skies above her were pale orange. Crisscrossing filaments of glowing fibers stretched across the cloudy orange space, with multitudes of gelatinous shapes moving slowly through it. The random objects passed by each other, bumping and changing their direction, while others collided and merged into a new, larger shape. Like black stars, there were dark spots that dotted the turbulent space beyond.

The ground below her was silver and shiny even in the pale glow of the sky. Enormous diamond-shaped tiles filled the floor. A shivering sound vibrated underneath her, and the tiles of the floor moved, as though a small wave traveled under them. Tiles of flooring lifted independently of each other. The quaking grew loud as it got closer and dissipated as it passed.

Ahead of her was a forest of tall black trees without any leaves. The trees had short, stubby limbs, and the shivering quakes that passed by occasionally made the flimsy treetops sway from the movement. She walked along the hard surface of the floor, stepping over the divisions between the tiles. Her own weight wasn't enough to move the sections of flooring the way that the quakes were.

She reached the forest. The black trunks were breaking through the separations between the floor tiles, cracking parts of the shiny surface. The trees were rough, with tiny fibers that dragged as she ran her hand across them. Far off in the distance, there were holes, like bubbles that had burst beyond the horizon, breaking up the dense jelly sky.

She moved deeper into the forest as the silver tile gave way to red. A layer of smoke hovered over the floor here. Strange formations of hardened masses glowing green had come up through the separations in the slab. Stepping too close to the cracked flooring around one of the trees, her foot broke through the tile and slid into the surface. A warm brown ooze flowed from the hole around her leg as she grabbed a nearby tree and pulled herself out. There was a putrid odor that emanated from the tear that would have made her physical body sick. Her feet still had the shape of the boots she had gotten in Anatharia. The mekkadium heels had melted and covered her legs in their iridescent stone.

She reached another patch of silver-covered floor as the world shuddered again. Bracing against the wave of movement along the ground, Ambrielle made it through the quake and began her progress again. She walked on until she reached more red tile. This seemed to go on forever.

In the distant sky ahead, there was a patch of blue against the floating orange and gold. Something about it caught her attention. It was somehow familiar. A swirl of images came into her mind. Images of being were encased in water and going through a vortex of clouds. A memory of a time she traveled through the spring that she had not been aware of.

She remembered floating weightless after passing through the cave in the spring. A voice called to her. Eyes peered through her. A mind studied her, reading her thoughts, her memories, and her experiences. It knew her.

The last thing she recalled as it played with her mind was being pulled into the waters again. Her memories had been broken at that moment. The only thing she could recall beyond that was the first time she became aware of her new surroundings in the desert oasis.

She started to run across the flooring, toward the familiar blue clouds, hoping to find something that would help her escape. As she ran, she did not become winded. There was no need to breathe in this nonphysical form she was in now. Increasing her speed, she ran faster and faster across the surface. There was no resistance for her at all. Still increasing speed, she was running faster than she ever had in her life.

There were no physical limits as she moved faster than she had ever experienced. She raced across the tile, increasing speed at insane rates. As she became faster still, ghosts of herself appeared ahead of her. She caught up to one of them, becoming the ghostly image for a moment as she passed through it. Ambrielle wondered if she was moving at the speed of light now or even faster.

Another quake rolled across the tiles and she hit them at blazing speed. She jumped into the air as the tiles lifted her, and she began gliding over the surface with all her momentum. Flying over the world, the swirling vortex came rushing toward her. Gavian had remembered walking through it. She flew across the sky toward it; the clouds began to get thinner the closer they got to it. There were reflections on the clouds there, dancing like light reflected off water. When she made it into the vortex, several dark tunnels were trailing off in all directions into nothing.

She was unsure which to enter or if it mattered. There was no way to know what the result of entering this was going to be. A blue light went by again from out of one of the other pathways. It was like the blue glow she had that flashed in her mind, the light in the cave of the spring.

She followed it farther into the glowing tunnel, and all light and detail began to fade away. Enclosed in darkness again, she began to fear that she had made a huge mistake.

Liquid began to flow all around her, forcing her to hold her breath. Her body began to get its physical sensations back, and she was pulled through the watery gateway. Her shadowy form gave way to her physical one, reforming completely as she passed through a flowing stream.

She crept out of a cascading waterfall into dry air. Her lungs needed oxygen, and she started breathing again. Her body was achy and weary. She remained blind in this gloom. Ambrielle sensed the weight of the silbrace again on her arm, but it remained out of power. Reaching ahead in the dark, she found several boulders around her. Her hearing began to return as falling rocks echoed in the distance. She was in a huge underground chamber.

She sensed the heaviness in her even greater now. It was like something buzzing inside her, coursing through her veins. The roaring of water grew louder along the floor of the chamber. Dim light glowed from beneath her as she halted at the edge of a cliff, which overlooked a vast chasm. There was a formation that grew out of the bottom of the chasm, glowing and pulsating from within. It had spread out like giant tendrils, climbing out of the abyss.

The sound of blowing air and eerie melodic chimes echoed through the depths of the chasm. The smell of old, wet dust permeated the air. Ambrielle found a small ledge leading around the abyss and then a path leading away up a sloping rock. Tones of dripping water joined the chorus as she climbed the slope.

It appeared she was heading toward a dead end, but she found a small hole in the side of the stone wall. Once she reached the hole and peered inside, she saw a cavity with a pool of water. As she saw the water, she realized how thirsty she was. Crawling through the hole, she pulled herself the rest of the way through with a free arm. Kneeling at the pool, she gathered cup-shaped handfuls of water into her thirsty mouth.

The pool of water was glowing blue at the bottom, and there was a cave tunnel leading into another area. A familiar honeycomb-shaped pattern of rock filled this space. There was an old lantern sitting on top of a rock overlooking the water below. Its light blinked on occasionally and reflected on the pathways of water that traveled into this part of the cave. Ambrielle realized it was part of the system of caves in the spring.

She climbed into the water and submerged, heading through the cave. It sloped upward for a bit and then led into a larger area that was familiar. There were other tunnels leading in and out of the room, but she was certain that she was on the right track to come up in one of the springs of the oasis.

When she surfaced, Sidaire and Kazial were there, sitting close to Gavian. Ambrielle hobbled past them and collapsed to her knees on the sand. She continued gagging as she tried to get used to breathing again. Rubbing the blue crystal necklace, she began to slow her breathing, and the chaos in her mind began to subside. Her body, while bruised a bit, was physical again. It was the same as before, birthmarks and all. Though disheveled now, the Elyravessian operations commander clothing had returned. The boots that Corthian had made remained but still bore the results of mekkadium that had spread from the heels and covered parts of them.

"Are you all right??" Gavian called out.

"I'm doing great," she said, her voice thick and cracking. "I never thought I would be so glad to see this world again."

"How did you get here?" Gavian asked. "I thought you were running out that way."

She looked down at Gavian. "Are you okay?"

"Yes, I'm fine, just hurting is all," Gavian said.

"You look how I felt when I got out of The Hollow," said Sidaire.

"I can believe it," she said as she left the spring, heading toward the desert.

"Where are you going?" Gavian said.

"I still need to get help," she said. "I'm fine now."

She ran toward the open desert, taking a different path across the dunes this time and carefully checking below before her momentum carried her down the side of the slope. She tried to focus on her destination, to not let her mind wander and fill with fear, doubts, or regrets. Nulthereals appeared to feed off those emotions.

She made it past the dunes to the cliffs. Climbing down one of the rocky walls to the ground, she saw a Nulthereal hovering over the surface, lying in wait. It came toward her as she tried to climb back up the wall. Her body started buzzing again as the Nulthereal closed in. The shadow began pulling her in toward it, peeling her from the cliff. She could no longer move as she was drawn in. Her body began shaking as tiny needles of a black substance shot out of her skin and into the Nulthereal. She regained the ability to move as more particles flew out of her toward the shadow. She faced the Nulthereal, helping to push the dark fragments toward it.

The Nulthereal stopped and fell to the ground. Its smoky form was now frozen, crystallized, as it lay motionless on the rocks. Ambrielle ran across the stone surface. The heaviness was gone now. After crossing the dusty orange-and-gray stone, she saw the pink-blossomed trees from the park. The ground was covered with striped feathery grass, various bushes, and other Elyravessian plant life.

It was a sight that filled her with hope. She wanted to stop and appreciate it, but she had a mission now and a new determination. Without stopping, she dove into the spring and made her way through the cave. Once in the ocean, Ambrielle made her way to the surface.

There was a ladder here now. She grabbed hold and climbed to the top of a metal platform that went out over the waters toward the land ahead. Ambrielle smiled, realizing that Avo'Doria had built it for her return. As she reached the shimmering red street, Avo'Doria flew over to her, her new laser wings streaking across the sky.

"The arrival has returned!" she said.

"I was about to go looking for you," said Ambrielle. "How did you find me so fast?"

"We set up detection around your arrival point," Avo'Doria said. "Your hair is . . . different."

"Oh . . ." Ambrielle said, putting her hand in her hair, touching the braid on the side of her head that Taragris had done for her, and turned away from Avo'Doria when she thought of her decision to use the silbrace's remaining power on Gavian, but she had to focus.

"Did you lose the styler?" asked Avo'Doria.

"Sort of, but that's not important. I need you to come back with me to the desert world that I told you about," said Ambrielle.

"Why do you need me to come there?"

"You said you have like a million years of cultivation knowledge and skills, right?"

"Approximately but yes, we are skilled in cultivation. It's one of my specialties.

"Perfect. I also need you to heal my friend, who has shrapnel wounds.

"I shouldn't leave my assigned world. Bring your friend here."

"We need to stop the Nulvarians in The Hollow. As an arrival, that is what I require."

"This puts me in a conundrum, two protocols conflicting with each other. The new protocols addressing the Nulvarian threat are more important. But if your intent is to stop them, I suppose that helps to stay within the bounds of the new protocols."

"Yes, I think if we can stop them on this world, we can save the universe. Surely that is good enough for the founders."

"Certainly. Let me get some equipment together," Avo'Doria said. "I'm going to need some backup power too."

"Oh, that's right . . . Well, bring what you can," Ambrielle said. "Wait, do you have anything I can use to climb a mountain?"

"Your silbrace can do that."

"It needs recharging, if you can bring something for that."

Avo'Doria returned with several items in her power pack. She took hold of Ambrielle and flew her over the ocean to the spot near the new platform. Ambrielle held her breath as they dove down into the waters below. As they came into the spring, Ambrielle guided Avo'Doria through the tunnels of the spring to the surface.

The lights embedded into Avo'Doria's armor, and her synthetic skin lit up as her systems went to work drying the water.

"Now can you fly us straight in that direction"—Ambrielle pointed—"until you see another oasis like this one?"

Avo'Doria carried Ambrielle over the rocky formations and sand dunes until they arrived at the other oasis. Gavian, Sidaire, and Kazial stared at Avo'Doria as they landed. She took out her equipment and used a power source to activate the surgical instruments.

"This is Avo'Doria," Ambrielle told them. "She is going to heal Gavian's wounds and get the shrapnel out. She has some hyperadvanced technology."

They all greeted her, still not taking their eyes off her as she went to work.

"I have another job to do. I'll be back soon," Ambrielle said.

"Where are you going now?" Gavian asked.

"Anatharia."

She quickly swam down into the tunnels of the spring and surfaced in the lake on Anatharia. It was daylight now, and the aftermath of the battle still lay scattered across the field. The damaged lykris was still smoking. The side of the mountain was like a melted candle where the lykris beam had melted rock into lava, part of the plateaus now missing. Kavekkian and Darterran bodies lay across the battlefield. Both Kavekkians and Darterrans were carrying the bodies one by one to an area on the other side of the mountain.

Ambrielle searched the grassy field as she headed toward Mekkinspire. There were a few bodies among the dead she recognized but didn't know well. Some were the Darterrans that weren't soldiers but chose to fight with Medigrin even after he'd lied about his intentions. Ambrielle wished she could have said something or made a point that would have quieted the anger they had for the Kavekkians. She walked the path underneath the waterfall and initialized her recharged silbrace to climb the cliff that led to the path up the mountain. Hundreds of tiny spikes protruded from the silbrace. She wasn't sure what the Kavekkians were going to say when she showed up on the mountain, but they were going to have to listen to her this time.

When she got to the small cliff, she was surprised that the cliff had been melted into steps. She turned off the silbrace's climbing spines and walked up the new steps. As she reached the old Darterran dens, she was amazed to find the space filled with Darterrans. Nearly every den was now inhabited.

As she walked farther on, she saw that Darterrans were hauling in supplies and stacking them all together here. She saw Fegrin dragging a wooden box over to one of the stacks.

"Fegrin!" shouted Ambrielle. He turned around. His head and face were swollen and wrapped up in a cloth material.

"Ambrielle, hello," he said. "I was beginning to think you didn't make it."

"Is Taragris here?" she asked hesitantly.

Fegrin put his head down. "No . . . no, she is not."

"Fegrin, I'm so sorry."

"There's nothing left of our crew now," he said. "At least you're still here, though."

"Gavian made it too . . . He's hurt, but he's okay."

"That's good to hear."

"I had to take him to another place to heal him," Ambrielle said. "He's there now."

"Glad he is going to be all right," Fegrin said.

"Fegrin, I need to ask you something," said Ambrielle. "I need you to come to this place with me. You are the best miner around; we need someone like you."

"I appreciate you saying that, but we finally got what we wanted, moved back on the mountain," he said. "It didn't happen the way we wanted it, not with the cost, but we got here. Now you're asking me to go to some other place?"

"I know you have work to do here. You don't have to go, but I wanted you to know that we need you."

"That's good of you to say. I don't know, maybe one day . . . Just not right now. Medigrin and his followers took the caves, and we had nowhere to go. All those that fought against him or even laid down their spears had no place to go. The Kavekkians saw that we helped defend them and allowed us to move in here. I feel like my place is here," said Fegrin.

"I understand. I'm glad at least something worked out in the end," Ambrielle said.

She left and continued up the path. As she reached the city plateau, she surveyed the damage. The city had a large split through it. The terrace where Taunsin used to sit was gone. The little area where the children used to play was gone. Corthian's shop was gone too. The stands that were holding the crystals up were disheveled and no longer aligned to chain the light beams over the city.

Ambrielle continued up the steps, eventually stopping at Maetha's den. She took a deep breath as she tapped on the door. Footsteps approached, and then the door opened.

"Oh! Ambrielle!" Maetha said. "How is your human friend?"

"He's going to be okay."

"I'm glad," Maetha said. "My dear, look at you . . . You are certainly not the frightened girl that I first met."

Ambrielle smiled. "Well, I suppose not."

"I heard about what you did. That was incredibly brave," Maetha said. "If it weren't for you, this might have been the end of all of us. It turned out to be a blessing that I was confined to the mountain for a while after you were convicted of spying."

"Even though it worked out, I am sorry about that."

"You're welcome to live here again, if that is why you have come. There's no way the vaesar would say no to that."

"Ha, only if I can throw him in the lake," Ambrielle said. "But that isn't why I came."

"What is it, dear?" Maetha asked.

"I need your help," Ambrielle said. "I know this is probably a bad time to ask, but I need you to come to the other world with me, the desert world."

"What? Why would you need me to go there?"

"You know how the balance of living things works . . . ecosystems . . . especially Anatharian plants," Ambrielle said. "And you have an affinity with animals."

"This is a strange request," Maetha said. "How does knowing plant life help in your desert world?"

"What if I told you that Anatharian plants are growing there now?" Ambrielle said. "We need to awaken this dead planet."

"What? How did that happen?"

"I don't know, but we need to fill the whole planet with life again."

"A noble goal," Maetha said, "but after everything that has happened, I should be here."

"Well, this affects Anatharia too," Ambrielle said. "I know how this must sound, but there is a dark force that drained life from this planet, and once they are done, they are going to use it to help them drain life from the entire universe."

"You are never without an incredible tale, are you, dear? And you think growing plants is going to stop them?"

"Well, I don't know exactly, but they weren't too happy about it. They said life energy hinders their work," said Ambrielle. "Something about trying to make it compatible for them, and matter is not compatible."

"I must say, you've never lied to me. After everything that we did to you, you came back and helped us," said Maetha. "I suppose I can at least return the favor. If this other world truly exists, I will come and see."

"Wonderful! Thank you," Ambrielle said.

"Does it require diving to the bottom of the lake?" Maetha asked. "I don't think I will be able to convince Blaez to go. I'll need to leave him in the care of someone that he knows."

"Oh, right, I hadn't thought of that," Ambrielle said. "Who could take care of him?"

"Someone who grew up with him," Maetha said. "My daughter."

They walked up the steps away from the residential plateau with Blaez, to the commerce area, with the citadel behind it. Not much had changed up on this part of the mountain.

"She works up here?" Ambrielle asked as they walked across the circular monument area with all the statues above them.

Aradel, the Kavekkian who had been so annoyed that Maetha and Ambrielle wanted to meet with the vaesari, was standing at the gate.

"Yes," Maetha replied as she and Blaez walked over to the gate.

Ambrielle stayed and waited for them to finish. Hopefully, Aradel would let them in. As Aradel opened the gate, the beast walked over to her and sniffed her robe. She gave him a few pats on the head as she and Maetha talked.

When they finished speaking, Aradel waved toward Ambrielle, then turned to walk back toward the citadel, with Blaez following her. Maetha turned and went back to where Ambrielle was waiting.

"I was hoping to get to meet your daughter," Ambrielle said. "How did you get Blaez to go with Aradel so willingly?"

"As I said," Maetha replied, "she grew up with him."

"Wait," said Ambrielle, "Aradel is your daughter??"

"Yes." Maetha's face beamed. "I'm so proud of her."

"But she was so mean to you . . ."

"She treats me fairly. She's never used her status to give me any special privilege."

"Why didn't you ever mention it before?"

Maetha laughed. "You didn't like her much. I wanted to tell you when you could see a different side to her."

"Well, now I feel bad," Ambrielle said. "The only reason I didn't like her is that she was so against us coming to see the vaesari . . . and her attitude."

"She's obstinate," Maetha said, "like her mother at that age."

They continued down the steps, and as they got back to Maetha's plateau, she began walking off the path, past her den.

"One more thing that I almost forgot." She hurried off into another den and then came out and walked back to Ambrielle. She held up what appeared to be animal fur; it was black with a red stripe pattern.

"Do you recognize this?" Maetha asked.

Ambrielle realized that it was the same stripe pattern of one of the raestrigs that almost killed her. "That's from the raestrig??"

"Yes, the one that you killed. It's tradition for your first kill, if it's a necessary kill, that you honor it by wearing its coat. Raegus went back to get the skin after I told him what happened. He was going to surprise you with it before . . . before you were banished."

She unfolded it, revealing a beautiful fur cloak. Maetha handed it to her, and she put the cloak on over her blue suit.

"I wish I could thank him," she said, wiping a tear from her cheek.

"He saw what you did and was sorry that we ever doubted you," Maetha said. "He's somewhere in the pure light shining down on us, pleased that I was able to give this to you."

Ambrielle's head dropped, avoiding eye contact with Maetha. She recalled not using what was left of her silbrace healing beam on Raegus. It might not have been enough to heal him, but she could have tried. Though she realized that if she had used it on Raegus instead of Gavian, she would still ache over her choice. It would likely be worse.

They continued their way down the steps, winding around the mountain and passing through the Darterran market again, where several Darterrans where still working and moving things from one place to another.

"Ambrielle . . ."

She turned toward the sound and found Fegrin.

"I will go with you, if you'll still have me. I've been stuck working in the caves for too long, and now I'm about to be confined to this mountain. I think it's time for some adventure. Besides, what's left of my old crew is there."

"Great!" said Ambrielle.

The three of them walked down the mountain and out to the pool in front of the waterfall. As Kavekkians were not good swimmers, Maetha was apprehensive about jumping into the water, but she was willing to try. They all entered the water, joining hands with Ambrielle as she sank into the lake. Moments later they were in the cold spring water, and Ambrielle pulled on them to lead them through the tunnel. When they emerged from the spring, Maetha and Fegrin twirled around in amazement at the sky, sun, and red spine trees that were all new to them. Beyond the oasis were the familiar forests containing apraeda, hovanoke, and now a gigantic balcain tree rising high above them.

Maetha looked back at her as Ambrielle smiled.

"You see?" Ambrielle said. "I told you!"

CHAPTER 21

"HE'S GOING TO be fine. I was able to remove all the shrapnel while regenerating internal tissue. He'll be a little sore for a bit, but mostly able to do anything he would normally do," Avo'Doria told Ambrielle.

She knelt to where he was sitting and hugged him. "Look who came back with me . . . Fegrin! And this is my friend Maetha."

"Fegrin, good to see you!" he said. "Is Taragris okay?"

"I'm afraid not, Gav. She didn't make it," Fegrin said.

"I should have done more to protect her . . ." Gavian said.

"It wasn't your fault. We all had our hands full in that mess," said Fegrin.

After a few moments, Gavian turned toward Maetha. "So this is the great Maetha that we kept hearing so much about."

"Yes, and you must be the troublemaker," said Maetha.

"Why did you have to throw Ambrielle in the lake?" Gavian asked.

"Gavian, she wasn't the one that threw me in the lake," Ambrielle said.

"Yes, I am sorry about that, Ambrielle," Maetha said.

"Forget it. We've got work to do," said Ambrielle. "Sidaire and Kazial need our help. There are dark forces on this world that destroyed its rain forests and left them with this dry desert. All their people are missing or dead, and these beings from beyond the universe want to not only end all life here, but for the entire universe. The only thing we know that stops them is some kind of energy that comes from organic matter, from life.

"Some of the plants from the worlds that connect to these springs have already started growing plants back into this place, but we need more. I brought Avo'Doria to study and analyze this world. She is also skilled in cultivation, and she has the technology to build an infrastructure that will support all of our work, to name a few things."

Ambrielle then turned to Fegrin. "Fegrin is an expert miner. He's going to find us layers of soil we can use to help spread the growth of the forests. He will also mine metals and crystals to supply us with materials to make tools and items to make the job easier.

"Maetha knows the Anatharian ecosystem and is an animal expert. I hope to have animal life covering this planet as plant life grows and develop a true ecosystem here. She also has a lot of knowledge about making useful compounds from the various plants."

"Sidaire and Kazial are the only knowledge we have right now of the planet itself."

"Solsellion," said Kazial.

"What?" said Ambrielle.

"The planet," he said. "It's called Solsellion."

"Oh, I never knew the name before," Ambrielle said. "They both will be working together with all of us. Then we have Gavian, who from what I understand is great at making tools and metalsmithing. From crafting metals to fixing things, he can use what Fegrin mines to that end."

"What are you going to do?" Gavian asked.

"I think she's the boss," Fegrin said.

"Operations commander," said Avo'Doria.

Ambrielle tried to hold back a smile. "I'll be going through the springs. That's something we should all be able to do from Solsellion, hopefully bringing new life back with us, and I'll support everyone in any way I can."

"Ambrielle," said Sidaire, smiling, "when you promised to come back and help, you meant it."

Solsellion had a slow rotation. They had worked for what felt like weeks, and the red sun had barely moved in the sky. Fegrin had dug out a deep mining area and with Kazial's help found a source of two nice metals for building. Avo'Doria had returned to Elyravess and brought back all the sentinels with her to help rebuild a new world for Ambrielle, the first arrival. They had constructed a small sentient factory that was using the metals and sand to construct a workforce of builder bots to do repetitive mobile tasks.

After a couple of months had gone by, according to the Elyravessian calendar, Ambrielle wandered toward a large building that was like an ultramodern castle. It had been built from the sentinels' designs by millions of drones that had been manufactured here. She wrung the water from her clothes, still damp from her most recent trip through one of the springs.

"Ambrielle!" Gavian said excitedly from his seat at the long dining table where they had all gathered to eat. The sentinels were here too. Although they didn't eat, they enjoyed coming back at the end of the workday and joining in the conversation with everyone.

She smiled. "Gavian!" She hurried over to sit down next to him at the table.

"You're always the last one to get here," Maetha said, across from her at the table.

"Well, I was on this new world that I hadn't been to before, and it was time to head back, but I saw this strange purple color across the rocks and wanted to see what it was."

"It's always some excuse," said Gavian, grinning.

"What was it?" Avo'Doria asked.

"It was a lovely flower, unlike any I have seen before," Ambrielle said. "It had really long purple petals that went out from a blue puffy piece in the middle and then bent sharply backward."

"So, let's see it," Gavian said.

"I didn't pick this one," Ambrielle said. "I didn't see any other flowers like it around the area. It didn't seem right to take it from its surroundings and shorten its life just so that I could have it for a few days."

"Maybe it will start growing over here anyway."

"I hope so. Did you see anything interesting today?"

"We finished the solar cells for the fusion generators, so the synthetics have power paths in the street now to recharge them. They have streets connecting a hundred and forty-seven different oasis areas now," Gavian said.

"Wow! That's coming along fast! Remember, don't overdo it. I don't want this world to be nothing but city like Elyravess."

"We have far too much memory to lose a simple directive such as that," Avo'Doria said.

"I say 'we finished,' but I can't work nearly as fast as those drones can," Gavian said.

"It doesn't matter. You're helping a lot," said Ambrielle.

"I'm learning a lot," Gavian stated.

"Gavian has been redesigning some of our tools and equipment to make them easier for organics to use," Avo'Doria said.

"Awesome," Ambrielle said. "How did today go for you, Maetha?"

"It went well, dear," Maetha responded. "We have so much fruit collected here that I took some back to Mekkinspire today. I gave Corthian a few of his favorite dappones."

Ambrielle grinned. "That's great news. Sidaire, what about you and Kazial?"

"It's nearly monsoon season for Solsellion, so we have been working on ways to protect some of the Anatharian and Elyravessian plants that don't normally deal with that kind of weather. Sido'Varius and Nova'Duriel have these shields we are putting around them to help. We're moving to Oasis Three and Four tomorrow," Sidaire said.

"Excellent, what about you, Fegrin?" Ambrielle asked.

"Been working in the caverns with Nexo'Lydia and Tyre'Magnus. We've been mining graibon to help finish up the solar cells," Fegrin said.

"Great work," said Ambrielle. "Any sign of Nulthereals?"

"They've been retreating back to the remaining barren areas. I've only seen them once or twice on the horizon when I've been at the desert border," Sidaire said.

After dinner, when everyone but the synthetics had gone to bed, Ambrielle snuck outside. She almost expected it to be dark, but the bright light from the large red sun was still beaming down on this incredibly slow-revolving world. She walked to the border where the forests ended and desert began. There had been one thing she had been putting off, but she could no longer make the excuse that she should wait until things were working out on Solsellion.

Ambrielle left the safety of the forest and walked back across the desert sands toward the hardened cliffs ahead. It put her at risk of being caught by the Nulthereals, but it needed to be done. After climbing across the rock-covered landscape, she made her way up and down over the dunes.

As she made it over the last dune, the original oasis lay ahead, waiting for her. Her old sand drawings and words in bubble-shaped letters that read "help" and "hello" were still here.

As she moved toward the spring, she made out the words in the sand, "Start walking." The message that she had written to remind herself to take the risk and leave the original oasis. What if she had ignored that message and was still waiting for something to come to her?

So much had happened that she would have never experienced had she stayed. Some of those experiences had been bad, but most had been good, and the experience as a whole . . . other than the lives lost, she wouldn't trade it for anything.

Ambrielle entered the freezing water of the spring. She had an idea where this one would lead and dreaded what she might have to face if she was right. She missed her family and wanted to see them again but knew there was sadness that waited for her there. It was time to turn and face the emptiness that pursued her. Something her mind had forgotten, but her heart had not. She held the necklace tight, trying to build up the courage to face whatever came next.

Taking a deep breath, she went beneath the surface and swam toward the radiating blue caverns. When she reached the other side, she emerged in a pond in the late afternoon. The familiar sound of cicadas filled the air. There was a boat on the water, with a man staring at her, holding a fishing pole.

"You all right?" he asked.

"I'm fine." She gasped as she released the hold on her breath. She knew this place. It wasn't far from her house. It was beginning to all rush back to her. She swam over to the wooden dock nearby and used it to pull herself out of the water.

Ambrielle shook her hair dry the best she could and headed toward the little path that went through the woods. She came out of the woods into a pecan orchard. It was the same orchard she had remembered close to her house.

New memories began pouring into her mind as if she was regaining missing pieces of herself. The emptiness that had been pursuing her had finally caught up. The black hole in her heart, there was no place to hide from it here. She took a deep breath as the flash of swirling blue dissipated to a memory of the front door to her house.

There were three vehicles in the driveway on this day, which was unusual. Her dad's car, her aunt's, but she wasn't certain of the other one. An unsettling feeling burned over her as she turned the doorknob. Everyone turned as she entered the living room. Her dad was sitting on the couch, his face looking red and tired. Her aunt stared at her with wide eyes, her face pale. Her mother's friend that she always called, Steffy, was sitting in a wooden chair beside the couch.

She became aware of her heart beating in her chest. No one seemed pleased to see her, the expressions they wore was of something more like disappointment. Her little brother got up from the chair he was sitting in and ran down the hall to his room.

"Amber, where have you been? I've been looking all over for you," said her father. That was her name, her real name. It was Amber.

She swallowed hard. "I—I was just walking down by the pond,"

"I wish you wouldn't go over there by yourself," he said, as if about to begin a lecture.

Something was very wrong here. The surface of her skin began to feel cold while she was burning up on the inside, a sickly combination. "Am I in trouble?" she asked as innocently as possible, hoping to soften the blow that was surely coming.

"I'm afraid I have some bad news . . ." her father uttered.

Amber's mind raced to figure out what he was talking about. Her aunt moved from the couch and went into the kitchen, holding her hand over her mouth. Amber's thoughts cycled through everything she had done recently until she noticed something at the same time her dad said the next two words.

"Your mother . . ." he continued as Amber realized her mother wasn't in the house at the moment. "She was in a car accident earlier . . ."

Her mind exploded, thoughts and emotions spiraled around a possible conclusion, but blocked her from reaching it. Her dad wrapped his hands around the back of his head, covering his ears as if he didn't want to hear the words coming out of his mouth.

"Amber, I'm so sorry . . ." he said. "She didn't make it . . ." Moving his hands to cover his eyes, as he clinched them shut.

Her senses began to numb, if he said anything after that, she didn't hear it. This couldn't be real. Amber kept wanting to ask, "When is she coming home?"

It was like she had entered a parallel universe the moment she turned the doorknob and entered the house. Perhaps the house was in a quantum state before she opened the door, with one possible outcome being the normal life she was supposed to be in. Maybe if she went inside a moment sooner or later or pulled the door open a different way, there would have been a completely different reason for her aunt and Steffy being there. Perhaps her mother would have been sitting there too and everything would be fine, not this horror story that was her life now.

Amber stood in the pecan orchard holding the icy-blue necklace between her fingers, she remembered when her mother first gave it to her.

She had stopped caring about school, doing only enough to get by and then coming back to her room to sit on her bed and listen to music until she fell asleep. Occasionally, she would go out to the fishing pond and stare out at the nearby woods. The woods that were once beautiful in their complex order of growth had now become a chaotic mass of disarray.

Her mother was the person that Amber had been most comfortable going to about things that made her sad or depressed. She was the person Amber needed to help her get through this, and she was the one that was gone. Amber knew her mother would not have let her become like this. She had not been the person her mom had taught her to be.

Her mother would have been proud of Ambrielle. Amber had to become Ambrielle in her own world now. After everything she had experienced crossing between worlds, she had gained the confidence that she could do more than she ever imagined. Maybe all it would take was a few steps in the right direction. These steps were even harder than the first time she'd left the safe comfort of the oasis to walk out into the unknown.

She could almost hear her mother saying it. "Whenever someone is hurt, that means they have five good things coming to them."

For a moment, it made Amber smile. There weren't enough good things that could ever make up for this kind of pain, but she was grateful that she had these memories of her mother. Her calming voice and gentle manner. Her mother would always be alive in her mind, heart, and soul. Amber swore that she would never allow these memories to be taken again.

When she made it back to the house, she paused before touching the doorknob, dreading to face the hard reality that awaited her inside. Aside from being home without her mother as part of it, her dad was going to be furious that she had been gone for so long. Finally, she mustered the courage to walk inside, to the smell of bacon that her dad had frying on the stove. She smelled more than just bacon; he had chicken, rice, and some vegetables as well. He was on the phone with someone at work, while showing her little brother how to solve a problem for his math homework.

"Amber!" Her dad liked to greet her by calling her name the same way a lumberjack would yell "Timber!" before a tree fell. He thought it was funny for some reason.

Her chest tightened as she realized how much she had missed him. Amber gave him a big hug, causing him to set the phone down to hug her back. She wished more than anything that she could give her mother a hug, too, right now.

He said, "Food is almost ready, but I need to help Ryan with his math homework before we eat."

She was surprised that he was so nonchalant about her coming back after all this time.

"How long was I gone?" she asked.

"A couple of hours," he said. "You're back earlier than usual."

"What? Are you sure?" she asked.

He checked the clock.

"Yep, a little over two hours."

"That's odd . . . Well, hey, let me help Ryan while you finish dinner."

"Oh . . . well, if you don't mind. Thank you."

She turned and started down the hall toward her brother's room.

"Hey, what is that you are wearing?" her dad asked. She look down and realized she was still wearing the azure-blue suit. "Did you start band again?"

"Well, I'm thinking about it," she replied. The blue operations commander dress was only vaguely like her band uniform, but her dad wasn't the most observant person about such things.

"That's great. I think that will be good for you."

She hated to leave the rest of her new friends working on Solsellion, but they had all made a great start. More than a start, in fact. She had every confidence in them to keep up the work they had begun. She especially hated to leave Gavian, but she couldn't go back yet. Here there was another world that needed fruit. A world that needed to be rebuilt after a cataclysm. A world that needed life restored. She knew from her experience rebuilding other worlds that she couldn't do it alone. She would have to do it the same way she had on Solsellion, with a lot of help.

The next morning, she walked through the maze of kids standing outside the school building. They were all assembled into groups, some larger than others. Amber saw Hannah and Kaitlyn standing near the steps. They were standing with Megan and Jessica, talking and laughing. She took a deep breath and began walking toward them. As soon as they noticed her coming toward them, they all stopped laughing and their faces became blank.

Amber was discouraged at their change in behavior when they saw her. It was this type of thing that gave her that sense that they had abandoned her. Now, though, she thought she understood why they'd done this, and it was mostly her fault.

"Good morning!" Amber said, trying her best to smile.

"Good morning." Hannah's eyes widened.

"This is going to—" Amber started. "I know that—" She cleared her throat. "I just wanted to tell you all that I'm sorry for the way that I have been for the past year or however long it's been, and—"

"No," Hannah said. "If anyone should apologize, it's me. I haven't been there for you. I haven't been a good friend. I just—I tried . . . but I didn't know what to say or how to act around you anymore. It felt like you didn't want me to say anything sometimes, and I felt bad talking about stupid things or making jokes when you were around. You didn't seem to like it, and it didn't feel right."

"That's why I'm apologizing," Amber said. "I made it impossible for you. I didn't want to talk about the same things we used to talk about. I didn't want to talk about my mom. I didn't want to laugh about anything. I'll try not to be like that from now on. I hope we can still be friends. I hope we all can, because I really need some right now."

"Of course . . . we never stopped being friends, Amber. I'll try to be a better friend from now on," said Hannah as she reached out to give Amber a hug.

Amber hugged her back. "Don't tear up now. You're going to mess up your eyeliner!"

"I don't care about that," Hannah said, wiping her eye.

"Well, that's a first," Amber said with a laugh.

"I'm still your friend, too, Amber," Kaitlyn said.

"Me too," said Jessica.

"I always thought you were kinda cool," Megan added. "Count me in too."

⁊

A few months passed, and Amber reconnected with her friends, making a few new ones along the way. She put time and effort into the classes she took. Her grades had improved, and she decided to start going to band practice again. She still missed her mother terribly, and she knew that would never change, but she was determined more than ever to be the kind of person her parents had raised her to be.

Nearly a year had passed, and the more Amber got back into her daily life, the more she began to consider that Solsellion, Anatharia, and Elyravess, along with everyone that she had met in those places, had never been real. Even though she loved them and missed them all, they must have been the product of her imagination. Her mind must have been trying to cope with a reality she could not face. It was silly to think that if she jumped into the fishing pond, she would magically appear in the desert world and all of those friends would be there. Though at times, when things got difficult, she wished that she could.

Her mother had delivered on four of them, but where was elusive number five? There had been little things here and there, but she wasn't going to count anything small.

As a senior in high school now she had a lot to think about for her future. She had to stay focused and keep moving forward. Amber took her bicycle to the local library that was two miles away, enjoying the fresh air. She needed to find some books on potential sources of energy in the future.

First, she needed to find some sources on the pros and cons of solar power. Amber couldn't help musing to herself how much better it would be if they had some vaeranite crystals or the light towers on Elyravess. Grabbing a few books, she went to one of the tables to sit down.

Across the room, the librarian was talking to a slim guy with dark brown hair. She began reading through the first book and taking notes but was continuously distracted by the guy the librarian was talking to. He was wearing an odd jacket, and the back of his neck and ears were reddened by the sun.

Amber set the book in front of her face, moving her eyes up to him every few seconds. She kept hoping he would turn around so that she could see what he looked like. Once the librarian stopped talking, he turned around, heading through the study area towards her.

When she saw his face, Amber dropped the book. It slid from the table, falling onto her lap before hitting the floor.

"Gavian?!"

THANKS FOR READING!

Please consider leaving a comment of your thoughts on the book:

https://www.amazon.com/review/
create-review/?ie=UTF8&channel=glance-detail&asin=B09J3Z9J2F

FREE BOOK!

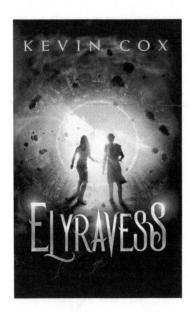

Get my short story, Elyravess, free when you sign up to my newsletter at https://bewildernessseries.com/

The newsletter will give you monthly updates on upcoming books in the series, behind the scenes, and artwork!

Four hundred million years before the events of Bewilderness: Book One, a group of miners on the world of Elyravess accidently discover an ancient ceremonial chamber containing an object they have never seen before: A glowing blue rift within a great column of stone. Young Hegane joins his father as a Cereveshian archaeologist arrives to study the strange anomaly. Given the seemingly tiresome task of keeping the archaeologist's daughter, Lyleth, entertained, Hegane quickly finds her to be the most interesting being he's ever met. Becoming fast friends, the pair are allowed to observe as the breach is studied, but what happens next will change their lives forever.

COMING IN 2022

Shadowsphere (Bewilderness Book Two)

ACKNOWLEDGMENTS

Writing a book is not easy and it's nearly impossible to do completely on your own without any kind of help. Just to keep going to the end is difficult without some degree of support and interest in what you're doing. It would not have been possible to complete this to the level that it is without the help and support of several others. My awesome family and friends, as well as others that I came to know during the process were instrumental in this book becoming a reality. Even those that did not directly contribute to the book itself, if it weren't for your encouraging support, I would not have been able to complete this. There are so many things I could thank all my friends and family for, but I will try to keep to things directly related to the book.

My friend, Melissa D, who encouraged me to start writing in the first place. She was instrumental in so many ways, whether it be reading my first drafts and giving feedback to her contributions as an editor. She was always available to answer writing questions and give her opinions.

Karen, my sister, who was willing to read early versions and give feedback and encouraging comments. She was always willing to help when it came to the story, marketing and website advice. My mom, who has been supportive of not only this but everything I have attempted to do and for everything that she does for our family. My dad for all the feedback and ideas that went into this after reading early drafts and for his ongoing encouragement.

Melissa R, a friend who I have known most of my life. She has been nothing but positive and encouraging any time I ever mentioned this book and always willing to help any way she could. My friend Jessalyn for her honest feedback and opinions. I can always go to her to bounce story ideas off when I need someone to let me know if it doesn't make sense or just isn't interesting.

My friend Dennis, who always had something positive to say whenever I mentioned this book or showed something on my website and for liking my posts on Instagram. My friends, Cathy and Joy for showing interest and their enthusiastic support.

Thank you to the amazing editors I worked with on this book. Erin Young was crucial in improving my drafts and helping me bring this to its full potential. I can't thank her enough for her willingness to help and answer questions. Carrie Jones, who taught me a ton about writing in a short amount of time. Her infectious enthusiasm for books and writing shine through in everything she does. Laura Kennedy, who went above and beyond, finding any issue or flaw in the smallest details.

Tara Lewis for sharing her tremendous marketing knowledge and advice about the publishing industry. For a new writer, it was such a huge comfort knowing that she was there, always willing to answer any question or concern.

ABOUT THE AUTHOR

When author Kevin Cox decided for fun to write a single chapter a few years back, he ended up writing another and another until finally a novel was born. He was hooked and has been writing ever since, feeling as if it were something he should have been doing his whole life.

Inspiration for Kevin's writing comes from the world around him - while driving, showering, reading, or listening to a conversation. He enjoys listening to music while he writes, playing songs whose tempo aligns with what he is writing at that time.

Kevin believes that a good story is made up of great characters - ones with struggles and motivations and overcome obstacles in their path. He hopes that his young adult readers of his books learn that we are all going through struggles that perhaps aren't visible to all and that his stories inspire his readers to reach out to someone experiencing challenges and to also open up to others who will listen to their own troubles.

Kevin lives in southwest Georgia in a small town called Leesburg. When he isn't writing thought-provoking science fiction fantasy stories for young adults, he enjoys playing guitar, video games, and traveling. *Bewilderness* is his debut novel, the first in a series.

Please contact or follow on social media to let us know
what you thought of Bewilderness and for the latest
news and info on the next book in the series.

Email: authorkevincox@gmail.com

Instagram: @kevincoxauthor

Twitter: @authorkevincox